P9-CZV-819

THE BARONS

family series from Harlequin Presents

RAISING THE STAKES
SANDRA MARTON

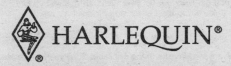

HARLEQUIN®

TORONTO • NEW YORK • LONDON
AMSTERDAM • PARIS • SYDNEY • HAMBURG
STOCKHOLM • ATHENS • TOKYO • MILAN • MADRID
PRAGUE • WARSAW • BUDAPEST • AUCKLAND

ISBN 0-373-83511-6

RAISING THE STAKES

First North American Publication 2002

Visit us at www.eHarlequin.com

Printed in U.S.A.

PROLOGUE

IN THE darkness of the hot summer night, Dawn lay curled like a baby in its mother's womb as she listened to the frantic slap, slap, slap of the silk moth's wings against the screen.

She couldn't see the moth, not from here in the back bedroom, but she knew it was outside the kitchen window, shredding its beautiful wings in a useless attempt to reach the light.

The silk moth had turned up at dusk, right after she'd fed Tommy and put him to bed for the night.

"Sleep tight, sweetheart," she'd whispered, and he'd given her his biggest, brightest three-year-old smile.

"An' don't let the bed bugs bite," her son had replied, as he always did.

Dawn had kissed him, loving his sweet, baby scent. Tommy had rolled onto his belly and she'd drawn a light blanket over his upraised rump. Her smile had faded as she'd shut the door to his room and looked around the cabin, trying to see it through Harman's eyes. Did she miss anything when she dusted earlier? Had she put all Tommy's toys away?

She'd paused beside the sofa, smoothed down the flowered chenille throw that covered the seat cushion where the spring had popped. Everything looked fine but what looked fine to her didn't necessarily look that way to her husband, especially on Friday nights when he cashed his paycheck at the Foodco and then stopped for drinks on the way home.

It didn't always happen that way. Once in a while, Harman just came straight home. Those times weren't perfect. He still liked things exactly as he liked them. "Everything in order," he called it, "the way a man's entitled, in his own home." But it was easier on nights when he didn't stop at the bar. Without liquor in him, he was still surly and he'd talk mean, too, but he wouldn't—he wouldn't—

Dawn blanked her mind to the rest.

The thing to do was keep busy, not notice that if Harman were heading directly for the cabin, he'd have been here an hour ago. She took a breath, glanced in the spotted oval mirror that hung over the table near the door. Did she look okay? Not too tired? Harman didn't like her to look tired. It was the baby's fault, he'd say, when she yawned too much or her eyes didn't sparkle the way he liked. The baby was sapping her energy. Once she'd made the mistake of saying no, no, it wasn't like that. The baby was the joy of her life.

"I am the joy of your life," Harman had said coldly. "You remember that, girl."

She would. Yes, she would. Because it wasn't how he'd looked at her that had scared her, or how he'd sounded. It was the way he'd looked at Tommy afterward, as if their son was a trespasser in a world that had been perfect until he'd been born. It had never been perfect, not ever, not from the day after the wedding when she'd thoughtlessly left her lipstick and comb on the bathroom sink...

Dawn spun away from the mirror, went into the kitchen, took a broom from the closet and stepped out onto the sagging porch. It would need sweeping. The tall oaks that surrounded the cabin were what made the mountain so handsome, but Harman didn't much care for seeing leaves and acorns on the porch.

"Got to be swept twice a day," he said.

So Dawn swept it, twice a day. Sometimes more than that, just to be sure. And that night, as she'd swept, she'd seen the silk moth.

It wasn't the first one she'd ever seen. Years ago, when she was a little girl, a moth just like it had come swooping in through the open trailer door. Her mother had screamed as if it was a creature straight out of hell, grabbed a rolled-up magazine and gone after it.

"Kill it," she'd yelled, "kill it!"

Instead Dawn caught the moth and took it outside, feeling the delicate pink wings trembling with terror in her cupped hands. She'd set it free in the stand of scraggly trees between the trailer park and the highway.

"Go on," she'd whispered, "spread your pretty wings and fly far, far away."

Her mother slapped her when she went back into the trailer, not very hard because she was already high on what she called her pain pills, but just enough to remind her that she'd been disobedient.

"I tell you to do a thing," she'd said, "you do it. You got that, girl?"

Dawn got it. Rules were to be obeyed. Still, she'd risked breaking another one the next day. She was supposed to go straight home after school. She had chores to do and stopping off anywhere, especially at the library to poke her nose into books that gave her, Orianna said, fancy ideas, was forbidden. But Dawn wanted to know the name of the beautiful moth whose life she'd saved. She found a picture of it in the encyclopedia. It was a Glover's silk moth, a thing of rare beauty, and though she'd always hoped to see one again, she never had.

She knew it was silly but tonight she wondered if, by some miracle, the moth on the porch might be the one she'd saved years ago. She paused in her sweeping, watching the moth with delight until, suddenly, she heard the sound of a truck laboring up the mountain.

Her heart leaped into her throat. Was it Harman? So early? That would be good. It would mean he hadn't stopped for more than a drink or two—but it would be bad, too. She wasn't done sweeping and just look, she'd somehow gotten a stain on her skirt.

It wasn't Harman. The sound of the engine died away. Dawn dragged a breath into her lungs and swept the porch until the unpainted boards were spotless. Not that it mattered. If he came home drunk, she could have swept a hundred times over and he'd still find a speck of dirt, a bit of leaf, something, anything, and when he did…

She switched the thought off, just clicked it to silence as if it were a station on a radio because she'd learned there wasn't any sense, really, in thinking ahead. Whatever happened would happen. Nothing she could do would change it. She could only sweep harder and faster and not do anything stupid, like hurrying back inside the cabin and waking Tommy so he could see the silk moth. Her son loved all the creatures that shared this godforsaken mountain with them, but why take him from his bed to see something that would surely be dead by morning? And it would be dead, drawn by the light Harman insisted must be on so he could be sure she wasn't in the arms of one of the nonexistent men he was convinced came around whenever he wasn't there.

Once, exhausted at the end of a day spent cooking and cleaning in hopes of pleasing him, she'd forgotten the light. Harman had come in late and dragged her out of bed, to the front room and the unlit lamp.

"Did you think you could hide in here without my knowin' what you were up to?" he'd said, and when she'd tried to explain that she hadn't done anything, that his preoccupation with her leaving on the light didn't make any sense, he'd called her a liar and a whore. He'd beaten her and then he'd unzipped his jeans, torn off her nightgown and pushed himself inside her.

She never forgot to turn on the light after that.

It was like a beacon, shining there in the blackness of the mountain night, luring the gossamer-winged creatures of the forest to their deaths. The silk moth would meet the same fate. It would beat its delicate wings to pieces in a fruitless attempt to reach a warm, shiny world that was only an illusion. Bad enough she knew that awful truth. Why would she want Tommy to know it, too? Her son had lots of time to learn about the world.

So she'd finished sweeping a floor that didn't need sweeping and now she lay in the dark, listening to the pathetic slap of the moth's wings, to the quick thud of her own heart as it grew later and later. At last, she heard the whine of her husband's pickup truck as it made its way toward the clearing.

Dawn shuddered, held her breath. If she could only feign sleep...

The truck door slammed. Booted feet stomped up the wooden steps and across the porch. The door opened.

Maybe it would be okay. Harman had been good to her, once. When he'd asked her to marry him, when he'd offered to take her away from her mother and the trailer park and the endless stream of men who slept in her mother's bed, he'd seemed the answer to her prayers.

"Shit!"

Dawn dug her face into the muslin pillow tick. Stay asleep, Tommy, she thought frantically, don't, oh don't wake up. Not that Harman would ever hurt their son, she was sure of that, but still...

Another noise. More cursing. The sound of Harman falling, then getting to his feet.

"Goddammit," he roared. "What the hell is this?"

Oh, God! Had he tripped over something? What? What could she have left on the floor? She'd put the broom away. The dustpan. The chairs were lined up under the table just so, all of them neatly arranged. Tommy's toys, such as they were, were carefully placed on the shelf in his room...

The red car.

The brand-new red plastic car she'd bought at the supermarket, even though it cost two dollars, because of the way her baby had looked at it, his blue eyes going all round with wonder. He'd played with it all afternoon, rolling it back and forth, back and forth while she folded laundry until, finally, he'd fallen sound asleep right there at her feet, the car clutched in his chubby fist. She'd smiled, scooped him up, carried him to his crib—and kicked the red car, by mistake. It had rolled toward the corner and she'd forgotten it, forgotten to look for it.

The bedroom door shot open. The light flashed on. Don't move, Dawn thought desperately, don't open your eyes, don't blink, don't stir, don't breathe...

"Get up!"

She scrambled up against the pillows, clutching the quilt to her chin. Her husband loomed over her, looking as big as the mountain he came from and as mean as the storms that blew across it.

"Harman. Please. I didn't mean to—"

The first blow caught her across her cheek. The second was better aimed and got her in the jaw. Her head snapped back; the coppery taste of blood was on her tongue.

"Where'd this come from, huh? Where'd it come from?"

He shook his fist under her nose, opened his hand, let her look at what lay in his palm. It was Tommy's red car.

"Answer me, dammit. Where'd you get this?"

"I bought it. In Queen City."

He hit her again, this time with the hand that held the toy. Dawn felt the skin split just above her eye.

"Ain't no toy stores in Queen City, bitch. Try another lie."

"I didn't buy it at a toy store." She was gasping for breath now. Harman was clutching her by the neck. He hoisted her to her knees and his fingers pressed hard into her throat. "Harman? Harman, please. I can't breathe."

"Who was here? What man came here and brought this to keep my son silent while you and he rutted in my bed?"

"Nobody. I swear it. Nobody was here. I bought the car. At the supermarket. They sell toys now, and Tommy saw this, and he wanted it so badly that I—"

She cried out as he lifted her from the bed and threw her against the dresser. Pain shot up her spine and into her neck.

"Liar," he snarled as he bent over her. The stink of his breath choked her.

"It's the truth. You know I don't have men here, Harman. Why would I? I love you. Only you. Nobody but—"

He punched her. Dawn's head jerked back and he hit her again, then curled his hand into the neckline of her nightgown and ripped it down to the hem.

"Whore! Harlot! Only a decent woman knows the meaning of love."

"Harman. Please. Please, oh sweet Jesus, don't—"

"Bitches like you ain't fit to use His name."

He hit her again. And again. By the time he tossed her on the bed and unzipped his pants, the world had become a gray blur.

"You won't learn," he said, as he came down on top of

her. "I try and try to teach you to be a good wife but you—
just—won't—"

Dawn moaned as he seated himself deep inside her. She
could feel her dry flesh tear as he pounded into her again and
again until, finally, she felt the hot spurt of his discharge. He
fell against her, his breathing harsh, the reek of him like sew-
age in her nostrils. She could feel wetness between her legs.
Was it from him, or was it blood?

I hate you, she thought, *God, I hate you, Harman Kitteridge.
I wish you were dead!*

No. It was wrong to think such things. This was her husband. She had taken vows that bound her to him. He was the
father of her child.

Maybe he was right. Maybe all this was her fault. She didn't
lie with other men, she didn't even talk to other men, but
surely she did things that made him angry. She could learn to
do things his way. The right way. She could—she could plan
a little better, look at the sink and notice that she'd put the
soap dish in the wrong place or see that she hadn't folded his
work shirts the way he preferred them folded.

She could leave him.

No. She could never do that. It wasn't right. A wife was
supposed to cleave to her husband. Besides, there was the baby
to consider. She'd grown up without a father; she knew that
a child deserved better than that. And Harman didn't mistreat
the baby. He'd never raised a hand to him. Tommy loved his
daddy. He loved him. Wasn't that worth the world?

Dawn lay stiff and silent under her husband's suffocating
weight. He was a heavy man, big and muscled from years of
working the timber on the mountain. She was small, just like
her mother. But she knew better than to complain that he was
crushing her and, after a long time, Harman grunted and rolled
off her.

Dawn waited. Then, slowly, carefully, she began inching
toward the edge of the mattress. She had to wash, put some
ice on her jaw and on her temple. Her little boy was getting
older. The last time Harman had beaten her, Tommy's eyes
had gone wide when he saw her in the morning.

"Mama hurt?" he'd said, as he'd touched his soft baby fingers to the cut on her lip.

"No, darlin'," Dawn had answered, "no, Mama's fine…"

"Where you think you're goin'?"

She gasped, jerked back as Harman's hand closed hard on her wrist. "Nowhere. Just—just to the bathroom."

"You was goin' to check on the kid."

"Well—well, yes. I thought the baby might have kicked off the blankets and—"

"He ain't a baby no more. Don't need you hangin' over him all the time."

"He's only three, Harman. I just want to—"

She cried out as his fingers bit into her flesh. "He's only three," he mimicked cruelly. His voice dropped, grew flat and cold. "Three's plenty big enough for him to know to put away his damn toys."

"Yes. Of course. I'll teach him."

"You'd better. 'Cause if you don't, I will."

A chill shuddered down her spine. "Harman. He's just a baby. He's just— Ahh. Harman. Please. Don't. Don't—"

Dawn closed her eyes as her husband climbed between her thighs and shoved himself inside her again. Each surge of his body was like a blow.

When he was done, she rolled away from him, rolled into a tight ball and lay shaking in the dark, her hand curled into a fist and shoved between her teeth to keep them from chattering. It had never been this bad before. Never. And it was her fault. Hers. It had to be. If she just learned to be a good wife…

"You're no good." Harman's voice rumbled in the silence. "You never will be. You're just like your mama. Don't know how in hell I came to marry a bitch like you."

Dawn bit back a sob. There was no sense in contradicting him, in reminding him that he'd seduced her into thinking a life with him would be better than the one she'd been living, that she'd gone to his bed a virgin.

"Don't know why I ever thought you'd make me a good wife or that you'd be a good mother to my son." The bedsprings squealed as he rolled onto his back. "The boy's turnin' out bad already." He yawned; his voice took on the blurry softness of alcohol-induced sleep. "But I'll fix that. I'll teach him the right way. I'll turn your little baby into a man."

"No." The word burst from her lips. "Harman, no. Not Tommy. You can't—"

"I can do whatever in hell I want. This is my house. The boy is my flesh and blood. Startin' tomorrow, I'm gonna start teachin' him that."

"Harman—"

A whimper drifted through the thin wall. Dawn grew rigid with fear as the whimper grew stronger.

"Wazzat?"

"The wind," she said quickly, "it's just the wind."

"Mama?"

The baby's cry was soft but it seemed as loud as a church bell in the silence. Tommy, she thought, Tommy, no, please, baby, no. Go back to sleep.

"Mama?" her son said, and began to cry.

"It's the kid," Harman grumbled. "Just listen at him, sobbin' like a girl."

"He's not. He's just—we must have woken him. He heard us and he's afraid. He's only a baby."

"I'll give him somethin' to be afraid of," her husband said. He rose up on one elbow, groaned and fell back against the pillows. "In the mornin'. I'm too wore out now. Man works all day, comes home for a little peace and quiet and does he get it?"

"Maaamaaa…"

"Go shut the kid up, you hear me, Dawn? You keep him quiet, or else."

Dawn sprang from the bed. She tugged what remained of her nightgown together and ran into the next room. Tommy was standing up in his crib. He was too big for it, really, and suddenly she knew why she hadn't suggested it was time to put him into a bed, because she'd been afraid of this all along, afraid of Harman taking a good look at their child and realizing he wasn't a baby any longer.

"Mama?"

Tommy sobbed her name, lifted his arms to her and she scooped him up, held him close, soothed him with whispers and kisses.

"Hush, sweetheart," she said softly. "Mama's here. She won't let anybody hurt you."

Except, it was a lie. Harman would hurt him and she'd be powerless to stop it from happening. Hot tears burned her eyes. Why had she denied the truth for so long? Her husband was a monster. He took pleasure from inflicting pain on those too weak to fight back. Tommy's life would be even worse than hers. He was a child, and helpless. Harman would brutalize him...and when he grew up, what kind of man would he be? One who'd learned to beat others into submission with his fists?

No. God, no. She couldn't let that happen. She was the one who had brought her baby into this and she was the only one who could save him. Dawn knew it as surely as she knew that the silk moth outside would be dead by morning.

Sounds came through the thin wall. Harman was asleep and snoring. He'd snore straight through to morning and wake up mean-tempered and even more dangerous than he was now.

Quietly she stole from the baby's room to the kitchen where the day's laundry lay neatly folded in a wicker basket, awaiting the touch of the iron. She always ironed on Saturdays. Harman preferred it like that. He liked to sit by the stone hearth and watch her iron. She'd told herself it was a charming, homey thing to do. Now, for the first time, she saw it for what it was, a fabrication that made them seem like a real family when they were actually something out of a nightmare.

Tommy had fallen asleep. Holding him carefully in one arm, Dawn dug into the basket for a change of clothes for her son and a cotton dress and underwear for herself. Gently she laid him in the basket while she stripped off her torn nightgown and put on the fresh clothes. She knew she looked a mess, not just because her dress was unironed but because her face had to be bruised. Almost as an afterthought, she looked down at her feet. No shoes. Well, that was all right. Shoes were easy enough to come by.

Life wasn't.

Dawn settled the baby in the crook of one arm as she took the flour canister from the cupboard and dug down inside it for the few dollars she'd managed to squirrel away from what she earned selling her blackberry preserves each season. She'd never let herself think about why she'd saved the money and hidden it; it had been a terrible risk that would surely have brought her a beating. Now, she knew she'd put the money aside in anticipation of this moment.

Harman's keys lay on the floor, glittering in the light cast by the lamp. She picked them up, opened the door and stepped onto the porch where the thwarted silk moth still beat against the window screen. Dawn hesitated, but only for a moment. Then she went back into the house and reached for the lamp.

The light blinked out. The awful sound of the moth's wings thudding fruitlessly against the screen stopped in almost the same instant. Carefully Dawn eased the door open and stepped outside. In the faint wash of the moon, she could see the creature hovering in confusion at the window.

As she had done so many years before, she scooped up the silk moth with her hand.

"Fly away," she whispered. "Fly away, and don't ever come back."

The moth's great wings beat. It lifted into the air, hung suspended before her for an instant, then flew into the night. Dawn climbed into her husband's truck, strapped her baby into the seat beside her. She took a deep breath, stuck the key into the ignition, turned it and stepped down, hard, on the gas.

In her heart, she'd always known it would come to this, that she would have to take her child and run for his life and for hers.

She was leaving the monster she'd married and she was never, ever coming back.

CHAPTER ONE

Four years later:

GRAHAM BARON stepped out of the terminal at the Austin airport and wondered how he'd ever survived spending the first seventeen years of his life in Texas. He was thirty-three and lived in New York now but whenever he came back here, the fact that he'd been born in this place always surprised him. It all seemed alien. The people. Their lazy drawls. The vastness of land and sky. The weather.

Oh, yeah, he thought, the weather, as the heat washed over him like an open furnace. And it wasn't really summer. Of course, there were those who said this wasn't really Texas, either. The guidebooks called the area hill country. So did people back East.

"Are you really from Texas?" somebody would say, if the subject of his birthplace came up.

"Yup," he'd reply, hooking his thumbs in his belt loops and putting on a John Wayne drawl, "ah surely am."

It always got a laugh, considering that he had no accent, didn't wear cowboy boots and had washed away the stink of oil, cattle and horses sixteen long years ago.

"Where in Texas?" they'd ask. And when Gray said he'd been born in Austin, someone would nod wisely and say, Austin, huh? Wasn't that, like, different? Weren't there green trees and rolling hills in Austin? It wasn't really the same as the rest of the state, right?

Like hell it wasn't, Gray thought as he put down his briefcase, peeled off his suit jacket, loosened his tie and rolled back his shirtsleeves. A man accustomed to a soaring Manhattan skyline had little use for the puny imitation of this one, and the hills of Central Park rolled as much as the land around here.

Dammit, he was in a rotten mood. For what had to be the hundredth time since he'd boarded the plane at La Guardia this morning, he wished he hadn't let himself get talked into making this trip...but he had. What was that old saying? Curiosity killed the cat. In his case, it had put him on a 6:00 a.m. flight to Texas.

A horn beeped at the curb. Gray looked over, saw a dark green Jeep with the Espada longhorns painted on the door. Abel Jones waved a hand. Gray waved back and trotted over.

"Nice of you to pick me up," he said as he got into the seat beside Abel and dumped his briefcase in the back.

Abel gave him a long look, then spat out the window and pulled into traffic. "Jes' part of the job," he said laconically.

So much for conversation. Not that Gray was surprised. Jonas Baron's foreman was a lot like the old man himself. Tall, spare, seemingly ageless, and not given to small talk. Well, that was fine. Gray wasn't much interested in conversation. He sat back, let the coolness of the air-conditioning wash over him as they made their way out of the airport and onto the highway that led from the city to the town of Brazos Springs, and tried to figure out what his uncle could possibly want.

Jonas had phoned late last night. The call had drawn Gray from the kind of deep sleep that came of having a woman lying warm and sated in his arms. The woman, someone he'd been seeing for several weeks, murmured a soft complaint as he rolled away from her and reached for the telephone, an automatic reaction that came of eight years of practicing criminal law.

You got a lot of middle of the night calls, when your clients weren't exactly the salt of the earth.

"Gray Baron," he said hoarsely.

The voice that responded was one he hadn't heard in a long time, an easy Texas drawl laid over a whip-sharp tone of command.

"Graham?"

"Jonas?" Gray peered at the lighted dial on his alarm clock, then sat up against the pillows. "What's happened?"

"Ain't nothin' wrong with your old man, if that's what you mean. Ain't nothin' wrong with nobody you care about, so you can relax."

"Gray?" the woman beside him murmured. "What's the matter?"

That was what he was trying to figure out. He reached back, smoothed his hand over her warm skin. Telephone at his ear, he got to his feet and walked, naked, from the bedroom.

"What's that supposed to mean? That there's nothing wrong with anybody I care about?"

"It's jes' a statement, boy. No need to try and parse it." There was a brief pause. "I guess you're wonderin' why I'm callin' so late."

"You guessed right," Gray said dryly.

"What time is it there, anyways? Midnight?"

"It's almost two. What's up, Jonas?"

There was another silence. "I just, uh, I just thought...I thought that we ain't seen you in these parts for a while."

Jesus, Gray thought, his uncle had finally gone senile. "No," he said carefully, "you haven't."

"Not since Samantha married that Dee-mee-tree-ose guy," Jonas said, turning the Greek name of his stepdaughter's husband into pure Texas.

Forget senile. The old man still had a mind like a steel trap. "So?"

"So..." More silence, then the sound of Jonas clearing his throat. "So, I wondered if you might be in the mood to pop down for a visit."

"Let me get this straight," Gray said carefully. "You phoned in the middle of the night to invite me to Espada?"

The old man chuckled. "You don't buy that, huh?"

"No." Gray walked through his dark apartment to the kitchen, tucked the phone against his shoulder and opened the refrigerator. He took out a bottle of mineral water, unscrewed the top and lifted it to his lips. "Hell, no," he said, wiping his mouth with the back of his hand. "Did you really think I would?"

"That's what I like about you, boy. You ain't like some people. You don't believe in treatin' me like I was God."

Gray laughed. What his uncle meant was that he didn't like the old man and he'd never pretended otherwise. He'd never toadied up to the Baron money the way his father did. Jonas whistled; Leighton came running. It had always been like that, all the years Gray was growing up. Sometimes he'd been hard-pressed to know which of the men he despised more, his father for sucking up or Jonas for wallowing in the pleasure of it. After a while, he hadn't bothered giving it much thought. All that mattered was that he hadn't done the same thing. He'd thumbed his nose at both of them and at a system that should have died out in the middle ages, and made his own way in the world.

"No," he said bluntly, "I don't." He put the bottle on the counter and made his way back toward the bedroom. "Look, Jonas, let's cut the crap, okay? It's the middle of the night. This is the first time you've ever phoned me. Come to think of it, this might just be the first time you've said more than three words in a row to me."

"Or you to me, boy."

"Absolutely. So, why would you expect me to buy into the idea that you called to invite me down for the weekend? Get to the bottom line. What's the deal?"

Another of those pauses hummed over the phone. Gray could hear the rasp of the old man's breath.

"You're some kinda hotshot lawyer up there in New York, ain't you?"

Was he? He was a partner in a prestigious firm, but did hotshot lawyers spend their days putting the scum of the earth back on the streets?

"I'm a lawyer, licensed to practice in the state of New York," Gray said brusquely.

"Well, I got a legal matter needs tendin'."

"A legal matter?"

"Uh-huh."

"Why come to me? For starters, I'm not licensed to practice in Texas."

"Don't need you to practice. Maybe I should have said what I need is legal advice."

"You have people to give it to you. Your son, for one."

"Travis is a lawyer, all right. But he lives in California."

"Yeah, and as we both just agreed, I live in New York."

"I don't want to involve Travis in this."

Did the old man know the effect that remark would have? Gray squelched the sudden rush of curiosity that shot through him.

"Well," he said, "you've probably got a powerhouse law firm on retainer in Austin."

"Damned right." A touch of pride crept into his uncle's voice. "The best."

"Exactly. Whatever legal advice you need, you'd be better off turning to them than to—"

"This here's a private matter. I want you to handle it, not my son or a passel of lawyers who got no more interest in the Baron name than when they see it on checks."

Another little flare of curiosity went through his blood but Gray ignored it. "That's very flattering," he said politely, "but—"

"Bull patties," Jonas said curtly. "I ain't tryin' to flatter you, an' you wouldn't give a tinker's damn if I was."

Gray sat down on the edge of the bed. The old man was good at this. He played people like a virtuoso played a Stradivarius, but Gray wasn't going to let himself be drawn in.

"You're right," he said, "I wouldn't. Look, whatever this is about, I'm not interested. I'm in the middle of a case."

"You could fly down in the mornin', fly back by nightfall."

"I'm afraid I can't. Besides—"

"Besides, you'd sooner work for a no-account horse thief than me."

The only good thing about Jonas was that he was always direct. Gray often thought it was the single quality he and his uncle had in common.

"Yeah." He smiled into the darkness. "That about sums it up."

"You know, boy, it ain't my fault your father's spent his life suckin' up to my money."

Gray rose to his feet. "It's late," he said coldly, "and I've had a long day. Good night, Jonas."

"Wait!" The old man huffed audibly. "I need your help."

Jonas Baron needed help? His help? Gray paused with his finger on the disconnect button. "In what way?"

"You fly down to Espada and I'll explain."

"I have no intention of flying down to Espada. Tell me the problem now."

"I can't do that."

"Jesus, I don't believe this! You get me up in the middle of the night, you mutter some crap about legal advice, and I'm supposed to drop everything and head for Texas?"

"Yes," the old man said sharply, and Gray suddenly realized his uncle's just-folks accent had disappeared. "That's exactly what you're supposed to do."

"Here's a news flash for you, Uncle. I've never done what I was supposed to do and I'm not going to start now."

"You might find this interesting."

"I doubt it."

"Gray." Another exhalation of breath, this one slightly ragged. "I'm an old man."

Ah, hell. Gray sat down again. "Look," he said, "it's true, you and I never really got along, but—"

"We'd have gotten along fine if we hadn't based our judgment of each other on your father."

Gray laughed. Definitely, direct and to the point. And maybe even dead-on correct. "I guess that's possible. But we did, and it's too late to go back and change things." His voice softened. "Jonas, I wish I could help you. But I really am in the middle of a case, and—"

"I'm getting old, boy. Real old." Jonas cleared his throat. "And—and I did something, a long time ago, that I need to atone for, before my time comes."

"Hell, I'm no clergyman."

"Dammit, are you listening to me? I don't want some candy-assed preacher to hear me confess my sins. What I need is a man I can trust."

"And you think that's me? Why? You and I hardly know each other."

"There's some of my blood in your veins, boy, even if you wish there wasn't. My brother was your grandfather."

Gray pinched the bridge of his nose between two fingers. "Jonas. Listen, if you need advice, I can recommend someone. One of my partners clerked for a Federal judge—"

"So did you."

That the old man would know so much about him took him by surprise. Still, he didn't want to get drawn into this, whatever "this" might be. Over the years, he'd kept his distance from his father, from his uncle, from Texas. He went back for weddings and big family parties but only because he liked his cousins. Other than that, he'd never felt part of the Baron clan, never wanted to be part of it.

"Graham?"

"Yes. I'm still here."

"I'm tellin' you again, boy. I need your help."

"And I'm telling you, Uncle. I can't give it."

The old man's patience slipped. "Damnation," he'd roared, "you fly down here and I swear, it'll take less time to tell you my problem than it's takin' you to tell me you ain't interested in hearin' it!"

Gray had known that was probably the truth. Besides, he couldn't quite repress that unwanted curiosity. After another few minutes he'd said okay, he'd take the first flight out of La Guardia in the morning.

"Good," his uncle had said briskly. "You're on Trans-America flight 1157, leavin' at 6:05 in the a.m."

The phone had gone dead and Gray knew he'd been had. He'd cursed, then laughed, finally climbed back into bed and when the woman in it rolled into his arms he'd made love to her. But part of him had remained at a distance while he'd tried to come up with a reason his uncle would go to such lengths to arrange for this command performance. At four-thirty, he'd risen from the bed, showered, dressed, left a note for his still-sleeping lover asking her to please let herself out and that he'd phone her in a day or two. Then he'd taken a taxi to the airport.

Yes indeed, he thought, as the Jeep pulled through the wrought iron gates that marked the entrance to Espada, curiosity killed the cat—but he was, just as Jonas said, a hotshot New York attorney, too smart to be drawn into anything against his will. He'd hear his uncle's story, offer some legal mumbo jumbo to soothe whatever twinge of conscience could plague a man at the end of such a long, powerful life and be back in New York by suppertime.

For all he knew, this little break in routine might just clear his head, make him feel better about the way he earned his living, twisting Justice's arm just enough to keep his next rich client from serving a stretch in prison.

The Jeep came to a stop in a cloud of dust. Gray nodded to Abel, grabbed his briefcase and headed for the house. When he was a kid, it had reminded him of Tara. It still did, he thought, and he was smiling when his uncle's wife opened the door. Gray was taken aback. He hadn't given it any thought but now that he did, he was surprised to see Marta, considering how secretive Jonas had made all this sound.

"Graham," his stepaunt said, "how good of you to come." Smiling, she held out her arms and hugged him. She smelled of expensive perfume and looked as if she were planning to lunch on Madison Avenue and he thought, as always, how surprising it was that such a woman would be happy in this setting. He liked her; he always had. Of all the wives the old man had gone through, Marta was the best.

"Marta." He kissed her cheek, put his hands on her shoulders and held her at arm's length. "You're as gorgeous as ever."

"Flattery will get you everywhere," she said, laughing. She linked her arm through his, shut the door on the hot breath of late spring and drew him into the elegant foyer. "I'm so pleased you decided to accept Jonas's invitation."

The old man's summons had been about as much an invitation as the Spanish Inquisition would have extended to heretics, but Gray kept the thought to himself.

"My pleasure," he said politely. "How have you been?"

"Oh, I'm fine. Everyone's fine." Her eyes clouded. "Except Jonas, of course."

Gray looked at her. "He's not well?"

"No. Not at all. Didn't he tell you?" She sighed and shook her head. "Of course he didn't. He seems to think he can pretend the years aren't finally catching up with him. And that his doctors haven't diagnosed—"

"Diagnosed what?"

Marta dropped his arm and folded her hands together at her waist. "Leukemia," she said softly. "That's the reason for all of this."

Hell. It was like sitting in at the Mad Hatter's tea party. Gray knew the characters but he didn't understand the dialogue. "All of what?" he said carefully.

"You know. The talk about what will happen after—after he's gone. Whether he's divided his assets properly. Whether he's left each child what that child truly wants." She looked up at him, smiling brightly. "I'm sure your chat is going to ease his mind. I mean, yes, certainly, Jonas has an excellent attorney. And he's given a great deal of thought to his will, but he seems to feel that discussing some of the specifics with you, as a member of the family, will help him be sure he's taken care of everything."

Gray's eyebrows rose. Was that what this was all about? Was he here to read the old man's will over his shoulder and offer advice on who should get what? He couldn't imagine any of Jonas's offspring quarreling over the disposition of the estate.

"Well," he said cautiously, "I'll do what I can."

"I know you will." Marta cleared her throat. "Now," she said briskly, "what can I get you?"

"Nothing, thanks." Gray glanced at his watch. "If you'd just tell Jonas that I'm here…"

"How about some coffee? Or something cold. Lunch won't be for another couple of hours. You'll join us, of course."

"I'm not sure," he said, although he knew that he wouldn't. "There's a two o'clock flight back to New York. If I can, I'd like to be on it."

"Ah. I'll be disappointed, but I understand. Well then, I'll have Carmen bring something for you to nibble on. Some of her pecan shortbread, and some lemonade. How's that sound?"

"Thank you, but it isn't necessary."

"Don't be silly." They paused at the closed library door. Marta turned to him and smiled, her eyes glittering with what he knew were unshed tears. "It's just so kind of you to do this for Jonas. Really, it's very generous."

Gray almost told her that kindness had nothing to do with it. Instead he took her hand and squeezed it. "I'll do what I can."

"I know you will. And Gray…try not to let him see your surprise at all the changes." Her voice quavered. "Will you do that, please?"

He nodded, and she rose on her toes and pressed a kiss to his cheek. Then she turned to the door and he could almost see her pulling herself together.

"Jonas?" She rapped her knuckles lightly against the wood, then turned the brass handle. "Darling? Graham's here."

Marta stepped back and Gray entered the library. The door swung softly shut behind him and as he looked around, his first thought was that he didn't know what she'd meant, warning him about changes. Everything was the same. He remembered when Marta had married his uncle. She'd redone the living room, the dining room, some of the rest of the big house, but this place—his uncle's lair, was the way he thought of it—had not been touched.

There were the same sofas and chairs he recalled from childhood, the leather cushions slightly worn and burnished by time. There was the same mahogany sideboard, and the big desk with the conquistador's sword that had given Espada its name mounted above it. The same draperies hung at the windows, the same old and beautifully faded silk carpet lay on the floor. And there was Jonas, seated in his favorite chair near the massive fireplace, a glass in his hand.

Nothing had changed at all…and then his uncle put down the glass and rose to his feet, and Gray caught his breath.

Jonas had shrunk. That was his first thought. The old man had gone from being six foot something to being five-nine or -ten…except, he hadn't. It was just that he was hunched over, those once-massive shoulders rounded, that proud back bent.

"Graham."

Jonas started across the room and Gray got his second shock. His uncle's stride had always been a proclamation that he owned the world. Now, he shuffled. His booted feet slid across the carpet. *Swoosh, swoosh, swoosh.* It was the sad, painful sound of age, and of a man who knew he was approaching the end of his life.

"Good to see you, boy."

Gray gave himself a mental shake and met his uncle in the center of the room. They clasped hands. Jonas's grip was still surprisingly strong but his fingers felt bony and cold. For the first time in his life, Gray felt a twinge of pity for him.

"It's good to see you, too, Uncle," he said.

Jonas nodded toward a pair of chairs. "Have a seat. You want somethin'? I can ring and ask Carmen to bring some coffee."

"No, thank you. I had enough coffee on the plane to float a ship."

"Good. I never did trust a man who'd sip coffee when he could be sippin' whiskey instead." The old man grinned. "Or ain't you a bourbon man, nephew? I can't seem to recall."

Gray smiled. Jonas recalled, all right. It was a standing joke that nobody would ever join the old man in a glass of the whiskey he favored. His sons preferred wine, beer and ale. Gray's preference was for single-malt scotch, but the memory of those cold fingers pressing against his made him reconsider.

"I'm not, usually," he said. "But I think some bourbon might be fine right about now."

Jonas nodded and shuffled to the sideboard. Gray saw his hands tremble as he opened the bottle of Jack Daniel's and warned himself not to let the signs of illness and age influence him. He'd come prepared to listen to whatever his uncle wanted to tell him, then to decline involvement and head home, and that was still what he intended to do. The last thing he wanted was to be dragged into sorting out some past mistake, real or imagined...unless Marta was right, and he was here to advise Jonas on his will. Hell, he wouldn't do that, either. He wanted no part in any of this.

"Here we are," Jonas said.

Gray took the glass, touched it to his uncle's and sipped the whiskey. There was more ceremony to get through, this time involving a box of Cuban cigars, which he refused. He waited while the old man bit the tip off one, spat it into the fireplace and lit up.

"Ain't supposed to drink or smoke, but what the hell's the difference? I ain't long for this world anyways."

"You'll outlive us all," Gray said politely.

A knock sounded at the door. Jonas opened it, took a quick look at the tray in his housekeeper's hands and waved her out.

"Lemonade," he said, his lip curling with disgust, "and cake. You'd think there was a couple of kids in this here room." He slammed the door and looked at Gray. "Where was I?"

"You said you wanted to talk."

"That ain't what I was saying. I was tellin' you there's not much point in me avoidin' a good shot of whiskey and a fine cigar." Jonas eased into a chair, motioned to the other one. "But you're right, I do have some talkin' to do. I suppose Marta told you I'm dyin'?"

"Uh, well, uh, she said—"

"Come on," Jonas said impatiently, "don't play games! There's just so much time a man has got, and I've used up most of mine. Remember what I said last night? That I liked the way you shoot straight? Don't disappoint me now, boy. I'm dyin'. That's all there is to it. And you know what? Dyin's okay. I lived a long, full life." He smiled, took a puff on the cigar and exhaled a cloud of smoke. "Had me five fine wives, four strong sons, built me this ranch and had me enough good

times for a dozen men.'' The smile faded and he sat forward.
''But the closer I come to the end, the more I've been thinkin'
that not all them good times was exactly good, if you catch
my drift.''

What was the old man getting at? A confession? A cleans-
ing of the soul? Gray cleared his throat.

''Yes, well, all of us do things we're not proud of, from
time to time. I mean—''

''Damnation, boy, get that panicked look off your face.''
Jonas scowled darkly. ''I told you, If I wanted a pulpit pansy
I'd have sent for one. I ain't about to drop a bunch of regrets
in your lap and ask for absolution.'' He paused, took a long
breath, then got to his feet. Slowly he walked to his desk and
picked up a paperweight. ''You ever notice this, Graham?''

Gray rose and followed his uncle to the desk. Jonas held
out the paperweight. Gray took it from him and, as he hefted
it, he realized it wasn't a paperweight at all. It was a chunk
of rock, pitted, rough and heavy, mottled with snaky streaks
of what he figured was some kind of mineral deposit.

''No,'' he said slowly, ''I guess I never did. What is it?
Granite?''

The old man chuckled. ''Hold it to the light.''

Gray moved to the window and lifted the rock toward the
glass. A beam of sunshine struck it, turning the mineral streaks
into dazzling ribbons of bright yellow.

''Gold?'' Gray said, looking at his uncle. ''Is that what this
is?''

''That's what it is, all right. Gold ore.'' Jonas took the rock
from Gray's hand and closed his fingers around it. ''Took it
from a mine in Venezuela, more'n half a century ago.''

''I didn't know you'd been a gold miner,'' Gray said, with
a little smile. The old man was right. He had, indeed, led a
long and interesting life.

''I been a lot of things.'' Jonas opened his fist, looked at
the rock, then put it down. ''I was a young man back then.
Already made me a pile of money in longhorns and some other
things nobody else thought would pay off so when my pal,
Ben Lincoln, asked me to go fifty-fifty on a mine in South

America, I figured why not give it a try? The mine was s'posed to be played out but Ben had reason to believe otherwise.''

He paused for a long moment and stared blindly out the window. Gray felt the hair rise on the back of his neck. It was almost as if the old man saw something out there that nobody else could see.

"So we took ourselves down to Venezuela and then up the Orinoco to this mine in the jungle somebody had worked an' then abandoned.''

He paused again, this time for so long that Gray moved toward him. "Uncle?" he said softly.

Jonas looked at him. "Yeah. I'm just thinkin' back.'' He cleared his throat. "Anyway,'' he said briskly, "turned out Ben was mistaken. We found some gold, but not enough. So Ben and me, we decided to end the partnership.''

Gray took another look at the rock. It was an interesting story, but what did it have to do with him? Jonas was still talking, something about him and Ben Lincoln, how they'd gone their separate ways and he'd come back to build Espada. Gray shot a surreptitious glance at his watch. An hour had gone by. If he didn't get out of here soon, he wouldn't make that flight to New York.

"Dammit, boy, how about payin' some attention here?''

Gray's head came up. A muscle knotted in his jaw. "You know,'' he said, as carefully as he could, "I don't like being called 'boy.' And I have been paying attention. I'm here, aren't I, when I should be meeting with a client—and I still don't know why in hell I came. What do you want, Jonas?''

"I'm getting to that.'' The old man hesitated. "Ben died a long time back. A few months ago, I heard—I heard he had some kin. A granddaughter.''

"And? What does any of this have to do with me?''

The old man's eyes met his. "I've owed a debt to Ben all these years, and I'm a man always pays his debts.''

Gray's eyebrows lifted. "It's a little late to worry about repaying this one, isn't it?''

"Ain't never too late to do the right thing, Graham. You live as long as me, you might just figure that out for yourself.''

"What kind of debt?"

"A debt, dammit," Jonas said irritably. "What's the difference?"

Things were starting to make sense. His uncle owed money to a man who was dead. For all he knew, he'd cheated Ben Lincoln out of some gold. Maybe he'd gone back later and found the mother lode. Maybe he'd done it without ever telling Ben Lincoln. Or maybe he'd palmed a couple of aces when they played cards. Knowing Jonas, anything was possible.

Now, with death looming ahead, he was having an attack of conscience. He wanted to make things right and he didn't want his sons or even his own lawyer to know about it for fear it would tarnish his image. Gray thought of telling him that there wasn't anything that could do more damage to an image like his, but what would be the point? The old man really didn't have much time left. It wouldn't hurt to do this simple thing for him.

"Okay," he said. He sat down again, picked up his briefcase and snapped it open. "You tell me the granddaughter's name, give me her address, and—"

"Don't know her address."

Gray sighed. "That's all right. Her name will probably be enough. I've got a couple of private investigators I use all the time. They'll find her."

"Don't know her name, neither."

"You don't know her name?" Gray repeated, trying to sound patient.

"Jes' said that, didn't I?"

"Okay. Okay, then, just tell me whatever you can about this Ben Lincoln. Where he was from. Where he went after you and he broke up the partnership. Anything you remember."

"Here." Jonas plucked a manila envelope from the top of his desk. "Figured you'd want whatever information I got. Wrote it all down for you."

Gray took the envelope and placed it in his briefcase. "Fine." He uncapped a pen, put a yellow legal pad on his knees. "These guys I know will find Lincoln's granddaughter."

Jonas nodded. "I was counting on that."

"And how do you want to handle this? After they've found her, do you want to mail her a check? Or do you want it hand-delivered?"

"A check?"

"Yes," Gray said, trying to disguise his impatience. "For his granddaughter. You want to keep it impersonal, or—"

"I don't intend to give the girl a check. If she's Ben's offspring, if she's a decent woman, I'll want to meet her. Write her into my will."

Gray looked up. Jonas was standing over him, one bony hand curled around the back of a chair. His eyes were flat, his mouth a grim line, but a dark blue vein throbbed in his papery temple. Something was going on here, something more than the old man had told him, but what?

"You want to write her into your will?"

"You deaf, counselor? How come I have to repeat everything I say?"

Oh, yeah. Definitely something was going on. There was the look on Jonas's face. The sudden ringing tone to his voice. More to the point, the on-again, off-again accent had just taken a hike, and that was always meaningful.

Gray capped the pen, placed it and the legal pad inside the briefcase and stood up. He'd been as tall as Jonas for years; now, he towered over him. It was a small but decided advantage, and wasn't that a crazy thing to think?

"And how will you be sure she's a decent woman, Uncle?"

Jonas's mouth curved at the corners. "I'll rely on your reports, nephew. What else would I do?"

"Now, wait just a minute. I'm willing to use one of my investigators to locate this woman, but if you intend to base your decision on the findings of a private detective…forget it. I won't take responsibility for somebody else's opinion of an unknown woman's moral fiber—assuming the investigator finds her at all."

"He'll find her. You just told me he would."

Hell. Gray ran a hand through his hair. "Okay. I'll put the best man I can think of on the case."

"I've already done that, Graham. I've put you on it." Jonas seemed to stand a little taller. "Your investigator will do the footwork." He grinned, and suddenly he didn't look quite so frail and old. "Wouldn't expect somethin' so down and dirty of you, boy. But you're the one who's gonna verify what the man says. You'll take a good, hard look at the lady once she's found. Observe her. Talk to her, check her out every which way. An' when you know what she's really like, why then, nephew, you'll report back to me and tell me everythin' I need to know." Jonas strolled to his chair, sat down and picked up his tumbler of bourbon. "Way I figure it, the whole thing shouldn't take you no more'n a couple of weeks."

"Jonas." Gray spoke gently. "Look, I'd like to help you. But surely you understand that I have a law practice. Clients. I have obligations, and I can't just—"

"You got an obligation to me, boy. Maybe it's time you knew that."

Gray narrowed his eyes. There was an ominous sound to the words. "What in hell is that supposed to mean?"

Jonas got up, walked to the sideboard and refilled his glass. "You never did get along with your old man, did you? Never did cotton to the idea of sittin' around, watchin' him grovel to me." He sipped the bourbon, smiled over the rim of the tumbler. "You ever stop to think how nice it was, gettin' away from here when you was, what, eighteen? When you went away to that there fancy college in New Hampshire?"

"I was seventeen," Gray said coldly. "And what does that have to do with this conversation?"

"An' how 'bout that law dee-ploma?" Jonas sighed. "The way I hear it, ain't ever'body can afford a Yale law dee-gree."

The hair on the nape of Gray's neck was rising again. "I had full scholarships to both Dartmouth and Yale."

Jonas chuckled. "Oh my, yes. You was a smart kid, Graham. You won them scholarships, fair and square." His smile faded. "'Course, you never did give too much thought as to who funded those scholarships, did you?"

Gray stared at his uncle. He felt as if the floor were dropping from under his feet. "You?" he said hoarsely. "You funded them?"

"And the pocket money that went along with them." The old man plucked what remained of his cigar from a heavy glass ashtray and stuck it between his teeth. "Your father did the right thing, son. He come to me, said you was smart and he couldn't afford to do right by you."

That his father had once said something good about him didn't seem to matter half as much as learning that he'd gotten where he was today—wherever in hell that might be—courtesy of the very man he'd grown up despising. Gray could feel a cold, hard knot forming in his gut.

"And now," he said softly, "you're calling in your markers."

His uncle shrugged. "Only if you make it seem that way."

Gray laughed. "Only if *I* make it seem...? You are some piece of work, Jonas, you know that? You're blackmailing me into taking God only knows how much time out of my life so you can soothe your conscience before you die, and you say it's payback time only if I make it seem that way?" His laughter stopped abruptly. "I don't suppose you'd settle for me writing out a check for whatever I owe you... No," he said grimly, when Jonas chuckled, "no, I guess not." Anger flooded through him and he balled his hands into fists, jammed his fists into his pockets before he did something he knew he'd regret. "I've got news for you, old man. You don't need to be concerned with your conscience because the fact is, you never had one."

Jonas took the cigar from his mouth and set it back into the ashtray. "Yes," he said softly, "I do, even if it seems to be catching up years too late." He walked toward Gray, his gaze locked to the younger man's, his hand outstretched. "You do this, we'll call things even."

Gray held his uncle's eyes for a long minute. Then he looked pointedly at the outstretched hand, ignored it and reached, instead, for his briefcase.

"You're damned right we will," he said, and he pulled

open the door and marched down the hall, hating Jonas, hating himself, but most of all hating his own father, a man he'd sworn he'd never emulate, because here he was, dancing to a tune Jonas Baron played and stuck with dancing straight to the very last note.

CHAPTER TWO

GRAY boarded the flight to New York still tight-lipped with rage.

If anybody had asked him how he'd gotten where he was today, a partner in one of New York's top law firms at such a relatively young age, he'd have said he'd done it all on his own. Good grades in college had led to his acceptance at Yale Law. A straight A average there and a stint writing for the *Law Review* had won him a clerkship with a Federal judge and then interviews at a number of important firms. He'd picked the one where he'd figured he'd have a straight shot at the top after putting in the requisite seventy-five hours a week of grunt work for a couple of years. He'd been right. Those years got him noticed; he landed a partnership even sooner than he expected without having to curry favors from anybody. Watching his father go through life as a suck-up had convinced him he'd sooner end up flipping burgers than repeat Leighton's pattern.

Now it looked as if he'd been blissfully living a lie, that his successes were all traceable to Jonas's largesse. Okay. Maybe that was an overstatement. He'd made it to where he was on his own, but his uncle's money was the reason he'd been able to get his foot on the bottom rung of the ladder. He was just where he'd sworn he'd never be, beholden to the old man, and now Jonas was calling in the debt.

"Sir?"

But facts were facts. You couldn't change them; you could only use them to serve your client's best interests. That was one of the things he'd learned in law school. First, make a dispassionate assessment of a case. Then use your knowledge to get the outcome you wanted. Well, he was his own client right now, and what would serve his interests was to do what had to be done so he could get on with his own life.

Truth was, he wouldn't have to spend much time dealing with Jonas's situation. He had all sorts of contacts, including private investigators whose fields of expertise involved tracking people even if the trail was old and cold. Actually he didn't have to do much of anything personally except give Jonas's information to one of those people, then sit back and wait for the answers to drop in his lap.

Then, if—and it was a huge "if," considering that Jonas didn't even know if this Ben Lincoln actually had a granddaughter—if there was such a woman, and if a P.I. could find her, Gray would meet her, spend ten minutes in conversation before contacting his uncle.

"Mr. Baron?"

What the old man did with his money was none of his business. All he wanted was to erase this debt. Hell had to be going through life, knowing you had an obligation to Jonas Baron.

"Mr. Baron. Sir, would you like to see the lunch menu?"

Gray looked up. The flight attendant, smiling politely, leaned toward him. For the first time since he'd stormed out of his uncle's library, Gray felt good enough to smile back.

"Sure," he said, "why not?"

Why not, indeed? A couple of days, maybe a week at the most, and he'd be able to tell Jonas to go scratch.

"Here's the report on the woman you wanted to find," he'd say. "And now, uncle, for all I give a damn, you can go straight to hell."

It was such a welcome thought that he went right on smiling, even after the flight attendant placed the airline's version of lunch in front of him.

The next morning Gray phoned Jack Ballard, a P.I. who'd done some good work for him in the past.

"I can come by on Monday," Ballard said.

Gray said it would be better if he could come by right away. Ballard sighed, said he'd be there in about an hour. When he showed up, the men went through a couple of minutes of inconsequential talk before getting down to business. Gray said he'd been asked to do a favor for a client. He told Ballard only as much of the story as necessary, mostly that he wanted him to locate a woman whose only link to his client was through a relationship half a century old, and shoved Jonas's still-sealed manila envelope across the desk.

Ballard lifted an eyebrow as he looked at it. "You didn't open this to see what's in it?"

Gray shrugged his shoulders. "You're the detective. Not me."

Ballard grinned, ripped the envelope open and peered inside. "Well, it looks as if there wasn't all that much to see."

Three pieces of paper fluttered onto the surface of Gray's always-neat desk. One bore notes in what Gray recognized as Jonas's hand. The other two were black-and-white photographs, the edges torn and yellowed. Ballard reached for the notes; Gray scooped up the pictures and looked at them.

The first was of two men dressed in suits, though neither man looked as if he belonged in one. They stood with their arms around each other's shoulders and grinned into the camera. The men were in their thirties or early forties, strong and young. Curious, he turned the photo over. *Ben and Jonas, Venezuela 1950*. The words were scrawled across the back of the picture, again in his uncle's handwriting.

Gray took another look at the photo.

Yeah, he could see it now. One of the men was definitely Jonas. The mouth, the eyes, the grin...none of that had changed. It was just weird to see him so young. Somehow, though he'd always thought of his uncle as fit and powerful, he'd never imagined him as anything but old. The other man, Ben Lincoln, had lighter hair and sharper features. Except for that, Jonas and he seemed like duplicates, tall and handsome and broad-shouldered, looking into the camera through eyes that said they already owned the world.

The second photo was of a woman. Gray flipped the picture over. *Nora Lincoln,* someone had printed on the back. She stood in a grassy square, maybe in a park somewhere, hands planted on slender hips, chin elevated in a posture of what seemed defiance. She was a pretty woman or she would have been, if she'd unbent just a little. Her expression was hard to read. Were her eyes cool? They seemed to be. Her hair was long and light-colored. It looked windblown and maybe in need of taming, but another look at those eyes and Gray figured everything about her had probably needed taming.

Two powerful, tough-looking men in the prime of life. And a woman who looked as if she'd be a challenge to either of them. Gray felt a stir of interest. What did these people have to do with a sample of ore from a Venezuelan gold mine?

"Well," Ballard said, "this sure isn't much to go on."

He handed the handwritten page of notes to Gray. Ben Lincoln, date of birth unknown, place of birth unknown, had been married to a woman named Nora sometime around 1950. They'd been divorced early in 1952 and Nora had given birth to a child she'd named Orianna in the summer of that year. Orianna had given birth to a baby girl, too, in 1976 or '77. The father was unknown. The child had probably been born somewhere in southern Utah or northern Arizona. That baby girl, if she existed, if all the other information was correct, Jonas had written, would be Ben Lincoln's granddaughter. But, he'd added, there was no way to be sure. Ben Lincoln had died a long time ago. He'd heard that Nora and Orianna were dead, too.

Gray turned the page over. The reverse side was blank. "That's it?"

"That's it," Ballard said, and grinned. "This one's gonna cost a bundle. I'll have to hire a bunch of guys to do the legwork. There'll probably be a couple of dozen leads to check out and the odds are good they'll all go nowhere long before I can find something usable." He tapped a pencil against his teeth. "We're talking six figures here."

Gray tossed the paper on the desk, tilted back his chair and folded his hands over his flat belly. "That's okay, Jack. Just do it and send me the bill." He smiled tightly. "Don't worry about the cost."

Ballard laughed. "I never do."

"Good. My client deserves to pay through the nose."

The investigator chuckled as he scooped the photos and the

single sheet of information into the manila envelope, then got to his feet.

"You disappoint me, Gray. Here I thought you defense attorneys were supposed to be protective of your clients."

"Nobody needs to protect this one," Gray said. He rose, too, and came around his desk. "As always, this is confidential, okay?"

Ballard clapped his hand to his heart. "Man, you wound me. Aren't I always the soul of discretion?"

He was right. Investigators didn't last long if they weren't discreet but Ballard was even more circumspect than most. It was one of the reasons Gray employed him.

"Yes, you are." Gray held out his hand. "What I meant was, if you should manage to find this woman, don't talk to her. Don't let her know you're watching her. Just keep everything under your hat. I'm supposed to check the lady out myself. Client's orders."

"No problem."

The men shook hands. "Truth is, though, I suspect you're not going to come up with anything."

"The odds are that you're right, but you know me. I'll put all the stuff I don't find into a fifty-page report, fit the report into a shiny binder and your client will be impressed."

Both men grinned. "Keep me posted," Gray said, and Jack promised that he would.

Two weeks later, Ballard phoned late one morning.

"Got some stuff," he said.

Gray suggested they meet for lunch at a small Italian place midway between their offices.

"So," Gray said, after they'd ordered, "what do you have? Information? Or fifty pages of B.S. in a shiny binder?"

Jack chuckled. "Information, surprisingly enough. Not enough to fill fifty pages, but solid."

"You found Lincoln's granddaughter?"

"No, not yet. But I figured you'd want an update. I found the town where Orianna Lincoln lived and died, and some people who knew her."

"Orianna Lincoln," Gray said. "So, even though she was born after Ben and Nora were divorced, he acknowledged the child as his flesh and blood?"

"Careful, counselor." Ballard sat back as their first courses were served. "You're leaping to conclusions. All I know is that Nora Lincoln put Ben Lincoln's name on Orianna's birth certificate." He stabbed a grape tomato, lifted it to his mouth and chewed vigorously. "Orianna was born in '52, same as your uncle said, in a little town in Colorado. Her mother—Nora—died in an auto accident not long afterward. Orianna was bounced from foster home to foster home, grew up into what you might expect."

"Her father didn't raise her?"

"Ben Lincoln? No. He lit out for Alaska in '53, died up there in a blizzard a few years later. The kid—"

"Orianna."

"Right. She grew up, got herself into a little trouble. Nothing much, just some shoplifting, a little grass, a couple of prostitution convictions."

"Sounds like a sweetheart."

"Right. NCIC—the National Criminal Investigation Center—has her getting busted for petty crap all over the southwest. Eventually she ended up with some bozo in Fort Stockton, Texas. He walked out on her and the next record we have shows she set up housekeeping in a trailer park in a place called Queen City, up in the mountains in northern Arizona."

"Alone?"

"Yup." Ballard speared another tomato and grinned. "But that didn't keep her from leading a full life, if you get my drift." The detective took a sip of water, swallowed and leaned over the table. "The lady believed in an open door policy. One man in, another out, no stopping to take a breather in-between. No kids to slow her down until 1976, when something must have gone wrong with her planning. She gave birth to a girl she named Dawn."

Gray raised his eyebrows. "Classy name."

"Yeah, and I figure that was all that was classy in the kid's life. Dawn lived in the trailer with mama until she was seventeen. Then she married a local name of…'' Ballard reached into his breast pocket and took out a small leather notebook. ''Name of Kitteridge. Harman Kitteridge.''

''In Queen City?''

''Yup, Queen City. Two traffic lights and half a dozen cheap bars. And local branches of every whacko political organization you ever heard of.'' He grinned. ''Plus some you're lucky you haven't.''

Gray put down his fork. ''It sounds like heaven.''

''You got that right. Two days there, I was ready to grab a rifle and go looking for black helicopters. Kitteridge lives on the outskirts of town, on top of a mountain. He's got a cabin up there. Apparently his grandpappy built it with his own hands.'' Ballard put down his notebook and turned his attention to his salad. ''You can almost hear the banjoes playing in the background.''

Gray nodded, picked up his fork and poked at his antipasto. Just what he needed, he thought glumly, a trip to the ass end of nowhere for a stimulating conversation with Dawn Lincoln Kitteridge. If he'd thought about her at all during the last weeks, he'd imagined a more up-to-date version of that defiant, almost beautiful woman in the photo, but this conversation had put things in perspective. He could almost envision Dawn Kitteridge, country twang, lank hair, bare feet, gingham dress and all.

''Lucky Dawn,'' he said, ''she got to trade her trailer for a shack.''

''Yeah, she got herself a shack, and a hubby ten years older than she is.'' Ballard paused as the waiter cleared away their appetizers and served their main courses. ''But she got tired of both,'' he said, tucking into his *spaghetti carbonara*. ''She left Kitteridge and the mountain almost four years ago.''

Gray looked up from his *pasta alla vongole*. ''She missed the trailer park?''

''If you mean, did she go back there, the answer's no.''

''Damn,'' Gray said with a little grin, ''and here I was, happily anticipating a trip to a sophisticated metropolis called Queen City.''

"Well, actually, I don't know where you're going to be taking that trip to meet up with the little lady—that is still your intention, isn't it? 'Cause the thing is, she didn't exactly leave a forwarding address."

Gray put down his fork. He'd been telling himself this was all over, that he'd go to Arizona, spend an hour talking with Lincoln's granddaughter, then fly to Espada and end his unwanted obligation to his uncle.

"Are you saying you don't know where she is?"

"I'm saying I haven't located her yet, but I will."

"Damn." Gray shoved his plate aside. All at once, he had no appetite. "How much longer will it take?"

Ballard shrugged. "I can't say for certain. Four years is a long time and when the lady left, she seemed determined to cover her tracks."

"Kitteridge doesn't know where she went?"

"I didn't talk to him. Not yet, anyway. He was out of town but from what I picked up from local chitchat, he has no idea what happened to her." Ballard patted his lips with his napkin. "Hey, don't look so sour. I promise, we'll find her. I've got three men looking for her."

"Yeah, yeah." Gray sighed, sat back and rubbed his hand over his forehead. "I just don't want this to drag on forever."

"You said money wasn't a problem."

"It isn't. Time is my concern. I want to get this done with."

"Gray, my man, don't I always deliver?"

It was true. Gray had no doubt that Jack would find Dawn Lincoln Kitteridge. He just had to be patient.

"Yeah, you do. Look, put another couple of people on it, okay? Do whatever it takes to locate the lady."

"Absolutely."

"Meanwhile, what's this Harlan Kitteridge like?"

"It's Harman. I told you, I didn't meet him, but I did some checking. He's got some stuff on his record."

"Such as?"

Ballard opened his notebook again. "Some DWIs. Two bar fights. He broke up a guy pretty bad in one of them but witnesses said it was self-defense so, you know, case closed. An assault on a woman he'd been living with. Beat her up and she called the cops but when it came to the courtroom, she said she'd hurt herself taking a tumble down the stairs and all she wanted was Harman out of the place.'' Jack looked up. ''Nothing once he married our girl. Dawn either swings a heavy bat or she reformed him.''

''Yes,'' Gray said lightly. ''They sound like a real nice couple.''

The bus boy cleared their places. The waiter stopped by. Gray ordered espresso; Ballard ordered a cappuccino and cheesecake.

''So,'' Ballard said, ''the next thing I'm going to do is fly on back to Queen City and have a chat with Mr. Kitteridge. He's on his mountain again.''

''I thought you said he doesn't know where his wife is.''

''I said that's what the town says. Besides, even if he doesn't, maybe he can give us some clues. Maybe she talked about wanting to see someplace special. Maybe she has friends in places outside Queen City.'' The investigator peered at the slice of cake the waiter put in front of him, then dug into it. ''At the very least, he can probably fill in some blank spaces while my guys look for her.''

''That sounds reasonable, I guess.''

''Trust me, Gray. It *is* reasonable. Just tell your client to keep his pants on, okay?''

Gray laughed. ''I'm sure he'll love the advice, Jack. Anything else?''

''Nope. Oh. Yeah, before I forget…'' He patted one breast pocket and then the other. ''Here,'' he said, and held out a small white envelope.

''What's this?'' Gray opened the envelope. Inside were the photo of Jonas and Ben, and the one of Nora Lincoln. ''Ah. The pictures. You don't need them anymore?''

''Not really. Besides, I made copies. I figured your client might want these back.''

Gray nodded and pocketed the photos. ''You've done fine, Jack. To be honest, I didn't think we had a chance of coming up with anything, but you've managed to find the girl.''

"Not yet. I found where she lived and who she lived with."
Ballard took a sip of his cappuccino. "She's still among the
missing."

"Among the…" Gray looked up. "You think something
happened to her? That Kitteridge did something?"

"Hell, no. Jeez, you've been associating with lowlife too
long. No, Gray. I just mean I haven't located her yet. But I
will."

"Fine. Call me when you do. In fact, call me after you go
to Queen City and speak with Harman Kitteridge. I have to
admit, I'm curious."

Ballard grinned. "Your wish is my command, counselor.
Say, is this lunch on your client's expense account?"

"Why?"

"You think I could have another slice of that cheesecake?"

That night, Gray phoned Jonas and gave him a brief update.
When he finished, there was a long silence. Then his uncle
cleared his throat.

"So," he said, "the girl really exists."

"Yeah. So it would seem. Do you still want her found?"

"Yes, of course. Find her, talk to her, see what she's
like…" Another silence. "This husband of hers. He doesn't
sound like anybody's idea of Prince Charming."

"No. He doesn't."

"You're gonna meet with him?"

"No," Gray said coldly, "I am not. The investigator I hired
will do that. There's no reason for me to talk to the man."

"You got a good way of seein' inside people."

Gray laughed. "Don't try to con me, okay? If I did, I'd
have figured out, years back, that the only way my father could
have come up with money for my schooling was by begging
it from you."

"You know, boy," Jonas said, his voice hardening, "maybe
you ought to be grateful he did, otherwise what would you be
doin' right now? Not livin' high on the hog in New York City,
I bet."

"I'll call you when I know more," Gray said, and hung up the phone.

Hours later, he gave up trying to sleep. The old man certainly had a way of getting to the heart of a thing. He'd grown up disliking Texas and despising his uncle, congratulated himself for getting free of both...and now it turned out he hadn't actually escaped either one.

He went into the kitchen, switched on the light, took the pictures Jack Ballard had given him from the kitchen table and stared at the faces frozen in time.

There was more to this tale than his uncle admitted. Gray had suspected it. Now, he was sure of it. He'd been a lawyer long enough to sense when a client was omitting pieces of a story. Sometimes, you were happy to leave it like that. You wanted the truth, but you didn't want to hear things that might keep you from doing the best possible job. Defending a man against a charge of murder was a lot easier when you believed he hadn't actually committed it. There was no murder involved here but something dark and distant was gnawing at Jonas's innards. And, like it or not, he was being drawn further and further into the situation.

He sat down at the table and stared at the picture of Jonas and Ben Lincoln. Was there a whisper of hostility hidden inside those smiles? And the picture of Nora Lincoln. He touched the tip of his finger to her face. Were her eyes cool, or were they infinitely sad? Maybe that chin wasn't tilted in defiance but in self-defense.

"Dammit," Gray said, and kicked back his chair. What did it matter? The story, whatever it was, dated back half a century. And it sure as hell didn't involve him. He had better things to think about than a dead woman who might have a secret in her eyes and a granddaughter who had run away from a mountain in the middle of nowhere.

The case that had consumed his time for the past few months was winding down. Tomorrow, he'd present his closing argument to the jury. His client would walk free. Gray wasn't foolish enough to think you could predict how a case would end but sometimes you could make a pretty shrewd guess. His client had been accused of felonious assault with intent to kill; he'd sworn that the witnesses had misidentified him. Gray hadn't been concerned with the man's guilt or innocence. That wasn't his job. His duty was to convince the jury that the witnesses were wrong, that there was reasonable doubt that it was not his client who had committed the crime. Every instinct he had assured him that he'd done that.

He'd be free of the case in a few days. He'd thought about taking a break, getting away from the city and the stress of his job, maybe doing something different enough to get the juices flowing so he'd feel the way he once had about his work. He'd even had a talk with his travel agent, who had given him a stack of brochures about things that ranged from running the rapids in Alaska to mountain trekking in Nepal.

He'd been to Alaska. And there were mountains in northern Arizona.

He looked at the photo of Nora Lincoln. What would she think, if she knew her granddaughter had spent most of her life in a trailer park? That she'd married a man with an arrest history and then left him?

"Life sucks," Gray said softly, "and then you die."

He went into his study, flicked on the light, looked up Jack Ballard's phone number in his address book and dialed it. Ballard answered on the second ring.

"It's late," Ballard said in a gravelly voice. "This better be good."

"Jack, it's Gray Baron. Look, I'm sorry to bother you at this hour but…" Gray cleared his throat. "You know that trip you were going to make to Arizona? The thing is, my client— well, I have a personal connection to him. And, as a sort of favor, I've decided to talk with Kitteridge myself. Uh-huh. I'm going to fly out there, probably within the next couple of days. No, no, I'm not pulling you off the case, Jack. Far from it. I want you to locate Dawn Kitteridge for me. Absolutely. Right. Yes, do it just the way I asked. Find her, but don't approach her. You just tell me where the lady is and I'll take it from there. Great. Thanks, Jack. I appreciate it."

Gray hung up the phone and headed back to bed.

Definitely, he could use the change in routine. He was starting to get curious about where this was really going. Jonas might be dying but he still couldn't quite accept him as a man bothered by a prickly conscience, especially when it involved something more than fifty years old. And then there was that look in Nora Lincoln's eyes. Would he see it in her granddaughter's eyes, too? Gray needed to find out, not for Jonas but for himself.

Three days later, with another acquittal in his files and the directions to Queen City in his pocket, Gray flew to Arizona.

CHAPTER THREE

IF TEXAS was hot, Arizona was the gateway to hell.

Gray flew into Phoenix in early afternoon. He could have saved time by flying into Flagstaff but he decided that the extra half day it would take him to reach his destination was worth it. He'd get the chance to decompress after the rigors of the trial and to work on the excuse he'd thought of to explain to her husband why he was looking for Dawn Lincoln Kitteridge.

He picked up his rental car and dumped his bag in the trunk. Desert heat was dry heat, people always said, as if without humidity a temperature of one hundred and six would be no problem. Gray was dressed for comfort in chinos and a white shirt with an open collar and rolled up sleeves but he still felt as if he was standing in front of an open furnace.

He set the AC on high and headed north on Highway 17.

After a while, the land opened up into true desert, broken only by occasional roads that seemed to arrow through the scrub and cactus toward the distant mountains. Eventually the highway began to climb. Pines towered overhead; patches of snow glistened on the higher ridges. Gray turned off the air-conditioning, put down the window and drew in deep breaths of cool, clean air.

The countryside was spectacular, and all that open space coupled with the scent of pine was soothing. He could almost feel his tension starting to drain away. Coming here to see Harman Kitteridge had been the right decision. He could satisfy his curiosity, ask some questions Jack couldn't because there had been no reason to tell him he was looking into this for his uncle. He didn't plan on telling Kitteridge, either. It was always best to play your cards close to your chest.

Gray took one hand off the wheel, dug in his pocket and took out the map his travel agent had faxed him. She'd booked him into a place called the Drop-On Inn for the night. That was the only place available in the vicinity of Queen City, she'd written, and he'd visualized how her elegant eyebrows must have lifted at the news that he was going to such a hole in the wall. She'd also included the names of a couple of resort hotels between Flagstaff and Queen City, along with a polite note saying he might prefer one of them to the Drop-On Inn.

Gray knew she was probably right but he figured it would be simpler to stay near Queen City for the night. With luck, he'd meet with Kitteridge in the morning, and how long could a conversation with the man possibly take? An hour? Two? After that, he might just check out some of those hotels his agent had mentioned. This was beautiful country, high, rugged and untouched. A little time off here could be just what he needed.

He turned on the radio, searched for a station that played the kind of cool jazz he liked and settled instead for some guy singing about a love gone wrong. A couple of songs later, he was humming along with the melody. Yessir, making this trip had been a fine idea.

The Drop-On Inn dimmed his enthusiasm only a little. The sign out front said Motel but it was just ten small rooms strung together like links of sausage. Still, the place was clean, his room had a TV that received two channels, and there was even a café next door. Gray and a trucker who apparently owned the eighteen-wheeler parked at the other end of the motel were the only customers. He ordered a steak that overflowed the plate and mashed potatoes floating in enough butter to make him feel guilty so he passed on dessert, had a cup of coffee, went back to his room and slept as well as a man could when his feet hung off the end of the mattress.

He awoke to sunshine but by the time he'd finished off a stack of pancakes and three cups of coffee at the café, a bank of charcoal clouds had rolled in. Clouds or not, he felt pretty good when he set off for Queen City. He'd definitely make a short vacation out of this trip. If there was a camping equipment store in Queen City, he'd stop there after he finished with Kitteridge, buy himself some boots and some simple gear, use one of the hotels his agent had recommended as a base and head into the mountains. Gray liked the isolation of hiking but he also liked hot tubs, soft beds and the company of beautiful women. A few days in the wilderness, followed by another few days in a luxury resort, would feel just fine.

He found the station that played country love songs again and tapped his fingers against the steering wheel in rhythm with the music. It was hard to believe he'd wasted time the other night, sitting in his apartment, looking at a picture of a dead woman and speculating about what kind of life she'd have led, or what life she'd have wanted for her granddaughter.

The first fat drops of rain hit the windshield as he passed a sign welcoming him to Queen City, population 3,400 and home of the Patriots Regional High School Championship Football Team. Jack Ballard had given him a phone number for Harman Kitteridge. Gray had laughed and jokingly expressed surprise that the cabin would have a phone and electricity. Now, slowing for the first of the two traffic lights Ballard had mentioned, he thought the same thing again. This time, he meant it.

To call this place a city was not just an overstatement, it was a pathetic dream.

Queen City had seen better times. At least half of the shops on Main Street were vacant. The only living creature in sight was a dog relieving himself on a teetering pile of boxes in front of a boarded-up store. If it was a comment on the town, Gray agreed with it. Even the mountains that ringed Queen City were depressing. Their colors were sullen and their looming presence made him feel claustrophobic.

He drove into the only gas station in sight and stopped beside a self-service pump. While he gassed up, he dialed Kitteridge on his cell phone. It was Sunday and he figured the odds on finding the man at home were good. He hadn't called in advance because the less time he gave him to think about this visit, the better. In fact, the less Kitteridge knew about the real purpose of this visit, the better.

Kitteridge answered on the first ring. "Yeah?"

"Harman Kitteridge?"

"What's it to you?"

So much for the social niceties. Gray tucked the phone against his shoulder as he pulled the nozzle from the gas tank and hung up the hose.

"My name is Gray Baron."

"I don't want none."

"Excuse me?"

"Whatever it is you're sellin', I don't want it."

"I'm not a salesman, mister—"

Gray winced as the phone slammed in his ear. He got into the car and hit Redial. Again, Kitteridge answered immediately.

"Mr. Kitteridge," he said quickly, "don't hang up. I'm not selling anything."

"You think I'm an idiot? Of course you are. What is it? Insurance? Home repairs?" Kitteridge's voice took on a nasty edge. "Or maybe this is about that there loan you bastards give me last year."

"It's nothing like that. This is about your wife."

"My what?"

"Your wife. Dawn Lincoln Kitteridge."

There was a long silence. "Who is this?" Kitteridge finally said, so slowly that Gray could feel his suspicion through the phone.

"I told you. My name is Baron. Gray Baron."

"What do you want with my wife?"

"I'd like to talk with her."

"So did that other guy, couple of weeks ago, folks tell me. Or are you gonna claim you and he don't know about each other?"

Gray thought about playing dumb and decided it would only heighten Kitteridge's mistrust. "No," he said, "I'm not. He worked for me."

"And the both of you want to talk to my wife? Well, anything you got to say to her, you can say to me."

"I'm afraid not," Gray said politely. "This is a legal matter. I can only discuss it with her."

"She don't talk to nobody unless I say she... What kind of legal matter?"

Kitteridge's tone had gone from hostile to sly. So far, so good. A horn tapped behind Gray. He glanced in the mirror, put the car in gear and pulled away from the pump.

"Well," he said, as if saying more would violate his code of ethics, "I suppose I could explain it to you... But not over the phone."

"You a cop? 'Cause if the bitch got herself in trouble, I ain't interested in hearin' about it."

"No trouble," Gray said easily. "I'm not a cop, I'm a lawyer."

"A lawyer? An' you want to see Dawn?"

"Yes. I'm trying to find her for a client."

"What in hell for?"

"I really can't say too much, Mr. Kitteridge, but since you're her husband, I suppose it's all right to tell you that this involves settling the estate of your wife's grandfather."

"That's nuts. Dawn ain't got no..."

Kitteridge stopped in midsentence. Bingo, Gray thought, and waited.

"Are you sayin' somebody left my wife money?"

"I'm sorry, Mr. Kitteridge," Gray said politely. "I have to meet with your wife."

"Yeah. Okay. Uh, where are you? I mean, are you comin' to town?"

"Actually I'm already here. I'm in a gas station on the corner of Main and Liberty."

"Uh-huh. Ah, there's a diner across the way. See it?"

Gray peered out the window. A red neon sign blinked the words Victory Diner through diagonal sheets of rain. "Yes, I see it."

"Go on in, get us a booth. I'll be there in fifteen minutes."

"Be sure your wife is with you," Gray said, as if he had no idea Dawn Kitteridge had flown the coop.

Kitteridge hung up. Gray let out a breath, checked for non-existent traffic and drove across the road to the diner.

Almost twenty minutes later, he was nursing a cup of inky

black liquid the waitress had poured him when the door opened. A man stepped inside. He was maybe six-three with a rugged, work-hardened body and a face Gray figured men would call nasty and some women would call strong. The guy shook himself like a wet dog as the door swung shut, thumbed an oily-looking lock of black hair from his forehead and scanned the room even though Gray and the waitress were the only people in it.

"Coffee," he barked in the general direction of the counter. He walked toward Gray with a loping swagger. "You Baron?"

Gray got to his feet. "Yes." He forced himself to hold out his hand. He had the irrational feeling he'd want to wipe it off after Kitteridge shook it. "Harman Kitteridge?"

Kitteridge looked at Gray's hand as if he'd never seen a lawyer's hand without a subpoena in it before. Then he grasped it and fixed his eyes on Gray's.

"That's my name."

He squeezed Gray's hand hard. Harder, when Gray didn't flinch. What Gray really wanted to do was laugh. Was he actually being invited to have a pissing contest in a run-down diner on Main Street, U.S.A.? He was going to have some interesting tales to tell when he got back to New York.

Kitteridge grunted. Gray wasn't sure if it was a sign of dissatisfaction or pleasure. He let go of Gray's hand, slid into the opposite banquette and sat back while the waitress served his coffee. He poured in cream, added half a dozen heaping teaspoons of sugar, stirred the coagulating mess and licked the spoon before dropping it on the table.

"What's this all about, Baron?"

"It's about your wife's grandfather's estate."

"What about it?"

"Sorry. I can't discuss it with anyone but her." Gray looked past Kitteridge, as if he expected to see Dawn standing near the door. "Where is she? I told you to bring her with you."

Minutes passed. Kitteridge's stare was filled with venom. Finally he drank some coffee, then put down his cup.

"She ain't here."

"Where is she, then?"

"Listen, man, my wife is out of town. You want to waste this whole trip?" Kitteridge grinned, showing off sharp, yellowing teeth. "Or you want me to think you always hang around places like this diner and Queen City?"

Okay. Kitteridge wasn't really stupid. Gray could only hope he was greedy, greedy enough to swallow the story he was about to tell him. It was one part truth, nine parts fantasy, and—he hoped—sufficient to get information without giving any.

"Well, I guess it won't hurt if I fill you in on some of the details. This is about Ben Lincoln."

"Who the hell is Ben Lincoln?"

Gray reminded himself that losing his temper and telling this asshole that he *was* an asshole would be counterproductive.

"Your wife's grandfather," he said calmly. "On her mother's side."

"What about her mother?" Kitteridge's eyes narrowed. "Who you been talkin' to?"

Definitely an asshole, but he needed him. Take it easy, Gray told himself, and just keep smiling.

"Nobody. I'm trying to give you some background, make sure you understand the importance of this conversation."

"Yeah, yeah. I got that. Go on. What's the deal?"

"Your wife's grandfather left her something in his will."

Gray could almost see the dollar signs light up in Kitteridge's eyes. "Dawn's got money comin'?"

"The inheritance isn't much. Not by most standards. Look, I can't actually discuss it with you, so if you'd just tell me where I can find your wife—"

Kitteridge shot out a hand and grabbed Gray by the front of his shirt. "Listen here, Mr. Lawyer, I've about had it with your games. How much is comin' to her? I'm her husband. I got the right to know."

Gray closed his hand around Harman's wrist and pressed his thumb against a pulse point. He could see the shock in the other man's face as he began exerting pressure. When he was a kid, he'd worked his father's pathetic excuse of a ranch, branding cows, neutering bulls, breaking the few horses Jonas usually let Leighton buy for next to nothing each year. He'd played rugby at Princeton, soccer at Yale, and as soon as he found himself chafing at the sedentary boundaries imposed by his profession, he'd taken up handball, racquetball and Japanese aikido. His body was honed and hard, his grip strong and unyielding and he knew, with a little rush of satisfaction, that the prick seated across from him had not expected any of it.

"Let go of the shirt, Kitteridge," he said softly. "Right now, or you won't be able to use that hand for a month."

Kitteridge stared at him through eyes flat with pain and rage. After a minute, he smiled. It made him look like a Halloween mask designed to scare the pants off kids who had seen one horror movie too many.

"Sure. No harm meant."

Kitteridge dropped his hand to the table. Gray let him settle his shoulders back against the cracked vinyl of the banquette.

"Guess we got ourselves off to a poor start, Baron. It's just that I don't like somebody comin' around, askin' about my wife without me knowin' what's up."

Gray nodded. He could still feel his blood pumping hot and fast through his veins but he was here for information and beating the stupid son of a bitch across from him to a pulp wasn't the way to get it.

"Yeah. Okay. I understand, but *you* need to understand my position. I'm legally charged with seeing to it that your wife gets what's coming to her."

"Trust me, Baron. I want her to get what's comin' to her, too."

Harman saw the lawyer's eyes narrow. Stupid, he told himself, stupid, stupid. He had to watch what he said around this slick bastard. The guy wasn't from around here. He was from a big city, Phoenix or L.A. or even someplace on the East Coast. He wasn't as easy as he looked, either. He had a lazy smile, clean fingernails, a way of talking that made him sound as if he'd been born with a silver spoon in his mouth, but he also had an iron grip and a hardness to him that had been a surprise. And what in hell was this talk about that bitch, Dawn, and some kind of inheritance?

He still had trouble saying Dawn's name, even thinking it, without wanting to put his fist through the wall. Goddamn slut, taking off in the middle of the night, walking out on him as if she had the right to do whatever she wanted. He should have slapped her around more often. That would have kept her in line, same as it had done for her mama.

And all these damn fool questions about Dawn's grandfather. She'd never talked about a grandfather. Hell, she hadn't talked about her own mama much, never mind anybody else, and now, from out of nowhere, she had a grandpa who had left her money? Hot damn, that was something to think about. Some dead presidents would go a long way toward making up for what the bitch had done to him, leaving him with an empty bed, leaving him to cook and clean for himself, stealing his son even though he'd been able to see, even four years back, that the kid was going to grow up soft, like his mother.

Well, he'd have changed that. He'd still change it, when he found Dawn. And he would. He'd always intended to; he'd be damned if he'd let her think she could get away with walking out on him. But now, if there was money on the line, there was more reason than ever to find his sweet wife.

If she had money coming, it belonged to him. A man had the right to be king in his home. Dawn had never understood that but she would, once he got her back. He'd bring her home to the mountain, beat the crap out of her and the kid, too, until they both understood he was the one law in their lives.

He lifted his coffee cup, took a sip of the rapidly cooling liquid and did his best to conjure up a smile.

"Dawn's going to be real upset when she finds out you was here and she wasn't."

Gray nodded. "Uh-huh."

"'Course, there ain't no real problem. You probably got some papers for her to sign, right?"

Gray gave another nod, more noncommittal than the first.

"Well, you can leave 'em with me. I'll see to it she puts her name where she ought to and mails them to you."

"Yeah. Well, I wish I could do that, Kitteridge, but the law…'' Gray leaned forward and flashed a man-to-man smile. "As long as we're being honest, I have to tell you that I talked with some people around town."

Kitteridge's eyes turned cold. "People ought to learn to keep their mouths shut."

"They seem to think your wife left quite a while ago."

"If she did, it ain't nobody's business but mine."

"You're wrong. It's my business. I mean, this inheritance…'' Gray sighed. "Well, that's a pity."

"I'm here," Kitteridge said sharply. "And I'm her husband. Whatever's comin' to her should come to me. That's only right."

"I agree," Gray said pleasantly, "but the law…''

The law, Harman thought. The goddamn law. What he ought to do was drag this son of a bitch attorney out of his seat, do it fast, before he knew what was happening, and beat the crap out of him—but that wouldn't get him what he wanted. The question was, what would? The thing to do was calm down and think. What would soften up a hotshot lawyer? A little hearts and flowers, maybe. Yeah. A sad story, complete with violins. That might just do it.

"Okay," Harman said. He wrapped his hands around his cup and looked down into its murky depths. "I'm gonna tell you the truth, Baron. I don't talk about it much 'cause it near to kills me to do it, but my wife run out and left me four years back."

"Ah. That's rough."

"It is, for a fact." Harman lifted wounded eyes, locked them on Gray's. "She was everythin' for me, you know? I loved her like I never loved another woman. But she weren't no good. She catted around, paid no mind to her wifely obligations or to our son."

That did it. He saw the lawyer's eyes go dark.

"She had a child?" he said.

Harman pulled a sad face. "Oh, yeah. A little boy. Sweetest thing you can imagine, but she didn't give no more thought to the kid than she did to me."

"You mean, she didn't take the boy with her when she left you?"

Harman didn't even blink. "No." Violins, sad stories and a leap to abandoned babies the lawyer had taken all by himself. Fine. Whatever would work. "You can see why I don't talk about it much."

Oh, and it *was* working. Baron was nodding in agreement, clearly thinking bad thoughts about a woman who had slept around and dumped her kid. Well, the sleeping around part was surely the truth, and there wasn't a way in hell Baron would ever find out she'd taken the boy with her.

Harman took out his wallet. "See this?" He took out a dog-eared photo of a woman with a baby in her arms and pushed it across the table. "That's what she left behind. That innocent babe. Boy's seven now an' there's times he still wakes up in the middle of the night, cryin' for his mama."

It was the perfect touch. The lawyer was staring at the picture as if it was the Madonna and child.

"Yeah." The attorney cleared his throat. "So, where is she? Where'd she go?"

"If I knew, don't you think I'd have brought her back?" Harman's mouth twisted. "Teach her a lesson for walkin' out on me?" He saw the way Baron's head came up. Dammit. He'd overplayed his hand. "I mean, I'd tell her how much she hurt me. How I still love her. How I miss her. How I 'spect her to keep the promises she made when we was married, is what I'm saying."

"The bottom line is that you don't know where she is, do you, Kitteridge? That's what *I'm* saying."

Harman smiled slyly. "I don't, no. But I bet a hotshot lawyer like you got ways to find her."

"Maybe, but I'll need your help."

"Anythin' I can do, you just ask."

"You said she catted around. How about the names of some of the men she slept with?"

"Don't actually got names. She was sneaky."

"Well, how about places she'd been and liked, that she might have gone back to?"

"She never went nowhere. Not that I wouldn't have taken her, if she'd been a good woman, but—"

"Places she talked about visiting," Gray said impatiently. "Nothing? Come on, man. Think. Didn't she ever look at a picture in a magazine or someplace on TV and say how much she'd like to go there?"

"If she spent time on such things, she was smart enough not to let me know. Wastin' time makes the devil happy."

Gray started to answer, thought better of it and, instead, took his wallet from his back pocket. Coming here had been pointless. He'd wasted two days and he didn't know anything more about where to look for Dawn than when he'd started. The only thing he'd learned was that her husband was the shithead Ballard said he was, and that Dawn wasn't much better. She'd slept around, run off, abandoned her child... So much for the lure of Nora Lincoln's sad eyes and defiant chin, or for the fact that he'd thought he'd seen those same eyes, that same chin, in the photo Harman had shown him.

"Well, thanks for your time, Kitteridge." Gray dropped a five-dollar bill on the table. "I'll give you my card. If you think of anything that might shed some light on your wife's whereabouts..."

"Wait just a damn minute, Mr. Lawyer."

Gray looked up. Kitteridge flashed a smile as phony as the wood graining in the plastic tabletop.

"I mean, you ain't just gonna run off, are you? Now that I told you about my wife, surely you can tell me what her grandpa left her, right?" Harman looked around, then hunched his shoulders and bent over the table. "It's only right and proper I should know. For the sake of my son, you understand?"

Gray had an answer ready but he made it look as if he didn't. "Well," he said slowly, "I suppose it's okay, all things considered."

Harman licked his lips. "How much?"

"He didn't leave her money."

"He didn't... Ah. I got it. He left her a house, right? What do you call it, real estate?"

Gray tried to look soulful. "No," he said, "no real estate. Actually your wife's grandfather died broke." Was it a lie? Maybe. Then again, maybe not. But the answer would defuse Harman's curiosity. That was what counted.

"Broke?" Harman's eyes narrowed. "Give me a break, Baron. You want me to believe you come here to tell my wife her grandpa didn't leave her nothin'?"

"I didn't say that."

"Yeah, you did. You just told me the old man died broke."

"But he did leave her something. A music box." That part had come to him just this morning. He thought it sounded pretty good.

Harman's face was a blank. "You're shittin' me."

"I guess it had sentimental value to him. It's a nice music box, actually. Walnut, with mother of pearl inlay and a revolving dancer on the—"

"You want me to think you come all the way here to tell my wife she inherited a music box?" Harman said in a soft, ominous voice. "I guess you think I'm pretty stupid."

"I don't have any opinion of you," Gray said pleasantly, lying through his teeth as he got to his feet. "You're right about one thing, though. Given a choice, I sure wouldn't have come all the way here but, as my client's representative, I'm obligated to fulfill his wishes. He stipulated that I was to locate his granddaughter and give her the box. That's what I'm trying to do."

"Yeah. Sure."

"I'm sorry if you're disappointed, Kitteridge. I'd love to have told you your wife was sitting on a fortune. Unfortunately, she's not."

Harman wanted to lunge over the table and stomp the crap out of the smart-ass city attorney. Instead he curled his hands into fists in his lap. It was the only way he could manage to smile.

"Well, that's somethin', ain't it? And here I was, feelin' good for my Dawn, thinkin' she was comin' into easy times. It just goes to show, you never do know, ain't that right?" He stood up, put out his hand. "Nice meeting you, Mr. Baron. Good luck, findin' my wife."

"Yeah. Same to you."

"You get any word, you'll let me know, right? My boy and I sure do miss her."

"I will." Gray took a card from his wallet and handed it to Kitteridge. "I wonder... Could I have that photo?"

"Photo?"

"Of your wife and son. It might help me identify her, if I find her."

Harman smiled. "I'd like to help you, but it's the only picture I got to remind me of her. It's very valuable to me, if you know what I mean."

The lawyer wasn't dumb. He dug a hundred-dollar bill from his wallet and Harman handed over the photo.

"I can use the money to buy somethin' nice for the boy," he said somberly. "You take care now, Mr. Baron. These roads can be slippery in the rain."

He waited until the door closed after the attorney. Then he sank down on the banquette.

"Son of a bitch," he muttered. Did the man really think he'd fallen for that lie about a music box, or that he'd bought him off with a hundred bucks? There was lots more to this story. Nobody, especially not a lawyer from—Harman glared at the card—from New York City, came all this distance to tell a woman her grandpa had left her a wind-up toy.

Dawn had come into money, and probably one hell of a lot of it.

Harman got to his feet, walked to the counter and slid onto a stool. "Gimme two eggs," he said to the waitress, "over easy. Bacon. Flapjacks." He leaned toward her. "And more coffee, only it better not be this crap from the bottom of the pot, you understand?"

The girl damn near clicked her heels, which was just as it should be. The bible said it best. A woman was meant to obey. Wives, especially. And what a wife possessed belonged to her husband. Her body. Her spawn. All her earthly possessions.

Harman scowled as the waitress put a cup in front of him.

Dawn was coming into an inheritance, and it was only right and proper he was there to take care of it for her, and to take care of the boy, too, see he was raised up proper. It was time to find the bitch and put her four years of loose living at an end.

Outside, in the parking lot, Gray got behind the wheel of the rental car and drove a couple of miles north before he pulled onto the shoulder of the road, took out his cell phone and dialed Jack Ballard.

"Jack? Gray Baron here. I just met with Harman Kitteridge. Oh, yeah. He's just what his rap sheet suggests. Mean. And stupid as the day is long, except when he thinks he smells money. Nope. He hasn't a clue as to where Dawn is. Trust me, Jack. I had him salivating. If he knew, he'd have— You did?" Gray smiled and gave the steering wheel a light tap with his fist. "Las Vegas, huh? Terrific. Too bad you didn't call me. I'd have been able to skip my scintillating meeting with Kitter— Oh. Did you? Well, I was in a diner at the ass end of nowhere, which is probably why your call wouldn't go through. In fact, I'm losing you now. Jack? Jack…"

The line went dead. Gray put the phone into his pocket, felt something papery and took out the photo of Dawn Lincoln Kitteridge. She didn't look much like a woman who would walk out on a man and a child, but that only went to show you how misleading a picture could be. He had a photo of his own mother tucked away at the bottom of a drawer. He'd found it years ago, when he was ten or eleven, and she hadn't looked like a woman who would have done those things, either…but she had.

Gray checked his mirror, did a U-turn, sped straight through Queen City and headed south, to Flagstaff and the airport. Forget staying on for a few days. Ballard had found the woman. He'd fly home, put things on hold for a week, then fly to Vegas and check out Dawn Kitteridge, though it wouldn't take much checking before he'd know what to tell Jonas. How much doubt could there be as to the morals of a woman who slept around and then deserted her son, and never mind the way she looked in that photo.

He knew all about women like that. His own mother had slept her way through Brazos Springs before she'd walked away, left him behind and never once looked back.

Gray stepped down hard on the gas. Soon, very soon, he'd be able to put this entire incident behind him and get on with his own life.

CHAPTER FOUR

Las Vegas, Nevada

DAWN'S alarm was set for six but when she opened her eyes, the bright green numbers on the clock's face read 5:03.

Her heart pounded as she sat up and looked around her tiny bedroom. What had awakened her? Footsteps? A voice? The sound of someone outside the window? She held her breath and listened but she couldn't hear anything. Nothing but silence.

She exhaled and fell back against the pillows with relief. That was what had awakened her. Not a noise. The silence. The AC had shut off. The unit was old and noisy. It died with startling regularity and when it did, the lack of sound was like an assault on her eardrums.

Even after four years, she still couldn't decide what was better, noises that startled you or silence that shook you. No, that wasn't true. You could get accustomed to noise. Silence was different. If it was too quiet, you started to hear things. A creak that might be a footstep. A tap that might mean someone was at the window. A whisper that could be a voice you prayed you'd never hear again...

"Stop it," she said, and she sat up and tossed the covers aside.

The creaks were from the floorboards. Her apartment had been carved out of the first floor parlor and maid's room of an old house, old by Vegas standards, anyway. The only thing tapping at the window was the branch of the indigo bush. She probably should have lopped the branch off when it first started growing toward the house, just as Cassie had suggested, but she was happy letting the Indigo go its own way.

She'd had to plead with the landlord to let her plant it. The woman had looked at her as if she was crazy but she'd finally said yeah, okay, you want an indigo bush? You buy it, plant it, take care of it, you can have it. Dawn had done all that and provided the tough little shrub with the nurturing it needed to gain a foothold, and it had thrived.

The Indigo had the right to grow in any direction it wanted. So did every living thing on the planet.

As for hearing that voice, Harman's voice, well, it was better to be alert than complacent. Every now and then, she'd see some half-buried item in the paper about a woman who had run from a husband or a boyfriend, been found by him and beaten senseless. Or killed. And even as she'd feel pain for that poor, faceless woman, Dawn would know that what she'd just read was a reminder. She'd have to spend the rest of her life being careful, never letting down her guard, never forgetting that Harman was still out there, hating her because she'd done the unthinkable.

She'd defied him. Worse, she'd left him. That was the worst sin of all.

Her husband had owned a dog when she'd married him, a scared, skinny hound that made the mistake of creeping to her for comfort one day after Harman kicked it. Enraged, he'd beaten the poor thing half-senseless and when it ran away, he'd gone after it, dragged it back to the mountain and shot it.

"Bad enough it weren't loyal to me," he'd said, while she'd sobbed and begged him to spare the dog's life. "What's mine stays mine till I say otherwise. You got that, bitch?"

She should have left him then, but where would she have gone? She had no money, no job skills. Her mother was dead and even if she'd been alive, Orianna had never been able to help herself when a man abused her. How would she have helped her daughter?

Dawn swung her feet to the floor. What was wrong with her this morning? She hadn't wasted this much time thinking about Harman in months. It was one thing to be cautious, another thing to be paranoid. Besides, thinking about him, worrying about what he might or might not do, only gave back some of the power he'd once wielded over her. She'd learned that sitting through some counseling sessions at the women's shelter in Phoenix, the second stop in her flight four years back.

"Remember," the counselor had said, "the best way to break with the past is to take control of your life. Educate yourself. Make plans. Learn to be independent. You are a whole person, no matter what your abuser wants you to think."

Dawn had done all that. The proof was in what was going to happen today, her very first day on her own at her new job. That's what she'd think about, not Harman.

The new job was going to be a challenge, but she was up to it. Keir thought so. Cassie did, too. Even Mary O'Connell had given her a wink a couple of days ago, when she'd breezed past the Special Services office where Dawn was standing at Jean's shoulder, listening while she phoned to arrange for the Desert Song's private jet to pick up a VIP and fly him from Boston to Vegas.

"Good luck," Mrs. O'Connell had said softly, which had to mean that even the Duchess was aware she'd taken a more responsible position but then, not much that went on at the Song escaped the Duchess's attention, even during the months she'd been ill.

"Thank you," Dawn had replied, and the Duchess had smiled in that way of hers that made you feel as if she really cared about you.

Dawn laid out her clothes for the day. She ran her hand lightly over the blue jacket and beige skirt she'd bought with part of the clothing allowance that went with her new position. She just hoped she'd live up to everybody's expectations.

"You're going to be great at this," Cassie kept saying. Keir had pretty much told her the same thing when he'd interviewed her. By then, she'd already passed the other hurdles: a clean employment record at the Song, votes of approval from Becky, who headed up Special Services, but Keir had the final say and what he'd said was, yes, the job was hers.

"You're good with people," he'd told her. "I think you're going to be an excellent addition to the Special Services staff."

Remembering, Dawn let out a breath. She hoped he was right. She really, really wanted this job. Better pay, which she sorely needed. Better hours, which she needed, too, and a bonus she'd never mentioned to anyone but Cassie.

She'd never really liked dealing cards, even though she'd been good at it. She had quick hands, she didn't get ruffled. It was just that it always felt, well, wrong to be part of a process that separated people from their money, even in the classy area where she'd worked, the casino-within-a-casino at Desert Song, the high stakes tables where most of the players could easily lose tens of thousands of dollars without blinking.

"It's just wrong," she'd told Cassie one night over takeout Chinese.

Cassie put down her chopsticks and stared at her. "What's wrong about it?"

"I don't know. It just is."

"That's nuts," Cassie replied bluntly. "What, are you gonna worry about jerks who have money to throw away?"

"I know," Dawn said, "but—"

"But you grew up poor, like me."

"Well, yes. But that's not all of it. I mean, I know it's their money. It's just that it seems so—so—"

"Wong," Cassie said, so deadpan that Dawn couldn't help laughing. Cassie had sighed, then dug back into her shrimp with lobster sauce. "You are *such* a Goody Two-Shoes. Sometimes I wonder what you're doing in Sin City."

Hiding, that was what. Of course, Cassie didn't know that. Nobody did.

Dawn stepped into the shower and lifted her face to the spray. She turned around slowly, let the water beat down on her hair, then worked in a dollop of shampoo.

Hiding right out in the open, because this was the perfect place for it. Las Vegas was always crowded. Phoenix hadn't been this jammed with people, or even Los Angeles, and certainly not Santa Fe. Heaven knew she'd been in all of them in the days when Orianna bounced from town to town. She'd never seen streets more packed than the Vegas Strip or crowds any more dense than the ones that jammed the casinos. And there was a bonus. Harman wouldn't come here. Calling Las Vegas "Sin City" was Cassie's idea of a joke, but her husband would surely believe the devil walked these streets. He'd never come here unless he somehow learned where she was...

"Oh, for goodness' sakes," Dawn said briskly, and shut off the water.

Why waste any part of this exciting morning on a part of her life that was over and done with? She had to dry her hair, put on makeup, dress...but first, she'd begin her day the way she always did, with a call to the Rocking Horse Ranch so she could say good morning to her baby. Her son. The love of her life, the one good thing, the only good thing, Harman had ever given her.

Dawn reached for the telephone. And when, a few minutes later, she heard Tommy say, "Hello, Mama," in his sweet, eager voice, she made the same silent vow she made each morning. Someday, she'd find a way to keep her child safe without having to be separated from him, without having to keep him a secret...

"Hello, sweetheart," she said, and her heart almost overflowed with love.

By the time she left for work, the temperature had already climbed into the nineties.

She was in luck. Her cranky old car started up right away.

Nothing stirred in the arid brown and beige land that ringed the city. The creatures of the desert took to their nests and burrows during the day, waiting for nightfall and the coolness it would bring, but humans weren't that sensible. The roads and streets grew more crowded as she got closer to the city's heart, the area known as the Strip, which was already thronged with people.

Dawn parked in the employees' lot behind the Desert Song. The security guard at the back entrance touched the brim of his cap as she walked toward him.

"Mornin', Miss Carter."

She'd plucked the name from a display of baby clothes in a store. It had taken her months to grow accustomed to it. Now, the name felt as if it had always been hers.

"Morning, Howard." She smiled at the burly man. "I missed you yesterday. Everything all right?"

"Yes, ma'am." The guard grinned. "Took the day off so I could go to the doctor with my wife. Seems as if we're gonna have a baby."

"Oh, that's wonderful!" Impulsively she kissed his cheek. "Congratulations."

"Thanks. Got to admit, we're mighty happy. How about you? You must be feeling pretty good this morning. The word is this is gonna be your first day alone with all those VIPs."

"Uh-huh." She held up her hand, showed him her crossed fingers. "Wish me luck."

"You'll do fine, Miss Carter. Special's got to be a fun place to work. Getting to rub shoulders with the rich and famous... The grapevine says that Arab prince is checking in later today."

"That's some grapevine," Dawn said, and laughed. "It knows more than I do. Take care, Howard. And tell your wife I wish her well."

She stepped through the door, took a deep breath of air so cool it felt like a soothing liquid slipping down her throat, and set off down the corridor. Guests thought of the Desert Song as a fantasyland resort and it was, but it took a small, efficient army to keep it that way. This part of the hotel was very different from the public area. It was given over to administrative services. No blinking lights, no slot machines and their electronic chortles, just the occasional hum of a printer or the soft ringing of a telephone. Offices opened onto both sides of the hallway. The Special Services office—her new office, Dawn thought, and her step quickened—was at the end of the corridor. She stopped at the door, took a deep breath, then stepped inside.

There were five Service Specialists and they all shared an efficient, behind-the-scenes workspace. Dawn had already be-

gun adding her own touches by tacking things on the cork-
board that hung over the desk, the small section of it, anyway,
that belonged to her. She'd put up a few notes and a calendar
with a photo of Tommy beneath it. It was just a small picture
and he was only one little cowboy in a bunch of other little
cowboys dressed up for one of the Ranch's monthly cookouts.
If anybody happened to see it, which she figured was unlikely,
she could always point to one of the other kids and say he
was her cousin. It was an awful way to live, but Tommy's
safety was everything.

She paused now, smiled at the picture and touched it lightly
with one fingertip.

"Hey there, sunshine," she whispered. Tommy almost
seemed to smile back.

Okay. It was time to get to work. She had—she glanced at
her watch, then at the clock on the desk—she had fifteen
minutes to read through whatever faxes or e-mails were waiting. The Specialists worked rotating shifts and covered for
each other on days off and vacations so that one of them was
always available, day or night, to handle the needs of guests
like the Arab prince that Howard had mentioned, not that
Dawn or any of her sister Specialists would confirm that the
rumor was right and the prince was, indeed, arriving today.

Aside from providing guests like the prince the Desert
Song's finest suites and most elegant service at no cost, the
hotel also gave them privacy if that was what they wanted,
publicity if that was their preference. Part of Dawn's job was
to know when to provide one or encourage the other.

"It's not easy," Keir had warned her during the interview.
"It sounds glamorous, to hobnob with some of these people,
but it isn't."

"Oh, I know that," Dawn had replied. "I've been dealing
at the high stakes tables for a year. Sometimes it's fun…"

"And sometimes it's hell." He'd grinned, his black eyes
snapping with amusement. "By the way, I heard how nicely
you handled that little scene the other night. My compli-
ments—but did the senator really try to slide an extra chip
across the table after you showed seventeen?"

Dawn had given her boss a wide-eyed smile of innocence. "Surely not. The chip just fell out of his hand when he reached for his drink. Perfectly understandable, don't you think?"

"Uh-huh." Keir's grin had broadened. "Good thinking, Carter." His expression had turned serious. "Okay, the position is yours. Just remember that we want you to keep our VIPs happy but not at the expense of taking any kind of guff. Do you understand what I mean?"

She did. Men hit on you in this town. Finding ways to put men off, but politely, was a necessity when you worked in a place where the food, the drinks, the good times all seemed not just free but endless.

Cassie was the person who had taught her how to do it.

They'd met right after Dawn passed the test the Song offered employees who wanted to learn to be dealers. Dawn was still a waitress at the Reveille coffee shop; Cassie had just taken a job as a cocktail waitress in the casino after deciding she'd had enough of dancing behind a bar. They'd hit it off so well that Dawn had moved out of her cramped furnished room and into Cassie's tiny apartment while she looked for a place of her own.

"I swear," Cassie said one night, "more guys think they can cop a feel now that I'm serving drinks than when I was wiggling my ass behind that bar."

Cassie sounded annoyed more than anything else but Dawn felt a chill dance down her spine. Nobody had touched her since she'd left Harman. Nobody ever would. Even remembering how he'd slobbered on top of her made her feel sick.

"I never thought about that," she said carefully. "Is it a problem? Men, you know, trying to touch you when you work in the casino?"

"Is it a problem?" Cassie repeated, rolling her eyes. "Is the sun going to shine tomorrow? Yeah, it's a problem. Well, I mean, men are men, right? They see a good-looking woman, they figure, hey, why not? It was bad enough when I was dancing—you wouldn't believe how many idiots think a woman who strips down to a G-string in front of maybe a thousand people a week is actually trying to personally turn them on—but now that I sashay around the casino floor with a tray in my hand, dressed in a little black skirt and fishnet stockings…'' She gave a noisy sigh. ''Like I said, men are men.''

''Oh.'' Dawn hesitated. ''But when I'm a dealer, I'll be wearing pants and a jacket. You know, the standard uniform. So I won't have to worry about—''

''Are you kidding?'' Cassie grinned. ''You're good-looking. You're breathing. You wear a giant paper bag, maybe they won't come on to you. Look, don't worry about it. You learn to deal with it.''

''How?''

Cassie's smile faded. ''Oh, honey, what is it? You've got a look in your eye that says some son of a bitch laid his hands on you wrong.''

Dawn put on what she thought of as her neutral face. Nobody was going to know anything about Harman. Not ever. That was something else she'd learned in the shelter, not from any of the counselors but from the other women. Don't trust anybody, they'd told her, don't tell them who you really are or where you really come from or why you left your man because even if they don't mean to, they'll whisper it to their closest friends and their closest friends will whisper it to their closest friends, and before long your secret is out and your man will find you, he'll come for you, he'll—

''No,'' she'd said a little more earnestly than she'd intended. ''No, it's not that. I just—I never thought about having to deal with—with men as part of the job.''

''Dealing with men is *always* part of the job,'' Cassie had replied, with a look that suggested Dawn had been born under a cabbage leaf. ''Listen, guys are idiots. And some places I've worked, well, the management's made up of idiots, too. But not here. You develop a line of patter, you know, stuff about having a boyfriend who's six-foot-six, or a sick mother waiting at home, whatever works for you, and if you've still got a problem with some bozo, you tell Keir. Or security. Dan Coyle's guys will handle it.''

Becky had offered similar advice when she'd started training in Special Services. And, sure enough, on her second day a VIP had asked, very politely, if she'd like to come up to his suite and join him for champagne and caviar. Dawn had thanked the man and demurred in such a way that he understood that drinking with guests—more to the point, sleeping with guests—wasn't part of the plan. Not the hotel's, and definitely not hers.

"Carter? Good morning."

Dawn swiveled her chair around. Keir O'Connell was lounging in the doorway, arms folded, taking up most of the space, which was only reasonable when a man was that tall and that broad-shouldered.

"I'm fine," she said. "Just fine."

Keir grinned. "Liar."

"No, no. It's true. I'm fine. I'm…" Color flooded her face. "You didn't ask me how I was feeling, did you?"

"Nope."

"You only said good morning,"

"That's what I said, all right." He smiled. "So, you're a nervous wreck, huh?"

"Me?"

"You, Carter. And don't panic. I couldn't tell by looking at you."

"Why would you? I don't feel—I don't feel…" Dawn blew out a breath. "Okay. I'm nervous."

"Yeah, I figured. You don't need to be."

"That's probably what the executioner told Marie Antoinette."

"He probably told her exactly what I'm going to tell you," Keir said, laughing. "The crowd's going to love you."

"I hope."

"I know. Trust me, Dawn. You wouldn't have gotten this job if I didn't think you could handle it. Oh, before I forget…my mother said to tell you to break a leg." He smiled. "But not literally."

"Oh, that's nice of the Duch—of Mrs. O'Connell. Thank her for me."

"Sure. She'll probably stop by at some point, just to say hello and see how things are going."

"She's really better, then? Her heart—"

"Is healing just fine."

Dawn smiled. "I'm glad to hear it."

"Yeah." Keir nodded. "Me, too." He moved into the small office, peered at the open appointment book on the desk and raised an eyebrow. "Initiation by fire, I see. Prince Ahmat from Suli-Bahr," he added, when she looked blank. "Don't tell me you haven't been filled with stories about the guy."

"You mean that he generally brings all seven wives with him and that each wife must have different flowers in her rooms? That he only drinks Cristal champagne from a Baccarat flute? That two eggs, cooked for precisely three minutes, two slices of whole-wheat toast, unbuttered, and a pot of coffee—"

"Kona coffee," Keir said, deadpan.

"—a pot of *Kona* coffee, must be delivered to his suite at 7:58, not 7:59 or, heaven forbid, eight on the nose?" Dawn batted her lashes. "No. Nobody's told me a thing."

Keir grinned as he started for the door. "Give me a call when he gets here. And stop worrying. I mean it. I don't anticipate any problems but just in case you run into trouble—"

"Holler. I know." Dawn touched the tip of her tongue to her bottom lip. "Keir? Thank you for giving me this job. I promise, I won't let you down."

"I'm sure you won't but I didn't 'give' you anything, Carter. You interviewed well, and your pit bosses wrote terrific recommendations—not that they didn't all say they kind of hoped you'd change your mind and go back to dealing cards."

"Tell them they're sweet but I think I'm going to like it here."

"If I tell those guys they're sweet, I'll never live to see tomorrow. Seriously, I hope you do like it here. I think it's the right place for you."

"Me, too. Oh, and Keir, would you do me a favor? Tell your mother I'm glad to see her getting back into the swing of things. I'd have told her myself the other day but she swept by the desk so quickly—"

"I'll tell her. And just remember what I said. You're going to do fine."

Keir walked down the hall and through the door that opened onto the area behind Reception. The front desk supervisor was on the phone. She smiled and waved and he lifted a hand in salute as he stepped out from behind the counter and onto the deep blue carpet that covered the hotel's vast lobby.

It was crowded, which was always good, but the lines at the reception desks were too long. He did a quick count and made a mental note to meet with his manager and discuss adding staff to the day shift. The Desert Song prided itself on treating all its guests with courtesy, not just the VIPS, and that included not keeping them waiting in line longer than three minutes. His father had instituted the policy and called it part of the hotel's hospitality. His mother had added her own touch by occasionally strolling through reception and personally welcoming guests to the Song.

She was back to doing it, despite Keir's concerns that she was pushing her recovery. The Duchess had been the family's rock-hard core since his father's death more than six years ago. Her heart attack had shocked the hell out of them all, his sisters and brothers, the staff, even guests who had been coming here for years. After four months, the doctors said Mary Elizabeth O'Connell was doing just fine, that she'd be as good as new. Keir wanted to believe them. It was just that he couldn't get past how she'd looked in the intensive care unit of the hospital that first week, her skin pasty, her breathing labored, her body hooked up to all those damned tubes and lines.

Keir knew his mother was getting old but somehow, he'd never imagined her dying.

But she'd come through it, fighting for life with the tenacity that was in the O'Connell blood. Now she was on a new regimen. Plenty of exercise. A diet purged of fat. No liquor. No smoking. No living, she said, and grumbled she'd been sentenced to purgatory. Lately she showed signs of chafing at the bit. She'd begun showing up on the casino floor and in the hotel lobby, chatting with the staff, charming the guests and greeting Keir's suggestions that she take it easy with snorts of derision.

"Taking it easy is all I've been doing," she'd told him. "Any more of it and I'll turn into a vegetable." She'd given him a wary look. "Or is this a polite way of telling me I'm stepping on your toes, now that you're in charge?"

"You know better than that," he'd said and meant it. "You're the boss. You always will be."

It was true. He'd been running the casino prior to her illness but the Duchess held overall command of the Desert Song. It was an arrangement that sometimes chafed. Keir had been on the verge of making plans to move on when she'd had the heart attack.

"You'll take charge," she'd whispered to him as she lay ill, "not just of the casino but of the whole place," and he'd said yes, of course he would and he'd thought, just for a moment, about the dozen things he wanted to change but he'd done none of them. It was an old battle, Keir contending that innovation was the key to success and his mother contending that things that worked should not be changed. She was wrong. He knew it, but he'd never have done anything she wouldn't like, not while she was ill.

Promoting Dawn to a highly responsible desk job was something the Duchess had not only approved but suggested one evening when they'd discussed the day's business over drinks. Under the new rules, Keir had the drink and Mary Elizabeth had club soda—and unfailingly reminded him, each and every time, that she hated club soda.

A few weeks back, he'd tried a diversion and mentioned that one of the Special Services people was quitting. His mother had asked the reasons. She'd always taken a special interest in the staff that worked the hotel part of the Song, right down to the check-in clerks. They were, she said, the hotel's first opportunity to impress its guests. Keir had grinned, assured his mother that the girl was leaving the Song because she was pregnant, not because she was unhappy with the hotel or the hotel with her.

"Good. And who are you replacing her with?"

"Well—"

"What about Dawn Carter?"

It had seemed a good suggestion. Dawn was hardworking. She learned fast. She had a pleasant way with people and she was easy on the eyes—not his type but a man would have to be blind, not to notice. Good looks were definitely a bonus when it came to dealing with pampered VIPs, and to hell with what the PC Police said. It was one thing to be politically correct and another to be stupid. Keir had never been stupid, which was why he also suspected there was more to his mother's suggestion than the obvious. It struck him that the Duchess took an inordinate interest in the Carter girl.

"What about her?" he'd said lazily, and waited for a reaction. It had come, quick and hard.

"For goodness' sakes, Keir, can't you see that the girl is bright? She's pretty and personable. All in all, perfect for the job."

"Maybe."

"Maybe? *Maybe?*" His mother had bristled. "Don't be silly. She is and you know it. Why not talk with her and see if she wants the position?"

Keir had given Mary Elizabeth a brisk salute. "Your wish is my command, your ladyship."

"Keir." His mother had reached for his hand and clasped it in hers. "I don't mean to tell you what to do."

"Of course you do, Ma," he'd said with a gentle smile. "But you're right. The girl's perfect for the job. I'll talk to her this afternoon."

Dawn had leaped at the opportunity though, just for a minute, when he'd said she'd be in a highly visible position, something had clouded her eyes.

"Is that a problem?" he'd asked carefully.

"No," she'd said quickly, "not at all." Then she'd smiled a little too brightly for comfort. "It's just that I'm not used to being, well, visible. Nobody really notices me now. They're all too busy watching the cards.''

"Are you concerned about clothes? I should have mentioned that the hotel provides a clothing allowance to Special Services employees.''

"Oh, that's lovely." Still, she'd hesitated. "I'll only deal with VIPs. I mean, that's the policy, right?''

"Right," he'd replied, while his brain clicked away at what he'd seen in her eyes again at that last question. She was afraid. He wasn't a betting man—damn near growing up in a casino had taken care of any interest in gambling—but he'd have been willing to bet a bundle on that. She was afraid, but of what? Or was it, of whom?

Keir looked over at the elegant alcove where VIPs could use a special phone to ring for assistance. Dawn was standing at the French Provincial desk tucked into the alcove, her smile bright, her strawberry-blond hair swept back neatly from her face. She was talking to a man in flowing robes. Keir recognized him as Prince Ahmat's personal secretary, meaning that the prince himself would be coming through the doors any minute accompanied by a small army of wives and servants. He made a mental note to check back in a couple of hours and see how things were going, but he got caught up in the usual problems that went with running a place the size of the Song and it was a little after noon before he made the circuit through the lobby again. The Special Services alcove was empty so he strolled into the behind-scenes office. Jean was at the desk, just hanging up the phone. She looked up, saw Keir and smiled.

"Hi, boss.''

"Jeannie. How're things going?''

"Oh," she said, sighing dramatically, "the usual.''

Keir grinned. "That bad, huh?''

"No, seriously, no problems so far.''

"Great. Dawn made it through the morning okay?''

"She did just fine. A little nervous, but fine. She checked the prince in, got all his wives settled, and I figured she ought to take her lunch break a little early, give herself a breather.''

"Good idea."

"I told her to have lunch someplace other than the Song. Sort of escape the pressure cooker for a bit, you know?"

"Makes sense." Keir rapped his knuckles lightly on the desk. "Okay, kid. If you need me, I'll be in my office. Tell Dawn I'm glad her morning went well."

Jean shot a look at her watch. "You can tell her yourself, if you want to come back in fifteen minutes or so."

"I have a meeting. Besides, I just thought I'd see how she was doing. If you say she's doing fine, that's cool."

Jean gave him a thumbs-up. "Cool is the word, boss. Definitely cool."

Hot was the word. Definitely hot.

One oh six already, according to the disgustingly cheerful DJ who'd announced the temperature just before Dawn's car and radio died without warning. She'd been in the right hand lane on Las Vegas Boulevard, waiting at a red light. When it turned green, she put her foot on the gas, the engine coughed convulsively, and that was that.

"No," she'd said softly, "no, no, no..."

Yes, yes, yes. For the past five minutes, she'd tried every trick she knew to make the engine turn over but nothing worked. She was stuck with cars piling up behind her, horns blaring, drivers giving her the finger as they swerved around her.

Idiots!

Did anybody really think she'd stopped here on purpose? That she'd been driving along and suddenly decided, hey, why not see what it's like to block traffic? That she'd willingly sit inside a car with its windows sealed tight—and a curse on the head of the guy who'd invented power windows! Did those honking idiots think she was as crazy as they were? She wasn't—but another few minutes inside this sauna on wheels and anything was possible.

Dawn thumbed a trickle of sweat from her forehead. She'd be a mess by the time she got back to the Desert Song, her suit creased, her makeup melted, her sprayed-into-submission hair an unruly tangle. That was assuming she managed to get back to the hotel in this lifetime, which was starting to seem unlikely.

And what would she do about her car? She couldn't just leave it here. Well, she could, if she wanted some wandering car thief to get lucky, or if she was in the mood to let the city tow it away to never-neverland. Forget the thief. Nobody would be dumb enough to want to steal a wreck. The city, on the other hand, would be happy to take the car and demand hostage money she didn't have.

"Dammit," she said through her teeth, and slapped her hands against the steering wheel. Day One of her new job and she was totally, completely, irrevocably up the proverbial creek without a paddle. Even if she left the car here, the seven dollars in her wallet wasn't about to pay for a cab ride back to the Song.

The sweat was pouring off her and if there was any breathable air left, she couldn't find it. Okay. Dawn slipped off her jacket, folded it neatly and laid it on the back of the passenger seat, behind Space Cadet Teddy.

"I know it's hot," she said to the button-eyed bear. "But we'll be at the hotel in no time."

Teddy didn't look as if he believed her. Smart bear, she thought, and she put on her sunglasses, undid her seat belt and stepped out into the oven that was Las Vegas in early June. A horn honked behind her as she slammed the door. She jumped, looked up in time to see the white-haired driver of a big Buick shake a fist as his car squeezed past hers.

"Thank you for your concern," Dawn muttered, and popped the hood. Great. A tangle of wires, hoses, and strangely shaped hunks of metal. The only thing she recognized was the transparent container of blue windshield washer fluid. Cars were alien territory. Harman had a thing about women and automobiles. He'd only taught her to drive because he said it was beneath a man's dignity to shop for the groceries. Still, people whose cars broke down always peered under the hood and Dawn thought—well, hoped—something obvious would pop out at her, some cable connection that all but shrieked *Reattach me!* when she saw it.

No such luck. No luck at all, considering that she was supposed to be back in—she checked her watch and groaned—in ten minutes. If only she hadn't driven to the mall...but she had and the truth was, she had no regrets. Space Cadet Teddy had been available on a first-come, first-served basis at a giant toy store. She'd arrived in time to grab the last one. No matter what happened, that was something to feel good about.

She'd learned about the popular toy's unheralded, one-day-only appearance thanks to Prince Ahmat's third wife. Dawn had been riding in the elevator with her, her lady-in-waiting and the bellman when the princess, looking straight ahead, suddenly made an announcement.

"You will acquire a Space Cadet Teddy for me," she said.

Dawn lifted an eyebrow in surprise. A teddy bear for the royal wife? And who was she addressing? The lady-in-waiting, evidently, because after a bit of foot-shifting, the woman whispered that she would do her best but she understood the toy was difficult to come by.

The princess folded her arms. "The Crown Prince wants one. You will acquire it."

The lady-in-waiting seemed to shrink. Thankfully, the bellman came to the rescue. "Heard the radio this morning," he said. "Supposed to be a one-day sale of them bears at that store near Belson's mall. "

Dawn had come within a breath of asking the lady-in-waiting if she'd please purchase two Teddys. She hadn't, of course; it wouldn't have been proper. More importantly, there'd have been questions to answer about why she'd want a teddy bear at all.

When Jean urged her to take an early lunch, she pocketed her ID badge—you weren't supposed to wear it out of the hotel—hopped into her car and raced to the mall, already imagining the look she'd see on Tommy's face when he saw the bear. Her little boy had fallen in love with the toy in its first incarnation three years ago. Dawn had managed to buy every Teddy since, even when she'd had to pinch pennies to do it. Tommy had Fisherman Teddy, First Baseman Teddy, and Sleepytime Teddy. Now, she'd managed to snag the last Space Cadet Teddy from the shelf in the toy store...

And, on the way back, to strand herself far enough from the Song that she might as well have been the far side of the moon.

She sighed, closed the hood and dusted off her hands. The heat was unbearable. Everyone said you got used to it but she hadn't. When she had to be out in midday, she dressed for it. Shorts, if she worked in the tiny patch of yard that fronted her apartment; long cotton skirts, sandals and a floppy straw hat if she went to the market. What she was wearing now—a suit, silk blouse, panty hose and heels—was fine for the air-conditioned office and lobby of the Song but it was a killer anyplace—

A horn blared in fury.

Dawn spun around. A car was flying toward her. It wasn't true, she thought with terrifying clarity. When you were about to die, your life didn't pass before your eyes. Your heart lodged in your throat, and all you could do was wait for the moment of impact.

CHAPTER FIVE

GRAY'S plane had been delayed more than an hour by a line of heavy thunderstorms that rumbled through New York that morning.

He sat in the first-class lounge, annoyed and edgy, knowing he was overreacting to the delay but he didn't give a damn. All he wanted was to get to Vegas, find Dawn and write Paid to his debt to Jonas.

"How much longer until flight 1740 boards?" he kept asking the ground attendant.

Her response, the same as her smile, was constant. "Just as soon as the weather clears, Mr. Baron."

When he found himself on the verge of telling her she could save time by putting her answer on tape, he knew he needed to calm down. Pacing back and forth wasn't helping, and he had enough caffeine in his system so that he'd probably start twitching if he had any more. He took a small bottle of water from the minifridge and found a chair in the far end of the lounge where he couldn't see the departures board or the rain beating against the window.

When the weather cleared and outbound flights resumed, he'd know it.

The water cooled his throat, if not his impatience. He finished it, put the bottle on the floor beside him and took a file out of his briefcase. Jack had faxed him the last information on Dawn late last night and he'd tucked it away after a cursory glance. He'd intended to go through the information on the plane but why wait? He had the time right now.

The first few pages were duplicates of stuff he'd already seen. He thumbed through them quickly. The last pages were the ones that interested him. The data was new and defined the woman he was flying to Vegas to meet. It was fascinating stuff.

For starters, the lady wasn't Dawn Lincoln Kitteridge anymore. She was Dawn Carter. She had been, ever since she'd spent a couple of months in Phoenix where she'd somehow managed to acquire ID in that name: driver's license, social security card, a gasoline credit card. Everything you'd need to assume a new identity.

Whatever else Dawn was, she wasn't stupid.

She'd stopped at half a dozen other places after Phoenix, worked at a waitress in a couple of diners and at a Denny's before she'd landed in Vegas more than three years ago and got a job waiting tables at the Desert Song. She'd made the most of the opportunities at the hotel and casino, shifting from waitress to blackjack dealer, then to dealer in what Jack's investigator called the high stakes section of the casino. Now she was off the casino floor, working at something called Special Services where she "offered private attention to VIPs and big spenders," Jack's man had written, and underlined it.

Gray's mouth thinned. He wouldn't read anything into that, not yet, but he had his suspicions of exactly what special services she provided.

The personal data on Dawn Kitteridge—Dawn Carter, he reminded himself—was skimpy. There was nothing about who she had lived with, who she had been involved with during the months she'd spent working her way to Nevada. If what Harman said was true, she'd probably left a trail of men behind her but that wasn't his business. She lived alone in Vegas. She had one seemingly close friend, a former stripper named Cassie Berk who was now a cocktail waitress at the Desert Song. She also seemed to have, in the sterile language of the report, a "significant personal relationship" with the hotel's manager, Keir O'Connell.

What was that supposed to mean? Was she sleeping with her boss? Maybe that was why the lady had gone from waitress to dealer so fast. At least, Gray figured it was fast. He didn't know very much about the way casinos or hotels op-

erated, but it was a possibility. Harman had said his wife had
been unfaithful. Why should that change now? Gray rubbed
his forehead. There was nothing new in the report, nothing to
help him get a better grasp of the woman he was going to
meet. Actually the most telling piece of information was the
one Jack's man had omitted.

Dawn was beautiful.

He looked at the picture Ballard had faxed him. The investigator had obviously taken it at a distance and the black-and-
white fax transmission was of such poor quality that he could
see the grainy dots that made up the image. Jack had tucked
in a note explaining that he knew the picture wasn't very good
but that he figured it might be of some use since it was more
recent than the photo Gray had bought from Harman.

Lousy quality or not, one thing was clear. Dawn was no
longer a shapeless girl in a simple dress. She'd been replaced
by a woman with one hell of a body. A clinging T-shirt and
short—very short—denim cutoffs made the most of high
breasts, a slender waist, almost boyish hips and legs that went
on forever.

Was that why she'd left her husband? Why she'd abandoned
her son? Because she'd grown up and wanted a different life?
Because she preferred the excitement of a wide-open city to
the isolation of a mountaintop?

"Ladies and gentlemen, your attention, please. The weather
has cleared. The following flights are ready for immediate departure..."

Gray looked at the faxed photo again. The accompanying
note said Jack's man had taken it in the front yard of a house
at 916 East Orchard Road, where Dawn rented an apartment.
The picture showed her watering a shrub that looked as if what
it really needed was a quick and merciful death. The photog-
rapher had caught her as if she were staring straight into the
lens. Too bad the image was so blurry. Gray couldn't read her
eyes. Did they hold the same mystery as Nora's? That blend
of sorrow and defiance that seemed to say more than words
ever could?

Jesus. His mouth twisted with disgust as he stuffed the picture and the rest of the report back into the folder. What was with him? This was no mystical experience. He was going to Vegas to talk to Dawn, though he couldn't figure out what they'd talk about any more than he could see much reason for it. He already had a good idea of what she was like. What more could he learn? Something good, maybe? That she was kind to animals, or that she bought Girl Scout cookies?

"Flight 1740 to Las Vegas now boarding. All passengers, please report to…"

Gray tuned into the voice coming from the speakers. The storm was over, planes were back in business, and his was boarding. About time, he thought, and headed for the door.

He read a book part of the way to Vegas, a bestseller by a lawyer who obviously knew more about fiction than the law, closed it when he found himself yawning and slept until the flight attendant woke him to say they were about to land.

If only this were a real vacation, he thought as his plane touched down. But it wasn't, and when he exited the terminal at McLarran Airport, he felt the heat and thought wryly that he'd be ready for a vacation in the Arctic by the time he finished with this mess.

Gray turned the AC in his rental car to high.

He didn't like Vegas. He'd been to the neon oasis in the desert once before, to meet with a client. The flashing lights and phony glitter, the crowds hell-bent on a good time and the electronic noise of the ubiquitous slot machines had impressed him but not the way he suspected the city fathers would have liked. Everything he saw convinced him that the town was a monument to self-indulgence.

No wonder Dawn had come here to live.

He edged into the long line of traffic headed for the Strip and the Desert Song Hotel and Casino. He'd blocked out five days for this trip, figuring it might take him that long to check out Ben Lincoln's granddaughter, but he hoped he could cut out sooner than that, fly straight to Austin, write some notes on the plane, hand them to Jonas and tell the old man what he could do with his blackmail and his philanthropy.

"Here's the information you wanted," he'd say, "and by the way, Uncle, I'll send you a check to cover the money you spent on my education. Goodbye, good luck, and to hell with you."

Just thinking about it made him feel better.

The only thing he still had to do was decide on a way to approach Dawn Carter. He'd been wrestling with that problem for days. The straightforward approach was out. He certainly wasn't going to come at her with blunt questions any more than he'd walk up, introduce himself and say that he here to take a good, hard look at her and see if she was worth, oh, six figures, maybe even seven, to an old man who had too much money and a bad case of the guilts.

Years in the courtroom had taught him that misdirection was often the best way to uncover information, especially from a hostile witness. And yeah, this wasn't a courtroom and Dawn wasn't a witness, hostile or otherwise, but it wasn't much of a stretch to figure she wouldn't want to explain herself or her life to a stranger.

He could always fall back on the story he'd told Harman, that her grandfather had left her a keepsake. Just for a minute, he thought about finding the kind of junky gift shops this town was sure to have in abundance. He could buy a music box, tear off the inevitable made-in-a-third-world-country-you-never-heard-of sticker, and present her with it.

Traffic opened up ahead. Gray gunned the engine and the car shot forward. What a scene that would be. He, acting his part to the hilt, solemn and sincere as he handed her the box. She, eagerly anticipating something old, maybe priceless. Her reaction when she saw what she'd supposedly inherited…

He'd love to see it play out, but it would never happen. In a pinch, he could tell her the story but actually giving her a phony legacy would be pushing the boundaries. He was a lawyer, not a shyster. All right. He'd play it cool. Forget telling her anything. A man didn't need an excuse to talk to a woman.

A smile, a couple of minutes of idle chitchat, and he could parlay that into an excuse for a drink and some conversation. The unadorned truth was that he had an easy time with women. It was only relationships that were hell.

And he wouldn't feel so much as a twinge of conscience about the decep—

"Shit!"

He came up a low rise—barely a bump in the road, he thought, in the instant before surprise gave way to shock— and saw a woman and a stalled car directly ahead of him. He hit the horn, she whirled toward him, and he knew he'd never forget the white blur of her face, the look of horror that transformed it as he hit the horn, stood on the brakes, and prayed for a miracle to any god who might be listening.

His car came to a shuddering halt inches away from her. The stop threw him forward; the seat belt bit into his shoulder and hip. Adrenaline pumped through him, hot and fast, as he unlatched the belt, flung open the door and jumped out.

"Jesus Christ," he roared, "what's the matter with you, lady? You almost got both of us killed!"

"I didn't realize—" She took a step back. "I—I'm sorry."

She was shaking from head to toe. Good, he thought viciously, let her go into convulsions for all he gave a damn. She'd scared the crap out of both of them. His heart was still trying to beat its way out of his chest.

"You're sorry? *Sorry?* You leave your car in the middle of the goddamned road and you think you can say you're sorry and that's the end of it?"

"I'm *terribly* sorry. I didn't mean—"

"Did you ever think of setting out flares?"

"I don't have—"

"Well, you should. Or was the poor son of a bitch who came over that hill supposed to have ESP?"

"My car broke down. It just—it just…" She flung out a trembling hand. "It just stopped."

"Yeah, well, *you* almost stopped. And if you think I want to sit around a police station and explain how I came to cream

a woman too stupid to move her car off the road, you're—
What's the matter?''

''Nothing.''

Hell. Gray hurried toward her, caught her by the shoulders
as she swayed. She flinched, and he tightened his grasp.

''Let go,'' she said in a tiny voice.

''So you can pass out on me? Yeah, that would be perfect.''
None too gently, he walked her to the curb. ''Sit.''

''I don't need to—''

''Sit, dammit!''

Dawn felt his hands press down on her shoulders. It was
the first time anyone had touched her in anger in four years
but it didn't matter. The old instincts were still there, trying
to suck her down into submission. No. God, no, she wasn't
going to let it happen.

''Don't touch me!''

''Lady, don't be an idiot. You're going to faint.''

''I'm not…'' But she was. The world was spinning. She
heard him curse, felt his hand wrap around her arm as she
sank to the curb.

''Put your head down, dammit.'' He put his hand on the
back of her head and shoved her face toward her knees. She
felt as if she were on an out-of-control merry-go-round. Any
second now, her teeth would chatter. How could the sun feel
so hot and she feel so cold?

''For God's sake,'' the man said, his voice thick with disgust. ''Stay where you are, you hear? Don't try to get up.''

Stay where she was? If she could have, she'd have laughed.
It was hard enough to keep from pitching into the gutter. The
last thing she was going to do was try to stand.

''Here.''

She felt something warm drop around her shoulders. Grate-
fully she burrowed into it.

''Do you have anything to drink in your car?''

She nodded. Big mistake. The merry-go-round took another
spin. ''Bottle of water,'' she whispered.

He was back a few seconds later. ''Drink,'' he ordered.

He put the bottle to her lips and she clutched it, drank greed-ily, gulping down the warm, life-giving fluid, feeling it spill over her chin. When the last drop trickled down her throat, she lifted her head and looked at the man standing over her. His hands were propped on his hips and he was slit-eyed with hostility.

She could deal with hostility.

"I'm okay now."

Her jerked his head in what she assumed was assent.

"Thank you."

He jerked his head again. Apparently he'd run out of names to call her. Without a word, he walked to his car. She heard a door slam, followed by the sound of the engine starting. Good. Her Bad Samaritan was leaving—but he'd forgotten whatever he'd draped over her. Dawn reached up, felt the soft-ness of cotton. A shirt? A sweater?

"Leave it on."

She looked up, startled. He was back.

"I checked my trunk." Just for a moment, his mouth curved in what might have been the first stages of a smile. "Turns out there were no flares in it, either. You sure you're okay?"

Dawn nodded. The world had stopped spinning. "It was just the heat."

"And the sight of me coming at you at a million miles an hour."

The sight of you coming at me in a rage, she thought, and hated herself for discovering that she hadn't gotten past that. He smiled, and she forced herself to smile in return as she rose to her feet. He reached out a hand but she pretended not to see it.

"Okay," he said, "here's the deal. You go sit in my car while I move yours to the curb."

"No. That's all right. I'll—I'll—" She widened her smile and told the lie with aplomb. "I'll phone and have it towed."

"Good." He reached into his pocket, took out a cell phone and handed it to her. "Make the call. I'll move the car."

Dawn stared at him blankly. There was no reason to tell

him she couldn't afford to have her car towed, not until she figured out her current finances or borrowed some money from Cassie. "Actually…" She cleared her throat, smiled brightly and returned the phone to him. "Actually it'll be simpler if I get to my office and call from there."

"Are you sure?"

"Positive." She took a breath and went for broke. "But if you could help me move the car, maybe just up to that side street…"

He sighed. "Yeah. No problem."

Dawn could tell he was just being polite but really, what choice did she have? She couldn't leave the car where it was. Moving it away from the No Standing/No Parking/No Doing Anything signs that bristled like metal tree stumps along the boulevard would be a big help.

"Great." She pulled off the garment he'd put around her shoulders—it was a navy sweatshirt, faded and frayed—smiled and held it toward him. Her lips hurt from all the smiling. What was there to smile about, when your car was dead and you were at least a two hours' walk from the office that was certainly not going to be yours by the time you finally put in an appearance? None of that was the stranger's problem. She was just lucky he'd agreed to help her when nobody else had.

"You sure you don't need it?"

"I'm fine." Another smile. God, her lips were going to stick to her teeth. "I'll take the right side."

"The right…" He smiled and shook his head. "You just hop into the car and steer. I'll push."

"By yourself? But—"

"Steer, or you're on your own. No more saving you from passing out. When the weather's hot, I have a one a day limit on rescuing swooning damsels."

He really was being pleasant. This time, her smile was real. "Well," she said, "I guess I don't have a choice."

She got behind the wheel. He got behind the car. Dawn flashed a quick look into the mirror. Sweat was beaded on the man's forehead; muscles strained in his arms as he got into position. "Ready?" she called.

"Ready. Just steer for the corner."

The car rolled to the end of the street. Dawn turned the wheel and the car curved to the right and snugged against the curb, safe for a little while, at least. She gave a sigh of relief, opened her door and almost walked into the stranger.

"Whoops," he said with a little smile. He put his hand on her arm to steady her and she forced herself not to jerk away. She knew he wasn't trying to hurt her. He wasn't even angry anymore. He was flirting with her. Four years in the real world had taught her to recognize the signs. The easy smile. The appraising look. The little touches—touches that always set her skin crawling, the way it was doing now, even though she never let on. She was an expert at getting out of the game without any collateral damage. She smiled—another false lift of the lips—and stepped around him.

"Well," she said briskly, "thank you for your help."

"You're very welcome."

"And really, I'm sorry you had such a scare."

"Uh-huh." He grinned. "Me, too. Can I give you a lift?"

"A lift?"

"Yeah. To wherever it is you're going." He glanced up at the blue-white sky. "Unless you'd rather broil while you wait for a cab."

"Oh," she said, as if the possibility of going with him was completely foreign.

Did such a simple offer require such careful consideration? Gray watched the woman's face, what he could see of it. Not much, thanks to the oversize black-lensed sunglasses, but what was visible—a pert nose, high cheekbones and a silky-looking mouth—was very nice.

So was the rest of her. Her hair was a soft-looking reddish-blond, swept into some kind of fancy knot at the nape of her neck, and he wondered how she'd look if she let it down. He tried not to be obvious as he scoped her out but it was impossible to keep from noticing the high, rounded thrust of her breasts under a cream-colored blouse and the long, slender legs showing beneath the hem of her skirt.

He felt a pleasant tingle in his groin. Maybe he'd stay the full five days in Vegas. Check into the Desert Song, find Dawn Carter, talk to her and get all of that out of the way, then relax a little. God knew he could use a break. There was nothing to rush back to. He hadn't begun another case yet and his social life was at loose ends, now that the woman he'd been seeing for the past few months—a reporter with the *Times*—had been transferred to London.

"I'll miss you," he'd said to her, their last night together.

"Me, too," she'd replied, and they'd both smiled and known that the truth was that nobody would really miss anybody, not after a few days.

So the timing was right. A little vacation in Vegas, an attractive woman…a woman who was taking forever to say yes, she'd appreciate a lift to wherever she was going.

Gray smiled. "Big decision," he said lightly.

She blushed. "I don't normally… I mean, you've been very kind, but—"

"But, for all you know, I'm a serial killer."

"No. I mean, I wasn't—"

She stammered, and her color deepened. He knew the courteous thing would be to bail her out of the hot water she had tumbled into but he liked watching her. He wasn't enjoying her embarrassment, it was just that he couldn't recall the last time he'd seen a woman blush. What would she do if he plucked those sunglasses from what looked like a very nice little nose so he could get a real look at her?

"I promise," he said solemnly, "I'm not wanted for anything but littering in any of the forty-eight states."

That won him a slight smile. "But there are fifty states."

"You got me." He grinned. "Truth is, I dropped a lei into the Pacific at Honolulu. And I dropped a candy bar wrapper in Juneau, hightailing it away from a polar bear."

Her smile broadened. It was a good smile. "I don't believe you."

"Would a man lie about something like that?"

"I don't know. Would he?"

"Okay. It wasn't a real bear, it was a stuffed one outside a store, but the judge said stupidity was no excuse for littering and sentenced me to a hundred years anyway. I did my time quietly. Now can I give you a lift?"

Dawn laughed at the story. He smiled in return. He'd been nothing but kind. Really, what was there to fear?

"Well," she said slowly, "you have to promise you won't try to run away from any polar bears."

"I'll let them eat me first," he said solemnly.

"In that case... Yes. Thank you. A lift would be great."

"Good. I was afraid I'd be reduced to a puddle by the time you made up your mind."

She blushed again. Damn, but that was a nice thing to see.

"I'm sorry. I didn't mean—"

"Hey, you don't have to apologize. I understand. A woman can't be too careful these days." Gray made a sweeping gesture toward his car. "Your chariot awaits, m'lady."

"I just need to get some things from my car..."

"Oh. Sure." He reached past her and opened the door. "Need any help?"

"No. There's not much."

She leaned past him, her bottom poking enticingly into the air. He told himself a gentleman would look away but he wasn't a gentleman, he was a lawyer. Everybody knew lawyers were sleazy bastards, which meant he could look his fill. After a minute, his damsel in distress backed out of her car with a creased jacket in one arm and a teddy bear...

A teddy bear?

"Ah-ha," Gray said.

She swung toward him. "Ah-ha, what?"

"Ah-ha, it looks as if I'm not the only one with a secret to hide." Surprised, he watched the color drain from her face. "The bear," he said quickly. "We seem to both have bears in the closet."

For a couple of seconds, she looked blank. Then she nodded. "Oh." Her cheeks began to pinken. "Oh, I see. Your bear story. And—and this bear…"

She gave him another small smile, though she tried to disguise it by sinking her teeth gently into her bottom lip. He thought how much he'd like to do the same thing.

"It's—it's for me."

"What is?"

"The bear."

"The bear is for you?" he said inanely. Frankly he didn't care if the bear was a peace offering to the alien king of the planet Zabu. He just hoped she'd bite her lip again. Or maybe not.

"Yes. I, uh, I collect them."

Her blouse was damp. How come he hadn't noticed that? Damp, and clinging. A woman with a great smile and a lush mouth, and the faintest hint of pebbled nipples beneath that blouse…

Gray cleared his throat. "Okay," he said briskly, "if that's everything—"

"Just one second." She transferred the bear to her other arm and reached into the car. Her bottom pointed at him again but not for long. When she backed out this time, she had a small shopping bag dangling from her fingers. "For the bear," she said.

"Oh." He cleared his throat again and searched for something to say that would make sense. "Don't you think he'd enjoy the view from inside my car?"

That had been the right thing to say. It made her laugh, which made him laugh, too.

"I'm sure he'd love it, but—but I don't want to walk into my office with him under my arm."

"Too much ribbing to face?"

Too many questions, Dawn thought, but she wasn't about to tell him that. "Exactly."

He shifted his weight from one foot to the other. It brought him closer to her. "Is Teddy my competition?"

His voice was suddenly soft and low. It made her think of

gravel laid over thick velvet. She looked up and her pulse leaped. Her rescuer was watching her through dark-lashed, pale blue eyes. His hair was coffee-brown and thick. With a little start of surprise, she realized that he was good-looking. Very good-looking.

The back of her neck tingled and she was trying to decide whether the sensation was pleasant or not when he reached out and touched his finger first to the bear's button nose and then to hers. That was all he did, just brush her nose with the tip of his finger, but terror raced through her. She took a step back but there was nowhere to go. The car was behind her; he was in front of her. He was big and strong, he was crowding her, and suddenly the old panic was clawing for purchase in her throat.

"Don't!"

She thought the word had come out a shout but the look on his face told her it hadn't, that it had been a pathetic whimper, and for the second time since the stranger had come into her life, she had reason to despise herself.

"Hey." He stepped back. "I didn't mean—"

"I know you didn't," she said quickly. "I just—it's the heat. And this thing with my car. My boss will be—"

"Sure."

"—he'll be wondering if I—"

"Absolutely. Come on. I'll get you to work in no time."

Stupid, she thought as she followed him to his car. She'd fought so hard to come this far—was the simple touch of a man's hand really enough to send her scuttling back into her cave? Giving in to the fear was like giving in to Harman. It was letting him beat her into submission without lifting a hand, and she had long ago decided she'd choose death over that. Besides, she knew how to handle simple flirtation.

"Are you coming?"

She looked up, smiled, got into the car and waited until he'd gone around to the driver's side and settled behind the steering wheel.

"Actually," she said lightly, "you were right." He looked

at her questioningly and she felt foolish. Obviously he'd already forgotten that teasing line about the bear being his competition. "About my bear." God, if only the floor would open and swallow her. "About—about him being…" She took a breath. If he didn't remember what he'd said, she didn't have to explain it. "I love teddy bears," she said inanely. "I always have."

That eased the tension. He laughed, turned the key and blessedly cool air washed over her.

"Well, that's good to know. Still, I have to admit, I've never gotten the brush-off because of a stuffed bear."

She almost said she doubted if he'd ever gotten the brush-off at all. It was hard to imagine a woman—a normal woman—not being flattered by his interest.

The nape of her neck tingled again. Once, years back, Harman had lunged at her and she'd tumbled backward and grabbed a frayed electric cord as she fell. The sensation that had shot through her body had been something similar to this. Not pleasant. Not unpleasant. Just—just incredibly startling.

The memory, not of the sensation but of Harman, made her shudder.

"You okay?"

Dawn blinked. He was staring at her. By now, he most likely regretted offering her a ride. He probably thought she was crazy.

"Are you cold? I can turn down the AC, if you are."

"No. No, I'm fine." She flashed a bright smile. "I was just thinking about how late I'm going to be."

"I'll talk to your boss, if you'd like. I can verify your story about your car dying."

"Oh, he'll believe me. It's just that this is my first day on a brand-new job." She hesitated. "I wonder… Could I use your cell phone?"

He handed her the phone, watched while she punched in a number. She was a puzzle. She'd jumped like a cat when he'd touched her, but other times there was an unsettling stillness to her, as if part of her was standing back and observing things.

He tried not to listen while she spoke to someone. Her boss, probably. She sounded worried; she said she was sorry a couple of times and that she'd be happy to work the night shift to make up for it. He glanced at her, taking in the blouse, the tailored skirt, the jacket lying across her lap, the long legs encased in silky-looking stockings. She was dressed for an office. What kind of night shift did a woman work in a suit? In stockings? Or was it panty hose? His imagination kicked in, took him on a brief but fascinating trip, and he looked away from her and stared straight out the windshield. She was edgy and he was thinking about stockings and pantyhose. It wasn't a good combination.

"Thank you."

Gray looked up. She held out the phone. He took it and put it back into his pocket.

"Everything okay?"

"Uh-uh."

"You sure? My offer still stands. If you need me to talk to your boss—"

"Thanks, but it'll be fine."

"Yeah." He reached for the radio, then changed his mind. He didn't know why but he had the feeling almost anything, even a wrong choice in music, could spook her. "So, what kind of work do you do? No, don't tell me, let me guess." He looked at her. "You repair slot machines."

"Me? No! I don't…" She saw his mouth twitching and she laughed. "Try again."

"First tell me where to go. Left? Right? Straight ahead?" He smiled. "Better still, point me toward some quiet little restaurant where we can have a glass of wine, a long lunch and get to know each other better."

"Straight ahead," she said, because it was turning out she didn't know how to deal with this man's flirting at all, because she knew she was blushing, because she wondered why she was behaving like such a fool. "Just continue toward the Strip."

He sighed. "Struck out again."

"Look. I'm really…" Really what? Not good at this stuff? "I'm really grateful for your help, but—"

"But you have a boyfriend named Teddy and a boss named Scrooge and you have to get back to your office. I'm right about that, aren't I? That you work in an office?"

"Yes," she said.

He smiled. It was a nice smile and he was a nice-looking man with a nice sense of humor. Everything about him was nice. A winner, Cassie would say. Maybe Cassie would like to meet him. She could ask him his name, where he was staying, invite him to meet her at the Song for coffee and arrange for Cassie to be there…

"You're an accountant."

"Bad guess." Dawn laughed. "I need to take off my shoes to balance my checkbook."

"Yeah, well, so do I. That's what pocket calculators are for."

"In that case," she said, with a little smile, "are *you* an accountant?"

"Nope." He shook his head. "It's almost as bad, though. I'm a lawyer."

"There's nothing bad about being a lawyer."

"No?"

"No."

"That only means you haven't heard the jokes."

Dawn turned toward him, as far as the safety belt would permit. "What jokes?"

"Let's see." The light ahead turned red. Gray eased the car to a stop. "What do you call a thousand lawyers at the bottom of the ocean?"

She smiled. "I don't know. What?"

"A good start." Her laughter was so genuine that it made him laugh, too. Don't stop while you're ahead, he told himself, and fired off another. "Why do they use lawyers instead of rats in experimental labs?'' He gave her just enough time to shake her head. "There are some things you just can't get a rat to do." She laughed even harder and he thought how nice it would be to take her to dinner tonight. "You never heard those jokes, huh?"

"They're terrible," she said, on a last chuckle. "Are you here on vacation?"

He said he was, that he'd decided he needed a change of scene for a few days. He asked her to recommend some places to see, not because he gave a damn about seeing places but because he liked the softness of her voice. He liked the way she smelled, too. He had the fan turned high and the air had taken on her scent, a delicate mix of flowery perfume and female musk. What would the lady say if she found out that he was sitting here saying all the right things while he inhaled the essence of her, and that doing it was turning him on? Maybe she'd admit that she was interested, too. He'd seen it in her smile, in her sudden awareness of him when he'd leaned over her.

The teddy bear didn't know it, but it didn't have a chance.

"So," he said, "are you from Vegas originally? I mean, is this home?"

"It is, now. But nobody's actually from Vegas. Well, nobody I've met, anyway."

"Yeah. I guess it's the same as New York. There must be people who were actually born there but I've never met any."

"Is that where you're from? New York?"

"Yes. I clerked for a judge there, after law school, and—"

"If you take the next right, we can avoid the traffic. Sorry. I didn't meant to interrupt. You clerked for a judge in New York?"

Gray made the turn. "Uh-huh."

"But you were born in...Texas?"

He shot her a startled look. "How'd you know that?"

"I have a good ear for accents. I guess it's from living here and talking to people from different places."

"Yeah, but I don't have an accent."

"Well, you do. Just a tiny one."

"So do you, now that I think about it. I just can't place it. Is it California?"

"Take the next left—"

"Utah? New Mexico? Arizona?"

"—and just pull in here, into this parking lot, and stop."

"That's not fair. You pegged me as a Texan. Don't I get the same shot at you?"

"Thank you for all your help," Dawn said. She opened the door and stepped out. "And have a wonderful vacation."

The door closed. Gray hit the window control. "Hey," he shouted, as she ran across the lot toward a white building, "aren't you even going to tell me your name?"

She turned toward him, waved and went inside the building. That was when Gray saw the sign and realized he was at the back entrance to the Desert Song Hotel.

CHAPTER SIX

DAWN was exhausted by the time she tottered into her apartment at eight that night. It had been a long day, but at least things had worked out better than she'd expected.

For openers, she had her car back.

She'd taken a few minutes to make herself presentable after she'd arrived at the Song in the afternoon. Then she'd hurried to her office and found Keir waiting for her. She'd started to apologize for being late but he said Jean had already explained.

"Things like that happen to everyone," he'd said pleasantly, "but it might be a good idea if you have your car checked over to make sure it's reliable."

She knew it was a polite way of telling her that getting to work on time was part of her job. The raise she'd just gotten was significant. She could set some money aside each week and, eventually, either repair her old car or trade it in on a newer model, but it would take a while. She couldn't explain that, not without explaining, too, that she had expenses nobody knew about because she had a son and she was paying a pretty hefty tuition to keep him in a small private school not too far from Vegas but far from any possibility his father would ever find him.

All she could do was nod at Keir's graciously worded reminder of her responsibilities and assure him she'd have the car fixed and that she'd be on time from now on.

"Fine," he replied, and then he'd stunned her by saying he'd have someone take a look at her car, tow it in, if that was necessary, and fix it. When she stammered a protest, he reminded her that the hotel had its own small fleet of vehicles, that it had a contractor who serviced the fleet and that it was simple enough to send one of his men to do the job. He said he'd tell the contractor to charge her the special rate he charged the hotel, and to bill her separately.

Dawn knew the O'Connells had a reputation for fairness to employees but Keir's kindness amazed her. She'd wanted to say so but she was afraid she'd cry and embarrass them both, so she just smiled like an idiot and choked out a thank you.

A little while later, a man in coveralls came to get her keys. A few hours after that, when he returned them, he said her car was in the employee lot, all fixed and ready to go.

"What was wrong with it?" she'd asked, and he launched into a mind-numbing recitation that involved a dirty air cleaner and something called a ballast resistor. Dawn listened, nodded once or twice as if she understood what sounded like a foreign language, and finally the mechanic grinned and said the bottom line was that they'd bill her at the end of the month.

The good news was that her old car still had plenty of life in it. Good news? It was wonderful news. And it was heaven to be home at last.

Dawn kicked off her shoes, waggled her toes and sighed with relief. Wearing heels every day was something new. Her dealer's uniform had consisted of a shirt, vest and pants. Flat had been okay. The new job required heels. Nothing outrageous, just pumps, but she wasn't used to heels at all. Summers on the mountain, she'd gone barefoot; winters, she'd worn heavy walking boots. Never heels, no matter what the season. Harman hadn't approved. They made a woman look like a slut, he'd said, but then he'd said that about almost anything she wore, even the shapeless dresses she'd sewed herself in hopes they would be acceptable…

Dawn took off her jacket and carefully placed it on a hanger. She was doing it again, wasting energy thinking about the past. Was it because she'd missed her Sunday visit with Tommy last week? She always saw her boy on Sunday. Always. She got up at five, was on the road by five-thirty, arrived at Rocking Horse Ranch at seven and they spent the entire day together, just she and her son.

Sometimes she took him to a wonderful place Tommy called their hideaway, where water rushed down over smoothly sculpted rocks and things were so green and lush you forgot you were in the desert. Or they drove to what remained of a mining camp, where Tommy had found a battered tin cup that made his eyes shine. If the weather was iffy, they drove to the mesa not far behind the ranch, followed a steep path to the bottom and explored the little canyon at the base.

She saw her son during the week, too, if time permitted, but those Sunday visits were what she lived for—and she'd missed the last one. Becky had asked her to come in and spend Sunday reviewing things. For one wild moment, Dawn almost said she couldn't do it, that she had a little boy waiting for her... But nobody knew Tommy existed, not even Cassie.

He would always be her secret. It was his only protection.

It still amazed her that she'd made good her escape from the mountain.

That night, she'd known Harman would go after her. He had friends; one of them would surely lend him a car or a truck. As she'd huddled with Tommy in the dark parking lot of the Victory Diner, waiting for the 1:00 a.m. bus that would take her to freedom, she'd feared every pair of headlights that came down the street. Sure enough, once the bus was on the highway, she'd looked out the window to see a familiar old car racing alongside. It belonged to Harman's best drinking buddy, but her husband was at the wheel.

"Harman," she'd whispered. She shrank back in her seat as he glanced at the bus, even seemed to look right into the window where she sat with her baby in her lap, but then he'd pulled ahead. She'd almost sobbed with relief. Harman had been watching for the truck. His truck. He hadn't thought she would have abandoned it and taken the bus instead.

The look of him, wild-eyed at the wheel of that car, haunted her. It was how she imagined him still, driving through the night in search of her. It was why she would never tell her secrets to anyone, why she'd said no, she wouldn't mind giving up her Sunday when Becky asked. She'd called the ranch, told Tommy she had a cold because she was afraid he'd think she put her job before her love for him, and gave him a big *mmmwha* that she said was a superduper giant kiss to tuck under his pillow—it was a game that always made him giggle.

Maybe she couldn't wake up mornings to see her boy's smiling face or tuck him in last thing at night, but she had saved him from his father. That was all that mattered. As for her edginess tonight...well, the incident this afternoon had shaken her. A perfectly pleasant man had teased her a little and she'd almost gone to pieces. She'd thought she was past all that, the feeling of suffocating terror when a man leaned too close, when she saw that look, that tautness in a man's face that meant he was thinking of taking you to bed to do whatever would give him pleasure...

"Stop it," she said briskly.

The apartment was hot and airless after being closed up for so many hours. Dawn hit the switch for the AC, listened as it gurgled and groaned to life, then checked her answering machine. The red light was blinking. Dawn felt her heart in her throat, told herself she was letting her imagination run wild but sagged with relief when Cassie's voice flowed from the speaker.

"Hi. It's me. I know I said I'd come by for pizza but one of the girls called in sick, so I probably won't make it. Oh, I got your message. That's great, about your car. Keir's terrific, isn't he? Okay, gotta go. Talk to you tomorrow. Maybe we can meet for lunch, you think? *Ciao.*"

The machine clicked off. Dawn pressed her hand to her throat. "You really have to stop this," she said softly.

A blinking light on an answering machine didn't have to mean bad news. There were a thousand reasons for someone to leave a message. The hotel called with schedule changes. Salesmen phoned to try to sell her siding and insurance. She and Cassie were in touch almost every day. In her heart, she knew all that. In three years Mrs. Wilton had only phoned a couple of times, and the calls had been about simple things, like Tommy needing new sneakers or jeans.

It was just that she'd had this—this uneasy feeling all afternoon, the sense that something was wrong. Not wrong, exactly. Maybe just off-kilter. At work, she'd looked up a couple of times with the feeling that someone was watching her but nobody ever was, except for a harried reception clerk who had come to tell her a guest with blue hair and a free drink card was driving everyone crazy, insisting she could swap the card for dinner at La Chanson.

Dawn unzipped her skirt and hung it alongside her jacket.

Her mother would have said she was as jumpy as a long-tailed cat in a room full of rocking chairs. She would have told her to knock on wood three times or spit over her shoulder, whatever. Dawn had never been able to keep Orianna's endless superstitions straight, nor had she wanted to. She'd never wanted to be like her mother in any way, which made it even harder to understand how she'd ended up with a man like Harman.

To hell with Harman. He was out of her life, and hadn't she promised herself she wasn't going to waste another moment thinking about him?

She snatched up the phone, stabbed the programmed number of the Rocking Horse Ranch. Mrs. Wilton answered on the second ring. Yes, Tommy was fine. He was sleeping. What was new? Well, he'd decided he wanted to be a cowboy when he grew up. Or maybe a fireman, but only if firemen could ride horses, too.

Dawn laughed as she imagined her little boy's earnest face. By the time she hung up the phone, she felt fine again. She had to stop seeing shadows where there weren't any. That man who had helped her today, for example. So what if he'd asked her where she was from? She'd asked him the same question. It was just conversation; it didn't mean a thing.

He was a nice guy, that was all. Nice, and nice-looking. Definitely nice-looking. No question about it. Her Good Samaritan was what Cassie would call a hunk.

She took the pins from her hair and shook it loose, stripped off the rest of her clothes and stepped into the shower. There was a time, however brief, she'd have noticed how handsome he was right away. When she was fifteen, sixteen, before Harman came into her life, she'd just started becoming aware of those things. Other girls her age at Queen City High School had been standing in little knots, eyeing the boys and giggling for quite a while before she'd wanted to eye them herself.

Of course, she never had.

Dawn rinsed off and wrapped herself in a towel.

She didn't belong to any of those cliques. There was a pecking order even in that squalid town, and she was at the bottom of it. She would have died of embarrassment, anyway, if she'd looked at a boy and he'd noticed, though embarrassment would have been the least of her worries if her mother had caught her. Orianna had set out the rules the day Dawn first got her period. It was just about the same time her breasts began to develop and her waist to curve in above her hips.

"You're a woman now," she'd said.

Dawn hadn't felt much like a woman, not at twelve, but she'd known better than to talk back.

"Boys'll start comin' around you. Men, too. And I don't never want to see you showin' them any notice."

"Yes, Mama," she'd answered.

"You do and I'll beat you till you can't sit down. You got that?"

Dawn got it, even if the message hadn't made much sense. Years later, she'd figured out that it was Orianna's way of trying to keep her from leading the same life she did but back then, she'd wondered why her mother would warn her about men when she almost always had one in her bed, behind the closed door at the end of the trailer. The door wasn't much of a barrier. Sounds came right through. Smells, too, that musky stench of sweat and sex that made her gag the first time Harman laid hands on her, even before she'd learned how horrible it was to be with a man.

"Dammit!"

She was back to thinking about Harman again when what she should be thinking about was tomorrow, and her new job, and what she and Tommy would do together this Sunday...

The doorbell rang.

Dawn swung around and stared in the direction of the front door as if she might be able to see through it. Who would come visiting at this hour? Who would come visiting her at all? Only Cassie, and Cassie had left a message on the machine saying she wouldn't be coming by. Had she put the chain on? She couldn't remember. She'd been so glad to be home, so impatient to phone Mrs. Wilton...

The bell rang again.

Your abuser can't control you unless you let him. The steady voice of the Phoenix counselor echoed in her head. Dawn tossed the towel aside, slipped into her old terry-cloth robe and went to the door. Yes, the chain was on. She'd done it automatically.

"Who is it?"

"It's me. Cassie."

Cassie! Dawn almost laughed with relief as she undid the chain. "I thought you were working late."

"Yeah, so did I, but here I am." Cassie stepped into the living room and closed the door with her hip. "I figured I'd take the chance you hadn't eaten yet," she said, holding out a square white box. "Dinner."

"Not only haven't I eaten yet, I am positively starved." She was, too, now that she thought about it. "That pizza smells wonderful."

Cassie grinned and strolled past her. "Pizza?" she said dramatically, as she deposited the box on the kitchen table. "For shame, *mademoiselle*. Would I bring something as mundane as pizza?" She flung the lid back. *"Regardez! Pizza à la francaise!"*

Dawn peered into the box. "Mmm. Onions. Garlic. Black olives. Ham. Cheese." She took a deep breath, looked up and smiled. "It's pizza, and it's glorious."

"Not glorious. *Magnifique.* You keep forgetting those sixteen weeks I spent at the Sands, strutting across the stage with the Eiffel Tower on my head. I know French when I see it.''

''Uh-huh.''

''Uh-huh, my *derrière*. These are olives *niçoise*.'' Cassie took one of the little black olives and popped it into her mouth. ''And three different kinds of *fromage*, if you please.''

''And the ham?''

''You mean,'' Cassie said, batting her lashes, *''le jambon, oui?''* She grabbed a piece and ate it. ''It's Parma.''

''Parma ham's Italian.''

''Yeah, well, France is pretty close to Italy, isn't it? You have any soda?''

''In the fridge.''

Dawn put a handful of paper napkins on the table while Cassie opened the refrigerator and took out two cans of soda. They sat down opposite each other and dug in.

''So,'' Cassie said after a while, ''I guess you had a memorable day.''

''Only if breaking down on Las Vegas Boulevard is your idea of memorable.'' Dawn drank some soda. ''How come you didn't end up having to work tonight?''

''Jane—the girl who called in sick—decided she suddenly felt better and showed up.'' Cassie grinned and tucked a strand of jet-black hair behind her ear. ''Actually I think she heard that Prince Ahmat was in the house. He's a big, and I do mean big, tipper.''

''Well, that's nice. Not that he tips big. I mean, it's nice she decided to work. You certainly didn't want to work a double shift.''

''No.'' Cassie leaned forward, delicately removed a mushroom from the pizza and put it in her mouth. ''I met this guy. A Frenchman.''

Dawn laughed. Cassie's tastes in food inevitably reflected her love life. ''I never would have guessed.''

''He's tall, dark and gorgeous.''

''Mmm.''

"'Mmm' is for pizza. *Magnifique* is for handsome, loaded Frenchmen."

"It's for pizza, too, according to what you said two minutes ago."

"You're too picky for your own good, you know that?" Cassie sat back and crossed her legs. "So, are you gonna tell me how things went today?"

"They went fine." Dawn scooped up a gooey blob of cheese and sucked it off the tip of her finger. "Well, mostly fine. I had a couple of tough moments but all in all, I think it was okay. Jean said so, anyway."

"And your car?"

"All fixed. Something called a ballast resistor and some other stuff had to be replaced."

"Great." Cassie raised an eyebrow. "I heard that a knight in shining armor came to your rescue."

Dawn looked up, blushed, and looked down again. "You heard wrong. It's too hot to wear armor in Vegas."

"I also heard he was gorgeous, and that he was riding a black horse."

Dawn laughed. "It was a black Mustang."

"That's what I said."

"And you can't possibly know what he looked like 'cause he dropped me off at the employee entrance."

"Well, it was just a hopeful guess." Cassie cocked her head. "So, what *did* he look like? Warts? A potbelly? Ears like an elephant?"

"How'd you guess?" Dawn said, deadpan. She grinned when Cassie's eyes widened. "I'm joking. No warts. No belly. No ears like Babar's, either. He was okay looking."

"Okay, how?"

"Okay, that's all." Dawn took another piece of pizza and bit into it. "How many kinds of 'okay' can there be?"

"You really have led a sheltered life." Cassie refilled their glasses. "There's 'okay' as in that dealer who still tells me how much he'd like to take me out."

"I can't remember what he looks like."

"Exactly. Then there's Mario. The headwaiter."

"What's wrong with Mario?"

"What's right with him? Average looks. Average person-ality. Average everything."

Dawn finished the last bit of her slice of pizza and licked some sauce from her thumb. "And?"

"And, there's 'okay' as in Keir O'Connell."

"Meaning?"

"Meaning, okay, yes, perfect. Drop-dead gorgeous. You still want me to believe you haven't noticed?"

"I haven't. I don't think about Keir that way."

"I know you don't and a good thing, too, or I'd have to buy you pizza every night until you gained two hundred pounds and took yourself out of the running."

"I'm not *in* the running, Cass. Not when it comes to Keir or anybody else."

"Yeah." Cassie sighed, reached for another olive and in-stead slapped down the box cover. "I'm going to dump this, otherwise that two hundred pounds will be a reality. A hun-dred for you, a hundred for me, and even though it won't matter to you because you're determined to lead a nun's life, it'll matter to me because I'm not."

"You've already landed that Frenchman."

"Untrue. He spent four hours playing craps, kept asking me to bring him drinks, tipped me a hundred bucks...and just when I knew I was in love, his girlfriend came along and claimed him."

"Ah."

"Ah, indeed. But you'll see. Someday, I'm gonna land me a big catch."

"For a woman who says that, you've dumped an awful lot of fish back into the sea." Dawn smiled. "You know what I think?"

"Yes. You think I should save what's left of this pizza for your breakfast."

"I think that the heart of a true romantic beats somewhere under that supposedly tough shell."

"If your shell's not tough, what's the sense in having one? Just ask a soft-shell crab what he thinks sometime. Anyway, you're trying to change the subject."

"What subject? Pizza?"

"Men, and why you're afraid of them."

Dawn looked away. "I'm not afraid of men."

"Yeah, you are." Cassie sighed. "Look, we've been friends long enough for me to have noticed some things."

"I am *not* afraid of men. Just because I don't go out a lot—"

"You don't go out at all."

"I'm busy."

"With what? I work, too, remember? It's not exactly brain surgery that ties up your head twenty-three hours out of twenty-four."

Dawn rose to her feet and collected the soiled napkins. "I'm happy with my life."

"Miserable as the species is, a man could make you happier."

"You don't believe that any more than I do," Dawn countered, and dropped the napkins into the trash can.

Cassie sighed. "No. No, I don't. But locking yourself away from the world is no way to get a bad marriage out of your system."

"Cassie, I know you mean well. But—"

"But, you don't want to talk about it. Okay. I accept that. The thing is, you can't let your ex ruin your life, Dawn. Just because he was a bastard doesn't mean they all are."

"I never said…"

"No, you never did. Actually you haven't said anything about the guy, except that you were once married. Well, so was I. The difference is, I remember that I'm not married anymore. You don't."

"That's not true."

"What's not true?"

"That I'm not married anymore." It couldn't hurt to admit

just this much, could it? "I still am," Dawn said in a small voice.

"What? Well, then, that's the first step. Get a divorce."

Get a divorce. Dawn didn't know whether to laugh or cry. Cassie made it sound so simple, but she could never get a divorce. You had to file papers for a divorce. They would be sent to Harman. He'd know where she was. Where Tommy was. And he'd come after her and her baby.

"It's not that easy." She dumped the empty cans in the sink, rinsed them and propped them, upside down, on the drain board. "My husband would never give me a divorce."

"You mean, you're terrified of asking him for one."

"I didn't say that."

"You didn't have to. I wasn't born yesterday. I don't know why it took me so long to figure it out. You never date. You jump if a guy so much as looks at you."

"I don't."

"You do. You get this phony smile on your face—"

"Would you prefer I slug him? I don't have a phony smile, I have a polite one. You're the one who told me that was the way to go, remember?"

"I didn't tell you to treat perfectly nice guys like they were Jack the Ripper."

"Dammit, Cassie—"

"Dammit, Dawn, you're too young to lock yourself away like this." Cassie took a breath. "Oh, hell. Okay, I'm out of line. I know I am. I'm sorry."

"You don't have to be," Dawn said, trying not to sound stiff and knowing that she wasn't succeeding. "We're friends. You can say whatever you want."

"That's why I said it. Because we're friends, but the truth is, it's none of my business." Cassie carried the box containing the uneaten pizza to the trash can, hesitated, and put it into the fridge instead. "I don't know what made me say all this tonight. Well, maybe I do. It's the way you looked when I asked you about your knight."

"My what?"

"Your knight in shining armor."

"Do you know why armor shines?" Dawn said sharply. "It's plated with tin. Shoots a big hole right in that 'knight-in-shining-armor' theory, doesn't it? I mean, a tin-plated knight doesn't sound half as romantic."

"So call him your Good Samaritan. Who cares about names? I'm simply telling you that you said he was okay looking, but your eyes said something else."

Dawn grabbed the sponge and scrubbed the table free of nonexistent crumbs. "Great. Now you're into reading eyes."

"Look, I don't care. Deny it. Pretend you're living in a convent but do yourself a favor, okay? Dig a six-foot-deep hole in the front yard, right next to that pathetic thing you call a shrub—"

"It's an indigo!"

"Yeah, well, whatever it is, dig that hole and put your memories of the SOB you married inside it. Shovel the dirt back in, jump up and down on it a couple of times and you'll be rid of him once and for all. And do it before he completely poisons your life."

"Who would believe it?" Dawn threw her arms wide. "Oprah comes to Las Vegas," she said dramatically. "Tune in tomorrow while she solves the world's problems."

"It's good advice and you know it."

"Honest to God, Cassie…"

"Yes?"

The women glared at each other. Then Dawn felt her eyes fill with angry tears. She tried blinking them back but they flowed down her cheeks. She saw the stunned look on Cassie's face and then the words she'd never spoken to anyone burst from her lips.

"I hate him," she said, "I hate him! And I'll never be free until he really is buried in a hole six feet deep."

The words were so terrible, so unlike anything she'd ever permitted herself to think, that she began to tremble. Cassie flew toward her and gathered her into her arms.

"Oh, honey," she crooned, "oh, Dawn…"

"I shouldn't have said it. I know that. It's wrong, to want someone dead, but—"

"It's okay."

"It isn't. It's not okay. That's an awful thing, to wish somebody—"

Cassie led Dawn to a chair. "Sit down, honey. I'll get you something to drink."

"He did that, this afternoon," Dawn said unsteadily. "The man. He—he sat me down on the curb, and he gave me something to drink."

"That's what I said before." Cassie filled a glass with water and handed it to her. "The guy's an absolute knight in shining armor."

"It could be tin," Dawn said, and made a sound halfway between a laugh and a sob. "But I admit, he was—he was very kind."

"Take a drink."

Dawn sipped at the water, then handed back the glass. "Thank you."

"You're welcome." Cassie paused. "So, what's his name?"

"Harman."

Cassie smiled. "Harman, huh? That's a funny name for a knight."

"A name for a..." Dawn looked up. "No. Harman is—was—my husband." She licked her lips. "I shouldn't have told you that."

"Why? Do you think I'm going to take out an ad in tomorrow's paper?" Cassie held up her hands and stretched out an imaginary banner headline. "News flash! Dawn Carter's Ex Is Named Harman!"

Dawn didn't smile. "It's just better if you don't know anything about him, that's all. And I told you, he's not my ex."

"Yeah, well, he is. My ex was my ex long before I walked out on him."

"You said he walked out on you."

Cassie shrugged. "Same thing," she said, sitting down beside Dawn and taking her hand. "The point is, as soon as you start thinking that the marriage is over, it's over. Harman is definitely history."

"I wish."

"I know." Cassie hesitated. "Do you want to tell me more? Like, what he did to make you so gun-shy?"

"I'm not…" Dawn sighed. There was no sense in lying and less sense talking about it. "No."

"Well, that's straightforward."

"Cass." Dawn squeezed her friend's hand. "Honestly, there's no point in discussing it."

"There is, but if you don't want to, that's fine." Cassie grinned at Dawn's raised eyebrows. "Yup, it's another Oprahism. Well, I probably heard it on Oprah, anyway. You talk about a bad thing, you purge it from your system."

Dawn tugged her hand free and got to her feet. "Sorry, Dr. Freud, but that isn't always the way it goes."

"Okay, fine. Let's talk about something else."

Dawn filled the coffeepot. Cassie swung her foot and hummed. "So," she said brightly, into the deepening silence, "did you lose those five pounds on that new diet we both started last week?"

"No."

"Me, neither." Cassie tapped a finger on the tabletop. "How about that baseball game last night? That incredible ninth inning? Did you see it?"

Dawn looked at her. "No."

"Yeah." Cassie sighed. "That makes two of us." She hesitated. "Well, as far as I can tell, there's only one topic worth conversation. Let's talk about your knight."

"Give me a break, will you? There's nothing to talk about. Can't I convince you of that?"

"No, you can't. Let's see… For openers, what's his name?"

"I don't know."

"You didn't ask?"

"No."

"He didn't offer?"

"No. And this is silly. He's just a man. He helped me out. End of story."

"Humor me, okay? If he didn't have warts, a potbelly and ears that flap, what'd he look like?"

"I don't know." Dawn set the pot aside for the morning and took a box of cookies from the cupboard. "Want one?"

"What about the diet?"

She shrugged. "These are the low-fat kind."

"And probably good for the complexion."

The women munched their cookies in companionable silence.

"He's tall," Dawn finally said. "Maybe six-one, six-two. Dark brown hair. Blue eyes. Light blue."

"Matthew McConaughey-blue?"

"Uh-huh." Dawn ate another cookie and licked a spot of icing from her finger. "Anything else you want to know?"

"Of course. You don't think that's a complete description, do you? Let's see. We've got his height, his hair color, his eye color... How about his weight?" Cassie wrinkled her nose. "Don't tell me. He was soft, like he spends a lot of time behind a desk."

"Well, he probably does spend a lot of time behind a desk. He's a lawyer. But—"

"Big-time lawyer? Small time? No time?"

Dawn rolled her eyes. "How do I know? Big-time, maybe. He's from New York."

Cassie sprawled backward in the chair. "Be still, my heart. A New York lawyer with blue eyes, hair and, I'll bet, his own teeth! So what if he's soft and pudgy? I can survive."

"He isn't. Soft and pudgy, I mean. He's got great shoulders and a flat belly and these amazingly long legs..." Dawn fell silent. Color flooded her face. She stared at Cassie and then she closed the box, shot to her feet and jammed the cookies into the cupboard. "This is stupid."

"Anything that makes me drool can't be stupid. Go on. Did he have a nice face?"

Dawn closed her eyes and saw the man standing in front of her. He was leaning toward her, towering over her, watching her through those light blue eyes, looking at her in a way that told her he found her desirable. A knot formed in the pit of her belly. The last thing she wanted was to see desire in a man's face ever again.

"Dawn?"

"Yes." She turned and looked at Cassie. "You're wasting your time," she said in a low voice. The game had gone too far, and now it had to stop. "I know you mean well, Cass. But I'm not getting involved with anybody."

"A date with Sir Galahad isn't exactly getting involved."

"Whatever. I'm not doing any of it." Dawn took a breath, then slowly let it out. "Besides, I'll never see him again."

"Yeah, well, you should have asked him his name, at least. Where he was staying."

"I didn't care. I still don't. He gave me a lift. End of story."

"I meant so you could send him a thank-you note. That would be the right thing to do, wouldn't it?"

"You are so transparent, Cassie Berk! Just look at your face!"

"Well, you can thank him if you run into him. Las Vegas isn't really a big city."

"It's big enough," Dawn said firmly, "and the discussion is over." Her voice softened. "Thanks, Cass."

Cassie smiled. "Hey, what are friends for if not to stop by with pizza that put ten trillion fat calories on your hips?"

"I wasn't talking about the pizza. You know that. I mean, thank you for listening to—to that stuff about my husband."

"Your ex-husband."

"Right. My ex-husband. And thank you for getting my mind off the past."

"The best way to get your mind off the past is to think about the future." Cassie grinned. "Oprah says so."

"Well, for once Oprah and I agree." Dawn slid her arm around her friend's waist as they walked to the door. "I really do think about the future," she said softly. "All the time."

"Just promise me one thing. You bump into your knight, give him a chance to show you he's wearing sterling, not tin."

Dawn laughed. "Sterling tarnishes."

"Look, just give him a chance, okay?"

"Twenty to one says I'll never see him again."

The women paused at the door and faced each other, smiling. "I thought it was against the rules for the dealers to lay bets."

"I'm not a dealer anymore."

"You ready to put your money where your mouth is?"

"Absolutely."

"A buck," Cassie said solemnly.

Dawn nodded. "You're on."

They laughed and gave each other high fives. The next morning, within minutes of starting work, Dawn lost her bet.

CHAPTER SEVEN

GRAY opened his eyes, shut them again, rolled over and groaned as he buried his face in the pillow.

No good. The sun was pouring into his hotel room and the spill of golden light seemed to have lodged itself in his brain, right next to the little guy playing the maracas.

After a minute, he sighed, rolled onto his back and folded his arms beneath his head. The ceiling was white and easier on the eyes. Not that he deserved a break. The way he felt this morning was his own fault. The sun was coming in because he'd spent half the night standing at the windows or on the balcony, and he'd forgotten to draw the curtains before he'd finally tumbled into bed. He probably should have left that last miniature of scotch in the minibar, too. Not that it mattered now. He was awake, his head hurt and his mood sucked. Even a grizzly would have given him a wide berth.

After a while, he looked at the clock, sat up and headed for the bathroom. Maybe an icy shower and some aspirin would improve things.

They did, a little. The banging in his skull eased. He knew his attitude still needed work but a couple of gallons of coffee and a large glass of vitamin C in the guise of orange juice would help. The problem lay in getting to them. Just thinking about the crowds and the noise of the casino he'd have to endure on his way to the open-for-breakfast restaurant made him shudder.

Room service promised to deliver within fifteen minutes. The woman who took his order was so unfailingly cheerful, so eager to add pancakes or waffles or omelets to his Spartan meal, that he wanted to garrote her. Instead, to atone for the thought, he added a request for rye toast.

"Thank you, Mr. Baron," she chirped.

Gray dressed in a black polo shirt and chinos, decided that

120

shaving might be dangerous to his health and collapsed in one of the armchairs in the sitting area, determined to contemplate nothing more complex than his surroundings.

His room—a deluxe minisuite, whatever in hell that meant—was big and handsome, done in shades of sand and taupe, and almost austere except for the billowing ocher-silk canopy over the bed. A tent, he'd thought with some amusement when he'd checked in the previous afternoon. He assumed the scheme was meant to be reminiscent of the desert though no stretch of arid land or oasis could ever have been this luxurious. He was on the sixteenth floor and the room overlooked the pool and its surrounding gardens.

He'd spent a lot of time looking down at that pool last night.

A knock sounded at the door. He opened it and a waiter bearing a silver tray greeted him pleasantly. Gray did his best to be pleasant in return. Maybe he could get some information. God knew he hadn't come up with any on his own.

"Going to be hot today," he said, and winced mentally at the inane remark, though the waiter took it with grace.

"Yessir," he said as he arranged china and silver on a table near the window in the step-down sitting area. "Great weather for the pool."

"Or for the casino," Gray said, and smiled. "But I guess it's always great weather for the casino."

"That it is." The waiter made a minor adjustment to the single champagne-colored rose displayed in a slender crystal vase. "Would you like me to pour your coffee, sir?"

"No, that's okay, thanks. I'm not quite ready." Gray tucked his hands in his pockets. "So," he said, after a second or two, "I guess a place like this employs a lot of people."

"Oh, it does. A small army, you might say."

"Must be hard to know everybody."

"Well, you get to know faces." The waiter stepped back. "Some names, too. Not all of them, though. Just too many to deal with, you know what I mean?"

"Absolutely." Gray took a twenty from his pocket. "Here you go."

"Thank you, sir. Enjoy your stay."

"I'm sure I will. Oh, it occurs to me..."

"Sir?"

"A guy I know said he had a cousin he thought worked here, at the Desert Song."

"Really," the waiter said politely.

"Dawn something. Dawn Carter?"

The man shook his head. "I don't know her."

"She used to be a dealer."

"I don't know many of the casino people."

"But she works in the hotel now, in something called Special Services."

"I know mostly kitchen staff, sir."

"Pretty woman, this guy says.

"Sorry."

"She's a strawberry blonde. Tall. Long legs."

"I don't know anything about women, Mr. Baron." The waiter's tone had grown cautious. "All I do is deliver for room service."

"Yeah. Well, thanks anyway."

"Have a good day, sir."

Shit. Gray stalked back across the room as the door swung shut. He'd certainly screwed that. Now the waiter figured the guy in Room 1664 was in the market for a hooker. For a man who made his living pinning witnesses to the chair with carefully worded questions, he was turning out to be one sorry-assed detective.

He poured himself a cup of coffee, added a dollop of cream and stood looking out the window. It was early, barely seven, but people were already sprawled on lounges arranged around the free-form perimeter of the pool. Nobody was actually in the water, though a large woman in a suit a few sizes too small was sitting on the edge.

Maybe he'd take a swim. Maybe he'd lie in the sun. Gray's hand tightened around the cup. Maybe he'd fly back to New York, send Jonas a check and a note telling the old man that he could send some other sucker on this wild-goose chase.

"Dammit," he said, and drank some of the coffee.

It wouldn't be enough. Jonas had done him a favor he'd

never asked for, he was stuck with repaying it, and he couldn't do it with anything as simple as a check. The old son of a bitch was good at figuring people and he'd figured him to a T. The only way he could discharge this debt was by fulfilling his uncle's request.

He could feel his mood going from miserable to rotten. Nothing had gone right, not from the minute he'd hit Las Vegas.

The woman he'd rescued had brushed him off faster than a broom whisked away dust. On a personal level, he didn't much care. This town had two things in profusion: slot machines and good-looking women. She was no loss. It just pissed him off, the way she'd used first his muscles and then his car, and cut out without even telling him her name.

Gray refilled his cup.

As for finding Dawn Carter... He'd find her, all right. You could find anything, even a needle in a haystack, if you gave it enough time and effort. Any thoughts of cutting this little jaunt short were fast fading away. He'd walked through the hotel and the casino last night without spotting a woman who looked even remotely like Dawn. Admittedly the pictures he had of her were next to useless but still, he'd expected to be able to find some similarity. Her height. Her hair. Her eyes. He'd checked all the tables on the main floor as well as those in the special area set aside for high rollers on the assumption that Jack's guy might have gotten it wrong. Maybe Dawn still worked them when she wasn't providing those special services to special guests.

No luck. She wasn't around.

The high stakes tables had been interesting, though. He'd watched players raising the stakes to unbelievable levels and decided they were crazy.

He knew risk was exhilarating. Skydiving, mountain climbing, shooting class five rapids... Gray had tried them all and loved the adrenaline rush that came of dancing on the edge. You honed your body and mind in preparation, the same as you did for a courtroom showdown with a smart prosecutor or a tough judge. Risky, but you really were always in control.

Leaving everything to fate? That wasn't risky, it was crazy, plain and simple.

Chance decided where the little roulette ball landed, which number on the die came up, how many coins you had to feed into the maw of a machine before you came out a winner, if you ever did. Along about midnight, when he was damn near punchy from lack of sleep, it struck him that it was the same with relationships. No matter what you tried, you could never count on how they would turn out. A man never knew what was coming. Women saw to that.

Like that routine with Red. He didn't care if he saw her again or not. It just rankled, how she'd played him for a fool. Push my car, thank you very much. Drive me to work. Thanks again. Oh, no, I'm not going to give you my name. It's none of your business.

Gray tossed back the last of the coffee.

Basically, she was right. It was just that he'd felt stupid as hell, watching her bolt from the car and run through the rear entrance of the hotel. After a minute, he'd driven to the door, leaned out the window and spoken to the security guard who had let her in.

"Damnedest thing," he'd said, with what he'd hoped was a smile, "but the lady forgot to tell me her name."

"Really," the guard had replied, and Gray tried another smile.

"Yeah. Well, she was late for work."

"Uh-huh."

The SOB wasn't going to give an inch. "I'd sure like to know her name," he'd said, reaching for his wallet. "I'd be very grateful."

"Get lost, mister. You're trespassing on private property."

Just what he needed. Legal advice from a rent-a-cop. Gray almost told him that but sanity had prevailed. He gunned the engine, drove around to the front of the hotel, handed the car over to a blue-jacketed valet and checked in at the front desk.

A shower cooled him down. A meal helped, too. Then he'd started his trek through a casino the size of a small city and never came close to sighting his quarry. When he'd realized he was also keeping an eye out for the lady whose car had died on the road, he felt his bad temper coming back. He had problems enough, trying to find one woman. Why double the number?

At 1:00 a.m., with the slot machines and the tables still busy, he went to his room, stripped down and collapsed on the bed, tired by the endless day and his lack of success. He lay on his back, arms folded beneath his head, staring up at the silk canopy and wondering how in hell the fool who had designed the place thought a person would be able to sleep under a goddamn parachute without feeling claustrophobic.

After a while, he sat up and rubbed his hands over his face.

There was nothing wrong with the canopy and hell, he'd never been claustrophobic in his life. It was just that the silken tent was soft and sensual. It made him think about what it would be like to have a woman in bed with him, the draped silk enclosing them both in a world made up of whispers, tastes and touches. He closed his eyes and saw the woman, a redhead whose eyes were still a mystery, whose name he didn't know, who had made it clear she wasn't interested in him, and got a hard-on that sent him into the shower again.

Afterward, Gray wrapped a towel around his hips, opened the minibar and took out one of those ridiculously small bottles of scotch he'd always figured were made for Lilliputians. He thought about swigging the stuff straight from the bottle, decided he wasn't that bad off yet and poured it into a glass. He drank it while he stared out the window at the pool and at the sky that glittered with galaxies of neon, and told himself to get his head on straight.

Forget the mystery woman. She wasn't worth thinking about. As for Dawn... He'd find her. He wasn't an impatient man. He liked things done on schedule, yes, but his profession—hell, his life—had taught him that sometimes the best thing was to wait. So what if he hadn't located her right away? She was here; that was the bottom line. The probability was she worked a different shift, or maybe this was her day off. He'd figured five days. So what if one was already shot to hell? There were four yet to come.

What was so bad about that? Nothing, he'd told himself, and hit the minibar again...and felt at least one of his promises fly out the window.

He couldn't stop thinking about the woman he'd helped.

He knew there was no reason for it. Yes, she was good-looking. At least, what he'd seen of her was good-looking, but so what? Actually she wasn't even his type. He liked small, curvy brunettes; she was a tall, slender redhead. Still, there were things about her that were memorable. Great legs. A nice ass. Breasts that made his palms ache to cup them. A pink, soft-looking mouth.

Just thinking about how she'd touched her sharp-little teeth to that tender flesh was making him hard again.

Gray opened another scotch and polished it off. He was reaching for number four when he caught himself, took a mineral water instead and slid open the door that led to the balcony. The night was warm and sultry, like a woman's caress. He closed his eyes and thought he could almost smell the desert and the distant mountains.

He wished he'd been able to see more of the woman's face. What little he'd seen haunted him. Her mouth. Her nose. Her small, resolute chin. Sort of like Nora Lincoln's, or her granddaughter's. Once or twice, she'd even lifted it in that same gesture of defiance. Maybe it was a female thing, that tilt of the chin. Something else he'd never noticed about women, some of the ladies who had swept through his life would probably have said.

He wondered about her eyes. What color were they? Blue, he decided. Blue would suit the color of her hair and the creaminess of her skin. Would her eyes be filled with laughter? He doubted it. Coaxing a smile from her hadn't been easy. He hoped her eyes didn't hold the same shadowed sadness as he'd seen in...

''For God's sake,'' he said with disgust.

What the hell was with him? The lady had made it clear that she wasn't interested. Was that the reason she was lodged inside his head? Or was it her seeming complexity that had piqued his interest? He'd sensed that a man would have to go through layers and layers to get to the truth of who she was, what she was; that she'd never fully revealed herself and the man who broke through the barriers would find something special...

That had done it. "Baron," Gray had said out loud, "you are on overload, man."

He'd put on sweats and sought out the hotel's exercise room. Seven miles on a stationary bike followed by some fancy footwork with the body bag and he'd returned to his room a mental zero, finally ready to fall into a deep, dreamless sleep. Unfortunately three hours wasn't enough. That was why he'd awakened in such a foul mood, and with somebody playing the maracas in his skull.

Gray turned away from the window. The coffee had done its job. He felt almost human. He shaved, slipped his feet into a pair of moccasins, scooped up his wallet and room card from the dresser, and went in search of the elusive Dawn Lincoln Kitteridge Carter.

Five fifty-nine, Dawn thought groggily, eyeing her alarm clock with distaste. Did she really have to get up at six? What was the harm in closing her eyes for five more minutes...

There was no such thing as only five more minutes. "Up and at 'em," she muttered. She shut off the alarm before it could ring and stretched her arms high overhead. She hadn't gotten enough sleep. Her own fault, really. It was the price you paid for eating pizza just before bedtime.

She'd had bad dreams all night. Every now and then she'd dozed off, only to awaken abruptly in the darkness, heart pounding for no good reason at all, skin slick with sweat.

It had to be the pizza. Either that, or she was back to where she'd been after she'd first moved in here, scared of each creak of the floorboards, shocked into wakefulness whenever the light from a passing car hit the curtained window.

Her apartment was on the first floor. That had been enough to make her think twice about signing the lease. While the realtor talked about high ceilings and affordable rent, Dawn stared at the windows and their low-to-the-ground sills.

"Great cross-ventilation from those windows," the realtor finally said, and she knew he'd picked up on the way she kept looking at them.

Great access to the street, Dawn had thought, but she'd kept the words to herself and pretended she was concerned about noise because the apartment was on the ground level.

"Oh," the realtor said, waving his hand as if to erase any concerns she might have, "that's not a problem. This street's a dead end. No through traffic."

She'd nodded, as if her real concern wasn't that an intruder could break a window and climb into the apartment before anyone noticed. Something must have shown in her expression, though, because the realtor assured her that if she was worried about security, it wasn't necessary.

"Safest street in Las Vegas," he'd said, with a little smile. "Hasn't been a burglary in this area in five years."

Lying awake now, while 6:59 became seven and seven became 7:01, Dawn remembered how close she'd been to telling him it wasn't burglars she was worried about. She was only worried about Harman, and looking up to see him coming through a window, his eyes black with hate, a little smile on his lips in anticipation of what he was going to do to her, but there was no point in dwelling on such things. The apartment was perfect. It was an easy drive to work. The neighborhood was quiet and safe. The rent was as reasonable as she could find.

Right now, anyway, life was good. Harman was always there, but buried in her mind. Thoughts of him were sort of like the red-and-white hair ribbon she'd stolen from Ellen-Sue Bannister's desk in third grade. Dawn took the ribbon because it was pretty and she'd wanted something pretty with all her heart, but once the ribbon was hers, she hadn't wanted it anymore. Just looking at it made her feel sick, but she was stuck with it. She couldn't give it back; she couldn't make it disappear. So she'd wrapped the ribbon in a piece of old wrapping paper and buried it in the bottom of a drawer.

There had been entire days, weeks, even, when she'd been able to forget its existence.

It was like that with Harman. Wrapped up, safely tucked away, she could almost forget what life with him had been like. She could even forget how his rage at her leaving must fill his life, but she couldn't forget it all the time. Every now and then, something would remind her. A man speaking sharply to a woman; a woman with a cowed look in her eyes. Then it would all come rushing back and she'd remember that Harman was still out there, still thinking about her, still relishing what he'd do when he found her.

Dawn sat up in bed. She thrust her hands into her hair, shoving it back from her face.

These were not things you wanted dancing through your head first thing in the morning. She pulled on her robe—she slept in a T-shirt and panties but she didn't like walking around the apartment that way because it made her feel exposed—and went into the kitchen. She plugged in the coffee she'd set up last night and ran a glass of cool water from the faucet.

The only reason she kept thinking about Harman was because that man had helped her with her car yesterday.

She took a sip of water, then rolled the cold glass against her forehead.

It was an unlikely juxtaposition, to go from thinking about her cruel husband to a generous stranger, but she could see an awful kind of logic to it. She hadn't stood that close to a man since she'd left Harman, hadn't felt so vulnerable or so crowded by one, although—although, just for a moment, looking at his handsome face and his appreciative smile, she'd felt a stirring within herself that she hardly recognized.

Then he'd asked her all those questions about where she was from and she'd wondered why he wanted to know, if someone had sent him, even as she'd told herself how crazy that was. A man with all that polish and charm wouldn't be, couldn't be, involved in any way with her husband.

Dawn put down the glass and walked slowly through the little apartment, the worn linoleum early-morning cool against her bare feet.

Back to square one, and wasn't that pointless? She couldn't

go through life letting everything, even a fleeting attraction to a man, drag her thoughts in the same direction. The therapists she'd dealt with in Phoenix would probably say it was a healthy sign that she'd found a man interesting, although the women with whom she'd had whispered conversations in the safe darkness of the dormitory had all warned her to be careful if she ever felt turned on by a man again or she might find herself back in a relationship with the same kind of lying, deceiving, cruel bastard as the one who had sent her fleeing into the night.

"Women like us," said the world-weary black woman who had helped her gain a new identity, "are always going to end up with the wrong men. Forget all that therapy crap. I've been back and forth to this shelter enough times to know. There's no way out. If you're foolish enough to hook up with some guy, you'll end up regretting it."

Dawn wasn't going to test the premise. She'd had enough of one man to make her more than content to stay away from all of them. There would never be room or need in her life for an intimate relationship. That was what the therapists called the man-woman thing, as if by giving it a fancy name they could change it from what it actually was to what they claimed it could be.

No sir, she thought as she gulped down a cup of coffee and a slice of fattening, delicious, cold, bad-for-you pizza. No relationships. If her car broke down again and a man with Mel Gibson's looks, St. Francis's disposition and Bill Gates's bank balance dropped to one knee right in front of her and begged her to let him replace her old wreck with a convertible before he married her, she'd just smile and say no, sorry, but I'm happy just the way I am. No man, no worries, no trouble.

And no job, if she didn't get a move on.

Dawn dressed quickly, put on her makeup and pulled her hair into a low ponytail. Cassie could weave all the romance she liked into a simple encounter. She knew better.

Her car started up right away, which was definitely a good omen. Traffic was light, and she scored a Perfect 10 for the drive when she didn't hit one red light all the way to work.

Dawn put her purse in her locker, checked the calendar above the desk and went looking for Betsy. She found her in the lobby alcove, frowning at a sheet of paper in her hand.

"Hi. How's it going?"

"Slow, so far. I made a list of things you'll have to do. Like, a one o'clock limo for the guy in the Ella Fitzgerald suite."

"The banker?"

"Uh-huh." Becky thumbed through her notes. "And that couple from Brisbane's coming in later this morning." She looked up. "The Allisons. I told you about them, didn't I? He calls himself a sheep farmer. Well, he is, but he's got a farm—sorry," Becky said, raising her eyebrows, "a *station* the size of Rhode Island."

Dawn nodded. "Okay. I remember. He plays poker. His wife shops."

Becky grinned. "Succinctly put. What the lady shops for are gemstones. Rubies, sapphires, emeralds—the bigger, the better, and she likes to do her shopping comfortably, so I've alerted Roger."

"Roger. The Rock Hound's manager?"

"Uh-huh. He'll be ready to take some things upstairs whenever she phones. I figure on putting them in The Blue Note. You agree?"

Dawn lifted her eyebrows. "La-di-da."

"You better believe it. You'll like them. He's a little loud, she pretty much wears every sparkler she owns, but they're nice people."

"Anything else?"

"He likes Foster's. Make sure the fridge stays stocked with it, and with Somerset Rambler. It's cheese," Becky said, by way of explanation, "imported from England. Made from ewe's milk."

"Baaa. I should have known."

The women grinned at each other. "Okay." Becky tapped a finger against her lips. "Other than that... Oh, yeah. The woman from that balloon place stopped by." She dug into a pile of papers and dredged out a brochure. "She dropped this off."

"What is it?"

"Info about something they're calling their 'Breakfast for Lovers' package... Yeah, here it is. 'See the desert with your beloved from a gondola high in the sky,' blah, blah, blah. 'Greet the day with champagne and caviar in a balloon operated by one of our very discreet pilots...' Dawn? Are you with me?"

Dawn wasn't. Her attention was focused on a dark-haired man who had just emerged from the bank of elevators. Her heartbeat quickened. Was it the man who had helped her yesterday? He hadn't struck her as the type who would check into a Vegas hotel. Well, that was stupid, of course. This was Vegas; he was from New York. He'd told her that. A person wouldn't come all the way from New York and not check into a hotel, but he didn't look as if he'd come to gamble. There were always conventions in town. There was one taking place right now, something to do with computer software—but he was a lawyer. As far as she knew, there weren't any legal conventions or conferences or—

"Dawn?"

Dawn looked at Becky. "Yes," she said briskly, "I've got it all. Brisbane. Sheep stations. Jewels, Aussie beer and ewe's milk cheese. Possible hanky-panky in the balloon gondolas. Right?"

"Right." Becky smothered a yawn. "I'm off, then. I promised my mom I'd stop by on my way home. She's back on that should she or shouldn't she get a perm thing. Whatever I say will be a mistake anyway, but I have to—"

Dawn's gaze drifted to the man. It was hard to make out details at this distance. Besides the dark hair, all she could really tell was that he was tall. That he had a long-legged, self-confident stride... Her pulse rocketed. Yes. Oh yes, it was definitely—

"...whatever she wanted to do in the first place. Dawn?"

She didn't want to see him again. She didn't want to deal

with him, feel that breathless rush of fear or anything else unnamed and unwanted...

"Dawn?"

"Yes?" She looked at Becky. "Oh. The perm. Uh, I like your hair the way it is, Beck. I don't think you actually need—"

"Dawn," Becky said gently, "are you okay?"

"I'm fine. I'm just—just thinking about the day's schedule."

She could see that Becky wasn't buying the story and now—now the man was looking toward her, a little frown puckering his forehead, and she could almost hear him thinking the equivalent of what she'd been wondering a moment ago.

Is that the woman?

"Good morning, ladies."

Dawn dragged her gaze from the man and looked at her boss.

Keir smiled. "I had a call from Prince Ahmat. He says you are both jewels beyond price and if this were not America he would marry you both."

"Did he mention anything about a bonus spin through the jewelry shop?" Becky said, her eyes wide and innocent. "'Cause I might just consider it if the price was right."

Keir chuckled. "He also asked if you'd send up more beluga."

"Heck. I should have known he had an ulterior motive." Becky smiled. "That's Dawn's department. I'm off. See you guys tomorrow."

"Take care, Beck." Keir smiled at Dawn. "How's it going?"

Dawn glanced across the lobby. The man was gone. "Fine," she said. He really was gone. Maybe he wasn't the man who had helped her yesterday. There were probably ten thousand tall men with dark hair in town at any given moment. Maybe he hadn't even been looking at her. Why would he? She was nothing special to look at. "Nobody's complained," she said with a quick smile. "Not yet, anyway."

"A sure sign of success. How's the car?"

She lifted her eyebrows and tapped on the desk's shiny wood surface. "Like new. Keir, I can't thank you enough for—"

"Forget it. Hey, I was protecting the Song's interests. We spent time and money training you. The last thing we want is to have you unable to get to work because you don't have transportation."

"Well, thank you anyway. Really. I don't know what I'd have done without your—"

Her voice trailed away. Keir frowned and glanced over his shoulder. "Something going on behind me I should know about?"

"No. Nothing. Sorry. I just…" The man was there again, closer than before. And yes. It was him. There was no pretending. "I just… That man."

"What man?" Keir swung around. "The guy in the tux?" He grinned. "I guess he had a late night."

"Not him. The other one. See? The one standing near the photo shop?" She took a deep breath. "He looks like the man who helped me yesterday."

"Yeah?"

"Yeah. I mean, it *is* him. I didn't think he was checking in here. I mean, I suppose it's possible. I mean…"

Keir lifted an eyebrow. He'd never seen the unflappable Miss Carter flapped, or whatever you called it when a woman looked the way this one looked.

"What's his name?"

"Why?" She flushed and looked at Keir. "I mean, what does it matter?"

"Well," Keir said pleasantly, "I'm going to walk over and thank him for his good deed. I figured it might be a nice idea to greet him by name."

"I don't know his name." Dawn saw the surprised look on Keir's face. She picked up the papers Becky had left and unwittingly clutched them like a shield. "I didn't ask. And anyway, you don't have to thank him. I wouldn't want to—to embarrass him or any—"

Her protests were useless. Keir was already walking toward the stranger. She watched helplessly as the men exchanged a few words, then a handshake. Keir gestured toward her and she forced a smile to her lips. She felt awkward and on display. Every survival instinct she'd cultivated during the past four years was shrieking the same message.

Run. Run!

But she couldn't run. She wouldn't. There was nothing to run from, except her own imagination. She held her ground with a polite smile.

The man said something. So did Keir. Then he put his hand lightly on the stranger's shoulder and they began walking toward her.

CHAPTER EIGHT

GRAY stared across the lobby. There were lots of tall, slender redheads in the world. Vegas had to be loaded with them. But this wasn't just any redhead. Even at this distance, he recognized her.

This was the woman he'd helped yesterday.

He could tell by the way she held herself, by the tilt of her head as she looked up at the man who was talking with her. Her conversation seemed animated. She was smiling and Gray remembered how difficult it had been to coax those first smiles from her and how foolishly pleased he'd felt when he finally had.

Why should he be so surprised to see her? She'd gone into the hotel through the employees' entrance; he'd figured that she worked here. It was just that he hadn't expected to stumble across her so easily. The Desert Song was the size of a small town; after last night, he'd assumed he'd have to search for her the same way he was going to have to search for Dawn. Instead he'd stepped out of the elevator and there was the mystery woman, standing next to a desk and smiling, though not at him.

Definitely, not at him.

He knew the exact instant when she saw him because her smile disappeared and she stiffened. The guy with her said something. She didn't respond. She kept her eyes locked on Gray instead. The guy spoke again. She answered, and now the man turned and gave Gray a long, assessing look. Then he said something to Red. She shook her head and took a step back.

Gray's smile faded. What was going on? She acted as if he really might be the serial killer they had joked about. The hell with her. And the hell with being Mr. Nice Guy. Dammit, he was going to tell her that. If she was that distrustful, she shouldn't have gotten into his car in the first place.

He started toward her, his step purposeful, just as the man with her started toward him. Gray felt a quick pump of adrenaline. Had she sent a watchdog to chase him off? But the guy began to smile; the closer he got, the more he smiled, and he had his hand out even before they were close enough for Gray to decide whether he wanted to accept the handshake.

"Hello."

"Yeah," Gray said, his eyes still on the woman. He had the feeling she was ready to cut and run.

"I'm Keir O'Connell."

"Yeah," Gray said again…and then the name registered. He tore his gaze from Red and focused it on O'Connell. He was a big man, about Gray's own height, with a pleasant smile and watchful eyes, the kind you saw on some prosecutors and lots of defense attorneys—and on their more intelligent clients.

"I manage the Desert Song."

Gray took the hand O'Connell offered. The woman could wait. He was in Las Vegas to find Dawn Carter and this man was her boss or maybe her lover. He was Gray's best lead so far.

"Nice to meet you." The Desert Song's manager had a firm grip. No way did he spend all his time pushing papers. "My name's Baron. Graham Baron."

O'Connell's smile broadened. "The pleasure's all mine, Mr. Baron. I've been hoping to meet you."

"I'll bet you say that to all your guests," Gray said, and returned the smile.

"Only to the ones who perform good deeds."

O'Connell tucked his hand into the pocket of his trousers. He wore a navy-blue suit, well-cut and tailored in much the same conservative style as the discreetly expensive ones Gray usually wore in the courtroom. He realized he'd expected shiny Italian silk and flashy gold jewelry. A pinky ring, at least. So much for his stereotype about Las Vegas businessmen—or at least about Keir O'Connell, who looked as if he'd be equally at home here or in a New York City boardroom.

"It was very decent of you to help one of my employees," O'Connell said. He jerked his chin toward the alcove where the redhead stood, frozen, staring at them both.

"Oh." Gray shrugged his shoulders. "It wasn't much." *Not enough for the lady to have told me her name.* "Actually," he said, with a little man-to-man smile, the kind he figured would make it simpler to ease into a deeper conversation that would lead him to Dawn, "it's my conscience that deserves thanks."

O'Connell raised one coal-black eyebrow. "Your conscience?"

"Well, the lady's car broke down just past a rise in the road. I was barreling along when all of a sudden she was right ahead of me. I stopped on the proverbial dime. I'm afraid I said some pretty rough things in what I guess you'd call the heat of the moment. Once I calmed down, I figured I owed her one."

Keir laughed, just as Gray hoped he would. "I'm sure she doesn't blame you for that, Mr. Baron. She told me that nobody else stopped to help her."

"I'm sure someone would have, sooner or later," Gray said, with what he hoped was the right amount of modesty.

"Maybe, but you're the man that did. And I appreciate it. It may sound corny, but we like to think of ourselves as family at the Desert Song. Have you had your breakfast? I'd be happy to walk you over to the Reveille Café and buy you—"

"I've already eaten, thanks."

"Well, then, it would be my pleasure to arrange for you to have dinner at La Chanson."

"That's very nice of you, Mr. O'Connell, but—"

"Please. Call me Keir."

"Keir." Gray hesitated. He and O'Connell were grinning at each other like old pals. Now was the time to ask about Dawn. On the other hand, maybe not. Maybe he was better off waiting until the conversation went on a little longer. And maybe, what the hell, he could solve one problem before he moved on to the next. "Keir, actually, if you want to thank me—"

"Absolutely."

"Well, what I'd really appreciate is an introduction to the lady we've been talking about." O'Connell raised his eyebrows again. Gray gave him a big smile. Any more smiling, they were going to be carted off to the nearest funny farm. "We never got around to introducing ourselves. She was so worried about being late for work…"

"Ah. That sounds like her. Well, in that case…" Keir put his hand lightly on Gray's shoulder and the men began walking toward the desk. "I'll be happy to oblige, Mr. Baron."

"Gray."

"Gray. It'll be my pleasure."

No, Gray thought, as they drew near the redhead, it would be his. At least Red didn't look as if she'd seen a ghost anymore. Her color had gone from white to pink. Was she embarrassed to face him because of the way she'd given him the slip? Actually she didn't look embarrassed so much as she looked trapped. What was her problem? Better still, what was his? Why would he want to pursue a woman who acted as if he carried the plague?

But he wasn't pursuing her. He just liked things wrapped up, that was all. He'd already wasted more time thinking about the lady than she deserved. A handshake, an exchange of names, and that would be the last she would see of him.

By the time they reached the desk, she'd started fussing with some papers, thumbing through them, studying them, doing anything to avoid making eye contact, but that wasn't going to stop him.

"Good morning," Gray said. "Remember me?"

She looked up, clutching the papers to her like a shield or maybe a lifeline.

"Yes." She smiled, if you could call that twitch of her mouth a smile. "Of course I do."

"You certainly left in a rush yesterday."

Her color deepened. "I know. I mean, I apologize. It's just that…" She looked at O'Connell, hoping for assistance, but Gray had to give the guy credit. He was strictly an observer, watching the little tableau play out with his arms folded and an indecipherable expression on his face. "I, um, I was so late for work…"

"Don't tell me your boss docked your pay," Gray said, flashing a thousand-watt smile to make it clear that he was only joking. O'Connell got the joke and smiled, too, but not Red. She darted another glance at the boss, then shook her head.

"No. Of course not. Keir—Mr. O'Connell was very nice about—"

Hell, Gray thought, and took pity on her. "I'm sure he was," he said, and stuck out his hand. "I think it's time we introduced ourselves. I'm Gray Baron. And you are…?"

She looked from his face to his hand. He had to stop himself from actually checking his fingers for spots of soot but, finally, she made the decision.

"Hello." She put down the papers and clasped his outstretched hand. Her fingers were cool; he thought maybe they even trembled a little…and then, suddenly he was the one who needed a lifeline because now that she didn't have the papers clasped against her, he saw the name tag pinned to her lapel. It was enameled, he thought crazily, as if that mattered, in blue and gold.

"I'm Dawn," she said, when he raised shocked eyes to hers. "Dawn Carter."

Mary Elizabeth O'Connell watched her son pace from the Carrera marble fireplace to the window of her living room with its view of the city and distant mountains and back again. He'd been pacing ever since he'd entered her penthouse suite a few minutes ago.

"Mother," he'd said, and kissed her cheek, "I thought I'd drop by to say hello."

Mary didn't buy that for a minute. Keir never visited her this early in the day. Her eldest son was a man who enjoyed the stability of routine. He always spent the first hours of the working day strolling through the hotel and the casino, greeting guests and staff and making sure that all was running smoothly. That had been his pattern ever since his father's

death six years ago, when Keir came west to help her with the
Desert Song. He'd only varied it when she'd been ill.

He might be thirty-five but she could still read him like he
was eleven and crazy to be the next star center on the Chicago
Bulls. Keir had something on his mind and she knew it, but
asking straight out had gotten her nowhere. Well, she should
have figured that. He'd never been one to spill his concerns
in anybody's lap.

"Is there a problem?" she'd said, when she'd opened the
door to his familiar knock.

"Must there be a problem for a son to pay his mother a
visit?" he'd replied, and flashed a smile.

Mary pursed her lips. For a man who had no problem, her
eldest son certainly seemed determined to wear a path through
the carpet. He wasn't talkative, either. Except for saying yes,
he'd like some coffee—and she strongly suspected that had
been out of politeness, not desire—Keir hadn't spoken another
word.

Time to take some action, she thought, and cleared her
throat. "Keir?"

"Hmm?"

"You should have told me you disliked Kelim carpets."

That stopped him. "What?"

"You're going to wear a hole in my rug," she said gently.
"Come and sit down." Mary smiled. "Besides, this excellent
pot of coffee is going cold."

"That excellent pot of coffee which is surely decaffeinated,
as your doctor ordered. Right?"

"Right," Mary said blithely, lying through her teeth. The
doctor had ordered her to give up the cream in her coffee.
He'd suggested she also give up the coffee but suggestions
were only that, nothing more. "Will you have a slice of
Jenny's raisin cake?"

Keir sat down in the blue velvet chair opposite hers and
shook his head as he accepted the delicate porcelain cup and
saucer she handed him.

"Thank you, but no. Coffee's all I want."

Keir took a sip of coffee. One taste, and he flashed her a

look through narrowed eyes that said he suspected the brew was the real stuff. She returned his gaze with what she hoped was charming innocence and, after another sip, he sighed and sat back in the chair, all but dwarfing it with his size. Looking at him she wondered, as she so often did, how she and her Ruarch could have produced such a son. Such sons, she thought, correcting herself. They were all so big. Not that her Ruarch hadn't been big, too, and wonderfully brawny until almost the end, when he'd been so thin that it had broken her heart to see him…

"Mother?"

Lord, she missed him. Six years, and still she reached a hand out to touch him in the night. They'd spent more than forty-three years together, she and Ruarch. You didn't meet a man when you were barely seventeen, marry him two months later, bear him six children and not feel as if a piece had been carved out of your heart when you lost him…

"Mother?"

Mary blinked away the past and smiled at her son. 'Yes, love. Have you decided you'd like some cake after all?"

"Don't try to divert me. You had that look on your face again."

"What look?" Mary picked up a knife from the silver serving tray the maid had set on the low table between the two chairs. "Just a little slice, to keep Jenny happy."

"Not even a crumb. It's too early in the day." Keir's voice took on an edge of command. "None for you, either, Mother. You know what the doctor said."

Mary O'Connell clucked her tongue against her teeth. "What does he know? He's hardly out of diapers."

"He has enough diplomas from enough fancy places to paper these walls, and he's seen what your arteries look like."

"Looked like." Mary took a sip of her coffee. "Thanks to this bread and water diet, my arteries probably look magnificent by now. I can see the obituary already." Her voice dropped in pitch. "'Mary Elizabeth O'Connell, once feared for her sharp tongue, ruled the Desert Song Hotel and Casino until she grew old, weak and useless. She leaves behind three sons, three daughters, and an arterial system so beautiful that it won the praise of every high-priced teenaged cardiologist in Nevada, California and points east including Boston and New York…'''

Keir laughed, as she'd hoped he would. "You're not dying. And you're not old, weak or useless."

"I notice you haven't corrected that phrase about me having a sharp tongue."

"I prefer to think of you as having a rapier wit." He smiled, lifted her free hand to his lips and kissed the knuckles. "Are you sure you're feeling well, Duchess?"

"Wonderfully well, if painfully bored. I see Dr. Maudlin next week and when I do, I'm going to tell him it's time I started easing back into work."

"His name is Mandlin," Keir said, his lips curving in a grin.

"Whatever. I'm weary of sitting on my butt. It's time I began putting in an honest eight hours."

"Don't you mean twelve?"

Mary sat back, her hands clasping the carved arms of her chair, and fixed her son with an exasperated look.

"You've been helping me run this place ever since your father died, and doing it all on your own these past months. Can you look me in the eye and tell me it's an eight-hour-a-day job?"

"No," Keir said bluntly. What was the sense of arguing with his mother when she knew the truth as well as he did? "But you can't do it all by yourself. You'll need to delegate authority."

"I did. I delegated it to you."

And you'll need to delegate it to someone else, once you're back on your feet. That was what he longed to tell her, but how could he? She'd told him, dozens of times, that she'd never have been able to keep the Song without him. How could he tell her that he didn't want to spend the rest of his life running this place, especially when he had no idea what it was he *did* want to spend his life doing?

"Keir? Is that why you've been pacing like a caged tiger? Have you come to tell me you're weary of running the Song?"

"No," he said quickly, "of course not." Keir put his hands on his thighs, sighed and rose to his feet. "Something's come up."

"About?"

"About Dawn Carter. The girl I just put into that Special Services slot."

"I know who she is. I suggested her for the job, remember?" Mary stood up, too. "What's the matter? Has something happened to her?"

"No." He shook his head, saw the sudden pallor in his mother's face and cursed sharply as he went to her side and caught her shoulders in his hands. "Sit down, for God's sake."

"The girl—"

"The girl's fine. Jesus, I didn't mean to scare you. I only want to discuss a situation that involves her, that's all."

Mary nodded. She'd liked the girl on sight and what she'd subsequently learned about her had brought out all her protective maternal instincts. If Dawn were her daughter...

"Mother?"

"Yes, I heard you. Well, don't keep me in suspense. Sit down and tell me about it."

Keir folded himself into the chair and sat forward, his hands on his knees. "I want to know what you've kept from me about Dawn."

"Why?" Mary's slender white brows lifted. "Are you interested in her?"

"Yes. No. Not the way you mean." He laughed. "Will you ever stop trying to get me married off?"

"No," Mary said immediately. "How can I, if I'm to have a grandchild? Not a one of you, not Sean or Cullen or Meagan or Fallon or Briana, has seen fit to marry and give me babies, or even give me babies and then marry, if that's the only way I'm to see the O'Connell name carried on."

Keir grinned. "Why, Ma, I'm shocked."

"It would take more than that to shock you and we both

know it.'' Mary smiled and patted her son's hand. ''Now, tell me what this is all about.''

''I just did. I want to know what secrets you're keeping about Dawn Carter.'' His mother opened her mouth and he spoke quickly, before she could get out a word. ''Don't waste your breath lying, Duchess. You've hovered over the girl since she came to work for us. There's no sense denying it.''

''There's nothing to deny. She's bright, she works hard, she wants to make something of herself. Those are all qualities that suit our management style. We've always believed in promoting from the ranks.''

''Yes, yes and yes.'' Keir leaned closer. ''But we both know there's more to it than that. You *do* have a special interest in her. And just now, when I said I wanted to talk about her, you turned white as a sheet.''

''What you said was that something had come up.''

''So? That's hardly cause for panic. Something's always coming up. It's part of the business. Last month, when we found out that eye in the sky was malfunctioning. Or when the girl in the Reveille kitchen decided it might be more interesting to use a knife to cut up her former boyfriend instead of the potatoes...''

''Those things are different.''

''They are, for a fact, and you know the reason? No, don't bother answering. I'll tell it to you. It's because those incidents didn't involve Dawn. She's always on your mind, or so it seems. When I discussed moving someone into the high stakes tables, you suggested her. The same when I mentioned we'd need to add a new Special Services rep. And for every time you've asked me how some employee is working out, you ask that same question about Dawn at least twice.''

''I like the girl, is all. Is that a crime?''

''You know something about her—something important— that you haven't told me.'' Keir's eyes narrowed. ''And since Dawn works for us, yes, that's a crime, Duchess. To hold back on me when I'm in charge is definitely a crime in my book.''

Mary looked deep into her son's eyes. Was he right? She and Ruarch had never looked into the background files of their employees unless the head of security said there was a problem and in those instances, they'd never shared the information with anyone else. That was all she was doing with regard to Dawn...or was it? Keir was in charge now. She still owned the Song but the power was in his hands. Had she kept the information about the girl from him because she'd always done it that way, or because she didn't want to acknowledge how impotent she felt since the heart attack?

Whatever the reason, she knew she'd made a mistake. It needed to be rectified.

"You're right," she said softly. "You're in charge, Keir. I shouldn't hold anything from you."

"You'll always be the one in command," he said gruffly, "but as long as I'm responsible for the Song's day to day operation, I need to know what's going on."

Mary reached for the phone and hit a button. "Dan? Yes, it's me. Would you pull the Carter girl's file and bring it up? All of it, yes. Yes, thank you. Right now."

She looked at Keir, then stood. He leaped up and held out his hand but she smiled and brushed it aside.

"I'm perfectly capable of walking by myself." Her voice was gentle but there was no mistaking the warning tone it carried. Keir nodded and followed his mother through the doors that led onto the wide penthouse balcony and into the heat of midmorning.

"Too hot?" she said, looking up at him.

"Not if your middle name is Satan," he said, and grinned at her.

"Your father always said the same thing. He thought I was crazy, when I'd go out into the sun, but I love the feel of it." She clasped the railing and looked at him again. "When Dan Coyle gets here, you'll read Dawn's file. Then we'll talk."

"Can't you tell me what's in it?"

Mary shook her head. "I'd rather you read it for yourself. I'm a woman. I might put my own emotional interpretation on the details."

His mother was never emotional when it came to business but Keir waited, his curiosity growing by the moment. By the time he looked through the glass doors and saw Jenny bringing Dan Coyle, the head of security, toward them, he'd gone from imagining Dawn as a runaway heiress to imagining her as a reformed murderer. Knowing his mother, either was possible. If Mary thought a person was worth a chance, she'd offer it.

Dan slid the door open. Sixty-something, with a thatch of graying hair and looking as fit as if he were twenty years younger, Coyle was a man who always seemed glad he'd started a new career. Keir and his mother had hired him two days after he'd retired from thirty years with the New York City police department as a captain of detectives, and Keir had never had a moment's regret about the decision. Dan was a good cop with an honest soul and a kind heart. He was also the only man outside the O'Connell family who had ever had the guts to address Mary by her nickname and live to tell the tale, Keir thought wryly.

Dan smiled as he shook Keir's hand. "Keir. Duchess. I see you're both trying for heat stroke."

"I'd rather be trying out the deep-freeze, but you know my mother."

Both men chuckled. Mary clucked her tongue. "The sun's good for you," she said. "For me, anyway. It warms old bones."

"So I've been told," Dan said lightly, "but I don't see any old bones around here."

"Flattery will get you nowhere, Mr. Coyle."

"It's not flattery, it's the absolute truth."

Keir looked from his mother to Coyle. Dan was still smiling politely; Mary was looking her usual imperious self. No, he thought, as an impossible thought flashed through his head, no, never.

"So," Dan said crisply, "you wanted the Carter file." He glanced at Keir, then back to Mary. "The whole thing, right?"

"Yes. The whole thing. Give it to Keir, please."

"Is there some kind of problem with the girl?"

"Just give him the file, Mr. Coyle."

"Oh. Sure. Here you go, Keir." Dan cleared his throat. "*Is* there a problem with the girl?"

"I don't know yet." Keir slid open the balcony door. "Not until after I see what's in here. And if you don't mind, Mother, I'd rather not broil while I take a look."

Dan and Mary followed him inside. Keir went automatically to the one incongruously out of place piece of furniture in the elegant room, the big, overstuffed armchair that had been his father's. His mother had refurnished the place after Ruarch O'Connell's death. She hadn't asked Keir's approval but if she had, he'd have given it. He knew it was the only way she could put the loss behind her and begin to move on, but she'd never brought herself to dispose of the chair. Too many memories, she said, and Keir agreed. He'd spent a good part of his life watching his old man sit in that chair, his feet on the beaten-up hassock before it, reviewing the day's events or thinking through a problem.

Keir opened the file.

The first page was the usual stuff. A photo of Dawn, looking solemn and maybe even nervous, but most people did when taking driver's license and ID photos. Her personal data followed. Name, date of birth, place of birth, social security number. Married? No. Children? None. Educational history? High school diploma. Work history. A list of jobs, dating back eight years. Had she ever been arrested? No. Had she ever been hospitalized for a mental illness? No.

He looked up. "This is all standard stuff. What am I supposed to be looking for?"

Dan and Mary looked at each other, then at him. A muscle jerked in Dan's jaw. "You'll know when you see it."

Keir turned a page. This was the in-depth report, the one Dan always ran once the decision had been made to hire anyone who would have access to cash. Keir glanced at the first few lines, frowned, flipped back to the prior page...

"Hey," he said, "what is this?" He looked up. His mother and Coyle were watching him with interest. "This says her name isn't Carter. It's Kitteridge." He turned the pages again. "It says she wasn't born in Phoenix, that her D.O.B. isn't the one she gave..." He stood up. "What the hell is this, Coyle?

When'd you discover the girl lied, and why is she still an employee here?''

"Take it easy, Keir."

"Take it easy?" Keir slapped the file on the table. "The girl lied to get a job. A job in a licensed casino, for Christ's sake. You're supposed to keep that kind of thing from happening, and you tell me to take it—"

"I told Dan to bury this."

He swung around and stared at his mother. She stared right back, head up, arms folded, her very posture making it clear she wasn't about to back down from the confrontation. Keir reminded himself that this was his mother, that it was her heart that had suffered damage, not her brain, and that losing his temper wasn't going to get him any answers. He took a deep breath, jammed his hands into his pockets and nodded.

"I see."

"No, you don't."

"Yeah, I do. For reasons known only to you, you made a unilateral decision, an arbitrary decision, to hire a woman whose entire application is a lie, to put the Song into a vulnerable legal position—"

"Why don't you read all of it before you come to a conclusion?"

"If you really believe that pawing through glowing reports of how well she's done here, or how much she's liked, is going to change my mind—"

"For God's sake, stop being so self-righteous! Read Dan's handwritten notes at the very end."

Jesus, he was having a tough time holding his temper. If he'd been alone with Coyle, he'd have let it blow sky-high. The ex-cop knew better than to let shit like this happen. Nobody ran a casino in Vegas in a vacuum. There were rules to follow, Gaming Commission rules, if you expected to hold on to your license. His mother damn well knew better, too. What was the matter with the two of them?

"Read it," she said, and something in her voice made him pick up the file, open to the back of it and do as she'd asked.

Long minutes later, he lifted his head and stared at Mary.

"Christ," he said, his voice low and thick and filled with the kind of controlled masculine rage Dan Coyle recognized in a heartbeat.

"Yeah," Dan said. "That was pretty much my reaction, too."

Keir looked at Coyle. "Where'd you get all this stuff?" He almost tore the page, turning it so he could read the reverse side. "A broken collarbone. Two broken ribs. A concussion…"

"From a little shopping mall clinic in the town she came from, and no, she never reported any of it to the police, just said it was an accident every time. And no again," Dan said, reading the next question in Keir's eyes, "you don't want to know how I came by any of it, not her real name or the medical stuff or anything else. Just take my word for it, Keir. It's all true."

"She's not from Phoenix?"

"Not unless you count the time she spent there in a women's shelter."

"She was married to this—this piece of—"

"She still is."

"And…" Keir looked at the paper in his hands again. "And she has a kid?"

"Yes. A little boy. He's in a school somewhere outside Vegas."

"Somewhere outside Vegas covers a lot of territory."

"I know. I've deliberately avoided zeroing in on the kid." Coyle nodded at Mary. "Your mother and I decided that might spook Dawn, if she got word somebody'd come poking around to get a look at him. Your mother was afraid she'd pick up and run."

"She would," Mary said with conviction. "Any woman would. And then she probably wouldn't be lucky enough to land in a place where people would try to protect her."

"You don't *know* it, Mother. Not for a fact."

"For as good as a fact," his mother said coldly.

"How? I mean, Jesus, you know hotels. Casinos. You don't know—"

"Your father and I had a neighbor years back, in Boston. Lived right next door to us, a sweet little thing with two babies. She was shy. Quiet. Kept to herself, though I've often thought how differently things might have turned out if I'd taken the time to try to get to know her..." Mary took a breath. "One night—one perfectly normal summer evening— a man came to her door. When she opened it, he shot her dead. Then he shot her babies. It turned out he was her husband, that she'd fled after years of abuse but she made the mistake of not changing her identity."

Oh, hell. Keir put his hand on his mother's arm. "Mother," he said softly, "Ma—"

"This girl, Dawn, had the presence of mind to change hers. I had a feeling about her, that she was a good person, a decent young woman, and I told Mr. Coyle to seal this report. I haven't regretted it for a moment."

"Yeah, but..." Keir ran a hand through his hair. But what? Legally his mother had done the wrong thing. Morally she'd done the right thing. And what the hell had *he* done? A strange man was in the hotel, someone who called himself Gray Baron, someone who had conveniently turned up just when Dawn needed help.

Something had flashed across Baron's face when Keir introduced him to Dawn. Shock, maybe. Surprise. That's what Keir had thought but maybe it wasn't that at all. Maybe it had been satisfaction at finally finding her...

"Keir?"

He looked up. Mary was staring at him.

"What's wrong? What's this problem with Dawn you wanted to discuss? Does it have anything to do with what you just read?"

Did it? He didn't think so. What had happened, really? Nothing, when you came down to it. A man had stopped to help Dawn when nobody else had. He'd registered at the hotel where she worked. He'd spotted her and asked to meet her. Dawn hadn't wanted to meet him; she'd gone from white to pink when Keir had insisted on making the introduction. Normal stuff, all of it. The guy was a Good Sam; Dawn was a shy woman.

Keir put down the file, jammed his hands into his pockets, rocked back on his heels and stared at the skyline visible through the balcony doors. But there had been that one quick moment when he'd seen something in Gray Baron's eyes. A flash of—of what? Confusion? Distaste?

"Keir?"

Keir looked at his mother. "You haven't answered me," she said softly. "What's the problem that concerns Dawn?" She hesitated. "You don't think... Do you have reason to believe her husband's looking for her?"

A thousand questions but no answers. Keir told himself to calm down. The report hadn't contained much information about Dawn's husband except that he'd been arrested in the past, that he got pleasure out of beating his wife, and that he lived on an Arizona mountaintop. Could such a man, *would* such a man, hire someone to find her? Someone like Gray Baron? Looks didn't mean a thing; this business taught you that. But there was no ignoring the designer watch, the expensive clothes, the soft, well-educated voice.

No, he wouldn't be her husband's point man. Besides, the man he'd just read about in that file would surely take pleasure in finding his quarry and dealing with her himself.

"Keir," his mother said urgently, "is Dawn Carter in danger?"

Keir shrugged his shoulders. "I don't know," he said, because, really, it was the only possible answer. "Dan, I want you to check out a man named Gray Baron. Graham Baron. He's registered with us, so it should be easy enough to learn what we need to know."

"Which is?" Dan asked.

A muscle clenched in Keir's jaw. "Which is," he said, "everything from where he was born to what he eats for breakfast. I want to know all there is to know about this guy, and I want to know it pronto."

CHAPTER NINE

GRAY knew he'd blown it.

Ten minutes of smiling and doing his boyish best to convince Dawn that that he was Mr. Terrific got him no place.

He shoved his hands into his pockets as he walked through the gardens along a pebbled path that curved like the blade of a scimitar around the Desert Song's enormous pool.

He'd wasted half a night searching the casino for a woman who wasn't there...and the other half thinking about an elusive stranger with a shy smile who had gotten under his skin in, what, less than two hours? It was crazy, and even crazier now that he knew who that stranger was.

He'd imagined Dawn Carter as a flashy blonde, but she wasn't. Not on the outside, anyway, and what did that prove except that you couldn't judge the package by its cover? He'd known that for years. Every man knew it. It was like a little gift that came with puberty. Your voice changed, you sprouted hair on your face, and you figured out that women were never what they seemed.

But this particular woman was more complex than he'd anticipated. That was going to complicate things. He'd have to ditch plan A and segue into Plan B...and that wouldn't work, either. The Dawn he'd come to see had just made it clear she'd sooner sip hemlock than have a glass of wine in his company, and he sure as hell couldn't see her swallowing a story about her grandfather leaving her a music box in his will.

Now what?

Gray drew a deep breath, then blew it out. It was quiet here. No *ping ping ping* of the slots, no sound of voices like the distant roar of the sea in the background. He was pretty much alone: the gardens were all but deserted at this time of day. A

153

hot breeze carried occasional laughter from the pool. At least someone was having a good time, he thought grimly, and kicked at the small white stones that made up the path.

This whole mess was Jack Ballard's fault. If he'd sent a decent picture of the girl instead of a blurred faxed copy, Gray wouldn't have spent the best part of an afternoon with the woman he'd come to see without knowing it and somehow offending her enough to make her want to freeze him out. Or maybe it was because of Keir O'Connell. If the man was, in fact, her lover, maybe she believed in being loyal to him...and what twist of fate had put O'Connell into the picture at the worst possible moment? Gray figured he must have looked as if he'd been hit in the head with a two-by-four when he read Dawn's name tag. Life in the courtroom had taught him how to fake a fast recovery and that was what he'd done.

"Nice to meet you," he'd said.

"Nice to meet you, too," she'd replied, but the lie had been in the sound of her voice, in the look in her eyes. She didn't think it was nice to meet him; he had the feeling she'd have been about as eager to shake hands with a snake as with him, but he'd made some inane remark about what a small world it was, yadda yadda yadda, and she'd said yes, it was, and all the time O'Connell had gone on standing there, watchful as a mastiff on alert.

Was it because he didn't like the idea of someone hitting on his woman, or had he picked up on something? And what the hell did it matter?

Gray parked himself on a teak bench, tucked his chin on his chest, stretched out his long legs and folded his arms. O'Connell or no O'Connell, he wasn't going to get near Red. She'd made that absolutely clear. He'd gone on talking, saying nothing, really, just waiting for her to pick up her end of the conversation, but she hadn't. Her eyes had been cool and flat and he'd thought about how much he'd wanted to see what they looked like yesterday, about how he'd stared at that blurry photo and wondered if she'd have her grandmother's sad, mysterious look, and then he wondered why in hell it should matter. That was when his brain went dead, his mouth went dry and he shut up.

Red had taken that as her cue to withdraw her hand from his. "Well, it's been nice meeting you, Mr. Baron," she'd said. "I hope you enjoy your stay with us."

Yeah, he'd said, thanks, he was sure he would.

"If there's anything special I can help you with," she'd added, but he knew she was on automatic, that it was part of her job to make that meaningless offer to VIP guests at the Desert Song and now, as a matter of courtesy, to him.

She'd smiled again and then she'd turned to O'Connell and murmured that she needed five minutes of his time. O'Connell had stuck out his hand and said it had been nice meeting him and he hoped he'd see him around…

Gray's mouth twisted.

What crap. Bull patties, Jonas would say. Two brush-offs in twenty-four hours, and there wasn't a damn thing he could do about it. He had to talk with Dawn, size her up without her knowing she was being sized up, although he still couldn't imagine what he'd gain. Nothing he'd seen here changed his original estimation of her.

A high-pitched buzz sounded just beside him. Gray turned his head and saw a hummingbird, a brightly jeweled blaze of crimson, hovering over a crimson flower. His mind flashed to a client he'd had years before, a woman who had been into what she'd called birding and never mind that she'd also been into eliminating her rich as Croesus, old as Methuselah husband. He remembered walking through Bryant Park with her on a hot summer afternoon while she explained that she'd shot her husband five times in the chest and once in the face in broad daylight at a distance of no more than five feet because she'd thought he was an intruder, and while he'd been trying to digest that, she'd suddenly made a little sound of delight and pointed at a bank of flowers and the tiny bird working the blossoms.

"A hummingbird," she'd said. She'd told him the exact kind, too, but Gray couldn't recall it. All he remembered was that she'd said the fragile creature had flown a couple of thousand miles to reach its destination and then she'd gone back to calm recitation of the facts, including a description of how she'd had to toss out her favorite silk dress because her husband's blood ended up all over it.

Gray had figured the hummingbird was lucky, not because a greedy woman with a .32 wasn't interested in blasting it to smithereens but because it had the ability to get out of the way and keep on going. He felt that way again now. What he wanted was to drive straight to the airport and hop a plane that would take him home, but he couldn't. He owed his uncle, big time. Defending a woman who had deliberately offed an old man was tough. Compared to that, finding a way to sit down and have a conversation with a woman you didn't like and who didn't like you was nothing.

That was what he'd come to Vegas to do, wasn't it? Talk with Dawn? He wasn't here because, okay, she had the same look in her eyes that he thought he'd seen in her grandmother's, or to ask her why she'd married a man like Kitteridge and then walked away from her own kid...

"Shit," he said, and he got to his feet, strode back inside the hotel, brushed past a noisy gaggle of women wearing T-shirts that read Slaves To The Slots and made his way to the little alcove and its fancy desk. A small, framed placard stood angled on the polished fruitwood surface. Discreet gold script urged Special Guests needing assistance to pick up the white telephone and press seven seven seven.

Gray wasn't so sure about the "special guests" part, but he definitely needed assistance.

A woman answered on the first ring. He knew who it was even before she identified herself. He'd have known that voice in his sleep.

"Dawn speaking," she said pleasantly. "How may I help you?"

Gray cleared his throat. "I need some assistance out here."

He hung up before she could say anything, counting on her either not recognizing his voice or recognizing it and knowing she had no choice but to deal with him since he was a guest. A minute passed. Then a door in the alcove wall opened and she came toward him. One look at her face and he knew she'd identified him right away.

"Mr. Baron," she said politely, "how may I help you?"

"Miss Carter," he replied, just as politely. She was a concierge? He'd dealt with hotel concierges for years. Okay. Let her do her job. "I was wondering...what's the hottest show in town?"

She looked relieved. He knew she hadn't been expecting such a simple question.

"Well," she said, after a few seconds, "there are a couple of them. It all depends on your own preferences." She hesitated. He didn't say anything. "For instance, there's the national road show of—"

"Have you seen it?"

"No. No, I haven't, but I've heard that it's wonderful. On the other hand, if you'd like to see something you can only see in Las Vegas—"

"Let's put it this way." He dredged up a smile he hoped would identify him as one of the good guys. "If you were going to get tickets to see something, what would you pick?"

"I'm afraid I can't tell you." She smiled and he felt his gut knot at the kind of smile it was, dismissive and phony, a smile you flashed when you didn't want to insult the guy at the door who was trying to sell you ten magazine subscriptions for the price of one. He thought about yesterday, how good it had felt to coax an honest curve from that soft-looking mouth, and wondered what it would take to make that happen again. "I really don't have much time for that sort of thing, Mr. Baron."

"Gray," he said. "Surely the man who rescued Spaceman Teddy from certain death in the desert is a man you can address by his first name."

That put feathers of pink into her cheeks. Good. Let her be embarrassed. All this formality pissed him off. He'd been feeling pissed off a lot, thanks to her.

"Gray," she said, as if the word were a bone caught in her

throat. She reached for the phone. "I'll be happy to arrange for tickets, if you'll just tell me what you'd like to see."

"You pick it."

"I can't do that. I don't know your tastes."

He wanted to tell her that she did, that *she* was to his taste, all that hair he longed to unpin, that soft-looking mouth, but what the hell did that have to do with his business here?

"Of course you can," he said pleasantly. "I'm a tourist. You live in this town. You must have an idea what's good and what…" He stopped, took a breath. "Are you involved with O'Connell?"

The pink in her cheeks turned crimson; she stared at him as if he'd just committed a social faux pas of hideous proportions and maybe he had, but he had to do whatever it took to get past that shield, didn't he? Wasn't that why he was trying to get her to go out with him?

"I beg your pardon?"

"I asked you if you're involved with—"

"That's none of your business!"

"Is that a 'yes'?"

"No! It is not a…" That delicate chin angled upward just like her grandmother's. He knew she was trying to control her temper. Good. At least he was getting some reaction from her other than dismissal. "Do you want me to see about those tickets or don't you?"

"That's why I asked the question, Miss Carter. If you're involved with O'Connell, the answer is 'no.' If you're not— if you're not, I have another question."

"Which is?"

"What night are you free?"

"I'm not," she said, biting off the syllables with staccato precision.

"You're never free?" He shook his head in pretended disbelief. "That's one hell of a work schedule."

"Mr. Baron—"

"Gray."

"Mr. Baron," she said coldly, "I am extremely grateful for your generous assistance yesterday, but—"

"But, you wish I'd disappear."

Color rose in her cheeks again, straining the polite mask she maintained. Being polite was part of her job and he was making it hard for her to do it.

"No. Certainly not. Again, what you did yesterday was—"

"I know. I was a real Boy Scout. Now, I'm Jack the Ripper."

No smile, not even a false one. "I don't date guests."

"House rule?"

"My rule," she said firmly. "Is that all, Mr. Baron?"

"No, it isn't." Gray leaned forward and examined the white placard. "Special Services Desk," he said, slowly and distinctly. "Special Services for Special Guests. If You Need Our Assistance, Please Dial—"

"Seven seven seven," Dawn snapped. God, the man was impossible, standing there with his hands on the desk, a smug look on his face and a tone in his voice that made her want to tell him what she really thought of him. Didn't he get the message? "I know what it says. And I assure you, the Desert Song prides itself on courtesy to all its guests, Mr. Baron— Gray," she said quickly, correcting herself before he could, " but—"

"But I have halitosis. Dandruff. A social affliction you can see even though nobody else can?" He smiled, pleased with how light he was keeping it, telling himself the knot in his gut had everything to do with wanting to get under that cool, brittle exterior only so he could do his job and go home.

"But," Dawn said frigidly, "this desk serves as an adjunct to the Special Services office. It is not a dating service. And if you want tickets for a show, the concierge at Reception will be happy to help you."

"I'm happy being helped right here."

"I just explained that this is the Special Services office."

"I don't follow you."

"Obviously not." Dawn took a deep breath, let it out while

she reminded herself that part of her job was knowing how to deal with pests. "It's a VIP office."

"A VIP…" Gray's eyebrows rose. "Well, that's fine. What do I need? A platinum credit card? An airline mileage account? Do I have to check myself out of my room and onto another floor?"

"*You* don't have to do anything. The hotel makes the determination as to which guests are deserving of VIP treatment. Those are the guests with whom I work."

It took Gray less than a second to figure out what she was telling him. This was Vegas. Any other place, VIPs would be guests who were willing to pay for a room on a special floor where you got a little pampering for the extra bucks. Here, a VIP would be somebody willing to dump a small fortune at the tables. Things were different at the Song—and different for this woman, who dealt with wealthy men.

"Ah," he said softly, "I get it." His eyes met hers. "You offer your services to the highest bidders."

Her face whitened. He almost said he was sorry, that he hadn't meant that to sound the way it had…but maybe it was the truth. Harman said his wife catted around. Gray had envisioned a bored woman sleeping her way through a town filled with shifty-eyed Harman-clones. Now that he'd seen Dawn, he knew she was beautiful enough to pick and choose the men she slept with, and he'd have bet his last dollar that not a one of them would resemble her red-neck husband.

Something flashed in her eyes. Anger? Rage? Pain. Jesus, it was pain.

"You—you have no right," she said in a shaky whisper. "I've never—I would never…" She took a breath so deep he saw her breasts rise and fall; her eyes cleared and the mask fell over her face again. "Goodbye, Mr. Baron. I don't think we have anything more to say to each—"

"Wait!" He reached out, clasped her elbow. That was all he needed, that she'd bolt because he'd said something incredibly stupid. She stiffened under the pressure of his hand

and he let go. "Dawn," he said, and cleared his throat. "Miss Carter. I didn't mean that the way it sounded. "

"Didn't you?"

"No. I just meant…I guess it's different here, that the hotel determines if a guest is a VIP based on how much he spends. Am I right?"

"That's part of it."

"Only part?"

She nodded stiffly. "We give VIP treatment to celebrities. People who are famous."

"Well, maybe you shouldn't be so quick to write me off." He cocked his head. "For all you know, I'm a famous celebrity in disguise. Or maybe I dropped ten thousand bucks at blackjack last night."

"You aren't, and you didn't. I'd know, in either case."

"Yeah, but if I were…?"

She sighed and folded her arms. "I'd arrange for some complimentary upgrades, by way of expressing the hotel's gratitude."

"But you wouldn't go out with me."

"No."

Gray smiled. "Well then, it's a good thing I'm just me, Graham Baron, because, in that case, it's okay for you to say yes, you will."

She stared at him as if he'd lost his mind. "Will what?"

"Will have coffee with me. Notice, I said 'coffee.' You offer VIPs upgrades. Well, I'm not a VIP so I'm willing to settle for a downgrade. Forget going to a show. Let me buy you a cup of coffee."

She rolled her eyes, bit her lip the same as she had yesterday and, just like yesterday, his hormones went on full alert. "Honestly, Mr. Baron—"

"Honestly, Miss Carter, I'm only trying to fulfill my obligation here."

He had her going now. He could see it, the confusion in her eyes, and that was a lot better than the cool disinterest that had been there only a little while ago.

"I beg your pardon?"

"I guess you never heard that old Chinese proverb, huh?"

"What old Chinese proverb?" she said cautiously.

"The one that says, if you save a person's life, that person becomes your responsibility."

"Me, you mean? But you didn't save my life."

"Come on, Miss Carter. You were stranded in the middle of a Nevada desert, one hundred and fifty horses dead at your feet, their bones bleached by the sun."

"What?"

"Your car. It was dead as a doornail on the sand."

"It was asphalt," she said, her expression one of bewilderment, "on Las Vegas Boulevard, and I don't think that car of mine ever had that much horsepower, not even when it was new."

"Technicalities," he said, with a little shrug. "There's sand under that asphalt, if you dig down. Your horses were belly-up, your teddy bear was desperate for water and who came along and rescued you? Me." Gray tapped his thumb against his chest. "I saved your life, and that makes me responsible for you now."

He waited, never realizing he was holding his breath until she let out a soft, almost imperceptible laugh.

"I don't understand a word you just said. Even if all that were true, how does that make asking me out your—what did you call it? Your obligation?"

"Damned if I know," he said, smiling. "But you have to admit, it's a good line." He leaned over the desk, which put him almost nose to nose with her, close enough so he could smell the faint scent of vanilla on her skin. Would she taste like vanilla, if he touched his mouth to throat? "Coffee," he said softly. "Fair enough?"

She didn't answer and he thought he'd pushed his luck too far. Then he saw her chin drop just a little. The look in her eyes went from hostile to wary.

"I'm not going to get rid of you unless I agree, am I?"

"I'm an attorney, Red. If we're known for nothing else, it's tenacity."

"What did you call me?"

"What did I…? Oh. Red. Sorry. It's how I thought of you all last night. You know. Red."

He reached over, tugged gently on the tendril of escaped hair. She pulled away but she smiled. Really smiled. He knew he'd won, and he knew, too, that the elation he felt was out of line with reality.

"Espresso," she said softly.

"I beg your pardon?"

"The coffee in the Reveille—it's that little self-service place down past the elevators—the coffee's awful, but the espresso is fine."

"You've got it," Gray said, and felt as if he'd just reached the summit of Mount Everest.

She said she had to do some things back in her office and she'd meet him in the little café in a few minutes.

He got there first, debated whether to plunk money into the coffee machine and have her espresso ready or wait until she arrived. Wait, he decided, and he chose a table near a big wooden tub of pansies and myrtle, chose a different table beside the window that overlooked the pool, and finally decided he was behaving like a kid on his first date, which was insane.

He was here for a purpose. He had a mission. There was nothing personal in meeting Dawn for coffee and besides, she wasn't really the shy woman with the nice smile and the sexy mouth she didn't seem to know was sexy he'd met yesterday. She was an assignment he'd undertaken because he had no choice. She was also the runaway wife of a man she'd let abuse her and the mother of a little boy she'd abandoned like a stack of old clothes…

"Hi."

Gray stood up. Dawn was standing in the doorway. She looked demure and beautiful, and he knew it was time to admit the truth. She was nothing he'd anticipated and he was drawn to her even though he didn't want to be. He wanted to grab her by the shoulders and shake her until her teeth rattled. Forget Chinese proverbs. She was a Chinese puzzle, boxes within boxes within boxes, and he hadn't a clue how he'd figure out what that last box held, or if he wanted to find out.

"Hi," he said, and motioned to the small table beside the window. "Is this okay?"

"Yes, it's fine."

"You said espresso, right?"

"Yes, thank you."

He held out a chair. She slipped into it. He dug a couple of bills from his wallet, fed them into the machine and it spewed two streams of black liquid into a pair of paper cups.

"Cream? Sugar?" He smiled again. It seemed as if he'd done a whole lot of smiling in the past hour or so. Had any of it been real? "The pink stuff?"

"Nothing. Just black, thank you."

"Black it is." He sat down across from her at the little table. "Well. Thanks for agreeing to have coffee with me."

"You're welcome." She hesitated. "I'm sorry if I seemed, um, if I seemed—"

"No need to apologize." He lifted the cup and took a sip. "You probably have guys hitting on you twenty-four hours a day."

"Yes. No. I mean…" She took a breath. "What you did was very kind, Mr. Baron. But—"

"It's Gray. And I only did what anyone would have done, in the same situation."

"Not true. A whole bunch of cars just whizzed past. One man even shook his fist at me."

"Well, of course he did. You're supposed to pick a place to break down, Miss Carter. That's the polite thing to do."

She laughed. "The only place to break down is next to a service station."

"Exactly what the guy who shook his fist at you must have thought."

"Actually, that happened to me once. I was driving along

and suddenly my tru—my car started to make funny noises. I coaxed it along for a couple of blocks but it finally died, right outside a station.''

''Ah.'' Gray smiled over the rim of his coffee container. ''A well trained... Did you say truck?''

''No,'' she said quickly, ''I said car.''

He knew she'd started to say ''truck.'' He thought about Queen City, about the parking lot outside the Victory Diner where he'd met with Harman. It was easy enough to imagine a truck in that place but difficult to imagine the woman opposite him behind the wheel. She looked too urbane, too fragile; she looked like a woman who had never seen a hick town or a pickup cab in her life.

''And what was wrong with it?''

''Sorry?''

''Your car. Cars. The one that broke down near a station and the one that died in the middle of the desert yesterday.''

''Oh.'' She sipped her coffee, and he had the feeling she was sorry she'd mentioned the service station incident. ''I just ran out of gas, that other time.'' Ran out, and had no money to fill the tank. Harman doled out only enough money for groceries, and he was the one who had driven the truck dry but when she'd phoned and said she was out of gas, he'd been furious...

''Miss Carter?''

Dawn blinked. Gray Baron was looking at her and smiling, but there was an intensity in his eyes that made her uncomfortable.

''Sorry,'' she said briskly. ''I was just thinking that I don't seem to have much luck with cars. It's a good thing you came along yesterday, or I might still be standing on that street.''

''Desert,'' he said solemnly. ''Just picture it the way it was not too many years ago. Sand and cactus, buzzards and rattlers...''

She laughed. ''I get the feeling you don't like the desert. Were you born in one of those green, leafy parts of Texas?''

He was baffled, but only for a second. Then he recalled how neatly she'd managed to place his accent.

"Yes, I guess you'd say that. Austin. Well, near Austin. Do you know the area?"

"No, I don't."

"Well, it's green." He grinned. "But it's still Texas, where men are men and cows are cows, and anybody who doesn't wear boots is pretty much an alien species. What about you?"

"What about...? Oh. I'm from a lot of places. We moved around a lot when I was growing up." She took a paper napkin from the plastic container centered on the table and touched it to her lips. "Well, this was really very nice, Mr. Baron."

"Gray, please."

"Gray. It was a nice break."

"For me, too."

"And I'm sorry I gave you such a hard time. I mean, having coffee turned out to be—"

"Nice."

"Yes. It was..." She blushed. "Mr. Baron. Gray. Look, I don't want you to think I'm ungrateful for what you did, but—but I'm not very good at this."

Gray caught hold of her hand as she began to stand up. "At what?"

She took a deep breath. "Never mind. The point is, as I already told you, I don't date guests."

"You also said it wasn't against hotel policy."

"That's right." Carefully she disengaged her hand from his.

"But you do date."

"Yes," she said, lying through her teeth, "of course, but—"

"But, you don't date guests." Gray smiled. "No problem. I understand."

"Good. I'm glad you do. I wouldn't want you to think it was anything personal."

"Recommend a hotel, then."

"Sorry?"

"I'm going to check out of the Desert Song and into some

other place. I figured you'd be able to give me the name of a hotel I'd like.''

"But why...?" Her cheeks colored. "Don't be silly!"

"I'm not. I'm being practical. Until a few minutes ago, I figured the only way I'd get to see more of you would be to drop a bundle at the tables tonight and get myself designated a VIP. That way I'd at least run into you from time to time, but now it turns out I can stay at another hotel and you'll go out with me for an evening.''

She sat back and stared at him. "I never said that!"

"Didn't you?"

"No. Absolutely not. You've twisted things all around."

"Yeah, well, I told you, I'm a lawyer. We're not just tenacious, twisting things around is what we do for a living. Look, I'm not asking for much. Dinner, anywhere you like. Just think of it as a memorial to those horses of yours, their bones bleaching in the dust of Las Vegas Boulevard.''

He saw her mouth twitch and then she gave a low, throaty laugh. "You really don't know how to take no for an answer, do you?"

"No," he said simply, "not when I see something I want. Say you'll have dinner with me tonight."

He said it so easily, as if things like this happened every day. And they *did* happen every day; she knew that. Men asked women out; women said yes and went. It was simple, really, and it didn't have to lead to anything but a pleasant evening, a couple of hours of laughter and good food, and when was the last time she'd done anything like that?

Never. Not ever. She'd never dated a man, never sat across a table from one and smiled and joked, just relaxed and enjoyed his company.

Cassie was right. Gray was handsome. And nice. He'd helped her yesterday and he hadn't asked anything in return, hadn't tried anything, hadn't made an oily bubble of fear rise in her throat the way it sometimes did when a man looked at her or touched her or—

"Dawn?" She looked up. He was smiling, waiting for her

answer. "If not dinner, how about a drink? That's all, I promise. Just tell me where to pick you up and when."

The sounds of the hotel, the ever-present electronic songs of the slot machines, faded to silence. She could feel her heart hammering, wasn't that ridiculous? Almost as ridiculous as the idea of agreeing to meet him tonight...

Just do it, she thought, and the words burst from her throat. "Seven o'clock. I'll meet you just outside the front door."

She stood up. Gray rose, too, but she shook her head and he stayed where he was, watching her until she disappeared in a river of tourists flowing down the corridor. Then he sat down, picked up the cup that held the last of his espresso and wondered why his hand seemed to be shaking.

CHAPTER TEN

DAWN looked at the dress that lay across her bed, at the jeans and T-shirts tossed beside it, and decided she'd lost her mind.

One of them had, either she or Cassie, who was standing inside the closet and pawing madly through the few things still dangling from the rod—but it wasn't Cassie who had agreed to meet a stranger for dinner.

"Stop!" Cassie didn't so much as turn her head. Dawn scooped up the dress, put it on a hanger and marched to the closet. "There's no point in playing deaf, Cass. I know you heard me."

"I cannot believe this," Cassie muttered. "Don't you own anything except work stuff and jeans? Honestly, Dawn—"

"Honestly, Cassie," Dawn said as she put the dress away, "you can stop taking my closet apart."

"Suits. Dresses my mother wouldn't wear. For Pete's sake—"

"Cassie." Dawn grabbed her friend's hands and held on until she looked at her. "Cut it out."

"Cut what out? You cannot possibly meet this guy looking like a cross between Mary Poppins and Velvet Brown."

"That's exactly the point. I'm *not* meeting... Who?"

"Mary Poppins. The nanny with necklines up to her chin and sleeves to her wrists."

"I know who Mary Poppins is. Who's Velvet Brown?"

Cassie blew a strand of dark hair off her forehead. "Jeez, it's sweltering in here. Turn the AC up, will you?"

"It's up as high as it goes."

"Yeah, well, you need to buy a new unit."

"My landlady needs to buy a new unit, not me. And you didn't answer my question. Who's Velvet Brown?"

"National Velvet," Cassie said briskly, tugging her hands free.

"Huh?"

"Don't you watch old movies?"

"No. And will you please stop dragging stuff from my closet? I told you, I'm not—"

"National Velvet. Elizabeth Taylor. Do you know who she is? A gorgeous actress. She was maybe sixteen then, with this big, wonderful horse..."

Dawn sank down on the edge of the mattress. "I'm lost," she said, "totally lost."

"I told you, it's a movie. Makes me weepy whenever I see it, Velvet and her horse..."

"What does an old movie and a horse have to do with me?"

"Everything. You have stuff you wear to work—and then there's crud like this." Cassie stepped from the closet, nose wrinkled, a pair of well-used boots dangling from her fingers. "You mucking out stables in your spare time, or what?"

"Or what," Dawn said, trying to sound casual. She rode with Tommy almost every Sunday. She'd never been on a horse until she'd sent him to the ranch and she still didn't ride very well, but her son loved horses—and what was a woman with a son to protect doing, violating her own rules? No men. No dates. No desire for either. That was the comfortable pattern she'd followed for four long years. "Cass." She took a deep breath. "Listen to me. I am not going to meet that man."

"Yes, you are, and in less than an hour, so help me decide what you should wear."

"I'm not. I don't want to meet him for drinks and dinner. Drinks, for God's sake." Dawn groaned and fell backward across the bed, her arms stretched out in supplication. "I don't *drink* drinks! And if I did, I wouldn't drink them with him. What got into me? Why'd I ever agree to this?"

"You agreed because you're a living, breathing woman and he's the most gorgeous thing in Vegas."

"I thought you said Keir was the most gorgeous thing in Vegas."

"I never said that."

"Yes, you did. Why don't you ask him for a date?"

"Who? Keir?" Cassie went back into the closet. "Don't be ridiculous."

"I'm not being ridiculous. You've asked men out before."

"Keir isn't 'men,' he's—he's Keir. He's an O'Connell. And we're not talking about me, we're talking about... Aha!"

"Aha, what?"

"Aha, you've been holding out. You do, too, have real clothes. Female clothes." Cassie emerged from the closet and smiled triumphantly. "White jeans. Black silk T-shirt. Catch."

The jeans and shirt sailed into Dawn's lap. She'd bought the outfit for a Rocking Horse Ranch Parents and Kids dinner. The first time around, she'd bought a dress. A Mary Poppins dress, she thought wryly.

Everyone else had worn jeans.

"You look nice, Mama," Tommy had whispered shyly, slipping his hand into hers, but she'd known she looked as out of place as she felt. Each year since, she'd worn the white jeans and the silk T-shirt. Each time, Tommy said she looked beautiful. Would a man think so, too? Harman wouldn't. He didn't like her in jeans, didn't like her in silk, didn't like—

Dawn pushed the clothing aside. "Forget it. I'm not going."

"And you can borrow these," Cassie said, kicking off her shoes.

"Those? With the nine inch heels? No way."

"Three inch heels. And I know, it's not the most hygienic trade but I promise, cross my heart and hope to die, the nail polish on my toes works as an antiseptic."

Dawn laughed. "I didn't mean—Cass, this is just so silly..."

"Look, I just spent half an hour battling dust bunnies in your closet. The least you can do is let me see how you look in the only things you own that pass for date clothes, okay?"

Dawn sighed. "It's *all* I'm going to do." She slipped off her robe and stepped into the jeans, pulled on the T-shirt, slid her feet into Cassie's shoes and gaped down at them. They were all straps and heel. "How do you walk in these things?"

"Slowly. And carefully." Cassie grinned. "Sometimes, you just have to grab your date's arm for support, you know?"

"I don't have a date."

"This is silly. A perfectly nice man asks you to have dinner and you act as if a sex fiend invited you out for the evening. What's with you?"

"Nothing's with me. I just—I don't—"

"Whoa." Cassie's eyes narrowed. "You don't think he's dangerous, do you? That he's somehow connected to your ex?"

"No," Dawn said, and meant it. She'd discarded that idea almost as soon as she'd thought it. "I can't imagine Gray and Har—Gray and my husband in the same room." She laughed. "I can't even imagine them on the same planet. And you've got it wrong, Cass. I told you, I don't have an 'ex.' Legally, I'm still—"

"Married. Right. To some no-good bastard who still scares you, even though he's out of your life. What you need is to go out, forget the past and have some fun."

Dawn shook her head. Pulling on the T-shirt had loosened the scrunchie she wore. It slid off, and her hair swung loose around her face.

"I don't want that kind of fun," she said firmly. "I don't want to get involved with anybody. I'm perfectly happy just the way I am."

"Amazing," Cassie said, lifting her eyes to the ceiling. "A guy asks her for a drink and she hears Mendelssohn playing in the background."

"What?"

"Mendelssohn. The Wedding March." Cassie lifted one eyebrow. "Surprising the heck out of you today, aren't I? Old movies, dead composers…"

"And bad advice. There's no reason for me to meet this man."

"He has a name. Why not use it?"

"Fine. If it makes you feel better, I'll say the whole thing. There's no reason for me to meet Gray Baron."

"Gorgeous name. Gorgeous guy."

"You saw him for two minutes."

"Two minutes was enough. When I spotted you talking to him, I knew he was spectacular. And when I got closer... Mmm-hmm. Those eyes. That voice. That smile." Cassie clasped her hands over her heart. "Just to hear him say, 'Nice to meet you, Miss Berk,' was enough to turn me inside out."

"Fine." Dawn folded her arms. "*You* go out with him."

"Well, I would, except I think he'd notice that I wasn't you." Cassie jerked her chin toward the mirror. "You look terrific, by the way."

"I feel dumb. Jeans and heels? It isn't me."

"But it is. Go on, take a look."

She did. What she saw was a stranger, a woman with her hair streaming down her back and her cheeks flushed with color, wearing a pair of snug jeans and heels that were like nothing she'd ever worn in her life.

"I must have gained weight. The jeans are tight."

"They fit the way they should."

"They're tight." Dawn sucked in her flat belly and turned sideways. "And look at these shoes. They're—they're—"

"Sexy?" Cassie said helpfully.

Sexy was exactly the word. The heels were skinny and high; the straps crisscrossed her bare feet, left her toes peeping out. Dawn stared at her reflection. Sexy shoes. Sexy jeans. Her hair loose and wild. If Gray saw her like this, would he give her that little smile he'd given her yesterday, when he'd leaned in close and her heart had banged straight into her throat?

It banged now, just at the thought. What was the matter with her? Why would she ever want a man to look at her that way and want the same thing Harman had wanted? A little shudder of revulsion sliced through her. She turned away from the mirror and kicked off the shoes.

"Show's over," she said briskly. "How about if I phone for some Chinese?"

"What do you mean, how about if you phone for Chinese? You told this guy you'd meet him. You can't just stand him up."

"You're right. I'll call and tell him I changed my mind."

Dawn picked up the scrunchie and tossed it on the bed. "I'll order first. What's it going to be? Hunan Shrimp? Kung Pao Chicken? Would you rather have something light? I could put together a tuna—"

"Don't look to me to save you," Cassie said. "I have a date." She began taking clothes from the bed and putting them away. "Some of us believe in letting guys buy us dinner."

Dawn decided not to rise to the bait. "Who is he?"

"Someone I met last night. A dentist from Kansas. He's taking me to that steak house, the one that advertises—"

"Kansas City ribs. Yeah. I figured. Is he nice?"

"He seems okay."

"Just okay?"

"Okay is fine with me. I gave up looking for Prince Charming years ago...and stop trying to change the subject. Why are you canceling your date?"

"Are we back to that? It's not a date. I only said I'd have dinner with him."

"If it's not a date, why not go ahead and keep it?"

"For heaven's sake..." Dawn took a breath. She felt edgy and irritated, and why let it out on Cassie? If she'd let Gray fast-talk her into this, whose fault was it but her own? "All right. It's a date. And that's just the point. I don't do dates. I'm not looking for Prince Charming or even a reasonable stand-in. I'm happy the way I am, single and unencumbered, and that's that."

Cassie lifted her eyebrows. "Wow," she said, very softly. "I'm impressed. You're unen—whatever."

"Unencumbered, and don't play dumb with me." Dawn snatched a blouse from the bed and jammed it onto a hanger. "You know exactly what I'm saying. I don't want a man in my life. Not now. Not ever. Once was more than enough, thank you very much."

"You met this guy yesterday, he asks you out on a date and now he's trying to move into your life? Huh. That's amazing."

"I didn't say—"

"Look, he wants to take you to dinner. That's all he wants.

Well, okay. He's a man and you're a woman, and unless he's brain dead, he's hoping for more than that—but the rest is up to you. If you want to stop at a drink, fine. If you want to tack on dinner, great. And if it turns out that he makes your temperature climb and you want to end up in bed with him—''

"Never!" Dawn whirled around. "I don't want to go to bed with Gray or anybody else.''

"Hey. I didn't mean—''

"I'd sooner enter a convent than—than—'' Dawn's voice trembled. From the look on Cassie's face, she knew she'd said far more than she'd ever intended. "This is silly,'' she said, fighting to sound calm. "We've gone from why I should go out with a man to why I should sleep with him.''

"I never said that. All I meant was—''

"I know what you meant. And, trust me, I don't want it. None of it. Not the dating, not the sex… I'm happy the way I am.''

"I don't think you are. I think this guy turned you on.''

"Don't be ridiculous.''

"And why wouldn't he?'' Cassie continued blithely. "There isn't a woman alive who wouldn't react to a good-looking guy, especially when he makes it clear he's interested in her.''

"My God, you are so damned sure of yourself!'' Dawn slapped her hands on her hips. "Trust me, okay? There are lots of women who feel the way I do.''

"If that's true, I feel sorry for them. And for you, because it means that bastard husband of yours won the war.''

Dawn glared at Cassie. Then she grabbed the scrunchie and pulled her hair through it. "I don't even know what you're talking about.''

"Yeah, you do. If you're going to judge every guy you meet by the one you lived with, then that bastard still has you under his thumb. Oh, don't look at me that way. You haven't said more than three words about him but you don't have to. Men like him are all the same. They're control freaks. They're only happy when they're telling you what to do. Am I right?''

"I don't want to talk about this.''

"Maybe it's time you did. Dawn, you're letting your ex own you."

"I keep telling you, he isn't my ex. I'm still married to him."

"And I'm telling you that unless you start living your life for yourself, you might as will still be living with him." Cassie's voice softened. "Don't you see that?"

The women stared at each other. Then Dawn turned away and made a show of rearranging the hangers in the closet.

"I know you mean well," she said in a low voice, "but my situation is—it's complicated. Even if you're right—and I'm not saying you are—even if it might be a good idea for me to get out a little, I can't. I can't, Cass," she said, turning to face her friend, her eyes pleading for understanding. "I honestly can't."

"Listen to me, okay? You're not signing on for forever. You meet the man, you have a glass of wine, you smile, he smiles, you talk a little, laugh a little. Heck, you flirt a little and maybe you begin to remember what it's like to be a woman. You have dinner and then it's over. You say goodnight, you come home, and you have a couple of memories that you can call up in the middle of the night, when you're feeling alone." Dawn was shaking her head and Cassie reached out and caught hold of her hand. "Don't say no without thinking it through."

"I'm telling you, it isn't that simple. There are—there are things you don't know…"

"I don't suppose you want to tell me what they are." Cassie sighed. "No. I can see that you don't."

"Only because it wouldn't change things. My life is—it's—"

"Complicated," Cassie said, with a wry smile.

"Yes. And it wouldn't help either of us if I drew you into it." Dawn squeezed Cassie's hand. "Thank you, though."

"For what?"

"For caring about me. For giving me advice."

"We're friends, aren't we? Friends are supposed to care. And if my advice was any good, you'd be heading out the door to meet that hunk who's expecting you in—'' she checked her watch and looked up ''—in less than fifteen minutes.''

"Fifteen...?'' Dawn groaned and made a grab for the phone. She dialed the hotel, reached Gray's room, paced back and forth while she waited for him to pick up. After five rings, she disconnected. "He's not there. What now?''

"Call back. Leave a message. Maybe he's in the shower.''

"Right. In the shower.'' The thought of Gray, standing naked under the water, turned her face warm and she swung away from the knowing glint in Cassie's eye. "Okay. I'll call back.''

This time, she waited for his voice mail to pick up. Then she left a polite message. She was sorry, she couldn't meet him, something had come up...

"Of course,'' Cassie said, checking her fingernails, "he's probably already downstairs, waiting for you.''

"Not yet. I'm not supposed to meet him for another ten minutes.''

"Uh-huh. Well, maybe he stopped to buy you flowers.''

"Flowers?''

"Yeah. You know, colored petals, leaves and stems.'' Cassie grinned at the expression on Dawn's face. "It's been known to happen. Or maybe he just wants to be there first. Whatever, if he's already left his room, he's not going to get that message. He'll just hang around for hours and hours.''

"Oh, stop! He'll give up after a little while.''

"You mean, once he figures out that he's been stood up?''

"Yes. No. Oh, hell...''

"Exactly. I have to admit, that's a novel way to repay a gallant knight for an act of kindness.''

"Cassie. You're a cruel woman.''

"I'm an honest woman. And I've got to go. My dentist's picking me up soon. Unlike some people I could mention, I don't believe in turning down a free meal.''

"I was only going to have a drink,'' Dawn said, sinking down on the edge of the bed. "Just a drink.''

"My point, exactly.'' Cassie looked at her discarded shoes,

smiled to herself and slipped her feet into a pair of Dawn's sandals. "You don't mind if I borrow these, do you?"

"What? Oh. No. No, take them, but why? I don't need—"

"Yeah, I know, but I figure, just in case you change your mind—"

"I won't. I can't. It's too late, even if…" Dawn gave a troubled sigh. "I feel terrible. It's wrong to stand him up, isn't it?"

"As wrong as snow in July," Cassie said cheerfully. She gave Dawn a quick hug. "I'm off. See you tomorrow."

"Yeah, okay. Have fun."

The front door swung shut. Dawn leaned back on her hands, crossed her legs and swung one foot in a slow arc. Now what? She felt horribly guilty, picturing Gray waiting outside the hotel. She could call the front desk and ask someone to please go look for a tall man with dark hair, waiting near the main entrance. Better still, she could phone her office. Who was working tonight? Amy? She could ask Amy…

Sure she could. By tomorrow, the entire world would know she'd made a date with Gray and then called it off.

She looked at the clock. He'd be looking for her right about now. God, she felt awful. The right thing would be to drive to the hotel and tell him, to his face, that she was sorry, she'd changed her mind…but it was too late. Despite what Cassie said, she knew that Gray wouldn't wait around indefinitely. Okay, then. She could drive to the Song and leave a note for him at the desk. That, at least, would be polite. And there'd be no risk of running into him. Surely, he'd have given up waiting by then.

Wouldn't he?

The room was so quiet that Dawn could hear the thud of her heart. She stood up and looked in the mirror. The jeans and silk T-shirt really did look nice. Slowly she reached up and took the scrunchie from her hair, watched as the waves tumbled over her shoulders. If she were actually going to meet Gray, if this was a date, Cassie's shoes would be the finishing touch, but she wasn't doing that. She was only going to the hotel because it was the right thing to do…

Dawn spun away from the mirror, slipped her feet into Cassie's shoes, grabbed her purse and keys and ran for the door.

Gray looked at his watch and told himself to keep a lid on his temper.

It wasn't easy.

He'd been stood up. Or maybe it was better to say he'd been had. Dawn had grown tired of saying she didn't want to go out with him so she'd said yes, she would, and all the time, she'd intended to leave him cooling his heels outside the hotel as he'd been doing for the past twenty minutes.

The doorman caught his eye and smiled politely. By now, he'd probably figured out what was happening, that Gray was out here waiting for a woman who wasn't going to turn up.

"Taxi, sir?" he'd said, when Gray had first come out, and he'd said no thanks, he was meeting somebody.

Like hell he was.

A muscle flickered in his jaw.

She'd stood him up. It was a first unless you counted the time he was, what, fifteen, and he'd let his cousins drag him to a party where he'd spent the night gawking at a girl visiting from Chicago. Finally he'd worked up enough courage to go over and ask her to dance, and after that he'd taken his life in his hands and asked her if she wanted to go to the movies the next night. Yes, she'd said, that would be fun, except she'd never shown up in front of the Prairie Theater and he'd waited and paced and waited some more and gone from puzzled to embarrassed to out and out humiliated...

He wasn't fifteen anymore; he wasn't embarrassed or humiliated or puzzled. He was just pissed because he'd only asked her out because of his obligation to Jonas. Hell, even if she showed up now, full of apologies, he'd tell her—

"Hi."

She was coming toward him, smiling hesitantly, wearing some kind of silky-looking T-shirt and white jeans; her hair was loose and swinging against her shoulders, and he felt like he'd been sucker-punched. His anger drained away and he smiled and held out the gift he'd purchased at the shop in the lobby. He'd planned on flowers until he saw the little teddy bear holding a silk rose in its paw.

Perfect, he'd thought, and from the look on her face, he knew he'd figured right.

"Hi," he said. "You look beautiful."

She took the bear and stared at it. For one crazy minute, he was afraid she was going to cry.

"Oh," she said softly, "he's wonderful. Thank you. I never dreamed—I mean, I just never imagined…" She blushed, and it occurred to him that she did that a lot, and that blushing was something women didn't do much anymore. "Sorry. I'm babbling. I love my bear."

"He needs a name."

"Of course he does," she said, and laughed. "And I'll give him one, after I get to know him." She hesitated. "Gray. I know I'm terribly late. I tried to call you…"

"That's okay. I'm just glad you finally got here. Did you have car trouble again?"

"No. I—I just—"

"You don't have to explain." Gray took her hand and wove his fingers through hers. Her skin was cool and at first he thought she was going to pull away. Then, very slowly, he felt her relax. "You're here now. That's what matters."

"Actually, I just came to tell you that—that—"

"That you'd changed your mind?"

She nodded. "Yes."

"Well, I can respect that but, since you're already here, why not have one drink with me?"

She stared at him, her eyes wide. A moment passed, and then she gave a soft laugh. "You're a very determined man, Mr. Baron."

"And a very thirsty one, Miss Carter. So, how about it? One drink? I asked the concierge to name a quiet place. He said there's a little bar in the hotel just across the Strip—"

She nodded. "The Oasis."

"Right. Is that okay?"

"I've never been there, but I've heard it's very nice."

"You've never been there, huh?" He knew it was stupid,

but that pleased him. "Well." Gray tugged her toward him. "Let's see if what the experts say is true."

It was.

The Oasis was small, dark and surprisingly quiet except for the soft sound of the piano playing in the background and the discreet murmur of voices drifting from the round oak bar in the center of the room.

They took a corner booth. Dawn slid in across the soft leather banquette, sat her teddy bear on the table and watched as Gray sat down across from her and picked up the wine list. He was dressed casually in chinos and a black cotton shirt with a banded collar. He'd rolled up the sleeves and she could see that his forearms were muscled and lightly dusted with black hair. He was as handsome as she'd remembered, but very masculine-looking, and he had a smile that she could feel, straight down to her toes each time he flashed it.

She knew she was blushing and she picked up the teddy bear and buried her face in the scented silk rose in its paw. The bear was beautiful and expensive. She knew the price of virtually everything in the Song's flower shop. That Gray would have bought the bear for her, that he'd have recalled their first meeting and somehow known this gift would mean more to her than all the flowers in the world, struck her as—

"...wonderful."

Gray was leaning toward her on his elbows, his fingertips steepled under his chin, and smiling.

"Sorry. I didn't hear what you said."

"I said, this bar is wonderful and so are you." His smile tilted. "Do you have any idea how formidably efficient you look when you're at work?"

She laughed. "I'm supposed to look efficient, but not formidable. 'Friendly, efficient, courteous and accessible,' is what it says in the job description."

"Well, okay. Maybe 'formidable' is a stretch. And you certainly charm the customers. Just like you charmed me."

He was flirting with her, and she had no idea how to respond. Dealing with a guest was easy. Dealing with a man you knew, a man you found interesting, wasn't. Plus, she knew she was blushing. God, but she felt like an idiot!

"Thank you," she finally said, and because she couldn't think of anything else to do, she picked up a coaster from the table and stared at it as if the print weren't swimming before her eyes.

"Beer?"

She looked at him. She'd only tasted beer once, when Harman had insisted, and she'd hated it. Was it all right to say no, thank you, she didn't like beer? Or were you supposed to be agreeable to whatever your date selected? A little thrill of excitement danced down her spine as she realized that this was her very first date. Harman had never taken her anywhere, not even before they were married. He'd just shown up at the trailer and she'd make him coffee—and what was the matter with her, thinking about Harman tonight? Better yet, what was the matter with her, thinking she'd ever have to do or say anything she didn't want to do or say, just to please a man?

"No, thank you," she said firmly. "I don't like beer."

"Ah. Sorry. I just figured, since you're reading that coaster…"

"What?" She looked at the coaster, saw the list of beer brands on it and dropped it on the table. "Oh. Oh, no. I just happened to pick it up because—"

"Because you're nervous."

"Don't be silly. Why would I be nervous?"

"I don't know," Gray said softly. He reached for her hands, clasped them in his. They were icy-cold, and he remembered how he'd badgered her into agreeing to meet him. "I'm not going to bite." He smiled. "Not unless you want me to."

Her face turned bright pink. What was he doing? Jonas had asked him to talk with this woman, spend a little time with her so he could form an impression of what she was like. Well, he had that chance now but he was coming on to her instead of talking to her.

Maybe it would be a good idea to start thinking of this as an interview rather than a date. He let go of her hands and sat back.

"Okay," he said briskly, "no beer. What would you like, then? Wine? Champagne? A cocktail?"

"Mineral water would be fine."

"Come on. Have some wine." He grinned. "Let me show off a little. You know, the whole bit. I get to browse the wine list with a serious look on my face."

His brow furrowed; his mouth turned down. Dawn smiled.

"Then I have this long conversation with the waiter. Sorry. With the *sommelier*. I ask him about vintages. Maybe we talk about climates and terrains. Then he says, very solemnly, that they have half a dozen special bottles of an impossible-to-get *sauvignon blanc* from some rarefied California vineyard tucked away in the wine cellar."

"Not French?" Dawn asked, laughing as she got into the spirit of things.

"French whites are passé, compared to this stuff from California. That's what the *sommelier* would say, if I asked. But I don't ask because I know better than to let him know I'm not onto this stuff, so when he mentions the wine, I light up brighter than the Strip. He produces the bottle, we *ooh* and *ahh* and watch carefully as he uncorks it and presents the cork for me to sniff. I nod, he pours an inch, I sip, I nod again. He pours for you and fills my glass. You and I sip, we smile, we discuss the color, the bouquet, the fact that the wine reminds us of a rare vintage from the southwest corner of a particular vineyard in the Loire Valley where wines like this were produced, maybe five generations ago..." He drew a slow, deliberate breath. "Are you really going to deny me all that?" he said, and she stopped laughing long enough to say she couldn't possibly be that unkind.

"In that case..." He picked up the card she'd been reading, turned it over and read the wine selection. Then he signaled the waiter, ordered a wine without any consultation at all, and when it arrived, waved away the tasting and sniffing. "If it's no good," he told the waiter pleasantly, "I'll let you know."

Dawn smiled. "That's it?"

"Disappointed?"

"No. Actually I can never watch someone going through that other routine without wanting to laugh."

"Yeah, well, I'll do some of it for an expensive bottle but not for a nice, everyday wine, which is pretty much all this place offers." Gray lifted his glass. *"Salud."*

"Salud."

They touched glasses, sipped the cool, dry wine. Dawn said it was very nice. Gray said he was glad she liked it. Then they fell silent. She looked at her wine, then at him. His eyes were on her face, his gaze penetrating. *He wants something from me,* she thought suddenly, and she remembered what she'd told Cassie, that he wasn't dangerous, that he couldn't possibly have anything to do with Harman...

"It's a good wine, isn't it?"

"Yes. It's very nice." She hesitated. "I should warn you, Gray—"

"That's the first time you said my name without making it sound as if I dragged it out of you."

"Look, I know it must have seemed, well, strange. The way I acted about having dinner, I mean, but I really don't date guests."

He nodded.

"And, actually, I can't stay very long."

"Got a pumpkin carriage waiting for you at the stroke of midnight?"

"Pumpkin...? Oh. Oh, no." She smiled again, put down the glass and ran the tip of her index finger carefully around the rim. "Sorry. I guess I'm a little slow on the uptake."

He thought how nice it was, that she was slow on the uptake, that she wasn't quite what he'd figured her to be... Except, she was. He had to stop letting that fact slip away from him. She was a beautiful woman with a soft smile, but there was more to it than that. The truth about her was still shrouded in fog that stretched all the way from the lights of Vegas to an Arizona mountaintop, where a little boy wept for his mother.

The thought soured him. He put down his glass, folded his hands on the table and wished, for the first time in years, that he still smoked. He was here for information, nothing else, and so far he hadn't gotten any.

"Well." He cleared his throat. "How long have you lived in Las Vegas?"

"Four years. And you? How long have you lived in New York?"

"Long enough to qualify as a native, despite the fact that you seem to think I have a Texas accent." He smiled. She smiled back. "Where did you live before this?"

He'd asked her the same thing yesterday. Why did he want to know? "Oh, lots of places," she said, though she suspected she wasn't going to put him off so easily this time, not without a car door to fling open.

"For instance?"

"Why are you so curious?"

"Am I?" He gave a lazy shrug. "Must be the New Yorker in me. Nobody in New York is actually *from* New York. You sort of get in the habit of trying to figure out where people are from."

"Ah. Well, I'm originally from Arizona. Phoenix." It was close enough, and what she'd put on her job application at the hotel. The best background lies were always grounded in as much truth as possible. That was another thing she'd learned at the women's shelter.

"Did you move around a lot?"

"That depends on what you mean by 'a lot.'" Her gaze held his. "I tried some different places before I settled on Las Vegas."

"Funny place to settle down, Las Vegas."

"Not really. The Strip is just a small part of the city. There are real people living here, the same as anywhere else. You don't notice them until you get away from the lights and the casinos. Then you see the real stuff. Houses with mortgages, drugstores, supermarkets—"

"Schools and parks and kids?"

Was there an edge to his voice? No. He was still smiling pleasantly over the rim of his half-empty glass.

"Of course. Lots of kids, in fact. There's a school near

where I live. Sometimes, when I leave for work in the morning, I see them running around in the playground..."

Her voice faded; her expression changed and became, what? Wistful? Yes, he thought, that was the right word. She looked wistful. Was she remembering her own son? Gray almost asked her, then jerked himself back to reality. He wasn't supposed to know anything about her but, dammit, he had to know the truth, how she had been able to walk away from her child and never look back.

"You like kids?" he said, hoping he sounded casual, but he knew, as soon as he'd spoken, he'd touched a nerve. She became pale. Her fingers tightened around the stem of her wineglass and he half expected it to crack under the pressure.

"That's a funny thing to ask."

"Just making conversation," he said with a quick smile.

"Yes, I like kids. Why shouldn't I?"

Gray's eyes met hers. Here it was, the information he'd been looking for, information that might explain why he kept seeing the defensive tilt of Nora Lincoln's jaw, the sadness in her eyes, in her granddaughter.

"I don't know," he said quietly. "I was hoping you could tell me."

He wanted to call the words back but it was too late. She stared at him, eyes wide and, to his shock, suddenly filled with what could only be fear. Then her face went blank. Carefully she blotted her mouth with her napkin, put down the glass and stood up.

"It's getting late," she said politely. "Thank you for the wine."

"Dawn." He rose, too. "Wait a minute—"

"I'm sorry. I have to go."

He cursed, dug his wallet from his pocket fast, pulled out a couple of bills and dropped them on the table but by the time he reached the door, she was gone.

CHAPTER ELEVEN

MARY ELIZABETH O'CONNELL had reached a decision.

She was tired of being treated as if she were made of glass, tired of taking an occasional stroll through her very own hotel while keeping one eye out for a son who clearly was afraid she was going to swoon on the spot like a maiden in a Victorian melodrama. Mostly she was tired of playing the role of a woman who had managed to avoid death by the skin of her teeth, even though it was more true than not.

Mary frowned into the mirror. She'd come close, very close, to meeting her Maker. Right after her heart attack and the surgery that followed, she'd sometimes thought it might not have been so awful if she had. It was a blasphemous thought, she knew, and completely unlike her. When her doctor realized what she'd been thinking, he'd assured her she was only suffering a normal bout of postsurgery depression, but Mary hadn't been so sure he was right.

The thing of it was, she'd missed Ruarch something fierce in the years since his passing. She loved her children, her hotel, her casino and her employees, but not even all that could fill the hole left in her life by the loss of her handsome, pigheaded, impossible, wonderful husband.

There was a dot of lipstick on a front tooth. Mary leaned closer and rubbed it away with a tissue. That was better. So was her new hair do. She'd ignored the stylist's suggestion about coloring it; her hair was white and white it would stay. But she was pleased with the short length, and the way the soft waves fell back from her temples. In the old days she'd worn her hair long, for Ruarch. Whenever she grew irritated by the time it took to wash and dry and braid all its heavy length, and she'd threaten to cut it off, he'd smile and take her in his arms.

"I love your hair as it is," he'd say in that rough burr that could always turn her strongest resolve to butter. "Leave it alone, *mavourneen*."

Despite the doctor's assurances, her depression had continued. She'd learned to cover its signs and live with it. And then, a few weeks ago, she'd awakened one morning and known it was time to come to grips with the realization that Ruarch was gone. The finality of the admission was a wound sharp as one made by a knife, but with it came a kind of bittersweet peace. As she'd settled back against the pillows, she'd felt a weight lift from her soul. Her beloved husband was gone but she was still here, thanks to her children, her doctors, her God and, yes, thanks to her own feisty determination that had apparently not failed her, even in the depths of her despair.

It was time to move on.

Mary put down the tissue, gave herself one last look and liked what she saw almost as much as she liked what she felt. She was back, and everyone would have to get used to that.

A tap sounded at the bedroom door and it eased open. "Ma'am?"

"Yes, Jenny?" Mary said. "What is it?"

"Mr. Coyle is here. I've shown him into the sitting room."

"Ah. Fine. Thank you. Ask if he's had his breakfast or if he'd like some coffee or tea, would you, and tell him I'll be right there?"

Mary took a last look at her reflection. She didn't look a day over fifty. Well, not a day over sixty, she thought, and smiled, and wondered, out of the clear blue, how old was Dan Coyle? She knew so little about him, only that he'd lived all his life in New York until he'd come to work here, that he was a widower...

And that he was a very nice-looking man.

The unexpected thought put a pink bloom in her cheeks. She felt it heat her skin as she made her way through the penthouse apartment.

Dan was seated in a chair that was too small for him. When she refurnished the room after Ruarch's passing, she'd chosen French Provincial velvet chairs and sofas. Keir always had to sit down gingerly. Now, she saw that Dan had to do the same thing.

Perhaps it was time to refurnish again.

"Duchess." Dan rose to his feet and took the hand she extended to him. He held it lightly, as he always did, just a quick press of the fingers before letting it go, and smiled. "You look different."

"Do I?" Mary gestured him back into the chair and sat down on the sofa. Jenny was hovering in the doorway, a tray in her hands. A pitcher of iced water stood on it. She smiled at Dan. "Iced water? Was that all you wanted? No breakfast?"

"I had mine. You go ahead, though."

"No, I've had mine, too, about an hour ago. Still, are you certain all you want is water?"

"Well, to be honest, I'd have asked for iced coffee but then you'd have had a glass, as well." He smiled. "And Keir would scold the both of us."

Mary laughed. "Bring us some cake, please, Jenny. And a pitcher of that decaffeinated stuff." She looked at Dan. "It's not so bad, once you get used to it."

"I know it isn't. I drink it myself, sometimes."

"Do you?"

"Yes. I have, for years. My wife wasn't supposed to have caffeine, either, so I drank it for her sake and grew accustomed to it."

"Ah. Your wife." This was a day of firsts. Dan had never mentioned her before. Mary sat back while Jenny put the tray in front of her. "I do recall, from your résumé, that you lost her quite some time ago."

"Eight years." He took the glass she held out to him and nodded his thanks. "You and she would have liked each other, I think."

"Would we?"

"Yes, I'm sure of it. You're very different from my Flo, but—"

"Different? How?"

"Well, you're out in the world, so to speak. My wife never had a paying job. She was a homemaker, one of those women who takes all her pleasure in baking and cooking and cleaning.'' He smiled at the memory. ''She made this hash, from leftover roast beef—''

''So did I.''

Dan's eyebrows lifted. ''You?''

''Certainly.'' Mary cut a piece of pound cake, put it on a delicate Spode plate, added a heavy sterling cake fork and a linen napkin and handed it all to him. He took the things with care, a big man typically overwhelmed by such signs of delicacy, and she bit her lip to keep from smiling. ''I never threw out a bit of food that was edible. And I knew ways to stretch the smallest leftover into a filling meal.''

''You?'' he said again, and she chuckled.

''We were poor as church mice, my Ruarch and I, when we married.'' She cut a tiny sliver of cake for herself and spread a napkin in her lap. ''My father was a Boston Brahmin. Do you know what that means?''

His ruddy face split in a grin. ''I was born in the Bronx, Duchess. We were lace-curtain Irish, though my mother would have been mortified if she heard me say so. We knew all about the upper-class gentry who lived in Massachusetts.''

''Well, then you'll understand when I tell you I grew up rich.'' Mary chuckled. ''And *my* mother would have sent me to my room for saying 'rich' rather than 'wealthy.' Would you like more coffee?''

Dan nodded. ''Thank you, I would.''

The ice clinked in the pitcher as she filled his glass. ''We had a place on Cape Cod where we spent weekends and summers. When I was seventeen, my father hired a new groom to care for the horses we kept there.'' Mary put aside the pitcher and folded her hands in her lap. ''His name was Ruarch O'Connell, and he was fresh off the boat from the old country. One summer day, I decided to go riding. My horse threw a shoe and Ruarch came to my rescue.'' She smiled a little. ''That was all it took. I fell crazy in love with him, and he with me. My father found out and threatened to put me in a convent, but I knew he'd never do that. Instead he had Ruarch thrown off the estate, but it was too late. He got a note smuggled to me, I met him by the gate..." She sighed. "It was all so very long ago."

"Yes," Dan said gently, "but the memories are as real as yesterday. It's that way for me, too. Sometimes, when I look at my girls—and they'd kill me for calling them that, when they're both grown women—sometimes, when I look at them, I wonder where the years have gone."

They were both silent a moment. Then Dan cleared his throat. "So," he said briskly, "how did a groom and his runaway bride end up owning one of the biggest hotels and casinos in Las Vegas?"

Mary smiled. "It was a long, circuitous route, I assure you. Ruarch had a love for cards. It was his one weakness."

"Come on, lass, there's no need to be modest. I'll bet his true weakness was for you."

Dan could feel the color spread up over his collar and into his face. Had he really said that? But surely it was the truth. Mary Elizabeth was a beautiful woman still; he could imagine that she'd have stolen a man's breath away when she was a girl. He thought of apologizing and decided against it. What could she do to him, for saying such a thing? Fire him? Let her, if she wished; he was glad he'd spoken the truth.

But she wasn't going to fire him, he saw with some surprise, or even chastise him. Her lovely face had turned as pink as he knew his must be and there was a glint of pleasure in her china-blue eyes.

"That's a very nice thing to say," she murmured.

"It's nothing but the truth."

They looked at each other and smiled. "So," he said, "you were telling me how you came to own the Song..."

"Oh. Yes, yes, I was." She lifted her glass, took a long drink. "Well, we had a difficult few years. The children came along quickly. Ruarch worked at whatever jobs he could while I did all those things women do. Washed, cleaned, cooked, changed diapers..." She sighed. "They were hard years but good ones. Do you know what I mean?"

"I do, yes, though we never had as rough a time," he said,

a touch of surprise in his voice. "A man doesn't earn a fortune when he's on the job—"

"On the job?"

"Cop talk for being a policeman. It didn't pay a lot but it was enough to support Flo, my girls and me."

Mary nodded. "We talked about Ruarch getting a real job. He tried it, but he had an itchy foot so we drifted from place to place, always heading west. He gambled, too. I used to tell him he'd lose everything someday but the truth is, he never did. He won at cards, at the track, at odd bets with strangers and with some people whose famous names would surprise you." She took the last bite of her cake, placed the fork across the plate and put it on the tray. "And then we came to Vegas and, one night, he came home and told me he'd won us a hotel."

Dan blinked. "He won the Desert Song?"

"No. Oh, no." Mary laughed softly. "He won a little place. A motel, I suppose you'd call it today. But he saw the possibilities in this town, and he had friends who agreed with his vision. He worked hard—with me alongside him, I might add—and we woke up one morning and found ourselves the proud owners of a classy hotel and casino." She winked. "That's the story our publicity people gave out, anyway. They thought it wouldn't do if we talked about the years we sweated."

Dan nodded. "Well, I'm impressed."

"So was my father. He sent me a note—the first I'd had from him in twenty years—and told me he'd known, all along, that Ruarch was a man who'd make something of himself."

"And did that heal the rift between you?" He saw her face change and cursed himself for a fool. "Duchess. Mrs. O'Connell. I'm sorry for asking such a personal question."

"Don't be silly. And don't call me that, either."

"Duchess? I apologize. I think it, and it just tumbles out of my mouth."

"No, not that." Mary smiled. "Perhaps I'm still Brahmin enough to like the sound of the word. Just, please, don't address me as Mrs. O'Connell. I think we know each other well enough to dispense with such formalities, don't you?''

What he knew was that the day was opening up like a doorway leading into heaven. Dan smiled back at this lovely woman he'd admired for so long. "Yes, I believe we do...Mary.''

They smiled at each other and then she cleared her throat. ''Well,'' she said briskly, ''it's a pleasure seeing you, but I have the feeling you came here for more than iced coffee and the story of my life.''

Iced coffee and more of listening to her soft voice would have kept him happy forever, Dan thought, so unexpectedly that he felt the breath catch in his lungs, but a man didn't survive almost thirty years as a cop working the mean streets of New York City by doing or saying things precipitously. He patted his mouth with the napkin, placed the plate, fork and napkin on the coffee table and leaned forward, his forearms resting on his thighs.

''I've done the background check Keir requested on Graham Baron.''

''Ah. I thought that might be it.'' Mary leaned forward, too. ''Is Keir joining us?''

''No. I've already spoken with him. I hope you don't mind. I intended to report to you both at the same time but Keir called my office a while ago on a different matter and—''

''No, no, I don't mind. Well? What did you find out?''

Dan rose to his feet. He undid the button on his suit jacket, tucked his hands into the pockets of his trousers, walked to the sliding doors that led to the terrace. She recognized the signs. He was a man delaying his response, and knowing it sent a chill along her spine.

''Dan? Is it bad?''

''Is it...? No. No, it isn't bad.'' He shook his head as he turned around. ''I'm sorry, Mary. I didn't mean to imply that it was. It's just that, well, knowing more about the man only makes the matter more complicated.''

''I don't understand. What did you find out?''

''Nothing. Nothing that would explain things, anyway.''

Dan sat beside her on the little sofa and stretched out his long legs. "Baron's an attorney. He has an impressive résumé—Yale Law Review, clerked for a Federal judge—and now he's a partner in a high-powered New York law firm that specializes in criminal law."

Mary's mouth twisted. "You mean he represents criminals?"

The way she said it made Dan grin. "A woman after my own heart," he said. "You say those words as if they burned your tongue but, in truth, I can't fault the man for what he does. It's part of the system, and I faced enough hotshot lawyers in my time to hold a grudging respect for some."

"Would he be one you'd respect?"

It was an incisive question and went swiftly to the heart of the matter. "He would be, yes. I spoke with old friends who're still on the force. Baron's tough. He'll use everything at his disposal to defend a client but he plays by the rules...and, after all is said and done, getting his people off is what he's supposed to do."

"I suppose." Mary sighed. "But why does that make things more complicated?"

Dan thinned his lips, rolled them in over his teeth. "They had a date a couple of nights back, he and our lady."

"And?"

"And, it seems it didn't go too well."

"That's good, isn't it? I mean, that'll be the end of his interest."

"I don't know about that, Mary. And I keep wondering... Baron is interested in Dawn. Dawn's husband has a record. Could there be some connection between a man who is a criminal and one who defends them?"

"Oh God." Mary clenched her fists. "Do you think—"

"No, I do not." Dan lay his hand over hers. "I can't for the life of me think why a New York lawyer with his thousand-dollar suits and a fancy degree would even be in the same room as Dawn Carter's husband. Baron doesn't handle penny-ante apes like that. Just going on gut instinct," he said, patting her hand, "I'd say the odds of the two being connected is zero."

Mary sat back. "Then, why are you still worried?"

"Because nothing I've learned explains why Baron's focusing on Dawn, or the reason he reacted as Keir says he did when he learned her name."

"Do we know anything else about him?"

"His uncle is Jonas Baron. He's a big-time Texas rancher with a finger in half a dozen other pies. Real estate, mining, oil... The old man's right up there on that annual Fortune 500 list of the richest people in America."

"Are they close? Graham Baron and his uncle?"

Dan shrugged. "Not so you'd notice it and besides, I don't see how his being Jonas Baron's nephew has any meaning here." He looked into Mary's eyes and his hand tightened on hers. "Don't look so worried, Duchess," he said softly. "We'll keep an eye on Dawn. And on Baron, as long as he's in town"

Mary nodded. "Good."

"Besides, Keir might have misinterpreted the way Baron looked when he introduced him to Dawn. It's entirely possible the man's sole interest in her is...biological."

"Biological?" Mary watched the color stripe Dan's cheeks and she struggled to keep from laughing. "Do you mean 'sexual,' Mr. Coyle?"

He nodded. That was all he could manage because, all at once, he felt as tongue-tied as a boy. Was that the gentle sound of laughter in her voice? Was she flirting with him? And—he looked down at their hands, joined now that she'd gently laced her fingers through his—and, God in heaven, was he actually clasping this woman's hand? He'd admired her for a long time. More than admired her but though she'd always been polite, she'd never looked at him as if he were anything but her chief of security.

She was looking at him differently now. As if he were a man, and she were a woman, and she might enjoy spending some time in his company.

"That's what I meant," he finally said, "exactly."

She laughed. "Well, I think you're probably right. And I think your plan is excellent. To keep an eye on things, I mean."

"Well, it's all we can do without alerting Dawn to our concerns."

"And we must not do that," Mary said emphatically. "I have the feeling she'd flee if she thought we knew her secrets."

"I agree."

A moment passed. Then Mary eased her hand from Dan's and rose to her feet. "Forgive me, but I have an appointment with my doctor. Oh, goodness, don't look like that! I want to take off a little weight. I'm just going in to discuss diets."

"You don't need a diet," he said, rising also. "You look fine, just the way you are."

Mary felt her heart trip. It had nothing to do with illness and everything to do with the way he was looking at her. The sensation was one she'd never imagined experiencing again.

"Thank you."

"You're welcome."

Dan cleared his throat. "You'll be happy to hear that Keir agrees we should be watchful. Without being obvious, of course. Keir's promised to keep a low profile and not be confrontational toward Baron."

Mary nodded. "Fine," she said, but knowing her son, she wondered exactly how long his promise would last.

Gray was furious with himself. Talk about your mouth getting ahead of your brain...

He'd spent the past two days trying to figure out what had possessed him to say something so stupid to Dawn. Mentioning kids, asking if she liked them, Jesus, asking why she didn't like them...

He shoved aside the toasted bagel with cream cheese that he hadn't touched, the congealing bacon and cold eggs, wrapped his hand around his coffee mug and lifted it to his lips. From the start, she'd been as wary of him as a canary in a cage full of cats. He'd had to do everything but turn handstands to get her to agree to have dinner and a drink with him. She'd come close to not showing up. And then, after she had, after things were going well, he'd said something so dumb he still couldn't believe it.

It wasn't like him to do something stupid like that. Lawyers measured their words, if they wanted to keep their clients out of jail. If somebody had been around to hear him, he could have pretended he'd said it to smoke her out, get a reaction...

Except, nobody had been there to watch his miserable performance, nobody but him, and what was the point in lying to himself? The simple truth was he'd spoken without thinking. He'd behaved like a man trying to figure out a woman for his own reasons, not like one who had a job to do.

And she wouldn't come near him, now.

He'd tried. He'd stopped by that little desk in that alcove, picked up the phone and hit seven seven seven, but no matter what he did or said, the answer was always the same. Miss Carter was busy elsewhere.

The hell she was. Miss Carter was avoiding him.

Gray shoved back his chair, scribbled his room number and his signature on the bill, and left the coffee shop. Enough was enough. He was tired of thinking about what he'd done, tired of cursing himself...tired of wishing he could turn back the clock and still be seated in that dark little bar, with Dawn smiling shyly at him. He needed to do something to clear his head. A change of scene, maybe. It would help his sanity, if not his disposition.

Someone stopped in front of him. Preoccupied with thoughts of Dawn, Gray muttered "Excuse me," and tried to move past but the man moved with him.

"Excuse me," he repeated, the words taut with impatience.

"Baron."

With a rush, his thoughts returned to the here and now. Keir O'Connell stood before him, looking as if he'd been carved out of stone.

"I'm busy," Gray said sharply.

"I want to talk to you."

"Another time."

"Now."

Gray narrowed his eyes. O'Connell looked the way he felt, frustrated, angry and dangerous. This was just what he needed, a go-round with a man he hadn't liked before he'd even met him. Nothing that had happened since they'd shaken hands had changed his mind.

"Yeah, well that's too bad. I'm in a hurry."

"I noticed." O'Connell's voice was as cold as the look on his face. "This won't take long."

They were toe to toe and eye to eye. *If I swung now, it would be over before he knew what hit him,* Gray thought, and the very insanity of the idea made him take a steadying breath. He gave a quick nod and followed the other man through the lobby, to an unmarked door. O'Connell took a key card from his pocket, inserted it in a slot, and the door opened onto a small, sparsely furnished office.

Gray stepped inside. O'Connell followed, and closed the door behind him.

"Nice," Gray said tonelessly, looking around at the desk and couple of chairs. "Too bad they won't give you a real office but then, I guess you'd need to have a real job for that."

"Sit down."

"You give me one more order and I'll stop being polite and tell you what you can do with it."

The men glared at each other. Gray took a deceptively casual stance, legs slightly spread, hands loose at his sides. It was something he'd picked up studying aikido. He'd ridden New York subways at night and strolled dark Manhattan streets but he'd never felt the need to be ready for whatever was coming the way he did, right now.

"What do you want, O'Connell?"

"What do *you* want? That's a better question."

"Well, this is great." Gray flashed a quick, lazy smile. "Is that what you wanted to discuss? Hey, I'm easy. A million buck payoff from one of those slots would be a cool start but since I have the feeling you're going to say you can't tell a machine what to do, we're done talking. I have better things to do than stand here, playing games with—"

Keir wrapped a hand around Gray's arm as he turned toward the door. Gray jerked free, his smile gone and his face close to the other man's.

"I'm going to tell you this one time," he said softly. "You touch me again, ever, and I'm going to rearrange your face."

Tension, taut and delicately balanced as the web of a spider, crackled between them. Slowly, deliberately, Keir took his hand from Gray's arm.

"Why are you in Las Vegas, Baron?"

"None of your damn business."

"You're wrong, buddy. It *is* my business. I run this place. If I think you're bad news, you're gone. So let's start again. What are you doing here?"

"Amazing." Gray leaned a hip against the desk and folded his arms. It was a safer posture; it would keep him from what he wanted to do, which was put his fist into Keir O'Connell's face. "Such personalized service. Do you provide it for all your guests?"

"It's a simple question. Why not answer it?"

"Sure. I'm here on vacation."

"Don't hand me that crap. You're the kind that goes native on some Caribbean island nobody else ever heard of when you want to take it easy."

Close. Gray decided not to show his surprise and, instead, smiled with his teeth. "Good guess. I'll be sure to tell that to my travel agent. Should make it easier for her to figure out where to send me in the future."

"You don't know a damn thing about gambling."

"Is that a prerequisite for a stay at the Desert Song?"

Keir could feel his gut tightening. A couple of hours ago, he'd agreed with Dan Coyle that they'd keep a low profile, not let Baron know they were watching him. That seemed like a fine idea until he spotted the man in the lobby, his face grim, his eyes cold. He'd thought of how the girls at Special Services were becoming concerned about Dawn, of how she'd phoned in sick yesterday as well as today when she wasn't sick at all. He'd talked to Cassie, who said Dawn was home with a virus, but made it sound like a white lie.

It all added up to the fact that this man was trouble.

"You've got a smart mouth, Baron, you know that?"

"And you've got a nose you like to stick where it doesn't belong. This discussion is—"

"What's your interest in Dawn Carter?"

"That's definitely none of your business."

"She's my employee."

"Is that all she is, O'Connell? Or is this interview even more personal than I thought?"

"I'm told that the lady made her position clear," Keir said, ignoring the barb. "She doesn't like you."

"Really."

"She's tired of having you around. She wants you to stop bothering her."

Gray was sure that was true, but he had no intention of letting Keir O'Connell deliver the message. "She can tell me that herself, if she wants."

"She doesn't have to. I'm telling you for her."

"Why? Are you afraid of competition? What's your problem, O'Connell? Are you afraid that if a woman looks at another man, she'll discover you aren't much?"

Keir made a grab for Gray. Gray sidestepped quickly and blocked the move with his forearm.

"Don't," he said softly.

The men glowered at each other. Then, slowly, each took a step back.

"If I were you," Keir said quietly, "I'd cut my vacation short and go back where I came from."

"Isn't it a good thing you aren't me, then?" Gray said, with a tight smile.

He could feel the adrenaline pumping as he brushed past O'Connell, wrenched open the door and headed across the lobby and out the front door. O'Connell didn't follow him, which he'd half expected. It was just as well. He didn't need the hassle a street brawl would produce, especially if he was still going to make an attempt at talking to Dawn.

The valet brought his car around. Gray dropped a bill in the kid's hand, tried not to growl at the bright smile and "Have a nice day'' crap. He headed north for no better reason than that traffic seemed lighter in that direction. Still, it was stop-and-go all the way out of the city. Eventually the road opened up and he stepped hard on the gas. The car shot ahead, as if it were as glad to be free of the constraints of neon and concrete as he was.

Gray drove aimlessly for more than an hour, his eyes fixed on the distant mountains bulking up over the straight-as-an-arrow road. There were cars heading into town but only a few heading out and he passed them quickly. After a while, they were just dots in the mirror.

Except for a couple of tractor trailers going in the other direction, he was alone on the road.

It made him feel better. Less constrained, less angry. Funny, he thought as he eased back in the seat and flexed his hands lightly on the wheel. He was a creature of the city, at home and content in New York's concrete and glass canyons, but Vegas made him uncomfortable. Too many lights, too many structures that looked as if they belonged in an amusement park. Too many people, hell-bent on having fun, or pretending to.

Dawn seemed out of place in that setting. It was easier to imagine her on that Arizona mountaintop, the wind in her hair, the sun on her face. There would be no Harman in the picture but there would be a child, a shadowy little boy huddled just behind her...

Gray cursed and goosed the car up to ninety. There was a turnoff ahead and a gas station looking lonely on the intersection of Nowhere and Noplace. He slowed, took the turnoff and found himself on a two-lane dirt road with no traffic and no signs of life. Perfect, he thought.

After a while, he relaxed again.

Somebody had once told him the Nevada desert was depressing as hell. An alien landscape, the guy had called it, but Gray decided he kind of liked it, the open space in all directions, the occasional cluster of cacti huddled together as if for companionship, and the massive piles of boulders that looked as if they'd been dropped from the sky with no plan in mind.

The land was forbidding and barren but it had a hard, powerful quality he admired. For the first time in days, he began to relax.

He'd come here to solve a problem. Instead he'd created a mess.

Gray frowned and tapped his fingers against the steering wheel. What would he tell Jonas? How would he explain his lack of information? He'd scared Dawn off and learned nothing he hadn't known before he got to Vegas.

Who was he kidding? He'd learned more about Dawn than he'd wanted to learn, and none of it would help his uncle reach any kind of decision about whether or not to include her in his will. He knew that she had a softness to her smile and to her soul, that she was more beautiful than any woman had a right to be, that he was having a hard time remembering he was here on Jonas's behalf.

And that she had abandoned her own flesh and blood.

How could he be attracted to someone who had done that? He'd always chosen women with care. He knew men who would bed a woman strictly because of how she looked. He prided himself on asking for more than that. A woman he slept with had to be bright. She had to be kind and giving. Hadn't he broken up with a model he'd been dating because she told him she'd abandoned her cat when she moved into a new apartment that didn't permit pets?

Oh, yeah. He'd dumped a woman who had abandoned her cat and now he was hot for a babe who had abandoned her kid. It made no sense. He wanted Dawn. Hell, yes, he wanted her. Wanted to taste that soft mouth and gently nip that lush bottom lip, to touch that soft skin that looked as if it would have the texture of silk. He wanted to cup her face in his hands, raise it to his, watch her eyes turn to midnight-blue as he lowered his mouth to hers. He wanted to tunnel his hands into that spill of red-gold hair, feel it fall over his hands as he kissed her, to slip his tongue into her mouth until she whispered his name, clung to him, begged for his possession...

Gray shifted in his seat. He was hard as a teenage kid with a copy of *Playboy*. Next thing he knew, he'd be...

What was that?

A car was coming toward him. It was a Ford, an old model, one you didn't see much anymore. It was the same model as the car he'd almost creamed on Las Vegas Boulevard. The same color, too.

He felt an uneasy sense of déjà-vu. How many times in just a few days could a man see a car like that? Gray let up on the gas. The car drew closer and the sense of unease grew stronger. It sure as hell looked like Dawn's car.

Was it a mirage? Another few seconds, he'd be able to see the driver...

It was a woman. Gray stiffened. No. It couldn't be. But it was. He saw the mane of read hair, the pale face...

"Dawn," he whispered, and he put his car into a hard, quick U-turn and hit the horn.

He saw her head jerk up. She was looking into her mirror, trying to see what was happening behind her. He hit the horn again and, even though she couldn't possibly hear him, shouted her name.

She went faster.

Of course she'd go faster. She didn't know who it was, zooming up on her tail, honking the horn like a madman. She wouldn't recognize his car. What were the odds that a woman alone on an empty road would obediently pull over and stop when a car started following her? Would she figure the motorist behind her was trying to tell her something important? Or would she think he wanted to hurt her and try to outrun him?

Gray hit the gas, pulled abreast of the old Ford and tapped the horn.

"Dawn," he shouted, "it's me."

She looked over, saw him and her face turned into a mask of terror. Her car shot away from his. Gray cursed and put his foot to the floor.

They flew down the deserted road at sixty, seventy, eighty miles an hour, Gray slamming his fist on the horn, Dawn pushing the old Ford beyond anything it had been made to endure.

He knew he could get more speed out of his car and he thought about zooming ahead and angling it across the road...

Was he crazy?

Sanity returned in a rush. The way things were going, they'd both end up dead in a heap of twisted metal. He slowed down and fell in behind her. Dawn kept up the speed. He didn't. The last thing he wanted to do was encourage her to go on driving so fast.

The road was straight. He'd have no trouble following her back to Vegas, if that was what it took, though he couldn't imagine her old clunker could keep this up forever.

Her car couldn't keep this up forever.

It was rattling and groaning, and Dawn had given up looking at the speedometer because seeing the needle hovering at eighty had to be an hallucination, but she couldn't slow down, wouldn't slow down. She didn't want to deal with Gray, not out here in the middle of nowhere.

The only good news was that she was on her way back from the Rocking Horse Ranch, not heading to it.

She looked in the mirror. Yes! He'd slowed down and fallen in behind her. She was losing him! Who would have thought it possible? All she had to do now was make it to the gas station on the corner where the road intersected the highway. There would be somebody to help her.

By the time she reached the station, her car was making ominous noises. Dawn shot a look into the mirror. Gray was far behind her. She pulled into the station, threw open the door and ran to the office.

"Help," she yelled, "somebody, please, help..."

She skidded to a stop. There was a hand-lettered sign taped to the glass. A sob broke from her throat as she read it.

Sorry, it said, Closed Sundays.

Sorry? Dawn began to laugh. "Sorry," she said, "they're sorry..."

A car roared into the station. She spun around. It was Gray.

"Dawn," he said, as he stepped onto the asphalt, "listen to me..."

She hesitated, and he thought he had half a chance, but he was wrong.

"No," she whispered, and she took off, racing into the raw, endless expanse of desert that stretched behind the station.

Gray shouted her name again and she ran faster. She was quick but he was quicker and he began to gain ground. He could hear the breath pumping in and out of his lungs.

"Dawn? Dammit, don't run away. I won't hurt you."

His promise didn't slow her down. If anything, it seemed to give her the impetus to speed up until, finally, she began to falter. He pushed harder, got close enough to grab her by the shoulders, and he spun her toward him. She gave a little cry and struck out at him. A couple of blows landed on his jaw, one hard enough to rock him on his heels, but he caught both her wrists in one hand and clamped them against his chest.

"Don't," she sobbed, "please, don't."

Her eyes were wide with fear and shiny with terror. Gray knew he'd never rest until he'd killed the man who had put that terror into her.

"Dawn," he whispered, and then he did what he'd dreamed of doing since the day he'd met her.

He bent his head to hers and kissed her.

CHAPTER TWELVE

She tasted sweeter than he could ever have imagined, and her mouth was even softer than it looked. Honey, he thought, as the blood pounded in his ears, honey and silk…and then he stopped thinking and let himself sink into the kiss.

For a moment, a heartbeat, she let him. At least, that was what he thought, that she'd wrapped her hands around his wrists to lift herself to him, that she'd tilted her head so his mouth could more readily, greedily, angle across hers…and then his brain kicked in instead of his hormones and he realized that the woman he was kissing with such hungry need was fighting for her freedom.

He took his mouth from hers, lifted his head and saw fear shining in her eyes. No. It was much more primal. It was terror, and it turned the hot rush of desire in his blood to ice.

"Dawn," he said, but she was beyond hearing. She was making little sounds that he thought might have been words, digging her fingers into his wrists, gasping for breath as she struggled wildly against him. His first impulse was to take his hands from her face as proof he wouldn't hurt her, but instinct told him she would run the second he let her go. The last thing he wanted to do was go after her again and bring her to earth like a hawk taking down a dove.

"Dawn," he said softly, "baby, I'm not going to hurt you. I swear it."

She shook her head wildly as he slid his hands to her shoulders, held her as steady as he could without using any pressure, until she stopped trying to twist away from him. Slowly her eyes cleared and focused on his. She took a breath that shuddered from her body straight through his hands and as she did, he felt a rage so razor-sharp that he understood, viscerally, what he'd never understood before, despite all his years as a defense attorney.

206

Sometimes the need to kill was so all-consuming that it swept aside everything a man knew of logic and law.

Harman had done this to her. Harman, her husband. He had taken this woman and ripped out her soul.

She was trembling now, breathing in quick, shallow gasps. Gray stroked his hand down her back and she stiffened but he went on doing it, gentling her with his touch and with soft whispers, words he'd have used to comfort a frightened child or an injured animal. He felt the tension start to ease from her muscles. Carefully, slowly, he drew her to him until she stood in the curve of his arm, her body just brushing his.

"Shhh," he said. "Shhh, sweetheart, it's all right. I won't hurt you. Nobody will hurt you, ever again."

A raw, primal sound burst from her throat. She sagged against him and pressed her face to his shoulder. Gray slipped his other arm around her, let out a breath he hadn't known he'd been holding and buried his face in her hair as he held her in the light cradle of his arms. She shuddered, her breathing grew even, and he knew the storm was over.

"I'm sorry," he murmured. "Dawn, I'm so sorry."

She nodded. He could hear the sound of her swallowing. She put her hands against his chest and drew back. He didn't want to let her go. He wanted to keep holding her, comforting her, but he knew that would be a mistake so he gave her some room, let go of her so she would see that he wasn't a vicious bastard out to inflict pain.

No, he was just a hungry-for-her bastard, already wanting her in his arms again. Any other time, he would have laughed at the self-deprecating truth but right now laughter would have stuck in his throat. Instead he put a knuckle under her chin and lifted her head so her eyes met his.

"All right now?"

She nodded against his finger. Tears still glittered on her face and without thinking, he brushed his thumb gently over them. She jerked back.

"I'm sorry," he said gently. "I never meant to hurt you. I only—"

"I don't like to be touched."

She said it with an iciness that was all the more meaningful, coming as it did from such a delicate-looking woman.

"I understand."

"No." Her voice trembled, but she didn't. "You don't."

Like hell, he didn't. He almost told her that he did, that he'd met her husband, but then she would surely turn and run. Besides, why would he admit he knew Harman? Then he'd have to tell her the rest of it, either that inane story about a music box or the blunt truth, that she might be in line for a fat inheritance. He wanted her but that didn't mean he trusted her fully. Not yet. So he nodded in acceptance while she went on looking at him, her face pale, her eyes glittering with resolve .

"Yeah. Well, as I said, I'm sorry. What happened was…" He left the apology hanging in midair, cleared his throat and searched for something ordinary to say. 'So, I guess the gas station's closed, huh?"

That wasn't just ordinary, it was absurd. But it was safe. Apparently she thought so, too, because she grabbed it like a lifeline.

"Yes."

She turned away and walked toward the station and her car. He suspected she wasn't looking at it any more clearly than he was, but that was okay with him. They both needed time to pull themselves together. Need for her still burned inside him. He'd wanted women before but not like this—and how could he want her at all, considering what he knew?

"The car just quit," she said. "I don't know what's wrong with it." She put her hand on the hood as if the answer to the question might rise up under the warmth of her palm.

"Well, let's take a look." He forced a smile. "Maybe I'll see something under the hood that means something this time. You want to get inside and release the latch?"

She did, and he peered into the engine like a soothsayer reading chicken entrails. After a couple of seconds, he shook his head.

"Nothing seems out of place or broken."

"I don't suppose you have your cell phone with you…?"

He didn't. He could almost see the damned thing lying on the sofa in his suite, right where he'd left it, but he slapped his pockets just to make sure.

"No such luck. How about I get behind the wheel and try the engine?"

She nodded and stepped out of the car. He got in and turned the key. The engine stuttered, coughed and died.

"Come on," he muttered, "catch." But it wouldn't, and as soon as he checked the gauges on the dashboard, he knew the reason. "Well," he said, sitting back and slapping the heels of his hands against the wheel, "I know the problem."

"The ballast resistor thing? That's what it was the other day."

He shook his head. "Nothing so complicated. You're out of gas."

"What?" Dawn leaned past him and stuck her head in the window. Her hair brushed his cheek. It smelled of sun and of the desert, and he closed his eyes as he inhaled the scent. "That's impossible! I filled up—I filled up—"

Today, she'd almost said. But it hadn't been today. It hadn't even been yesterday. She'd filled the tank just before her world started to come apart, the day she'd had drinks with Gray and he'd asked that terrifying question about her liking children.

Of course she was out of gas. She'd been back and forth to Rocking Horse Ranch since then; she'd gone straight there from the Oasis bar. She'd phoned first, to make sure Tommy was okay. Mrs. Wilton assured her that he was but she'd driven there faster than she ever had before because she needed to see for herself. He was asleep when she arrived and she didn't wake him. Instead she made up a story about a custody fight to explain her presence to Mrs. Wilton, who nodded and sighed as if she heard such things all the time.

"From now on, no one's to be allowed to see Tommy except me," she'd said, and Mrs. Wilton had nodded again and said she understood.

Everybody understood, or thought they did, but how could they when they didn't know Harman, or what he was capable of? If he found her, there would never be a legal fight over

Tommy. Harman would just take him, and if he had to beat her to death in the process, he'd do it.

Dawn had thought about that while she drove a couple of miles down the road, to a motel that reminded her of the one in Queen City. In the morning, she bought a pair of stiff blue jeans, a white sweatshirt and a pair of too-large sneakers at the little general store nearby. Then she'd gone back to the ranch and when Tommy came into the dining room for breakfast, she'd swept him into her arms and kissed him until he squirmed and whispered that all the other guys were watching and would she please put him down?

"Sorry," she'd said abashedly.

"How come you're visiting during the day in the middle of the week, Mom?"

It was the first time he'd called her Mom, not Mama, and something inside her chest had constricted. Her baby was growing up, and he'd be harder to protect than ever.

She said she'd wanted to surprise him, and he grinned and gave her a quick hug before he sat down with his pals and forgot all about her.

"Will you be leaving now, Ms. Carter?" Mrs. Wilton had asked politely.

Dawn had taken her aside, embroidered the custody story just a little and said she'd hang around, if that was all right. Mrs. Wilton had agreed, but reluctantly. At night, she'd returned to the motel, phoned Cassie and asked her to say she'd come down with a virus if anyone asked about her. Then she sat in the middle of the sagging bed and gnawed on a fingernail while she tried to figure out what to do next. It was tempting to take Tommy and run but she knew what that would do to him. He'd made friends here. It was the first place they'd lived in long enough for that to happen.

Maybe she'd overreacted. Gray hadn't actually said he knew she had a child. His comment had been muddled; actually, she couldn't recall it with any clarity except to know it had suggested she didn't like children. Or had it? For the last four years, she'd lived in dread. She knew, from experience, that there had been times one word had triggered unnecessary

panic. She'd fled Santa Fe because a man had shown up at
the diner three evenings in a row and turned down tables she
didn't serve. She'd run, then, in the middle of the night, and
only realized months later that the guy had probably just been
working up his nerve to ask her out.

By the time morning came around, she'd felt calm again.
She'd driven back to the ranch, tried not to notice how Mrs.
Wilton's eyebrows had lifted at the sight of her, kissed Tommy
goodbye and set out for Las Vegas. It was a long trip, first on
a two-lane dirt road, then on the highway that led home. She
was tired; her eyes felt heavy, and she'd decided to keep herself alert by thinking about Gray.

Yes, she'd definitely overreacted. If there was one thing she
was convinced of, it was that Gray and Harman had nothing
to do with each other. They might as well have come from
different planets. Different galaxies, she'd thought, remembering the first part of the evening she'd spent with Gray, how
nice it had been to see his face light up when he saw her. And
that teddy bear. What a nice thing to have given her. She'd
smiled at the memory…and that was when a car behind her
began honking its horn. What did the driver want? He'd been
right on her tail, which had scared her…and then he'd pulled
alongside, and she saw that the driver was Gray.

All the assurances she'd just fed herself evaporated like a
desert mirage. Life had taught her there was no such thing as
coincidence. She'd been almost blind with terror, especially
when she fled him on foot and he caught her and spun her
around…and then she'd looked into his eyes and what she
saw had nothing to do with knowledge of Tommy and everything to do with the private hell she'd escaped four long years
ago.

Terror had closed over her like a giant wave, choking her,
drowning her…

"Dawn?"

She blinked, forced herself back from the edge of that terrible chasm. Gray was trying to open the door and get out of
her car. She stepped back and gave him room.

"Come on. I'll take you to the nearest—"

"Why did you follow me?" The words spilled from her lips. She wanted to call them back, but it was too late.

"I didn't."

"Of course you did. Do you think I'm stupid?"

"I think," he said gently, "you have a very active imagination."

"How did you end up on this road, right behind my car? You followed me, and I want to know the reason."

"How could I have followed you? You're heading for Vegas. I was heading away from it."

"Oh," she said. She caught her bottom lip between her teeth in a gesture that was becoming increasingly familiar to him. "Oh…"

"Yeah." He grinned. "Well, that's okay. I get a lot of that."

"A lot of what?" she said. A delicate furrow appeared between her eyebrows.

"Of women saying I followed them when the both of us know, with all due modesty, that it's they who followed me."

Dawn stood up straight. "I did not follow…" She saw him grin again. "You're teasing me."

"Uh-huh."

She drew a deep breath, then let it out slowly between her slightly parted lips. A loose tendril of hair lifted on her forehead.

"I guess I owe you an apology."

"You do, indeed."

"I thought… I don't know how to explain…"

"You don't have to," he said gruffly. "And, while we're at it, I'm sorry I scared you."

She nodded. The day was warm, but he saw a little shudder go through her and she crossed her arms and clasped her own shoulders.

"The breeze," she said, by way of explanation.

"Sure." He cleared his throat. "Well. Let's go find us a gas station that's open."

He walked her to his car and opened the door. She hesitated before she got inside. I'm not the reincarnation of Count Dracula, he wanted to say—but he might as well have been. He was a liar and a cheat, and the need to come clean with her burned like a flame in his belly.

"Seat belt," he said with a quick smile.

She put it on. He started the car, thought about the endless miles of nothing he'd passed and looked at her.

"What's behind us?"

"Behind us?" she said stupidly.

"Yes. Back where you came from."

"Another ten miles of dirt road, a little general store with a gas pump…and a sign that said Rocking Horse Ranch And Boarding School Five Miles Ahead…"

The lie came easily. "Not much. A couple of side roads that don't lead anywhere."

"Well, where were you coming from? A town?"

"A wildlife preserve." That, at least, was true. There was one, about forty miles from the ranch. She'd taken Tommy there several times. "No gas stations, if that's what you're asking."

Gray nodded and pulled onto the road. "In that case, we might as well head back to Vegas. I seem to remember passing some kind of blur in the road about an hour back."

She looked at him and smiled. "A blur in the road?"

"Yeah." He grinned. "You know, what passes for civilization in the middle of nowhere. A sign that says Home Cooking, another that guarantees you the biggest, nastiest looking rattlesnake heads…"

"Yuck."

"And maybe a gas station." He looked at her, a little smile on his lips. "You have something against home cooking? Wait. Let me guess. You don't like rattler heads."

"I just think they belong attached to rattler bodies, that's all."

"Wow."

Dawn shifted in the seat so she could turn toward him. "Wow, what?"

"Wow, a lady who likes snakes. Never thought I'd get to see such a creature."

She laughed. "I didn't say I liked them. Actually I don't like them or dislike them. It's just that there's something, you know, kind of barbaric about killing them just so you can mummify their heads. Or whatever it is people do to get them to look like that. Do you know what I mean?"

"To tell the truth, I never thought about it but—yeah. You're right. It does seem wrong…unless, of course, you eat the rest of the snake."

Her eyes widened. "Eat it?"

He grinned at the way her voice skidded up the scale. "Uh-huh. Cross my heart. Don't look at me that way. It's considered a delicacy."

"Rattlesnake," she said flatly. "A delicacy."

"There's this terrific restaurant in Boston…" Gray looked at her. "Tastes just like chicken," he said, his mouth twitching as he tried not to laugh.

"That's what they said in Phoenix, at a place that served armadillo."

It was the most, hell, it was the only thing she'd ever told him about herself without being asked. He didn't know what to say. Anything he could think of would probably close her down and he didn't want to do that. He needed to learn more about her, didn't he? For Jonas?

"Armadillo." He arched an eyebrow. "Did you ever taste it?"

"No." Dawn shuddered. "And I'll bet that you never tasted rattlesnake."

"You'd lose."

"No. You didn't. Rattlesnake?"

"Yup." He goosed the gas pedal just a little, torn between wanting to make the drive last and wanting what was the best of two worlds, a car speeding along an empty road with a beautiful woman beside him. "It was sort of a rite of passage."

"Were you in college?" Dawn eyed him suspiciously. "Was this one of those fraternity things you read about? You know, where some idiot drinks a gallon of beer and thinks he's a man?"

"My God," Gray said innocently, "are you telling me there are universities where... No. I don't believe it. Why would eighteen-year-old kids do such things?" He looked at her and laughed. "Actually, I was only about ten when I munched on roasted rattler."

"You mean, rattlesnake is one of the basic food groups in Texas?"

"Now you're hurting my feelings." He eased back on the gas. "Nah. Only if you've got a pack of crazy cousins like mine. We hung around together a lot when we were kids." His smile tilted as he thought back to those days with three of Jonas's sons—Travis, Slade and Gage. Those memories were pretty much the only good ones he had of growing up in Texas. "They had this club. I'd always wanted to be a member, but—"

"Why weren't you?"

"They were brothers," he said, as if that explained everything.

"Huh."

The "huh" held a world of meaning. He glanced at Dawn. She'd folded her arms, lifted her chin and her eyes held a glint of irritation, as if she were angry at three people she'd never met for what they'd done to him. It made him want to pull the car over, take her in his arms and kiss her again.

Jesus, he thought, and shifted uneasily in his seat.

"And I wasn't there. On their ranch. Neither were they, most of the time. We were all away in boarding school..."

Gray frowned and cleared his throat. Great. Another few minutes, he'd be telling her all about his life, and Jonas, and a fortune she just might collect.

"Anyway, it was summertime, so we were all back home. We got together one afternoon and Travis, I think it was, found a dead rattler in one of the paddocks." He sent his mind back through the years, tugged a thread of memory loose, focused on it as it began to unravel. "It was sort of trampled."

"Double yuck."

"Exactly. Well, we looked at it, poked at it, picked it up

with a stick, and Travis said Indians used to eat snakes, and one thing led to another, and—''

''And,'' Dawn said, with a little smile, ''it tasted just like chicken.''

''It tasted like an old boot that had maybe kicked a chicken once, but mostly it tasted like it had spent too much time in a horse paddock.'' He chuckled. ''But we were only kids.''

''I know. Little boys can be such characters...''

The words seemed to float in the air. Gray looked at her. She was staring straight ahead, hands folded in her lap, a wistful quality to her smile. A little while ago, she'd shown compassion for the child he'd been more than twenty years ago. How could she care about a stranger and not her own child? Was she thinking about her own son now? Questions buzzed inside his head like bees around a hive. The more he saw of Dawn Carter, the less he understood. It made him uneasy. More than that. It made him angry. Maybe it was time to confront her, and to hell with being subtle...

''Look!''

He followed her pointing finger. The place he'd remembered was just ahead, a tin-roofed clutch of falling-down buildings set on a sprawl of gravel. The tires crunched as Gray pulled up to the gas pump and killed the engine.

''Okay. Now all we have to do is hope they have a gas can somewhere and we're in business.''

They did. A kid with a baseball cap pulled over his eyes filled Gray's car, then filled a dented red gas can.

''Forty bucks,'' the kid said when the tank was full.

Gray looked at the pump. It said he owed twenty-six dollars. The kid grinned. ''That's life, mister.''

Gray handed him two twenties and was glad Dawn had wandered off in search of what she'd referred to as a rest room. He doubted anybody would want to rest within a mile of this magnificent oasis. He also doubted she'd let him pay for the can and the three gallons of gas it held, and he was right.

''How much do I owe you?'' she said, when she found him behind the wheel.

"Nothing."

"Thank you, but I'd prefer to pay for the gas myself."

He shrugged "Okay."

"Great. So, how much do—"

"Dinner."

"I beg your pardon?"

"You owe me that meal we never got to eat." He made a show of checking his mirror and the road, as if the arrow of blacktop was about to turn into the Indianapolis Speedway.

"That's out of the question."

"You're right," he said, trying to sound every bit as coolly polite as she did. "You don't owe me dinner. I didn't mean to make it sound as if you did. What you owe me is the pleasure of your company at dinner."

"No!" She swung toward him, her forehead wrinkled in consternation. "Mr. Baron—"

"Don't tell me we're going back to that."

"Gray." She took a deep breath. He was learning things about her. That deep breath meant she was readying a logical, reasonable, perfectly sane explanation for why she wouldn't have dinner with him. "Look, Gray—"

"It's a debt of honor."

"I know it is." She opened her purse, pulled out a wallet. "And if you'll just tell me how much—"

"I don't know how much." He looked at her, then back at the road. "What's it cost, do you think, to have your own private Triple A?"

"Your what?"

"Your private Automobile Association of America. A hundred bucks a year? A thousand? Take a guess."

"That's not fair."

"Nope," he said cheerfully, "it isn't. But you have to admit, there's something unusual about the same guy rescuing the same damsel in distress three separate times."

"Twice," she said quickly.

"Thrice," he said, just as quickly. Did she smile? He thought she might have, but it came and went in a flash.

"Two times. On Las Vegas Boulevard. And then today."

"Right. And now I'm driving all the way back to where your car conked out. What do you figure? Seventy miles, round trip?"

He could feel her glaring at him. Then she slouched in her seat, looked straight ahead and folded her arms, and he knew he'd won.

"Home Cooking."

"Huh?"

"I'll have dinner with you, and that's what you'll get. Home Cooking."

It was more than he'd hoped for. Dinner, at her apartment. He told himself it would give him insights into her he'd never get elsewhere, because it couldn't be the idea of being alone with her that was making his blood sing.

"Well. That's very nice of you. I didn't expect you to go to all that trouble."

She turned her head and looked at him, and he knew, as soon as he saw her face, that he hadn't won at all.

"It's no trouble," Dawn said sweetly. "Home Cooking. That charming little restaurant where we just got that gas." She gave him a blinding smile. "I just hope neither of us comes down with ptomaine."

He was, at the very least, a persistent and determined man.

Dawn pulled onto the highway with Gray's car right behind her.

Persistent, determined, better-looking than any man had the right to be—and he was crowding her. Another woman would probably love all the attention. Not her. There was no room in her life for a man, not even for one who would only be in Vegas for a few days.

She glanced into the mirror again. He was still there, following along at a safe distance and that was probably the only "safe" thing about him. He wanted dinner, but she knew that wouldn't be all. He'd want more. Expect more. And she had nothing to give. He could be as charming, as handsome as he liked but she wasn't going to sleep with him, and wasn't that a hell of a stupid way to describe what happened between a man and a woman in bed?

She took a breath.

Okay. Maybe she was jumping ahead. Maybe she was reading things wrong. Maybe he'd be satisfied with dinner, though she doubted it. Still, she'd made a decision four years ago. She wasn't going to let anybody get close. Well, Cassie, yes, but Cassie was a woman. She had her own secrets and they knew enough not to poke at each other's pasts the way Gray and his cousins must have poked at that dead snake.

Dawn smiled.

She could almost see him as a little kid, dirty-faced, wearing jeans with holes in the knees, screwing up his courage to take a bite out of the snake. Tommy would probably do stuff like that, too, when he was older. When she'd saved enough to buy a little house somewhere, on a patch of land big enough for him to have a dog although she knew what he'd really want was a horse. Gray would know how to ride, coming from Texas the way he did. She could almost see her little boy, up on the back of a pony, Gray on a big horse, riding alongside him…

A horn bleated behind her. She jumped, glanced in the mirror and saw Gray pointing toward a blur up ahead. There it was. The dilapidated diner, the gas pump, the souvenir stand.

All she had to do was return the can and keep going. Or hang on to the can, to make it easier. She could hit the pedal and drive on, and what could Gray do about it? Nothing, except finally realize that she wasn't interested in him or in playing the games men and women played. But she'd agreed this was a debt of honor. Dawn let out a sigh, turned into the gravel lot and parked. He pulled up alongside.

"You're sure you want to eat at this place?" Gray asked, as they got out of their cars and walked toward the restaurant.

"It's just dinner. Not gourmet…" She stopped and stared at the smudged window of the shack. Big black spots were moving purposefully across the surface. "Ants," Dawn said. "And they're inside, not outside."

"No extra charge," he said lightly, and smiled at her.

She could leave now. She'd done what she'd promised, gone with him, and whose fault was it that they obviously weren't going to be able to have dinner here? She didn't owe him anything, not really, and the truth was that she knew he didn't really think it, either. But... Dawn's heart edged into her throat. But, she didn't want to leave him. She wanted to be with him a little while longer. All the things she knew about men, about what they wanted, about what was safe and what was dangerous, weren't enough to hide the truth clamoring within her, that she'd felt more alive since meeting this man than she had in the last four years.

"Dawn?"

Their eyes met. He was giving her the choice, and she took her courage in her hands and made it.

"There's a little café near town... If you like Mexican food."

"Hey." He raised his hands, held them palms out. "I'm from Texas, remember?"

They both smiled, and then they got back into their cars. He followed her again, just another twenty miles or so. She tried not to think about what she was doing because it was crazy. Crazy, and wrong...except she couldn't come up with reasons why it was either. She wasn't compromising Tommy's safety. She wasn't promising a stranger anything more than dinner. How could what she was doing be dangerous?

She signaled a turn, looked in the mirror and saw him wave his hand. They pulled into the parking lot of a small restaurant that she and Cassie had discovered. It served the best fajitas in Las Vegas.

The hostess, a small woman with a big smile, led them to the patio. It was dusk, and the tables were lighted with fat candles stuck into a variety of small earthenware bowls; white fairy lights glinted in wooden latticework overhead.

Dawn hesitated. "Maybe we should eat inside," she said, and looked up at him.

He knew what she was thinking, that this was a meal not a date, that they didn't belong out here in this romantic setting. He decided not to crowd her.

"Whatever you prefer. I like it here. It's relaxed and pretty, but if you'd rather go in…"

"There are no tables available inside, *señorita*. If you don't mind waiting ten, perhaps twenty minutes…?"

The breeze blew a strand of hair into Dawn's eyes. She shoved it back. The choice wasn't hers, it was fate's, she thought, though she'd never believed in fate before.

"No, it's foolish to wait. This is fine."

Gray pulled out her chair. His hand brushed hers. It was accidental, but nothing could have prepared him for the electric tingle that shot from her fingers to his. She pulled away as if he'd burned her. Was she feeling the same kind of fear as when he kissed her, or was it different this time? He wanted it to be different, more than he could recall having wanted anything in a very long time.

The realization caught him off balance. He looked at Dawn, saw the same surprise mirrored in her eyes.

A waitress appeared beside the table and introduced herself with the kind of senseless good cheer that usually made Gray long for the days when nobody gave a damn if you knew what their name was. Now, he embraced the intrusion and when she handed him a wine list, he gave it far more attention that it deserved before asking for a California Chardonnay.

"Is that okay with you?"

Dawn said it was. Then she buried her face in the menu. He did, too. Something crazy was happening. He didn't know this woman. What little he did know was disturbing. What was he doing, sitting across from her, feeling as awkward as a kid on his first date?

"Well," he said, and almost winced. He sounded more jovial than the waitress. "Tell me about the weather here. Is it always so hot?"

Brilliant. Just brilliant. Now they'd talk about the weather, and then maybe the food, and after a while he'd catch her checking her watch and he'd do the same thing, and he'd wonder, later on tonight, why in hell he'd imagined wanting to be with her…

Except, it didn't work out that way.

They began with weather but quickly, easily, moved on to other things. Books. Movies. The impossibility of tourists squeezed into polyester bermudas, Hawaiian shirts, black socks and shoes. Dawn was easy to talk to. She had a nice sense of humor, and, after a while, an easy smile. They talked about the casinos, and gambling, and he felt something inside him soften when she explained, earnestly, how she'd once been a dealer and how she'd never felt comfortable about it because so many people didn't seem to know when to stop.

"I'd look at them and I'd think, will you be able to pay the rent next month? And, of course, that really wasn't my business."

"But you felt it should be," he said, and she smiled as if he were brilliant and said yes, that was it, exactly.

"I had the same feeling when I dealt at the high stakes tables, and I knew that was silly because only high rollers—heavy gamblers—play there, and they know, going in, that there's a big risk." She sighed, scooped some guacamole onto a corn chip and looked at him. "Raising the stakes is always a mistake."

"Is it?" Gray said quietly.

She could feel her skin heating under his steady gaze. She wanted to look away from him but she couldn't.

"Dawn," he said with sudden urgency, "I have to tell you—"

"Here we are," the waitress said, and the moment was lost.

The evening moved on. They drank a little of the wine, ate a little of the chimichangas and fajitas and the hot, spicy sauces and cool salads. A guitarist came to stand beside their table and serenade them with music that was full of *"mi corazons"* and unabashedly schmaltzy…and, somehow, just right.

It was late by the time they rose from the table. Without thinking about it, Gray took Dawn's hand. They strolled out to the parking lot, which was quiet and almost empty, and he knew he didn't want the evening to be over. Not yet.

"Will you be okay, driving home alone?"

She smiled. "I'll be fine."

"I'll follow you."

"No. No, really. I drive home a lot later than this, from the hotel."

Gray nodded. She didn't want him going with her. Okay. He wouldn't push.

"Tomorrow, then."

She hesitated. "Gray. I don't—"

He didn't stop to think. He took her face in his hands, lifted it and brushed his lips lightly over hers. She stiffened and drew back but before he could apologize, she made a little sound, moved closer and pressed her mouth to his in a closemouthed, innocent kiss that left him feeling as if the earth had just swung out from under his feet.

"Dawn," he whispered. He clasped her wrists, took a step back because God only knew what might happen if she felt what that sweet kiss had done to him. He wanted to tell her everything, why he'd come here, what Jonas wanted, but he couldn't. Net yet. She'd only just begun to trust him. If he told her he'd come to Vegas to meet her, that might frighten her off. "It's late," he said softly.

She nodded. "I know."

"Meet me for breakfast, at that little coffee place in the hotel?"

Her lashes swept down and hid her eyes, but he saw her teeth gently sink into her lip in that now-familiar action he felt right down to his toes.

"I shouldn't..." She looked up and smiled. "Yes."

"Seven o'clock?"

"Six-thirty. I start work at seven."

"Fine." He smiled, stroked her hair away from her temples. He kissed her again, gently, tilting her chin up with his finger, and almost went to his knees when he felt her mouth move delicately against his. "Dawn. I don't know your phone number or your address."

He did. Both were in Ballard's report. All he had to do was open the file and look, but he couldn't let her know that any more than he wanted to open the file Jack had given him and be reminded that he'd lied to her from the minute they met.

She hesitated. He sensed that she didn't give that information to many people, and if she gave it now it would mean as much, maybe more, than that she'd kissed him back.

"Nine sixteen East Orchard Road," she said softly. "Five five five, one two seven nine."

He wanted to kiss her again but he wasn't sure he'd be able to stop himself from wanting to taste more of her. Instead he repeated what she'd told him and turned her gently toward her car.

He stood watching after her until all he could see of the car was the faint glow of its taillights winking against the darkness. Then he exhaled heavily and looked up at the night sky.

He'd come to Las Vegas to learn things and he had. He'd learned all he needed tonight.

He knew that he wanted to make love to Dawn Kitteridge and show her what being in a man's arms—in his arms—could be like.

His jaw clenched.

And he knew that Harman had lied. Whatever had happened on that Arizona mountaintop, Dawn would never have walked away and left her child behind.

CHAPTER THIRTEEN

GRAY got to the coffee shop at twenty after six. Dawn wasn't there yet so he fed the machine some coins, bought a cup of coffee and settled in to wait.

He didn't mind waiting. It gave him time to think about last night, how she'd returned that last kiss with an innocence that hinted at the passion locked within her. He could see it in her eyes, in her smile; he felt it whenever he touched her, whenever he caught her glancing at him from under the sweep of her lashes. Behind the fear, beneath the cool exterior, a woman waited to be set free. And he wanted to be the man to do it. His senses were filled with Dawn's scent, with her taste, with the low, lovely sound of her voice.

He'd never felt such intense need for a woman as he felt for her.

Last night, he'd made a couple of phone calls, then tried to sleep. After an hour of tossing and turning, the bed was a tangled mess. He got up, showered, put on jeans and a T-shirt and went down to the casino. He'd wandered around aimlessly, watching the crowd gathered around a roulette table where a middle-aged guy with horn-rimmed glasses was raking in the chips and trembling with excitement. He'd even fed a few bucks into a slot machine that promised a two million dollar payoff and after a few desultory pulls at the handle—not necessary, he knew, but at least it gave him something to do besides stare at the apples and oranges on the screen—the machine had suddenly belted out a series of electronic whoops and trills and regurgitated what looked like a ton of half dollars.

"You won!" the woman playing the next machine shrieked.

He had, to the tune of four hundred bucks. And he had to admit, just for a couple of minutes, he'd felt a rush of adrenaline. The lady on the adjacent stool leaned in, all but lay her boobs on his arm and asked him if he'd like to celebrate. Gray took his first real look at her. She was pretty. More than that. She was what any man in his right mind would have called hot, and her smile made it clear she was his for the asking.

He hadn't asked. Instead he'd thought about a woman with a hesitant smile and a mouth as soft as silk.

"Sorry," he'd said, with what was almost genuine regret. "I appreciate the offer but I've had a long day." Then he'd nodded at the tray that held his winnings. "You celebrate for me," he'd said, and walked out, headed back to his room and what remained of the night. He'd spent it dreaming about Dawn and how it would be to awaken her to desire.

Just thinking about seeing her this morning had made it easy to get up after only a few hours' sleep. He'd even found himself singing while he showered, something he hadn't done since his college roommate had threatened to drown him if he ever sang another note.

Now it was six forty-five and he was still sitting here by himself, waiting for a woman he was beginning to suspect wasn't going to show.

At five past seven, Gray dumped what remained of his cold coffee in the trash and headed for the telephone bank. Maybe she'd overslept. Maybe she was sick. Maybe he shouldn't have let her drive home alone.

He dialed her home number. The phone rang six times before a mechanical voice informed him that no one was available to take his call.

At the tone, leave…

Gray slammed down the phone. A robot's voice had more warmth.

Calm down, he told himself. Calm down, there's probably a simple explanation…and there was. He turned his back to the telephone and saw Dawn standing near one of the shops, looking cool and polite and pleasant as she made conversation with a guy wearing a robe. She had a pad and pencil in her hand. She'd started her work day. Gray could feel his blood pressure soar. She glanced at him as he walked toward her and though she paled a little, she didn't flinch.

The man took her hand and kissed it. "Thank you for all your help, Miss Carter."

"My pleasure, Prince Ahmat."

Gray waited until the prince strolled off. Then he spoke softly and, he hoped, carefully.

"Did you get here late?"

Dawn shook her head.

"Was there some monumental problem with that gentleman, something you had to deal with or your job would have been in jeopardy?"

"No."

She spoke softly. He read the word on her lips more than heard it.

His control was slipping. Hell, it was racing away. She was looking at him as if he were a stranger and last night had never happened.

"You're not home sick. You're not an oil spot on the road. I mean, that's what I figured. That you were doubled over with some bug you picked up at dinner, or that I'd been an idiot to let you drive home alone..." He stopped, dragged in a breath and told himself to take it easy. "Where were you this morning? Did you forget you were meeting me?"

"I didn't forget." She folded her arms, though it looked more like she was wrapping them around herself. "And I apologize. I should have phoned, I know."

"You know." Gray's mouth thinned. "What is it with you? Do you get a kick out of letting men think you're interested and then standing them up?"

Her spine stiffened. "You have no right to say that."

"I have every right. This is twice you've done this, lady. How many chances does a guy usually give you to make an ass out of him?"

Anger flashed in her eyes. "I don't have to listen to this."

He caught hold of her arm. "Yes, you do."

"Gray." She sank her teeth into her bottom lip and spoke quietly. "Please, don't make a scene."

"Yeah. I'll bet that's what you count on." He let go of her and dug both hands into the pockets of his chinos. "You give a man that 'don't hurt me' look and you figure he'll just walk away with his tail between his legs."

It was a cruel thing to say, knowing what he did about her husband. He hated himself for it as soon as the words were out of his mouth but it was too late to call them back and besides, when had she given a damn about him? He stood his ground, teeth clenched, as she started to walk away and then he cursed, went after her and stepped out in her path. She tried to dodge around him but he wouldn't let her.

"Okay. Maybe that was pushing it, but—"

"It doesn't matter."

"Dammit, it *does* matter. Look, I'm sorry I said that, okay?"

Instead of trying to move past him, she stood still and put her hand on his arm. "People are watching," she said, and somehow it only made him angry, that the very first time she'd touched him it was in defense.

"Let them," he said gruffly. "I don't care."

"But I do. My job…" She drew a ragged breath. "Look. I owe you an apology."

Just that quickly, he felt his temper dissipate. He smiled, moved closer to her. "No. I owe you one. If you couldn't meet me—"

"Not about that. I mean, I should apologize for not telling you, to your face, that I was calling things off." She licked her lips nervously. "I can't see you anymore, Gray. That's why I didn't keep our date this morning."

"Can't? Or won't?"

"It's the same thing." She took her hand from his arm and stepped back. "And I'm working, so—"

"Dawn." He snatched her wrist as she began turning away. "What the hell's going on here? One minute you want to be with me. The next, you don't. "

"Nothing's going on." Her eyes flew to his. "I should have told you last night. I don't want to see you ag—"

"Miss Carter? Is there a problem?"

Gray swung around. A face-off with Keir O'Connell was the last thing he wanted right now, but it wasn't Keir who had come up behind him, it was a man in a dark suit with salt and pepper hair, a ruddy face and a smile that didn't come close to concealing the threat in his blue eyes.

"Mr. Coyle." Dawn breathed the name as if it were a prayer. "No. No problem. This gentleman—Mr. Baron—was just—he was just asking me some questions about the hotel."

"Mr. Baron." Dan nodded. "I'm Dan Coyle. Head of security at the Desert Song. Perhaps I can assist you."

"I don't need assistance," Gray said brusquely. "I was just on my way out."

"Ah." Coyle smiled, though his gaze remained icy. "In that case, sir, I won't keep you…but please remember that I'm always ready to offer whatever aid you might need."

Gray smiled thinly. The message was clear. He'd been warned to watch his step.

"I'll keep that in mind, Coyle, but it's not necessary. I assure you, I've had enough of this place and its people."

"I'm sorry to hear it," Dan said politely.

He watched as Baron stalked to the door. Then he looked at Dawn. He couldn't read the expression on her face. Was she angry? Frightened? Distraught? Whatever she was, the Baron man had put that look there, and Dan didn't like it.

"Dawn? Is everything all right?" he said softly.

He thought he'd never seen anything that took more effort than the smile she flashed at him.

"Yes. Everything is fine. Thank you for—well, thank you."

"Listen to me, girl. If you need me, you call me. Not just here," he added gruffly, before she could answer. "Anywhere. If you run into somebody who causes you grief, you call me and I'll be there before you can blink. Okay?"

Dawn said that she would. Dan didn't believe her but he smiled, gave her shoulder a fatherly pat and waited until she'd gone to her office. Then he picked up the house phone and dialed Keir's private office.

"Coyle here." He spoke softly, cupping the phone, his back to the lobby. "Keir, I need to see you. I think something's brewing with Baron and the lady. No, I don't know what it is but I'm going to tell Snyder to keep an eye on her." Dan dropped his voice even lower. "And I have some information... Yes. Fine. I'll be there in five minutes."

Dan hung up the phone. He hadn't wanted to believe that Baron had any connection to Dawn's past. It didn't seem possible that such a man would even know a scumbag like her husband but he'd put out feelers for more information and just this morning, he'd learned something that made no sense.

Gray Baron had flown to Queen City right before he'd turned up in Las Vegas. That had to mean he'd met with Harman Kitteridge. Why? He'd been turning the question over in his mind when he spotted Baron and Dawn. The anger in the man's face and the fear in hers had been as visible as the sign that blinked outside the hotel.

Dan rolled his thumb over his pursed lips. Should he tell Dawn what he'd learned? No. Why frighten her until he had some answers? From now on, he or his man would be watching her.

Slowly he walked to the front door of the hotel. Baron was just getting into a cab. It was probably too much to hope he was heading for the airport, and out of Dawn's life.

"The airport," Gray said, as the taxi pulled away from the hotel.

The cab's air conditioner was making noise but it didn't seem to be working. That was fine. The blast of hot desert air was a welcome jolt of reality. To hell with Dawn Kitteridge or Dawn Carter or whatever she called herself, and to hell with Jonas and the guilt trip he'd laid on him.

Enough was enough. There was only one way to end this, and no reason to put it off.

He was ticked off, maybe more than he had a right to be. He calmed down enough to know that as he walked into the terminal at McLarran. The truth was that Dawn didn't owe him anything, not even the courtesy of a "Sorry, I've changed my mind," phone call. He'd figured on leaving Vegas in a couple of days. What had just happened simply speeded his departure. As for his uncle...if Jonas wanted a snoop, let him hire one because he was finished playing detective. *Auf Wie-*

dersehen, adios, au revoir. If the old man didn't like it, he could bribe, browbeat or cajole somebody else.

Last night, he'd decided to fly to Espada to tell his uncle exactly that. Of course, his motives had been a little different at two in the morning. After that evening spent with Dawn, after those soft kisses, he'd decided he didn't want to go on with the deception. If he was going to get involved with her, he wasn't going to be Jonas's pawn...

Which only proved how unreliable middle-of-the-night thoughts could be.

Involved? Gray snorted as he got on the end of a Southwest ticket line. A fancy word for what he'd wanted. A few more days in Vegas, a week, maybe, a little time spent in introducing Dawn to the pleasures of sex, was all the "involvement" he'd intended. Well, that was over. He was leaving Vegas ASAP. He'd have headed back to his room and packed after the confrontation with Coyle but he'd be damned if he'd let it look as if the interfering old son of a bitch had run him off.

So he'd fly to Austin first, tell Jonas what little he knew. How much information did his uncle need before he decided whether or not to put the granddaughter of a long-dead friend in his will? Either he'd be satisfied or he wouldn't. Gray didn't give a damn anymore.

This whole quest, whatever you wanted to call it, had been crazy from the start, not just Jonas's desire to right a wrong but his role in it. He'd met a woman a couple of days ago and she'd turned his life inside out. He'd never let a woman have that kind of effect on him and now he knew why. Giving a woman such power was a hell of an uncomfortable feeling. A little while ago, he'd been torn between wanting to grab Dawn by the shoulders and shaking her, or hauling her into his arms and kissing her. That didn't make him happy. He wasn't the kind of man who liked emotional roller coasters.

He was done with digging into her life. What did it matter if he couldn't forget the feel of her mouth under his, the soft intake of her breath when he'd cupped her face in his hands? What if he still couldn't believe she was the woman Harman described...

…or believe her when she'd said that she didn't want to see him again?

"Good morning, sir." The ticket clerk smiled politely. "How may I help you?"

Gray cleared his throat. "I want to get to Austin as soon as possible."

The clerk's fingers flew over the keyboard. "I have a seat on a plane boarding in half an hour."

"That's fine," Gray said, and blanked his mind to everything but the business of buying his ticket.

He called ahead and reserved a rental car at Austin. By noon, he was walking up the steps at Espada. The housekeeper opened the door and smiled broadly.

"Mr. Graham, how nice to see you."

He'd given up trying to convince her to drop the "mister" years back, and he was in no mood to take up the battle today.

"Hello, Carmen. Is the old man in?"

"Yes, certainly. He's on the deck. Come in, please. I'll tell him you're here."

"I'll tell him myself."

Gray brushed past her, went through the house and out to the waterfall deck. His uncle was lying on a chaise longue, eyes closed, a light blanket drawn over him despite the warmth of the sun. He looked old and tired. The anger that had been building inside Gray toward the old man for getting him into this mess began to fade.

He sighed, sat down to wait, but Jonas must have sensed his presence because he opened his eyes.

"Graham?"

"Yes. Hello, Jonas. I guess I should have phoned to tell you I was coming."

"Why? You afraid I might be too busy for a chat?" His uncle laughed and sat up. "Good to see you. What brings you to Espada?"

"You sent me to find Dawn Lincoln Kitteridge, remember?"

"Carmen?" Jonas's voice cracked, but it had the same timbre as ever. "Carmen! Where in blazes are you?" He glared at Gray. "'Course I remember. It's my blood's gone bad, not my brain. I take it you found her."

"Yes."

"Good, good. You want somethin' to cool your throat? Beer? Bourbon?" Jonas made a face as the housekeeper poked her head out the door. "Not that *she'll* let me have bourbon, not even with Marta gone for the day. Ain't that right, Carmen?"

"I'll be happy to bring you water or juice, Mr. Baron, and to bring Mr. Graham whatever he wishes."

"Iced water would be fine," Gray said.

Jonas sighed heavily. "Yeah, yeah, make it two."

He sat back and turned his face to the sun. Gray thought he might have dozed off again but once Carmen brought the water, poured it and went back into the house, his uncle looked at him, the command of old glittering in his eyes.

"Tell me about her."

"Well, she lives in Las Vegas."

Jonas raised his bushy brows. "Vegas? What does the girl do? Is she a gambler?"

Gray thought of what Dawn had said, about the guilt she'd felt as a dealer. "No. She doesn't think much of gambling. She works at a hotel."

"Doin' what? Am I going to have to drag every detail out of you?"

"She's a Special Services representative."

"Meanin'?"

"Meaning, she makes arrangements for VIPs. She sees to it that they have whatever they want."

The old man's brows rose again. "You tellin' me the girl's some sort of expensive hooker?"

"No," Gray said sharply, "she's not." He paused, gathered the composure he seemed to be having a tough time hanging on to today, rose from his chair and walked to the deck railing. What right did he have to jump on his uncle for leaping to that conclusion, when he'd done the same thing? "I thought something like that, too, before..." He wrapped his hands around the rail, fingers biting into it as he recalled the swift flush of anger in Dawn's face when he'd said as much. "The best way to explain it," he said, facing his uncle, "is that she does what a concierge would do, only more of it, and only for celebrities and high rollers. That's the closest I can come to a job description."

"High rollers, huh?"

"Yes. And VIPs. She was talking to an Arab prince when I saw her this morning."

"An Arab, like one of my sons-in-law." Jonas nodded. "Girl must be pretty smart, to deal with them VIP types."

"She is."

"What's she look like? Don't suppose you thought to bring me a picture."

"I have a couple of old ones. They're black-and-white, and not very good." Gray opened his briefcase and took out the photos of Dawn. Jonas took them and looked at them for a long moment before handing them back.

"Can't tell much from these," he said, his voice rough, "'cept that she seems to resemble her grandma some. She's a pretty girl, I see."

Beautiful. She's beautiful. "Yeah. I guess she is."

"What the hell's that supposed to mean? Is she short? Tall? Curvy? Skinny? What color's her hair?"

"She's a little taller than average. I guess you'd say she's nicely built. Her hair's red. Well, maybe not red, exactly, but sort of a deep strawberry-blond..." He stopped in midsentence, met the old man's surprisingly clear gaze and flushed. "Okay. She's a good-looking woman, if that's what you're asking."

His uncle put his hands on his knees and rose slowly to his feet. "Not surprised. She has good genes. Well, go on. Tell me more."

"That's about it."

Jonas snorted. "The hell it is! You ain't said a word about what she's like 'cept that she's smart and pretty, and I had to practically drag that out of you. Is she nice?"

"Nice?"

"You heard me. Nice. She got a sense of humor? Does she smile a lot? What'd you think of her?"

Gray could feel a knot forming in his gut. "I don't see what any of this has to do with—"

"Is she married? Single? Come on, boy, tell me somethin'!"

"Married."

"And?"

"And what? You asked me if she's married. I told you, she is."

Jonas narrowed his eyes. "Okay. You want to play twenty questions, that's how we'll do it. Who's she married to? What's he do for a living? Is she happy?"

Gray drew in a deep breath, then let it out. "She's married to a man with a record."

"Whoa. A prison record?"

"No. An arrest record, but he's never done time. She doesn't live with him. She ran away from him four years ago."

His uncle leaned on the railing next to Gray. "Kids?"

"One. The father claims Dawn ran out and left him and the boy."

"But?"

"But, I don't believe him." Gray turned toward Jonas. It felt good, finally, to say the words out loud. "I don't know where the child is or what happened to him, but she wouldn't have abandoned him. I can't prove it—"

"Don't have to prove it," Jonas said softly. "Most times, a man knows all he needs to know about a woman without her telling him." Minutes passed. The old man gave a deep sigh. "I told you this girl was my old friend's granddaughter. Well, that's maybe the truth…and maybe it isn't." He looked at the railing, ran his hand back and forth over the smooth wood. "Ben Lincoln and me were partners, same as I said, but we didn't stop working together because we found out it would cost more to get the gold out of that jungle than it was worth. It was because I slept with his wife."

Jonas stood straight, his eyes fierce as a hawk's. The years seemed to drop away until he was as he'd been in his youth:

tall, strong and arrogant in his conviction that he was lord of his universe.

"I didn't just sleep with Nora, I fell in love with her. She was a gentle woman with a kind heart and Ben—well, he just had no time in his life for what she needed." His voice lowered. "She wouldn't leave him. She said he was a decent man and that it was bad enough she'd broken one vow… Anyway, he found out. He came at me and I couldn't blame him, so I didn't do much to defend myself and he beat me up pretty bad. I didn't want to leave without Nora but she begged me to go. She said she'd make it up to Ben, that he was her husband…but I could see the truth in her eyes, that she loved me, not him, that saying goodbye was going to break her heart but that she was a strong, decent woman and she'd do the right thing."

Both men were silent, Jonas recalling the past, Gray recalling the picture of Nora Lincoln, the sad eyes and the resolute tilt to her chin. After a while, he touched his uncle's arm.

"Jonas?" he said softly. "Are you all right?"

"Sure." The old man swallowed hard. "It didn't do her any good. Ben couldn't forgive her. He divorced her. I didn't know about it. Nora had written me off as a bad mistake and I suppose I was."

His uncle stared over the meadows and gardens beyond the deck but Gray knew he didn't see them. He was seeing another time and place, and a memory he'd carried inside him all these years.

"A few months ago, I heard from an old buddy. He talked about Nora, told me she'd had a baby after the divorce. Right after it, I mean." Jonas looked at Gray. "And I need to know, son. Was that baby mine—or was it Ben's?"

"Oh, Jesus," Gray said softly, and his uncle laughed.

"Exactly. This girl in Las Vegas may be my granddaughter. If she is, I got to make it up to her. To her mama. To her grandma, too. Mostly to her grandma. You understand? If Dawn's my flesh and blood, Graham, I got to do the right thing."

*   *   *

The right thing, Gray thought hours later, as he stepped out of the airport at Flagstaff. What the hell was that?

He knew what it wasn't.

Pretending he could just walk away from Dawn wasn't the right thing. It was the biggest lie he'd ever told, even if he'd only told it to himself. She'd said she didn't want to see him anymore and he'd let his ego do his thinking instead of his head.

She wanted to see him. It was in her eyes, even as she'd told him to go away. There had been something else in those haunted eyes, too.

Fear.

Dawn was afraid, but of what? Harman? That was a good bet. But of something else, too. He'd bet on it. Was her fear connected to the child she was supposed to have abandoned? He had to know the answer and she wasn't going to tell him. But Harman would, he thought grimly, as he drove east from the airport at Flagstaff toward Queen City. He'd beat the answer out of Kitteridge, if he had to.

A hum of pleasurable anticipation raced through his blood at the thought.

He reached Queen City in late afternoon but he didn't bother phoning Harman. Not this time. Instead he drove his rental car to that same gas station he'd stopped at before, bought a couple of bucks worth of gas he didn't need and stood around talking with a kid working on a truck that looked more like an ad for chrome accessories than a usable vehicle until a fat man with a greasy bandanna tied around his neck came out of the back and told the kid to keep his mind on his work. After that, he drove across the street, went into the diner and ordered a cup of coffee and a piece of apple pie. The coffee was as bad as he remembered and the pie was worse, but the waitress—a younger one than before—was bored and friendly, and more than happy to gossip while she chewed a wad of gum and blew big pink bubbles.

Then he got back in his car, took Main Street to the end and followed a dirt road all the way up the mountain. Gray figured the man at the gas station might phone Harman to warn him he had a visitor after talking with the kid, so he wasn't surprised to find him waiting on the sagging porch of a dilapidated-looking shack that gave cabins everywhere a bad name.

Dawn had lived in this place, he thought, and felt that knot of tension forming in his belly again.

He got out of the car, slammed the door and wasted no time on preliminaries.

"Kitteridge. You remember me?"

Harman's sly grin curled across his face. "How could I forget you, Baron? It ain't often we get such classy visitors in these parts."

"I have a question."

"Bet you do." Harman strolled down the steps, thumbs looped in the waistband of his jeans, and spat on the ground. "You had questions last time, too."

"You said your wife ran off and left you."

"Yeah." Harman gave a deep sigh and transformed his expression from sly to despairing. "She sure did."

"And that she left her son."

"That, too."

Gray knotted his hands into fists. "That's strange, because people in town say she took the boy with her."

Harman spat again, closer to Gray's feet. "People in town lie."

"You're the one lying, Kitteridge."

"Get off my property."

"Was it to impress me? Did you think I'd hand over Dawn's inheritance to you if you gave me a sad story?"

"Dawn, is it?" Harman's eyes narrowed. "And why would I give a crap about some old music box?"

"You used to beat her, didn't you?" Gray could feel the heat rising within him. "Did it make you feel big, to lay your hands on her?"

"I guess you found my wife, Baron. I can tell by that look in your eyes. She's good at dazzling a man, don't you think? At makin' promises she ain't going to keep?" Harman took a step forward. "Where is she? Where is that whore hiding from me?"

"Tell me the truth, dammit. Did she take the boy? Or did you do something to him?"

Harman laughed. "You think I...? I'm sorry to disappoint you, Baron, but I never laid a finger on the kid." His mouth twisted. "But I will, I promise you that. Once I find him, I'll teach him to be a man, not a sissy. And when I'm done with my wife, she ain't never gonna run away again."

"You touch her," Gray said, very softly, "and I'll kill you."

"Don't you go makin' threats, city man." Flecks of spittle flew from Harman's mouth. "I'll get that whore bitch an' my son back. Ain't you or nobody else gonna stop me."

Gray moved forward, grabbed Harman by the shirt and pulled him forward so their faces were only inches apart. "Remember what I'm saying, Kitteridge. You touch Dawn or her son and I swear, I'll never rest until you're dead."

He let loose of Harman's shirt, got into the car and slammed the door. The car shot forward. He could see Harman in the mirror, running after him, his fist raised to the sky.

Gray jammed his foot to the floor. The car shot forward and he drove fast, too fast, down the mountain. Dawn, he thought, Dawn.

Flagstaff was too far. He drove one-handed, pulled out a map, saw that Winslow was much closer. It was a small airport, meaning it was a good bet he could hire a small plane to take him to Vegas. A couple of calls on his cell phone confirmed it. He gave a guy at the charter service one hundred bucks to take his car to Flagstaff and return it to the rental office.

Half an hour later, he was airborne.

It was dark when he pulled to the curb in front of an old Victorian house with an indigo bush out front. He recognized it from the photo Jack Ballard had faxed him. Impatiently he rang the bell and when there was no answer, he went to the window that looked out on the indigo and shouted Dawn's name.

The curtains fluttered. Her face appeared behind the glass.

"Dawn," he said softly, even though she couldn't hear him,

and later on he figured it was the way he must have looked when he said it that made the difference because the next thing he knew, the door was open and Dawn, crying and laughing all at once, was in his arms.

CHAPTER FOURTEEN

"YOU came back," Dawn said, "Gray, you came—"

He kissed her with the urgency that came of knowing how close he'd come to losing her. It wasn't what he'd intended to do. Go slow, he'd told himself. Ask her to forgive you for being such a fool this morning, and that sounded fine until he pulled up outside her house and saw those dark windows. What if she wouldn't let him in? What if she wouldn't even talk to him? What if, what if, what if?

More than one prosecuting attorney—with a rueful touch of admiration—had referred to Gray as "arrogant." A couple of women had accused him of it, too. Holding Dawn, feeling the race of her heart against his as he kissed her, he wondered what any of those people would think if they saw him, wondered, too, what was happening to him, and then he told the lawyer inside him to shut the hell up and let the man emerge. This soft, sweet, incredibly courageous woman was all that mattered.

"I thought I'd never see you again," she whispered between kisses. "I thought you'd gone away."

"I almost did." Gray cupped her face in his hands and lifted it to his. Her eyes were enormous, shining with tears, but a tremulous smile curved across her mouth. He bent to her, brushed her lips with his, lingered to taste their sweetness. "I was such a fool, sweetheart. If I could take back the things I said this morning..."

"You were angry. You thought I'd stood you up—"

"No. Not angry. Not at you. Never at you. It was just a cover for the truth. I was angry at myself, for wanting you so badly—"

"Shh." She put her fingers across his lips. "You mustn't say that. You don't—you don't know—" She took an unsteady breath. "There are things about me..."

241

"There are things about me, too." He closed his hand over her fingers, kissed the tips, then pressed his mouth to her palm. "None of it matters. Not anymore."

"It does." Her voice trembled. "Gray, you don't understand. It's complicated—"

He kissed her, threaded his fingers into her hair, tilted her head back and kissed her again, and when she parted her lips, let the tip of his tongue slip inside her mouth, he groaned with pleasure.

"Then let's uncomplicate it." His words were a low, rough whisper in the darkness of the narrow hall. "Come to bed with me, Dawn. Let me make love to you and you'll see, baby, you'll see how simple it can become."

She put her hands against his chest. It almost killed him but he gave her the space she needed to take a step back.

"I'm married." She took a deep breath. "I left my husband long ago, but I'm still—"

"I know."

She blinked. "You know?"

Gray cursed himself for a fool. This wasn't the moment to tell her why he'd come to Vegas. He had to show her how much she meant to him before he admitted that he'd deceived her from the beginning.

"I know the kind of woman you are, sweetheart. You said you're married, and that means you still believe in the vows you took."

"I did, for a long time, but—"

He drew her into his arms again and moved his mouth over hers in a soft, silken caress.

"Kiss me back," he whispered.

She told herself not to, that this was a mistake, but his mouth was hot on hers, his arms strong, and every beat of her heart whispered yes, yes, yes.

"Dawn." He pressed his open mouth to her throat, to the pulse racing in its hollow. "Tell me what you want, sweetheart. Let me hear you say it."

No, she thought. Oh, no. This was nice but she didn't ever want to be with a man again. She didn't want sex, didn't like it, didn't need to lie on her back, staring at the ceiling, while somebody grunted and sweated and buried himself inside her...

Gray brushed his hand across the front of her T-shirt. Her nipples rose, stabbed the soft cotton fabric and she caught her breath, stunned by pleasure that swept through her, pleasure so intense it verged on pain. He dipped his head, kissed first one straining patch of cotton and then the other. Dawn rose toward him, head back, and buried her hands in his hair. Somebody moaned. Was it she? She knew the sounds men and women made. They were ugly. They weren't sounds like—

Yes. Oh, yes. Her breath hissed as Gray slid his hands down her back, inside her underpants. His palms curved over her bottom; the tips of his fingers sought more, almost found it, drew back. Don't stop. Don't stop, she thought, and then she was saying the words, sobbing them...

"Tell me you want me," he said thickly, and she wound her arms around his neck, pressed her mouth to his and answered with her body, her heart, her soul.

Gray swept her into his arms and carried her to the bedroom.

The room was dark, the curtains drawn tightly against the night and the street, the only illumination a soft light seeping from the half-opened bathroom door, but even that felt harsh against her closed eyes. Without warning, the old, familiar panic began rising in her throat and she waited for the pressure of the mattress against her buttocks, against her back, for the smothering weight of a man's body bearing her down onto the bed.

"Wait," she said quickly. "Gray? Maybe we should wait. Maybe—"

He kissed her, his hands in her hair, his mouth warm and soft and gentle on hers as he lowered her slowly to her feet. She felt the quick, potent kiss of his erection against her belly and the flutter of panic became more insistent. He was so hard. So big. He didn't want to hurt her, she knew that, but he would. She knew. She remembered. Oh God, she remembered...

"Dawn." Gray put his hand under her chin and lifted her face to his. "Sweetheart?"

She shook her head and kept her eyes downcast, as shamed by her fear as she was filled by it.

"Baby, please. Look at me."

His voice was soft, and she loved the sound of the names he used with her. Sweetheart. Baby. Such soft, loving words— but they wouldn't change anything. No matter how he tried, this would be—

"Look at me, Dawn."

It was a plea, not a command, and maybe that was the reason she finally lifted her lashes and did as he'd asked. Their eyes met and what she saw in his stunned her. She'd expected the hot blaze of conquering passion but what she saw was tenderness and concern...and a banked anger that she knew, instinctively, had nothing to do with her.

"Are you afraid I'll hurt you?" He traced her cheekbones with his thumbs. "I won't. I promise."

"Thank you." She swallowed dryly, then gave a hollow laugh. "I'm sorry. I know this isn't the way it should be."

"There's no script, baby. This scene belongs to us. We get to write it any way we want."

"You must think I'm such a fool—"

"What I think," he said gently, "is that it would be nice to find out what's under that amazing T-shirt."

She looked down at herself. A scowling Wonder Woman flew across her breasts in red, white and blue glory, ready to defend the world from evil.

"Oh," Dawn said foolishly, "this."

"Yeah. That."

There was a smile in his words and, when she looked at his face, a hint of one on his lips. She'd never imagined people could joke about sex. It was nice that he could, even if he was impatient. He was waiting for her to get out of her clothes. Harman had always just shoved up her nightgown. Or ripped it off, if he was drunk and angry and—

Gray's hands closed on her wrists as she reached for the hem of the T-shirt. "Don't think about him," he said fiercely. "He isn't here. This is our world, yours and mine." His voice softened. "And I don't want you to take that shirt off." Slowly his eyes never leaving hers, he slid his hands under the shirt, trailed them up her bare skin. "I'll do it." He bent to her, nipped lightly at her throat. "I want to unwrap you."

Unwrap her? What did that mean? She wasn't a gift he'd found under the tree on Christmas morning, except—except that was how he was looking at her, as if she were a present, one he couldn't wait to...

Her breath caught.

He touched her. Brushed the tips of his fingers up her spine. Just that. Only that. It made her knees buckle and she reached out, grasped his shirt and curled her fingers into the soft cotton.

"Your skin is like satin," he whispered. "Soft. Smooth. Warm."

A moan rose in her throat as he put his mouth against her skin again. Her head fell back; she felt the brush of his lips, the hot touch of his tongue, the quick, faint nip of his teeth.

"I love the taste of you. Sweet. Like cream. So rich and smooth..."

His hands slid down her spine, brushed lightly over her buttocks and she braced herself, waited for him to pull down her panties and push inside her. Instead he swept his hands up again, his fingers dancing lightly over her hips, her waist, her nipples. Oh God, her nipples. There. Just there. The lightest whisper of sensation over her nipples...

She moaned, and he kissed her while he touched her, stroked her, feathered his thumbs over the aching centers. When he clutched the hem of the shirt and drew it up, she lifted her arms to help him and swayed, unsteadily, after he'd bared her to his gaze.

"Dawn."

He wanted to say more, tell her how beautiful she was, but his tongue was thick in his mouth. Besides, beautiful didn't half describe her. She was everything he'd ever dreamed a woman could be, and more.

Her breasts were rounded and delicate; he knew they would just fill his palms. Her nipples were pale apricot, the tips pearling even before he stroked them. Her body was warming, coming alive to him, for him, and he could feel his own flesh swelling, rising, aching with need for her. Only for her, he thought fiercely, and he forced his gaze to her face, saw her parted lips, her glazed eyes—eyes glittering not with fear but with the awakening of desire.

"Do you like what I'm doing?" he said thickly.

She tried to answer. Couldn't. Something was happening to her. She could feel her blood turning thick, beating hot and heavy through her body. And her breasts. They were—they were lifting. Hardening. Her nipples were growing tight. They ached. They wanted. She wanted. Wanted...

That. Oh, yes, that. Gray's hands, cupping her breasts. Raising them even as he bent his head. Her body was waiting for this. This. Her breath hissed from her lungs as he tongued one hardened bud, then drew it into his mouth and suckled her. She was startled. She'd never known men did this to women, or that it could feel like this, like a bolt of lightning that speared from breast to belly. She ached. Throbbed. God oh God oh God...

Her cry rose into the silence of the room and Gray groaned against her flesh, told himself that it wasn't possible for a man to come just because a woman dug her fingers into his hair, rose to his touch and his mouth, cried out in ecstasy, but if he didn't hang on, that was what would happen, he'd never get inside her in time...

Think about something else, he told himself frantically. Tort law. Case law. Think about anything but this, the taste of her breasts, the feel of her belly under his hand, the way she trembled when he slid his fingers inside her panties, found her wet and hot, so hot...

He took her down with him into the softness of the bed. She was sobbing, whispering his name as he pulled off her panties, dipped his head and sucked at her nipples, found the damp satin petals he sought, found the flower they guarded, felt it bloom against his thumb and this time, when she cried out, arched toward him, eyes wide and blind, he crushed her mouth with his and drank in her cries, her pleasure, her surrender.

She fell back against the pillows and he lifted his head, watched her face, felt a fierce exaltation sweep through him. Mine, he thought, mine forever…

"Gray." She held up her arms. "Gray." Her voice broke. "Gray…"

He tore off his clothes, settled between her thighs, told himself to go slowly, enter her slowly. God, she was—she was… Hot. Tight. Wet. So wet. The breath hissed from his lungs as he eased inside her. He felt his body bead with sweat. What he wanted was to drive deep, put his mark on her in the most primitive way possible, but he knew not to hurt her or frighten her. What was she thinking? Feeling?

"Dawn." He took her hands, wove his fingers through hers. "Sweetheart. Are you all right?"

She opened her eyes and looked up at him. He could see the shock on her face. His heart constricted; he waited for his flesh to follow suit but his body was flying on its own. No. No. She wasn't ready. Slowly he began to withdraw. She whimpered, lifted her legs and wrapped them around his hips.

God, she was going to kill them both.

"Don't. Sweetheart." He swallowed. Still inside her, he willed himself not to move as he lowered his forehead to hers. "If you do that, I won't be able to stop."

"Don't stop." She reached up to him, clasped his biceps. "Please. Oh please. Gray. Gray…"

She arched like a bow seeking an arrow and impaled herself on him. Her cry of release rang through the room. Then, at last, Gray threw back his head and let himself tumble off the edge of the earth with the woman he loved in his arms.

"Nooooo…."

"Dawn?" Gray shot up in bed as the scream razored through the middle-of-the-night silence. "Dawn?"

He threw out a hand, found her beside him, thrashing and moaning. A dream. It was just a dream. Heart pounding, he switched on the lamp and reached for her. She fought him like a tiger, beating her fists against his chest and shoulders, fingernails raking his cheek as he clasped her shoulders.

"It's okay, sweetheart. You're dreaming. Come on. Wake up."

Her head snapped up. She stared at him but he knew she didn't see him. Her eyes were wide and sightless; her lips drawn back from her teeth in a rictus of fear. A memory came to him, all too vividly, of a coyote with its leg caught in the teeth of a steel trap. He'd been a kid then, riding his father's land, helpless in the face of the animal's terror and pain.

This, thank God, was different.

"Dawn." He drew her against him, held her tight, whispered to her, talked to her, told her that everything was all right, that she'd been dreaming, that he would keep her safe. After what seemed endless minutes, he felt her muscles start to relax.

"Gray?"

"Yes, baby. I'm right here."

"I had a dream…"

"I know." Her hair was tangled and damp. He stroked it back and kissed the tender flesh behind her ear. "But it's over. You're safe, sweetheart."

She gave a little sob that almost broke his heart and burrowed against him. "Hold me."

He kissed her mouth, rocked her gently in his arms. "Do you want to tell me about your dream?"

She shook her head. "No."

"How about if I get you a glass of water?"

"Thank you, but I'm okay now."

She wasn't. Her skin was clammy and every now and then, she shuddered. His arms tightened around her. He knew exactly what she'd dreamed about. Harman. Her husband, the man who had beaten her, brutalized her…

"Dawn." Gray slid down against the pillows, still holding her against him. "I'll never let anything hurt you again."

She sighed, her breath warm against his skin, and lay her

face against his chest. "I was dreaming about my husband,"
she whispered.

His jaw tightened. "Were you?"

"He's a—he's mean."

"Is he?" he said, while he stared up at the ceiling and
wondered how long he could lie here answering her with such
stupid questions, listening to her tell him her secrets without
admitting his.

"When I was with him... When he—when he touched me,
you know, when he took me in bed..."

"Don't, sweetheart."

"No. I mean, I have to." She lifted her head and looked at
him, her hair spilling over her shoulders and onto his chest.
"You need to know that I've never... I never imagined what
happened tonight could be so—so wonderful."

Gray rolled over, taking her with him, resting his weight on
his elbows as he looked down into her pale face.

"How long did you stay with him?"

"Almost five years. Then I—I left."

"Did you ever love him? I mean, when you married him,
you must have thought—"

"I don't know what I thought." She swallowed dryly. "I
was young. My mama was—she had problems of her own.
And when Harman began to pay attention to me..."

"Harman?" Jesus, the lies were catching in his throat. "Is
that his name?"

She nodded. "He seemed nice. He was older but at first he
treated me sort of like a father, and I figured that was okay.
Actually it was fine. I'd never had a father around and, well,
it's hard to explain but I always used to think how nice it
would be if I did." She cleared her throat. "I know how silly
that seems, but—"

"It doesn't seem silly at all." Gray took a strand of her
hair between his fingers. It felt cool and silky as it curled
around his finger. "I used to think the same way when I was
a kid."

Dawn's brows lifted. "You didn't have a father, either?"

"Well, I did, yeah. I still do, but he wasn't the father I wanted him to be, I guess."

"Then you know what it's like. To want someone to care about you, I mean." A few seconds passed. "Harman said he loved me. He asked me to marry him. I said I thought we should wait a while, until I was a little older and we knew each other better, but he said there wasn't any point in waiting and I knew—I knew my mama wanted me gone. We just had this trailer and—and there wasn't very much room and—and—" She licked her lips. "I figured I'd learn to care for him. I mean, before we got married, he was nice to me. He never—he never…"

Gray kissed her, felt her mouth tremble beneath his. God, how he wanted to tell her that he knew all about Harman, but he'd let things go too far. Or maybe not. Yes, there were endless explanations to make and yes, she'd be upset, but he could handle that. He could tell her that he'd come looking for a faceless woman and found, instead, someone who had changed his life, that in ways he couldn't begin to explain or comprehend, he knew that this—the two of them, together— was right, and that all of what had happened before they met was just a prelude to the future that stretched ahead.

"Dawn." He laid his hand against her cheek, curved it over the delicate arch of bone and rubbed his thumb across her mouth. "Sweetheart, there are things I haven't told you…" He paused, silently cursed himself. Where was all the fluency that served him so well in the courtroom? "Baby, we've only known each other a handful of days and yet—"

"I know." She smiled, caught hold of his hand and kissed it. "It's the same for me. We only just met and yet, I've told you things I've never told another soul." He kissed her. Her lips parted, clung to his, and she looped her arms around his neck. "I've never been so happy," she said softly.

The simple admission felt like a blow to the heart. "Dawn," he said, "sweetheart—"

"You're the first man I ever made love with. What happened with my husband wasn't… You're the first, Gray. And it was wonderful."

"Yes. It was."

"And you're the first man I've ever trusted." She gave a sad little laugh. "The first *person* I've ever trusted. I don't think you know what that means to me, to be able to trust someone."

"Baby, remember what you said before? About things being complicated? Well, it's true. Life never goes in a straight line. There are twists and turns and detours, and—"

She drew him toward her. "And you were right," she murmured, her lips a breath away. "We uncomplicated it, in this bed."

She kissed him again, and the sweet innocence of it pierced his heart. He wasn't worthy of her trust. He wanted to tell her that but if he did, God, if he did, he'd lose her. There had to be a way to tell her the truth without raising the stakes so high.

"Yes," he said gruffly, "we did."

Dawn smiled. "I love the way you talk. That accent," she said, when he lifted his eyebrows. "That little touch of Texas that you can't quite disguise."

"I don't try to disguise it," he said defensively. She was the one who raised her eyebrows this time and he chuckled. "Okay, maybe I do. Truth is, even when I was a kid, I couldn't wait to get out of Texas."

"Why? I mean, I can tell you're, well, that you were brought up in a nice home."

"A nice home?"

"Uh-huh. Don't look at me like that. You know what I mean."

He grinned. "That somebody taught me which fork to use for my salad? That kind of stuff?"

Dawn tapped his chin with her fist. "Go on, make fun of me. Yes, that kind of stuff. Those things matter. You don't know how much unless you have to learn them when you're all grown up."

His smile tilted. "Takes a lot of determination, I'll bet."

"A thick skin, is what it takes. You catch people looking at you when you do something dumb, and you want to just shut your eyes and pretend you're not there." She sighed. "You were joking, but I really did have to learn which fork to use. Which spoon. I even had to learn how to dress."

Gray ran his hand down her back, cupped her bottom. "As far as I can see," he said, his voice a little husky, "you dress just fine."

"I'm serious. When I got my first job..." Her breath caught. "What are you doing?"

"Just checking what you're wearing. Mmm. Feels smooth. Silky."

"Gray."

Her voice was breathy; he loved the sound of it, the way it changed when he touched her, like now.

"What?"

"I didn't know... I never thought a man would touch a woman where—where... Gray. Oh God, Gray..."

"I like to touch you there." He moved down on the bed, kissed her breasts, her belly, traced the faint line from her navel to the soft curls below it with the tip of his tongue. "I like to look at you there, too," he whispered, slipping his hands under her thighs, lifting her, opening her to him.

"No. Gray, you can't—"

"You're beautiful, sweetheart. Every part of you. Your face. Your breasts. This. This perfect blossom, with such soft petals and this hidden within it..."

She moaned as he touched her. He watched her eyes go blind, felt the answering tug of his own need shoot through his body. He whispered her name, put his mouth where his hand had been, and Dawn cried out in shock. He kissed her. Nipped her. Tongued her until she forgot everything but him and the night...and felt only how deeply she'd fallen in love.

The pale gray of early morning was creeping past the edges of the curtains when Gray awoke. Dawn lay sprawled half across him, her head on his chest, her hand splayed over his heart.

I love her, he thought, and the realization came so easily, so joyously, that he smiled.

He kissed her temple, curved his arm more closely around her, and stared at the ceiling. Maybe it was a good thing that he hadn't blurted out the truth during the night, not just because of how she'd have reacted but because he needed time to put together a plan. Actually he'd started roughing one out while Dawn slept in his arms after the last time they'd made love.

He knew she was convinced that keeping her child's existence a secret was the only thing that would save him from Harman. Gray's mouth thinned. She was probably right. The bastard would never stop searching, especially now that he thought there was money involved. But things were different now. He was in her life.

He would stop Kitteridge, and he didn't give a damn if he did it legally or not.

Because the law was his specialty, he'd try that first, all the tricks of the trade that lay buried in the leather-bound volumes in the law library back in his New York offices. And if those tricks weren't enough, he had other resources, clients who knew how to change the minds of even the most determined men.

Whatever it took, Gray thought grimly, Kitteridge was going to be part of the past.

"Gray?" Dawn's voice was thick with sleep. "Wha' time issit?"

"Shh." He bent his head and pressed a kiss to her hair. "It's early, baby. Too early to get up."

"Mmm." She rolled away from him, flopped over and sprawled out on her belly. Seconds later, her breathing was deep and slow again.

Gray smiled. A couple of hours ago, she'd told him she always got up early. "I'll try not to wake you," she'd said through a giant yawn.

He'd drawn her close into his arms. "Call in and tell them you're taking the day off."

"Uh-uh. Can't. Promised I'd go in at noon and take over for Becky."

"Then you don't have to get up early."

"Told you, I always get up early."

Another yawn. He'd grinned, sure he'd heard her jaw creak. "Good. We can get up early and fool around."

That had won him a soft laugh. "Fool around, huh?"

"Sure. Work up an appetite for breakfast."

"Don't want breakfast," she'd mumbled, just before she'd started to snore. "Jus' want sleep."

Remembering it, Gray smiled. What *he* wanted was to wake her with a kiss and do some of that fooling around, but he didn't have the heart. Besides... He lifted his arm and checked his watch. Things would be starting to move back East right about now. He needed to call his secretary, ask her to pull some case history volumes from the library. He wanted to talk to one of his partners, too, a guy who was as well-versed in marital law as anybody in New York. And, just in case all the legal maneuvering in the world didn't do the trick, maybe he should begin to think about those of his clients who would best know how to dissuade a man who didn't want to be dissuaded.

First thing, though, he had to phone Jack Ballard. He was surprised Jack had missed finding out about Dawn's son but then again, he'd been searching for Dawn, not for a kid. Gray wanted to know where the boy was. His meeting with Harman had left him feeling uneasy. He had the feeling that he might have stirred things up. It would be best to locate Dawn's child, keep some kind of watch on him.

Gray sat up, eased to the edge of the bed and turned for one last look at Dawn. How different she looked from those photos...photos in the briefcase he'd forgotten in the back seat of his rental car yesterday. The memory gave him a twinge of distress even though he knew the briefcase was safe. He'd phoned Winslow during the flight to Vegas and the guy he'd paid to drive the car to Flagstaff said he'd already found the briefcase and sure, he'd send it to Gray at the Desert Song, pronto.

He collected his clothes, dressed quietly, then made one last detour to the bed. How could a man fall in love when he'd never believed love existed? How could it happen in a handful of days? He didn't know. He didn't care. All that mattered was Dawn. Once he was sure she was safe, he'd tell her everything. She'd be angry but she'd understand...and if she didn't, he'd take her in his arms and kiss her until she did.

He tiptoed into the kitchen and quietly phoned for a taxi. "Tell the driver not to blow his horn," he said. "I'll be waiting outside." Then he found a pencil and piece of paper, scrawled a note and went back to the bedroom. The bear he'd given Dawn sat in a place of honor on the night table, and he tucked the note under its paw.

Goodbye, sweetheart, it said. *I'll see you later.*

He looked at her for a long minute before gently kissing her temple. Then he smoothed the blanket over her shoulder, made his way quietly to the front door, set the lock, and stepped out into the morning.

Outside, in the shadow cast by the indigo, a dark figure squatted, motionless.

Harman was pressed between the shrub and the wall of the house, silent and watchful. He'd been there for hours and it pleased him to think how other men would have felt cramps in their legs by now or at least a stiffness in their muscles. Not him. He'd grown up hunting in the mountains of northern Arizona. No deer, no bobcat, no wild critter could outlast him or spot him, when he lay in waiting. He knew how to become part of the scenery, how to be still as a stone...

How to be as deadly as a rattlesnake, coiled and ready to strike.

Bile rose in his throat when the door to the house where his wife lived swung open. Graham Baron stepped outside, yawned and stretched. Harman had spent a lifetime scenting game. Now, his nostrils widened as he took in the stink of sex and woman. Baron had come straight from the whore's bed.

Harman's hands closed into fists. The lying son of a bitch! All that crap about music boxes... Shit, all of it. Dawn had come into money. His mouth twisted. And Baron had come into her.

Ah, how good it would feel to kill him. How easy. The

street was deserted. Not even a dog wandering by. He could be on top of Baron before the bastard knew it. How he'd love to feel his hunting knife slip between Baron's ribs and watch his face as the blade pierced his heart, watch as shocked awareness turned to terror and, at last, to acceptance of his whoremonger's fate.

Harman shuddered, licked his lips. Then he'd go inside and take care of the whore herself. No knife in the heart for her. She didn't deserve a quick end. He'd do her slowly, let her beg for a merciful death. Just thinking about it made him hard as a rock—but it would have to wait. There were things to do before he dealt with the slut and her lover.

Baron was pacing the sidewalk, his hands in his pockets. After a while, a taxi turned up the street. Baron waved and it pulled to the curb.

"The Desert Song Hotel," he said, and climbed inside.

A grin spread across Harman's mouth as the taxi drove away. When the cab disappeared, he rose silently and turned a hungry gaze on the curtained window.

Yes. He could do it right now. Give his whoring wife what she deserved. Climb through the window—it had been easy to jimmy the lock last night. Climb through, come up to her, put his hand over her mouth and gag her, then tie her down, strip away her clothes with his knife and spread her legs so that he could see the place she'd always tried to deny him and then teach her the price a woman paid when she forgot the vows she'd taken.

He drew a breath, wiped the spittle from the corners of his lips with the back of his hand.

Except, his son would be lost to him. The bitch would sooner go to hell than reveal the boy's whereabouts.

He couldn't kill Dawn until he knew where Thomas was.

Harman smiled to himself. Dawn had never credited him with being smart, but he was. Smart enough to have let Baron start down the mountain before he climbed into his truck and tailed him to the Winslow airport and the place where rich men kept their planes, and to have one of his drinking buddies who worked there tell him where the plane Baron chartered was going. For twenty bucks, his pal had let him search the car Baron had paid him to drive back to Flagstaff, and it was worth it because the city lawyer had been in such a hurry to get to his whore that he'd forgotten his briefcase.

There were papers and pictures in it, and then he'd struck gold. The best thing in that briefcase was the name of the place where Dawn worked...and the mother lode, her address in Las Vegas.

Harman had driven like a madman, using back roads whenever he could to avoid cops and speed limits, racing through the night without stopping until he finally got to Dawn's street. He parked a block away from her house, walked back and felt the presence of his whore of a wife even before he'd jimmied the lock on the window and heard the sounds coming from her apartment. Her voice. Baron's voice. The grunts and groans of two animals rutting, noises she'd never made for him.

A rush of crimson flooded his vision. Harman closed his eyes, breathed deeply the way he'd trained himself to do when long hours waiting for game threatened to upset him. He had to stay calm, stay focused. He'd waited four years for this. A few hours more was nothing.

He tucked his hands into the pockets of his overalls and walked away. No need to rush things, not now that it was all falling into place. A man had the right to enjoy his rewards, and he fully intended to do exactly that.

By the time he reached his truck, he was whistling.

CHAPTER FIFTEEN

CASSIE dug into her chicken salad, swigged down a mouthful of iced tea, looked across the table at Dawn and decided she'd never find out what was happening between her friend and Gray Baron if she went on being subtle.

For days now, ever since Dawn had admitted she was seeing Gray, Cassie had said things like, "How're things going?" "Is the guy as nice as he seems?" "How long's he going to stay in Vegas?" In response to which Dawn, big talker that she was, said, "Fine," "Yes," and, even more succinctly, "I don't know."

Cassie took another forkful of salad. It was obviously time for a more direct approach.

"So," she said, "are you sleeping with him yet?"

Dawn choked on her grilled cheese, coughed and held up a hand while she gulped down some water.

"Ask me something personal, why don't you?" she said, when she could talk.

Cassie grinned. "You know me. Damn the torpedoes. Full speed ahead. Fire when you see the whites of their eyes."

"It's *don't* fire until you see the whites of their eyes."

"Either way it's the same thing. I could have asked you last night, on the phone, but I didn't. I figured I'd wait until I could look right at you and know if you were giving me a truthful answer or not."

"Why should I give you any answer?" Dawn said reasonably.

"Because I'm your best friend?"

"You are, yes, but that doesn't mean—"

"You're sleeping with him. Don't shake your head. I can tell. If you weren't, you'd just laugh and say I was crazy, or you'd give me that look you get whenever I try to convince you there's no reason for you to live like a nun." She beamed smugly, stabbed a piece of chicken and popped it into her mouth. "So, how is he?"

"I've already told you," Dawn said, deliberately misunderstanding the question. "He's a very nice man."

"In bed. How is he in bed?" Cassie rolled her eyes. "Wonderful, I bet. Gorgeous. Inexhaustible. Knows every page of the Kama Sutra by heart... What?" she said, when Dawn started to laugh. "The Kama Sutra isn't funny." She giggled. "Well, maybe it is. Did you ever take a really good look at some of those illustrations?"

"You're impossible, you know that?"

"I'm interested, only because I want you to be happy...and because my own love life sucks and I'm hoping for a couple of vicarious thrills. Seriously, is he wonderful?"

"Yes," Dawn said simply. "He is, Cass. I've never known a man like him."

"A stud, huh?" Cassie spoke briskly, but her smile was soft.

"He's—he's everything a woman could want. Strong. Tender. Caring." Dawn pushed her sandwich aside. "And he's fun, too. We went to the movies the other night—"

"The movies," Cassie said, and sighed. "A big date."

"That's the way it felt. I mean, it was just a movie but we had such a good time. It was that theater doing that romantic comedy retrospective, you know the one? They were playing *Sleepless in Seattle* and afterward, on the way home, Gray did the Tom Hanks part and I did Meg Ryan, and we laughed because he sounded more like Martin Short trying to do Tom Hanks than Tom Hanks, and..." She laughed softly. "Do I sound completely insane?"

"No," Cassie said. She put down her fork and reached across the table to give Dawn's hand a squeeze. "You sound like a woman in love."

"Oh, I'm not. In love. I'm—I'm..." Dawn caught her lip between her teeth. "I can't be in love," she said quietly.

"Jeez Louise, puh-leeze don't give me that 'I'm still married' routine again! You're not married, not in any way that matters. Besides, this is the twenty-first century. They don't burn you at the stake for falling for another guy, especially when your husband is such a bastard that you're terrified of even trying to divorce him." Cassie paused. "Unless there's a complication I don't know about, like, Mr. Right wants you to marry him."

"No." Dawn touched her napkin to her mouth and placed it on the table. "Nothing like that."

"Ah. But you wish, huh?"

Dawn looked up. Her smile had faded; her eyes glittered with distress. "He hasn't asked me. He's just here on vacation. And—and even if he wanted to—if he wanted something more permanent, even if I thought about trying for a divorce, I couldn't let it happen."

"Because?"

"Because there are things about me... There are things..." Dawn reached for their check and pushed back her chair. "I couldn't, that's all. Leave it at that."

"Back to Dawn the Mysterious," Cassie said, and sighed. "No, that's okay. I'm not trying to pry. Well, I am, but I know there's no point." She patted her lips with her napkin, tossed it on the table and reached for her purse. "Your turn for the check? I'll leave the tip."

The women walked out of the restaurant into the hot noonday sun. "I'm happy," Dawn said quietly. "Really happy."

"Yeah, but for how long? Whatever this thing is that you never want to discuss, it's still there. And, look, I hate to make like a wet blanket but, well, what happens when Mr. Right decides it's time to pack his suitcase and go back to New York?"

"I'll be fine."

"Oh sure. You'll be great. Four years, and you've never so much as looked twice at a guy and now you're walking around with Cupid's arrow stuck between your shoulder blades but you'll be fine when this guy leaves." Cassie looped her arm through Dawn's. "You really think I believe that?"

"No." Dawn's smile was shaky. "I don't. And I don't believe it, either, but that's the way it's going to be."

"And suppose he wants more than that? Suppose he says

yes, this has been great but it's not over? What if he wants you to go with him and be part of his life?''

Dawn took a steadying breath. ''I'd have to tell him I can't.''

''Oh, Dawn…''

''Don't you have to be back on the floor in ten minutes?''

''Five,'' Cassie said, glancing at her watch. She looked up and frowned. ''By the way, I think you have an admirer.''

''Cass, honestly, I don't want to talk about Gray any—''

''No. Not Mr. Right. Some other guy.'' Cassie made a face. ''Frankly I don't think you'd want this one.''

''Don't tell me.'' Dawn sighed dramatically as they checked the lights, crossed the street and hurried toward the Song. ''Another poor soul like that farmer last year who hung around the casino every night for a week and kept telling me I looked just like his wife when she was a girl?''

''This one looks more like something out of *American Rifleman* magazine.''

''American Rifleman magazine?''

''Yeah. He's big. Rawboned, I guess you'd say, but you can see lots of muscle hiding under these god-awful clothes. Plaid shirts. Camouflage pants tucked into hunting boots… Dawn? What's the matter?''

Dawn had come to a dead stop. ''What does he look like? His face? What color is his hair? His eyes?'' She gripped Cassie's arm. ''Cass? Tell me what he looks like.''

''I don't know. I got so caught up in the funny outfit that… Okay. Let me think. Dark hair. Dark eyes. Long, bony face.''

''That's it? Can't you be more specific? What does 'dark' mean, Cass? Black? Brown? You have to tell me!''

''Okay. I'll take a better look if he shows up again. He's been hanging around the casino the past couple of nights.''

''Asking about me?''

''Well, not exactly. Well, yeah. Maybe. I mean, he says stuff like, 'Where do they get all the pretty women to work in this place?' and we say—''

''We?''

''The cocktail waitresses. We figured he was coming on to

us and, yuck, we're all willing to smile for a big tip, so we say, like, 'Thank you, they found me in a Cracker Jack box,' whatever, but then he always says yeah, but where did they find that woman I see talking to those big shots from time to time, and then he describes you to a tee, and wants to know all about you... Ouch! Dawn? You're digging your nails into me!''

Dawn looked from Cassie's face to where her hand had closed around her friend's wrist. Slowly she loosened her grip.

"Sorry. I'm sorry, Cass. I just..." She licked her lips. It didn't have to be Harman. It couldn't be Harman. Why would Harman try to be subtle? He wouldn't hang around or ask questions. He'd come straight at her, beat her, kill her, worse than that, he'd drag her into his car or his truck and try to take her away...

"Dawn?" Cassie moved closer. "What's the matter? You don't think..." She caught her breath. "You think it's your ex?"

"I don't know. It could be."

"Oh shit." Cassie's eyes widened. "No. No. It's impossible."

"What?"

"No, it's crazy. I just—I mean, first Mr. Right turns up and works his way into your life and then, a couple of days later, this man—somebody who might be your husband—turns up, too..."

"You think that Gray and Harman..." Dawn shook her head and refused to think back to when she'd considered the same thing. "Never! Gray isn't—he'd never—Cass, no. That's not possible."

"That's what I just said. Forget I even mentioned it."

Dawn forced a smile. "The rest of it, too. Harman—my husband—would never... I can't imagine how he'd have found me. Even if he did, he wouldn't ask questions, he'd—he'd..." She looped her arm through Cassie's again. "We're both going to be late if we don't hurry."

Cassie nodded. By the time they'd entered the hotel, she was smiling and chattering about a dress she intended to buy when she got her paycheck at the end of the week, but as soon as they parted and Dawn disappeared into her office, she ran to find Keir.

Mary Elizabeth O'Connell was having a wonderful time and the best part was, she wasn't supposed to be having a wonderful time at all.

She'd knocked on the door of Dan Coyle's office a while ago, supposedly so they could discuss some security changes Dan had suggested and they'd done that for maybe fifteen minutes. After that, Dan had asked if she'd like some coffee.

"The low-test brew," he'd said, with that grin she found charming.

She'd said that sounded like an excellent idea and he'd phoned for coffee and, because it was almost noon and a working lunch seemed like a good plan, he'd asked the kitchen to send up a couple of salads and a sandwich assortment.

"Is that all right?" he'd said to Mary.

"Fine," she'd answered, and it had been, though they hadn't talked about anything remotely connected with work ever since.

Instead they'd talked about themselves. Mary now knew lots about Dan's daughters.

"Wonderful girls, the both of them," he'd told her, and Mary had wagged her finger and said, lightly, that he was the one who had admitted they would probably prefer to be called "women."

"You're right," Dan had replied, with another of those marvelous smiles, "but they tolerate their old man's sexist language because—or so they claim—they're crazy about me."

"I can see where they would be," Mary had answered, stunning both of them, but they'd recovered and now they were into a long, friendly debate over whether a person contemplating a trip to the old country should best plan it for the spring or the summer.

"Spring," Mary said, pouring them both second cups of coffee. "Ireland's beautiful then, with everything just coming into bloom. Ruarch and I always went that time of year."

"Summer," Dan said, adding a dollop of cream to his cup. "There's the rain, yes, but the countryside is such a shade of green, it breaks your heart. That's why Flo and I always traveled there that time of year." He paused and looked at Mary. "Of course, there's something to be said about going in the autumn, if one were interested in starting fresh, Mary. Do you know what I mean?"

Mary's eyes met his. She thought she knew precisely what he meant and her heart gave the sort of lurch that would never trouble her doctors, but before she could phrase a reply, there was an impatient tap at the door. It swung open, and Keir stepped into the room.

"Dan? Listen, I…" His glance fell on his mother. "Oh."

"Oh, indeed," Mary said crisply. "What's the matter?"

"Nothing. I just, ah, I need a few minutes with Dan, that's all. If you wouldn't mind, Mother…"

"I would mind. Very much. I can tell by the look of you, Keir, that something's upset you. Are you afraid it will upset me, too?"

Keir flushed. "Mother. Duchess…"

"Dammit," Mary said, with deliberate heat. She never cursed and her uncharacteristic use of the word made it sound like the worst kind of obscenity. "I am not an invalid. When will you get it through your head that I can handle bad news without clutching my chest and falling to the floor? If you've come to tell Dan something important, you're going to have to tell it to me, too."

A tiny vein throbbed in Keir's forehead. After a few seconds, he nodded. She was right and he knew it.

"You recall our talk about Dawn Carter?" He looked from his mother to Dan. "Well, I think something's about to happen."

Dan shot to his feet. "Where? In the casino? Did you alert the—"

"No. Sorry. I didn't mean…" Keir sank into a chair. "There are things happening, is what I should have said, and though it's possible they're meaningless, I don't want to take any chances."

"What things?"

"Well, you know we were trying to figure out what Baron wants with Dawn." Keir glanced at his mother. "It would seem he's, ah, seeing her."

"Seeing her?" Dan said.

"Yes. Ah, dating her."

Mary snorted. "What sort of delicate flower do you think I am? Do you mean he's sleeping with her?"

For the first time since he'd entered the room, Keir smiled. "Yes."

"And you know this because...?"

"Cassie told me."

"Who?"

"Dawn's friend, Cassie Berk. She's a cocktail waitress in the casino. She knows Dawn better than anyone, and she said Dawn and Baron are...that they've become intimate."

"That's not a crime," Mary said dryly, "certainly not in this town."

"Well, there's more." Keir got to his feet, stuck his hand into his pocket and began to pace. "Seems that Dawn has never been involved with anyone before."

"You mean, Mr. Baron swept her off her feet?"

"I mean, maybe he set out to sweep her off her feet." Keir narrowed his eyes. "And maybe it had little to do with his attraction to her."

Mary frowned. "I don't follow you, Keir."

"Cassie says a man's been asking about Dawn. Seems like quite a coincidence, two guys turning up here within, what, a week, both of them interested in the same woman?"

"Yes," Mary said softly, "I suppose it does."

"Cassie says this guy doesn't belong here."

Dan raised an eyebrow. "I've never seen a human being who didn't belong in this town, one way or another."

"I'm not saying it right." Keir frowned. "She says he looks like..." He thought for a moment. "Well, from her description, he sounds as if he just came down from the hills. Big, rawboned, cammo pants and combat boots, talks like a redneck and he's got a cold look in his eyes."

"Harman Kitteridge," Dan said softly. "Dawn's husband."

"Right. It's a good guess, anyway. Do we have a photo of him?"

Dan unlocked a drawer in his desk, took out Dawn's file and leafed through it. "No, dammit, we don't. But I can get one."

"In the meantime, I've told Cassie she's to call me if she spots him again."

"I'll have her take a look at the footage from the security cameras, let her see if she can find him."

"Good."

"Keir?" Mary began to rise from her chair. "If you haven't yet said anything to Dawn, let me do it. You know, woman to woman."

"There's nothing to tell her, Ma. If this is a false alarm, we'd just scare her. Worse, once she knew we'd found out about her problems, she might run to protect herself and her son."

"Yes. Of course." Mary settled back. "But we can't simply ignore things."

"No. We can't."

The three of them looked at each other. Then Keir shrugged his shoulders. "The best we can do is what we've talked about. Let Cassie ID this man, if she can. Get a photo of Kitteridge. And Dan? Tell your men to keep their eyes open for this guy."

"Right."

"And make sure Snyder sticks close to Dawn without letting her know he's watching her. That's all we can do just now."

Mary and Dan nodded.

"We're agreed, then?"

"Agreed," Mary Elizabeth and Dan said in one voice.

Keir hoped it would be enough.

Gray spent the morning doing his best to behave like a tourist. Considering that he'd spent the night with Dawn in his arms, it wasn't easy. How could a man concentrate on Hoover Dam when his head was filled with a woman?

He strolled through the lobby of the Desert Song, remembering how hard it had been to leave her, as he always did, just before daybreak. That was how she wanted it. She had this thing about keeping their relationship private; it was why he hadn't stopped to look for her when he entered the hotel. He teased her about it but he had to admit, he kind of liked it. Not the secrecy. Hell, no. He wanted the world to know they were together...but he loved that touch of old-fashioned modesty.

How could he ever have imagined Dawn was a woman without morals? She was probably the most principled person he'd ever met.

He just wished he had half her morality, he thought as he inserted his key card into the door of his suite. If he did, he'd have told her the truth about himself by now, but he was a coward. He kept postponing the moment she'd realize that he'd deceived her, right from the start, especially after all the things she'd said about trusting him.

"Damn," he said softly, as he tossed his card on the table.

He had to come clean, and soon. He'd hoped to wait until he knew more about her child, where the boy was and how best to assure his safety, but the longer he put it off, the worse the moment of truth would be.

Gray pulled off his T-shirt, took a can of soda from the minibar and headed for the shower.

Plus, he couldn't stay in Vegas forever and he wasn't leaving until everything was out in the open. Her secrets as well as his, because that had to happen before he could tell her that he couldn't imagine being without her, that she was going back to New York with him.

He bowed his head, put his palms against the glass wall of the shower and let the water beat down on his shoulders.

He'd never fallen so hard or fast in his life. Actually it made more sense to say he'd never fallen at all, because what he'd felt that first night they'd spent together hadn't diminished. If anything, it had grown more powerful.

He was in love.

He'd tried telling himself he wasn't, that his emotions had been stirred by great sex. Mind-blowing sex. It hadn't worked. It was love, not sex, and he knew, just knew, Dawn felt the same way. He could see it in her eyes when he took her in his arms, taste it on her mouth when he kissed her, feel it in the way she touched him…and wasn't that great? He was standing in the shower, turning himself on.

Gray turned the water colder and shivered under its merciless pounding. By the time he stepped onto the bath mat, he'd reached a decision. He hadn't heard from Ballard yet but what did it matter? It was reality time. Tonight, he'd tell Dawn everything. Why Jonas had sent him in search of her. Why that search had started with Harman, and what Harman had told him about her son. She'd be upset, maybe angry, maybe scared, but he'd take her in his arms, force her to listen to him, keep talking and explaining and telling her that he loved her until she got past everything and admitted she loved him, too, because he knew she did, dammit, he *knew* she did.

Then she'd tell him where she kept her kid and he'd be able to protect the boy. And then—then, they could move on with the rest of their lives, live in New York or anyplace else she wanted, because among the many things he'd discovered during this amazing week was that he didn't really like the city. He didn't like what he did for a living, either. He'd started out with some noble idea about defending the innocent and ensuring justice, and ended up defending anybody who had the big bucks to buy his services.

What would it be like, to be a lawyer in a small town? A place like, say, Brazos Springs? It was a crazy idea, considering that he'd run away from Texas and small towns, but everything was different now. He'd run it past Dawn and make sure she understood that they could live wherever she wanted, in a city or a town or the middle of the desert, just so long as it made her happy.

Gray chuckled. He reached for a clean shirt and a pair of chinos, put them on and looked at himself in the mirror.

"You're running ahead of yourself, buddy," he said. "Slow

down, tell the lady how you feel before you start putting down roots.''

He would, tonight. And if Ballard didn't phone by this evening... Why wait for evening? He zipped his fly, slid his feet into a pair of mocs and reached for his cell phone, frowning when he got Jack's answering machine.

''Jack, it's Gray. I need that data about Dawn Kitteridge's kid ASAP. I'm counting on you, man. Get the info to me fast, okay?''

Gray snapped the phone shut. Ten to one, she had the boy living somewhere along that road where he'd chased her and her car ran out of gas. She'd probably been visiting the kid that day. Thomas, his name was. Jack had learned that much. Tommy. Nice name for a boy. He'd be, what, six? Seven? What did kids that age like? Baseball? Football? He'd never thought much about kids one way or another except for his ever-expanding batch of cousins, but he could...

''Whoa.''

He blinked. He was going from being a bachelor to being a husband and father, and he hadn't even consulted with the lady he wanted to marry. Intended to marry. Gray shook his head as he switched on the light over the bathroom sink.

His friends back east would never believe it. Graham Baron, a study in domesticity. His cousins wouldn't believe it, either, although they'd all taken turns teasing him, saying that one day he'd fall and when he did, he'd fall hard. Wishful thinking, he'd figured—but they were right. He'd gone down like the proverbial ton of bricks and the craziest thing was, he was happy about it.

Whistling softly, he lathered his face and drew the razor along his jaw. One more hour until he saw Dawn. Until he went for broke and told her everything. What if he said the hell with waiting that hour? If he went straight downstairs, to where she worked, swung her into his arms and kissed her and never mind modesty and propriety or anything else. Would she kiss him back or would she slug him? Knowing Dawn, she might do both. First the kiss, because he wouldn't let her go until he felt her mouth soften under his and, yes, it would soften. She couldn't resist his kisses any more than he could resist hers. Then the slap, because no matter how wonderful the kiss, she'd be brimming with indignation. He loved that about her, all that fire and strength—

Gray cocked his head. Was that somebody at the door? He turned off the water, swabbed at his face with a towel, looped it around his neck and went to find out. Maybe it was the guy who restocked the minibar. When he fished out that can of soda, he'd noticed...

It wasn't the minibar guy or the chambermaid. It was Dawn. He'd thought about her, wanted her...and she was here, yet another small miracle in a week of them. He felt a foolish smile curl over his mouth.

"Sweetheart. Honey, I was just thinking of—"

The words died on his tongue. Something was wrong. Terribly wrong. Dawn's eyes were wild; her face was drained of all color. She was trembling. Visibly trembling, and when he reached out to draw her into his arms she jerked away from his hands. A chill lanced through him, drove straight to the marrow of his bones as a dozen explanations ran through his head, every last one of them bearing the name Harman Kitteridge.

"Dawn? Sweetheart, what's happened?"

She slipped past him, drawing in her breath as if she couldn't bear the thought of her body brushing his. He caught her by the shoulders. She tried to pull away but he held on tight.

"Talk to me," he demanded. "Tell me what's wrong."

Dawn stared at him. She'd come here on impulse. It was either that or go crazy. Lunch with Cassie had triggered it but the truth was that horrible questions and doubts had been tormenting her for days, buzzing around inside her head like tiny insects. She'd done her best to ignore them but, just like a swarm of mosquitoes, they kept coming back no matter how hard she swatted them away.

Who was Graham Baron? A lawyer from New York, he said, but the only thing she really knew was that he was a stranger who had entered her life with the force of a storm coming down from the mountains. Why had he come to Vegas? He said he was on vacation, but he didn't like gambling any more than she did. And then there was the most important question of all. Why her? In a town filled with beautiful women, why had he chosen her? She never deceived herself about her looks. She was attractive, yes, maybe even pretty, but competition for the showgirls, the models, the would-be actresses who were a dime a dozen in Las Vegas? No way.

Why would a man who was so good-looking, so intelligent, so obviously rich and eligible, pick her?

All those questions, and then her conversation with Cassie. It had left her shaken though she'd tried not to show it. She'd spent the afternoon doing the scut work of the wealthy and important guests who demanded her services, performing her duties by rote while she tried to make sense of things, but how could you make sense of a puzzle when the important pieces were missing?

For four years she'd led a quiet, careful existence. She'd been content with her job, happy with the little home she'd made for herself, and thrilled with the knowledge that her son was safe. She'd lived by a set of self-imposed rules meant to protect her and Tommy—and then, in what she could only think of as one explosive moment of madness, she'd broken them all.

She'd gotten involved with a man. Gotten involved? What a stupid, empty phrase. What she'd done was a thousand times more dangerous.

She'd fallen in love.

She'd been sitting in her office after lunch, talking on the phone with an up-and-coming Hollywood director who was babbling about how he could only drink water bottled in a spring that bubbled up in a particular valley rimmed by a particular set of mountains, and she'd been saying yes, uh-huh, I understand, when all at once she'd thought, *Cassie's right. I'm in love with Gray.*

And hot on the heels of that dizzying realization had come another.

A man who sounded as if he might be Harman was hanging around the casino.

How could those two things happen at the same time? Was Cassie right about that, too? Was it coincidence, that Gray had come into her life and now Harman had found her, or was it something else?

"You must understand," she'd heard the director say, "only that specific water…" and she broke into his stupid little speech and said all right, she'd take care of it. Then she'd dropped the phone and run from her office because if she thought too long about where she was going or what she was about to do, she'd have lost her courage.

Riding the elevator to Gray's floor, listening to the pounding of her heart, she'd tried to imagine what he'd say when she confronted him. Questioning him could be the most risky thing she'd done since the night she ran away from the mountain.

If Cassie was wrong and there wasn't a connection between Gray and Harman, she'd have a lot of explaining to do. Once Gray knew everything, how would he look at her? Her past. Her secrets. She'd kept the most important parts of herself hidden from him…and yet, that wasn't the worst of it.

What if Cassie was right? Could there be some awful link between Gray and Harman?

No, she'd thought as she hurried down the hall, no, there couldn't be. Just imagining the two men in the same room was impossible.

Gray, she'd say, *Gray, I have to ask you something and I know it's foolish…*

And then he opened the door and saw her, and guilt flashed in his eyes like lightning. He'd tried to hide it but she knew what she'd seen, and it terrified her.

"Dawn? Talk to me."

She took a deep breath. "Gray. I have to ask you something."

"Anything. You know that, sweetheart. Let me shut the—"

"No!" She shook her head and shifted free of his hands. "No," she said carefully, "don't."

"All right." A muscle ticked in his jaw. "What do you want to know?"

"Do you… Have you ever…" Her mouth felt as parched as the desert. Just do it, she told herself, just say the words and get it over with. "It's about my husband. Do you know him?" She kept talking; she knew she was babbling but she couldn't seem to stop. "Have you—have you had dealings with him? Gray? Please. Don't look at me like that. Tell me. Tell me that you don't know Harman…"

"Darling," he said softly, and reached for her.

She slapped at his hands. "You do!" She wanted to scream but she had to hold on, hold on; she needed to know everything. "You know him. And you came to Las Vegas to find me."

"Dawn. It's not that simple."

"Yes. It is. It's very simple. You and Harman. God, oh God, you know each other!"

"Dammit," he said, his word rough with anger, "will you listen?"

"I did. Oh, I did. I listened to all your lies, you—you—" She caught her lip between her teeth, bit down until she felt the tang of blood. "Did you come to Vegas looking for me?"

"Jesus, if you'd just—"

"Yes or no?" Her voice rose. "Just yes or no, Gray. You can manage that, can't you?"

He stabbed his fingers through his hair, paced in a tight circle before facing her again. "Yes. Okay? That's why I came to Vegas. To find you. And yes, I know Kitteridge, but… Dawn? Dawn!"

He reached for her as she swung away from him and she flailed out with her fists, pummeling him while she sobbed for breath. Gray cursed and caught her wrist. She kicked him in the shins and he grunted with pain but held on.

"Dawn," he said desperately, "listen to me—"

"I did," she panted, "I listened and God, I wish, oh I wish…"

She jerked a hand free, reached back and picked up something from the table. Gray saw the blur of her hand and then pain exploded in his temple. *She slugged me with the phone*, he thought in wonder. Then the room began to spin. His hand fell from hers and he dropped to his knees. Blood dripped to the carpet.

A couple of minutes dragged by before he could get to his feet, walk unsteadily into the bathroom and peer into the mirror. He had a cut over his eye and the odds were good he'd also have an impressive shiner in a couple of hours. The lady swung one hell of a mean telephone.

He winced as he soaked a towel in cold water and pressed it to the wound. Time to go to Plan B—except he didn't have a Plan B. He'd never imagined Dawn would confront him before he had the chance to—

"You son of a bitch!" Keir exploded through the door, slapped a hand in the middle of Gray's chest and shoved him against the wall. "What did you do to Dawn?"

"You've got the question wrong, O'Connell. It's what did Dawn do to me?"

Keir jerked his head back and took a look at Gray's face. "Jesus."

"Exactly. And if you don't get your fist out of my gut, I'm just liable to toss my cookies all over your shoes."

Keir dropped his hand to his side, took a step back and glared at Gray. "Security tells me you manhandled Dawn Carter."

Gray barked out a laugh. "You've got it backward." He dipped the towel in the basin and wrung it out. "And what's Security doing, keeping tabs on your guests?"

"They were keeping tabs on Dawn, Baron, not on you."

"I don't understand." Gray hissed as he put the wet towel against his temple. "Why would they do that?"

"Don't play dumb with me," Keir snapped. "You might have fooled her but I saw right through you from the beginning. You're up to something."

"Listen, O'Connell, I've got my hands full right now, okay? I've got to figure out a way to make a woman stand still long enough to hear the truth. You want to fight? Well, save it for another time." Gray looked into the mirror and caught Keir's eyes with his. "You'd be wasting your time, anyway. Dawn's in love with me."

"She's been hypnotized by you, is what you mean."

"Sorry, pal. She's in love with me." Gray dropped the towel into the sink and turned around. "And I'm in love with her."

"Sorry? You think I'm interested in Dawn as more than an employee? I mean, she's great, she's terrific, but…" Keir narrowed his eyes. "You're good, Baron. I come busting in here because I know you're up to no good and now you've got me explaining that you're wrong about what I feel for Dawn Kitter—"

Keir swallowed the name as soon as he said it, but it was too late.

"You know," Gray said in amazement.

Keir jerked his thumb toward the door. "I know that you're going to be out of here in five minutes."

"You know who she really is."

"Five minutes. After that, I'll have you tossed out on your—"

"Dammit, man, don't play games with me!" Gray clasped Keir's arm. "How much do you know?"

"Everything," Keir said coldly. He shook off Gray's hand. "That's why you've been wasting your time. Did you really think we wouldn't figure out that you were working with her husband?"

"That I was…" Gray barked out a laugh. "You're dead wrong, man. Her husband is scum."

"That's the only thing you and I would agree on. And after I throw you out of my hotel I'm going to find Harman Kitteridge and toss him into the gutter with you."

"Listen, O'Connell, you've got this all…" Gray caught his breath. "What the hell are you saying? He's here? Dawn's husband is in Vegas?"

Something in Gray's voice made Keir bite back the sarcastic retort that had sprung to his lips.

"Yeah. He's here."

"You're sure?"

"Ninety-nine percent. Give me a break, Baron. You expect me to think—"

"Does Dawn know?" Gray demanded, curling his fists around the lapels of Keir's suit jacket.

"Get your hands off me!"

"Answer the question, dammit. Does she know?"

"Yes. She—"

"Jesus Christ, O'Connell, she's going to run!" Gray jammed a wad of toilet tissue against the oozing cut over his eye, raced into the bedroom and grabbed a shirt. "You don't believe me? Call downstairs. See if she's in her office. I'm betting she ran straight out the door and into her car."

"What are you talking about?"

"Do it, man!" Gray swung toward Keir. "I'm not working with Dawn's husband. I'd just as soon beat the bastard to a bloody pulp as look at him. It's true, I came here to find her but it had nothing to do with Harman. It's too complicated to explain right now. You'll have to trust me."

"Yeah," Keir said grimly, "and the check is in the mail."

"I love Dawn. I want to protect her. And I can't, because she's gone after her kid and I don't know where the hell he is!"

"You don't know anything," Keir said, but without much conviction.

"But you do, don't you? You know where the boy is."

"Pack up, Baron, and get out."

"O'Connell. Listen to me. If Kitteridge is here, he's watching her every move. He sees her fly out of this place looking like she did when she left me, he'll know she's on to him. He'll follow her. She'll lead him straight to the kid and once she does... Dammit, are you gonna just stand there and let him beat her senseless, then snatch her and the kid?"

Gray glared at Keir. Keir glared back. Was Baron lying, or was he telling the truth?

"At the very least, you've got to know I'm right about Dawn going to her son."

She would. Keir knew that much.

"And if I'm right about her husband following her..." Gray

took a step forward. "Here's the deal. You know where the boy is. Take me there with you. You have security people? Let them come along. And if I make one false move when we find Dawn, tell your men to do whatever it takes to stop me." His mouth twisted. "O'Connell, I love this woman. I'd give my life for her. And if I lose her because you'd rather stand here than come to a decision, I'll kill you right after I beat her son of a bitch husband to death with my bare hands. Do you understand?"

The threat didn't work. The fear in Gray's eyes did. Keir grabbed for the phone and jabbed a button. No, Dawn wasn't at her desk. In fact, Becky said, she'd been trying to find Keir to ask him what was going on. Dawn had come flying through the lobby and the guard at the employee's entrance said she'd driven out of the lot like a bat out of hell. And oh yes, Mr. Coyle had left a cryptic message for Keir, should he stop by, something about a faxed photo of a man who had been identified on a security tape by a cocktail waitress...

Keir slammed down the phone. "Let's go. Take the fire stairs. It's faster."

They pounded down the steps. Keir grabbed his cell phone as they ran through the lobby. "Dan? I'm on my way out the door. I'm heading for Rocking Horse Ranch. Take a couple of your men and follow me."

Seconds later, the little entourage was on the road. Keir shot Gray a look filled with warning. "If this is all bull and you're working with Kitteridge, I promise you, Baron, your life won't be worth a damn."

"It won't be worth a damn without Dawn," Gray said softly, and then he stared out the window as the empty desert flashed by, and prayed that they'd reach her in time.

CHAPTER SIXTEEN

CARS. Cars everywhere. And trucks and people, all of them crossing the street against the light, laughing and talking and paying no attention to traffic because they were on vacation and she was going to go crazy if everything and everybody didn't get out of her way. Get out, get out, get—

Dawn slammed her fist against the horn ring. A woman stepping off the sidewalk jumped back. Her plump face reddened and you didn't have to be a lip-reader to know she'd said something short and ugly but Dawn didn't care.

All she could think about was Tommy. She had to get to him before Harman did.

Ahead, the light went from green to amber. She stepped on the gas, shot through it before it changed to red. Another minute and she'd leave the city behind. Then it was a clear shot along the asphalt until the turnoff that led to Rocking Horse Ranch. Harman couldn't have gotten there yet. Maybe he hadn't even located Tommy. He would, though. There was no doubt of that.

She'd made a terrible mistake underestimating him, thinking him vicious and cunning but not really clever. But he was, clever enough to have gotten together with someone like Gray, someone she could hardly imagine breathing the same air as her husband.

The road opened ahead. Dawn tromped down on the gas. She couldn't think about Gray. Not now. It was too dangerous to let herself realize how stupid she'd been. How careless. Four years spent erasing the past and then a man came along and she listened to his soft lies and now she'd compromised everything. She was about to turn Tommy's life upside down, go on the run, take him from the only stability he'd ever known... If she was right, and Harman hadn't yet found him.

A whisper of despair burst from her throat and she blanked

her mind to everything but the road arrowing across the desert and the child who waited, *had* to be waiting, at its dusty end.

Gray gripped the roll bar of Keir's SUV and stared blindly at the road ahead.

"You sure this'll get us there faster than the highway?"

"Yes."

"How much further?"

"Maybe another forty, fifty minutes."

"This damn thing's a track, not a road. What if we run into some kind of barrier? Downed trees? A gully?"

"You find a tree within fifty miles of this place, you'll make it into the Guinness Book of Records. We see a gully, we drive through it. Or around it." Keir shot him a cold smile. "That's what Sports Utility Vehicles are for, Baron. Even a city slicker like you should know that."

"You sure we won't miss that turnoff?" Gray said, ignoring the kind of insult that would ordinarily have wrung a sharp retort.

"We'd both have to be blind not to see a pair of boulders the size of Godzilla's balls."

"That's the first marker. You said there were two."

"The second's a mesa, about half a mile from the Ranch. Look, you want to do something useful, check once in a while to make sure Dan's still behind us. Otherwise, just shut up and count yourself lucky I let you come with me."

"Don't push it, O'Connell," Gray said softly. "That's my woman out there."

"Your woman?" Keir laughed. "You don't even know her. How long have you been here? A week?"

"Ten days," Gray said tightly. "And I know her, all right, same as I know that the man she's married to would as soon make her suffer as breathe."

Keir's hands tightened on the wheel. "Amazing how things worked out, isn't it? You turn up. Then he turns up, and it's all one big coincidence."

Gray looked at Keir. A muscle knotted in his jaw and he looked back at the road.

"It's no coincidence. I was stupid. I underestimated Kitteridge. I forgot that snakes aren't as smart as humans but that doesn't stop them from being just as deadly."

Keir glanced at Gray. There was pain in the man's voice. Okay. Maybe he'd cut him some slack.

"How about telling me why you came to Vegas looking for Dawn?"

Gray craned his neck, saw the fast-moving dust cloud that was Dan Coyle's SUV behind them. "It's a long story."

"And it's a long drive. We've got time."

"Yeah. Okay." Gray ran the tip of his tongue over his lips. "Well, I have an uncle."

"Wow. That's unusual."

"You want to hear this," Gray snarled, "or you want to do stand-up comedy?" He took a minute to collect himself. "My uncle's an old man. He's sick, he's rich and he's had what you might call an interesting life."

"I don't see what that has to do with Dawn."

"You will, if you stop interrupting me." Gray shifted in his seat and looked at Keir. "A few months back, he asked me to do him a favor. He told me this story about a love affair that went wrong half a century ago."

"I still don't see—"

"My uncle got involved with his partner's wife. When his partner found out, he divorced her. Months later, she gave birth to a child. A daughter. My uncle never knew about it until recently and he figures it's possible he fathered the girl. Her name was Orianna. She grew up and had a daughter, too. She named her Dawn."

Keir scowled as he worked it through. "Let me get this straight. Your uncle is Dawn's grandfather?"

"Maybe. He's not sure but if he is, he wants to include her in his will."

"I still don't see your involvement in this."

"Yeah." Gray sighed. "Well, neither did I but my uncle insisted on playing this close to the vest. He didn't want anyone to get wind of what was going on until he had some answers, so he asked me to find Dawn Lincoln Kitteridge—Dawn Carter—and check her out.''

"Check her out, how?" Keir looked at Gray. "You gonna tell me all you've been doing is getting samples of her DNA?"

"What I'm telling you is that I'm tired of your smart mouth," Gray said coldly.

"Okay. Take it easy. I guess that was a little out of line." A scrawny coyote darted across the track just ahead. Keir cursed, swung the wheel and missed the animal by inches. "Traffic hazards, even out here," he muttered. "Check her out, how?"

"See what she was like. Her personality. Her lifestyle. Don't look at me that way, man. I know it sounds nuts but if you knew my uncle—"

"Jonas Baron. Yeah. He's got a reputation for coming up with unusual requests before he makes an investment."

"That's right. I guess that's how he sees this, as an—" Gray frowned. "You know who I'm talking about?"

"Don't look so surprised. Did you think you could come sniffing around the Song and not attract our interest? I had you checked out."

"Were you worried about your hotel—or about Dawn?"

Keir looked at Gray, saw the tightly banked jealousy in his eyes, and laughed. "Take it easy. I was worried about Dawn but not for the reasons you think. Actually it was my mother who was worried about her and, believe me, that story's even longer than yours. Let's just say my interest in the lady is strictly fraternal.''

Gray thought it over, considered the openness in Keir's expression and nodded. "A good thing for you that it is."

Keir decided to let that pass. "So your uncle told you where Dawn was, and—"

"Jonas told me nothing, not even the truth about him maybe being her grandfather. He just said he wanted to settle an old debt and asked me to do the groundwork. I didn't want to do it—I'm not one of my uncle's fans—but it turned out I owed a debt, too, to him, so I agreed."

Gray told Keir the story, from his first meeting with Harman to the last. "That's when I underestimated him. I didn't realize it but I must have tipped my hand and—O'Connell? Those rocks up ahead. Is that the formation we're looking for?"

"Yes. Another ten miles, maybe less, and we'll be there. If we're right and Harman shows, I just hope—"

"Hope won't do it," Gray said coldly. "But I will."

Keir looked at the man seated beside him. Gray seemed deceptively still. Once, hiking a canyon just a few miles from town, he'd spotted a mountain lion ready to spring on a mule deer. He remembered how the cat had concentrated all its energy, reflexes and mental acuity on that one moment, that one purpose and what it was about to do.

"You really do love her," he murmured.

"Yes," Gray said simply, "I do."

"Baron?" Keir hesitated. "Look, if we're right and Harman shows—"

"He'll show, all right. I can feel it."

So could Keir. What worried him wasn't that Harman might not turn up, it was the icy determination of the man beside him.

"Yeah. Well, if he does... You let Dan and me deal with him. Okay?"

"Is that what you would do," Gray said quietly, "if Kitteridge was after the woman who'd become your life?"

The men looked at each other. Keir nodded, not only in acceptance but in understanding. Gray smiled thinly. Then he turned away and stared out the window until, at last, the buildings and corrals of the Rocking Horse Ranch rose in the distance, shimmering in the heat of the thin desert air.

Mrs. Wilton was doing her best to smile. Dawn was doing her best to be civil.

"If you'd simply call ahead, Ms. Carter," the owner of Rocking Horse Ranch said, the same as she had a little over a week ago during that other unannounced visit. "We do have a schedule. The boys appreciate holding to a routine."

"I'm sure they do, Mrs. Wilton." Dawn knotted her hands in her lap to keep them from shaking. She'd decided to treat her appearance here as nothing extraordinary, just another quick visit squeezed in during the work week. She didn't want anyone to realize she was about to take her son and disappear. "As I said, I managed to free up some time at the last minute and I thought Tommy would like to go to dinner and then to a movie with me."

"There's a hot dog roast tonight, and cake and ice cream for Barry Salter's birthday."

"That sounds lovely," Dawn said brightly, "but I really think Tommy will enjoy the special treat I've planned."

"You'll be back late," Mrs. Wilton said, looking down her nose with disapproval.

"I'm afraid so. In fact..." Dawn smiled again, though it felt as if her lips were sticking to her teeth. "I might just keep Tommy overnight instead of bringing him back after the movie."

Mrs. Wilton sighed. "You'll be taking him home with you for the night, then?"

"Yes," Dawn said blithely. How easy it was to lie, when lying was all that would save you. "I'll have him back tomorrow morning, bright and early."

"Very well, Ms. Carter." Mrs. Wilton rose from her chair. "Thomas is probably watching cartoons with some of the other boys. I'll take you—"

"That's all right. I know where he is. I'll get him myself." Dawn paused in the doorway. "Mrs. Wilton? Thank you for everything."

"You're welcome, I'm sure. After all, one night's disruption in routine—"

"I mean, thank you for all you've done for Tommy. He's been very happy here."

"Oh." Mrs. Wilton's face softened. "Well, that's nice of you to say. He's a fine little boy."

"Yes," Dawn said softly, "yes, he is."

Tommy threw himself into her arms when he saw her. She drew him outside, to where she'd left her car, and told him they were going to have a very special evening, just the two of them.

His face fell. "But we're havin' a cookout. An' cake and ice cream," he said. "Didn't Mrs. Wilton tell you? It's Barry's birthday. He's gonna be eight."

Dawn squatted down and brushed her son's soft golden curls from his forehead. "I know, baby. But think of the fun we'll have. We can have hot dogs, same as you'd have if you were staying here."

"I won't get to grill mine on a stick."

"No. You won't. Tell you what. You pick what you want for supper. McDonald's? Burger King? I know. We'll go to that place where they serve those delicious waffles. You can have one with strawberries and whipped cream and—"

"You can stay here and go to the party with me."

Dawn cupped her son's face in her hands. "Listen to me, Tommy. We're going to play a very special game tonight. Remember that movie about the puppies that ran away and had to hide from a bad person?"

Tommy's eyes widened. "Are we getting a puppy?"

"Sweetheart, pay attention, okay? We're going to pretend we're like those puppies. We're going to get into Mommy's car and drive away from here as quickly as we can."

Tommy pushed out his bottom lip. "I don't think I'm gonna like this game, Mom."

Mom. Her little boy had called her Mom again. He was definitely growing up and now he was going to have to grow up even faster.

"Thomas."

"You never call me that unless you're mad at me."

"I'm not mad at you, baby." Dawn pulled him into her arms and gave him a quick, hard hug. "I just need you to be as big a boy as you can, okay?" She sat back on her heels, smiled and adjusted his collar. "Now I want you to get into the car and put on your seat belt."

Tommy sighed. "Okay, Mama. Lemme just go get my jacket—"

"No!" She spoke sharply. Her son looked at her in surprise and she stood up, reminded herself that she didn't want to scare him, and held out her hand. "You won't need it. There's always that big old blanket I keep in the trunk that we use when we picnic. If you get cold, I'll wrap you in that. We can't waste time going back to your room. Remember, we're like those puppies from that movie, on the run and moving fast.'' Tommy looked doubtful and she flashed another smile and tapped him lightly on the bottom. ''Okay, baby. You go scoot right on into—''

''Hello, Dawn.''

She knew the voice instantly. The coldness of it, the menace inherent in the flat intonation, were as familiar as if four days had gone by, not four years.

Dawn straightened up and turned to face the man who haunted her dreams.

He hadn't changed at all. The empty eyes. The thin smile. The hands, flexing and unflexing at his sides in promise of what was to come. He was all that was evil, and he had come for her just as she had always known he would.

''You were real easy to follow,'' he said softly, ''all the way from that fancy hotel to here.''

''Mama?''

Tommy's voice was a soft question. Dawn realized she was clasping his shoulder, digging her fingers into his tender flesh.

''Go in the house, baby,'' she said softly.

''Mama, what's the matter?''

''Nothing. Go on, Tommy. Do as I said. Find Mrs. Wilton and tell her—''

''Hello, Thomas.''

''Hello,'' her son said, with all the innocence of his seven years. ''Are you a friend of my mama's?''

Harman squatted down. His teeth flashed in a smile that made Dawn's belly knot. ''You could say that, boy. Why don't you come shake hands?''

''Tommy.'' Dawn pushed her son toward the door without taking her eyes from her husband. ''Get into the house. Now.''

''But, Mama…''

''Do what I tell you, Tommy. Go inside. Tell Mrs. Wilton to call the police.''

''It's going to be hard to do that,'' Harman said lazily, rising

to his full height, "considerin' that the phones ain't working."
He reached for his belt and withdrew a hunting knife that
reflected the sharp glare of the late-afternoon sun. "Funny,
how a modern thing like a phone line just can't stand up to a
little wear and tear."

"Harman." Dawn's teeth chattered. She had to tear her eyes
from the blade. She knew how sharp it was; she'd spent endless evenings, watching her husband hone the steel to a fine,
deadly edge. "Harman? I'll do whatever you want."

"Damn right you will."

"Just—just let Tommy go."

"My truck's right back there." Harman jerked his head toward one of the outbuildings. "You and the boy get movin'."

"I'll go. Not Tommy. There's no need for you to take
him."

"No need?" Harman's face darkened. "What does a whore
know of a man's needs, save for the only one she's fit to
service?" He took a step forward. "Move!"

"Mama…" Tommy buried his face against Dawn and began to cry. "I don't like this man."

"'Mama,'" Harman mimicked, "'I don't like this man.'
Damn you," he roared, "you see what you've done here? You
took a man-child and turned him into a sissy. Stop that bawl-
in', boy." Tommy's sobs only grew louder. "Goddamn you,
stop that snivelin' or I'll start the lessons you need to learn
afore we get—"

Tires squealed. Dust flew. Harman whirled around as a pair
of SUVs roared across the hard-packed dirt and stopped. Dan
Coyle and two of his men jumped out of one; Keir and Gray
jumped from the other.

"Well, well, ain't this nice?" Harman said softly. "We got
ourselves all kinds of company." He smiled, locked his eyes
on Keir and Gray and tossed his knife from hand to hand.
"Welcome, gentlemen. I should have expected the both of
you'd turn up, considerin' how cozy I'm sure you've been
with my wife."

Gray looked at Harman. Their eyes met, and he realized

that he'd never understood the full meaning of hatred until
now.

"Kitteridge," he said softly.

Dawn gave a choked sob. Gray risked a quick look at her.
I love you, he thought fiercely, as if she could see into his
head, his heart, his very soul. He felt the power of that hope
sweep through him as he turned his gaze on Harman.

"Let them go, Kitteridge," he said.

"You're some piece of work, Baron, you know that?" Harman spat a glob of saliva at the ground. "All that crap about
wantin' to give the harlot a music box and here you ended up
givin' her what's hangin' between your legs."

Gray's eyes were flat. Harman laughed, reached out to
Dawn and wrapped a hand around her arm.

"It wasn't no music box brought you to my mountain. Did
you think I'd really believe that? She come into money. I want
to know how much."

"A lot." Gray flashed a quick look at Dawn. Harman's
fingers had to be hurting her but she was staring at Gray, eyes
wide, as the fabric of deceit he'd woven began to unravel. *I
love you,* he thought again. "A lot," he repeated, steadying
his gaze on Harman. "And it can be yours, if you play your
cards right."

"Damn right. She's my wife."

"Yeah, but you don't know where the money is or how to
get it. I do."

"Meaning?"

"Let my friend here take the boy and I'll tell you. It's impossible to talk with the kid making all that noise."

Harman's eyes narrowed. Then he jerked his head at Keir.
"Get the brat out of here."

"Keir," Gray said softly, without looking at him, and Keir
nodded, scooped the sobbing child into his arms and started
toward the house. "No," Gray said sharply. "Take the truck.
Get him out of here." Seconds later, the SUV roared away.
One down, Gray thought, and one to go.

"Now," Harman said, "you tell me about the money."

"It's in a safe-deposit box."

A shifty smile curled across Harman's mouth. "An' you got the key, I bet."

"Yes." The lies came easily, just as long as he didn't look too hard at Dawn, didn't let himself see the expression he knew would be on her face. "I do."

"But you'd give it to me."

"Yes."

"Why would you do that? The way I figure it, you been screwin' my wife so's you could get some of that money for yourself."

"You're a smart man, Kitteridge. You figured it out before anybody else. But the thing is, you do something to her and there's no way anybody can touch the money. She needs to put her signature on a piece of paper."

"An' you were gonna be the man who'd share that happy moment with her." Harman grinned, tightened his grasp on Dawn and yanked her closer. "Ain't that the way you planned it, city man?"

"Like I said, you're smart."

Gray could see Harman processing what he'd told him. Greed was a powerful motivator. In his line of work, he'd seen it make men who thought they were smart overlook the most damning details. He could only hope Harman would make that same mistake.

"Why should I believe you?"

"Because you don't have much choice."

Seconds dragged by. Finally Harman nodded. "First, you call off the cops."

"Coyle?" Gray spoke to Dan but kept his eyes on Harman. "Get your men out of here."

"I don't take orders from you, Baron."

"He's raised the stakes too high, Coyle. Don't be a fool. Do as I tell you."

More time slipped by. Then Dan motioned his men into the SUV. They drove away and silence descended on the desert, broken only by the distant cry of a hawk. A sudden gust of wind blew its heated breath across the sand; it lifted a tendril of Dawn's hair from her temple.

Time seemed to stop. Then Harman slid his arm across Dawn's chest and yanked her back against him.

"Now you give me the key to that safe-deposit box."

"Sure," Gray said, with an easy smile. "But you have to give me something first. Put away that knife and let her go."

"You got balls, Baron, I'll give you that."

"Do it, or the deal's off."

"You just finished tellin' me I need her to sign some papers. Now you want me to let her go. I ain't the dumb country boy you seem to think. How's she gonna sign papers if I let her go?"

Gray took a slow step forward. "Stop and think, Kitteridge. Take a look at the lady. She's terrified. How are we going to travel to Austin with a woman who looks like she's scared to death of us?"

Harman frowned. "Austin, Texas?"

"That's what I said, yeah. Come on. Get rid of the knife and let go of her. She knows we can stop her anytime we want, don't you, sweetheart?"

Dawn flashed him a look that almost killed him but it didn't matter. Saving her was all that counted. Harman's mouth tightened but he sheathed his knife and thrust Dawn aside. She stumbled against Gray, who caught her wrist. She lifted her eyes to his and he thought his heart would break. She was pale, except for two bright spots of color on her cheeks. Tears clung to her lashes.

"You son of a bitch," she said, and spat into his face.

"Remember what I told you once?" he said softly. "This scene belongs to us. We get to write it any way we want."

"What scene?" Harman demanded. "What're you talking about?"

"I'm just reminding the lady of what I expect. The last thing a man wants to deal with is Wonder Woman."

"Wonder What?"

"Wonder Woman," Gray said softly.

"I don't know what the hell you're talking about," Harman said sharply.

Gray waited, hardly breathing, his fingers hard on Dawn's

wrist. Slowly he saw something changing in the blue depths of her eyes.

"Gray?" she whispered, and he smiled, just for her.

"Yes, baby," he said softly, and he pushed her aside and launched himself at her husband.

Harman stumbled back. The men fell to the ground, rolling over and over, grunting as they exchanged blows. Harman was bigger and heavier but Gray had the advantage of surprise and a hot, deadly rage. He pounded his fists into the other man's gut, into his face. Still, gradually, Harman's size began to tell. He shoved Gray down on his back, knelt astride him and pulled out his knife. Dawn screamed and flew toward the men. She beat her fists on her husband's shoulders but he brushed her away as if she were a fly.

"I'll deal with you next," he panted, "after I finish off this son of a—" A horn blared. Harman jerked around. An SUV was racing toward them, clouds of dust billowing out behind it. He looked back at Gray. "Plenty of time to do what I've dreamed of doin'," he said, his lips peeled back in a thin smile as he lifted the knife, but now the scream of police sirens rose above the sound of the horn.

Harman looked over his shoulder again. Cars were speeding toward them, fanned out across the desert sand. "Son of a bitch," he yelled. He turned back to Gray and brought the knife down, but Gray had taken advantage of the moment and as Harman struck, as Dawn's shrill cry rose into the air, he rolled to his side.

The blade bit into the sand. Harman cursed, jumped up, ran to his truck and took off with the vehicles in hot pursuit.

"Gray," Dawn sobbed. "Oh, Gray—"

Gray scrambled to his feet and opened his arms to the woman he loved. She flew into them, as she had the first night they'd made love.

"Did he hurt you? Are you—"

Gray hugged her to his heart. "I'm fine."

"Oh God, I thought he was going to kill you!"

"Sweetheart. You have to know I didn't mean what I said to Harman. I'll explain every—" She kissed him, and he could taste her tears and maybe even his own. "I love you," he said, clasping her face in his hands. "Dawn? Do you hear me? I love you. I'll always—"

A booming crash shook the earth. Dawn and Gray swung around. In the distance, they could see Dan Coyle's men and the police piling out of their cars. They'd stopped at the rim of the mesa that ran behind Rocking Horse Ranch. Another sound rocked the ground beneath their feet. Flames shot up from the canyon.

"Gray?" Dawn said. She looked from the mesa to him, and he knew the instant she realized what had happened. "Oh God! Harman drove over the edge…"

Gray cupped her head and brought it to his shoulder. She wept as he held her. Gradually her sobs died away and he drew back, just enough so he could tilt her face to his.

"It's over," he said softly.

She nodded, though tears still glittered in her eyes. "I'm not crying for him. Is that wrong? I just can't. I know I should but—"

"The hell you should," Gray said fiercely. "He doesn't deserve anybody's tears, sweetheart, certainly not yours."

"I'm crying for—I guess for the years lost. For the terrible waste."

Gray took out his handkerchief, gently wiped Dawn's eyes. "Don't think about that. Think about what's ahead. You. Me." He smiled. "And a kid named Tommy. I think it's time I met him."

Dawn made a sound that was half laugh, half sob. "He's a nice little boy. I think you'll like him."

"He's yours, baby. How could I not like him?" He smiled. "I just hope he likes me. I figure it would help if a kid liked the guy who intends to marry his mom."

"I love you," she said. "I love you…"

Dawn grabbed Gray's face, pulled it down to hers and kissed him. Then, arms around each other, they walked away from the past and toward the future.

EPILOGUE

Jonas Baron looked past his wife's shoulder, at the mirrored wall in their dressing room, and made a grumpy face.

"I don't see why a man's got to dress up like a penguin to attend a wedding."

"Hold still, Jonas, or this bow tie's going to... There." Marta beamed, took a step back and regarded her husband with admiration. "The tie's perfect, and so are you. You're still the handsomest man ever!"

"Methuselah in a cummerbund," he snorted, but a smile tugged at his mouth. "You look pretty good yourself. What do you call that color? I know it can't be somethin' as simple as red."

"It's called poppy." Marta laughed as she twirled before him, then smoothed down the skirt of her silk and chiffon dress. "And you're right. If they called it 'red,' nobody would buy it." Her smile tilted as she looked up at her husband. "You did remember to take your medicine, didn't you?"

"Yes ma'am, I did."

"Because you know what your doctors said, darling. That wonderful new transplant treatment cured your leukemia but you need to take those pills every—"

"Marta," Jonas said, in a voice so gentle none of his sons would have recognized it, "I'm old and sometimes I'm foolish, but the one thing I ain't is in any particular rush to meet my maker." He gave her a tender kiss. "Now, come on, gorgeous. Let's go show the younger generation a thing or two. What's the sense in havin' Gray's wedding at Espada if we don't get out and enjoy it?"

Marta smiled. "Sounds like a good idea." She took her husband's arm, then held back. "Jonas? I'm glad you told me why you sent Graham to find Dawn."

"Yeah, so'm I. I s'pose I should have said somethin' right

away but I wanted to be sure first. You understand, don't you?''

"Of course." Marta brushed a bit of lint from his tuxedo jacket. "Are you very disappointed?" she said softly.

"That Dawn isn't my granddaughter?" Jonas smiled. "No. Tell you the truth, I'm kind of relieved. When it turned out that Orianna—Dawn's mama—was born in August '52—''

"Meaning that Nora Lincoln was almost two months pregnant when you and she became lovers.''

"Yeah." Jonas sighed. "When Dawn told me her mama's birthday, it was like somebody took a big rock off my chest. I felt guilty as sin, thinkin' I'd abandoned a woman carryin' my child.''

"You didn't abandon anyone," Marta said gently. "Besides, look how well it's all worked out. I've never seen Graham so happy. Dawn's perfect for him. She's a lovely young woman.''

"She is that. I'm proud to have her join our family.''

"Her little boy is a sweetheart.''

"He's a charmer, all right. A hell-raiser, too." Jonas grinned. "Fits right in with our own grandkids.''

Marta peered into the mirror and smoothed down a stray curl. "Isn't it lovely that they've decided to make their home in Brazos Springs?" She smiled. "The party chairwoman says Graham's a wonderful candidate for district attorney.''

"That he is.''

"And I'm so pleased he and Leighton are getting on well.''

"Well, Gray's goin' out of his way to deal nicely with his old man. I expect that might be Dawn's doin'." Jonas lifted his wife's hand to his lips and kissed it. "A good woman can be a powerful influence on a man, like you've been on me, Mrs. Baron. I don't think I tell you that often enough.''

Marta squeezed her husband's arm. "I'm kind of fond of you, too," she said, and blinked back tears that came not of sorrow but of joy.

Twenty minutes later, in the gardens behind Espada, Gray stood at an altar bedecked with white and pink roses, watching as his bride took Dan Coyle's arm and waited for the pianist to begin playing the music they'd chosen for her walk up the aisle. Dawn wore a slender column of ivory lace; her hair was drawn back from her face and when she looked up from her bouquet of palest pink roses and smiled directly at him, Gray felt his heart lift into his throat.

"Beautiful," he murmured to his best man, Keir, who stood beside him.

"Yes," Keir said solemnly, "she certainly is."

"Hush," the maid of honor said, scolding them both.

Keir looked at her. Actually he'd been looking at her for the past half hour, ever since the wedding party assembled on the deck. He'd never seen Cassie look so, well, so beautiful. So softly feminine. So—so...

Something seemed to lift the hair on the nape of his neck. A breeze, he thought, though his sister, Meghan, would have said it was the breath of the little people teasing his senses. A good thing she wasn't here, then, Keir thought wryly, and turned his attention to the groom, who was whispering to the little boy standing on his other side.

"Tommy?" Gray said, out of the side of his mouth. "Have you got the rings?"

A small hand snaked into his. "I got 'em," Tommy whispered back.

Gray squeezed the boy's fingers. Four months had gone by since Dawn had introduced them and he already felt as if the child was his own flesh and blood.

"You know what, Gray?"

"What?"

"My mom was crying last night. Happy tears, she said, an' it was true 'cause she kept laughin' and huggin' me while she cried. She says it's because she loves you so much. Isn't that weird?"

"Weird." Gray cleared his throat. "But that's the way it goes, pal."

"That's what she said, too. Gray?"

"Uh-huh?"

"I'm glad we're marrying you."

Gray looked at the earnest little face. It wasn't part of the ceremony and he figured he was probably going to upset the wedding planner but he'd already done that by insisting on having two best men.

"Me, too." He bent and gave the kid a quick hug. Then he straightened up, watched his bride come toward him on Dan's arm. "Hello, sweetheart," he said.

Dawn smiled. "Hello, my love." Her voice trembled with emotion. Who could have imagined so much happiness? She rose on her toes and pressed a kiss to Dan's cheek. "I adore him," she whispered.

Dan grinned. "I'd never have guessed," he whispered back. He shook Gray's hand, then eased into one of the little white chairs in the front row, directly next to Mary Elizabeth O'Connell, who was quietly weeping. Dan rolled his eyes and dug into his pocket for a snowy-white handkerchief.

"I don't know why women cry at weddings," he mumbled, handing it to her.

"Because we're happy, you idiot," Mary mumbled in return.

Dan took a deep breath. "And would you cry at your own wedding, Mrs. O'Connell?"

Mary looked at him. "Is that a proposal, Mr. Coyle?"

"It is. Will you marry me, Mary?"

She smiled. "Yes, Dan," she said simply, "I will."

Dan took her hand, lifted it to his lips and kissed it. Then, fingers clasped, they turned their attention to the altar, where Cassie was weeping joyfully into her bouquet of roses. She'd been weeping all morning, except for the moment Dawn had hugged her, smiled, and tucked a crisp new dollar bill into her hand.

"I lost that bet," she'd said, "remember? The one we made when I said I'd never see Gray again."

"Oh," Cassie had replied, "of course you did." She'd laughed, then gone right back to crying, but they were happy tears. Her best friend had found happiness and deserved every bit of it. Not everyone was that lucky. She shot a quick look at Keir, who flashed her his usual polite smile. No, she thought, not everyone.

And then the guests rose to their feet, applauding, even laughing, because Mr. and Mrs. Graham Baron were in each other's arms, sharing a kiss that surely marked the start of a long and wonderful life, while a little boy locked his arms around their legs and beamed.

Harlequin invites you to experience the
charm and delight of

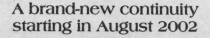

A brand-new continuity
starting in August 2002

HIS BROTHER'S BRIDE
by *USA Today* bestselling author
Tara Taylor Quinn

Check-in: TV reporter Laurel London and noted travel
writer William Byrd are guests at the new Twin Oaks
Bed and Breakfast in Cooper's Corner.

Checkout: William Byrd suddenly vanishes and while
investigating, Laurel finds herself face-to-face with
policeman Scott Hunter. Scott and Laurel face a painful past.
Can cop and reporter mend their heartbreak and get to the
bottom of William's mysterious disappearance?

HARLEQUIN®
Makes any time special ®

Visit us at www.cooperscorner.com   CC-CNM1R

The world's bestselling romance series.

HARLEQUIN®
Presents

Seduction and Passion Guaranteed!

SOCIETY WEDDINGS

**They're gorgeous, they're glamorous...
and they're getting married!**

Be our VIP guest at two of the most-talked-about
weddings of the decade—lavish ceremonies where the
cream of society gather to celebrate these marriages
in dazzling international settings.

Welcome to the sensuous, scandalous world
of the rich, royal and renowned!

SOCIETY WEDDINGS
Two original short stories in one volume:

Promised to the Sheikh
by *Sharon Kendrick*

The Duke's Secret Wife
by *Kate Walker*
on sale August, #2268

**Pick up a Harlequin Presents® novel and you will
enter a world of spine-tingling passion and
provocative, tantalizing romance!**

HARLEQUIN®
Makes any time special ®

*Available wherever
Harlequin books
are sold.*

Visit us at www.eHarlequin.com

HPSW

Three masters of the romantic suspense
genre come together in this special
Collector's Edition!

Unveiled

NEW YORK TIMES BESTSELLING AUTHORS

TESS GERRITSEN
STELLA CAMERON

And Harlequin Intrigue® author

AMANDA STEVENS

Nail-biting mystery...heart-pounding sensuality...and
the temptation of the unknown come together in one
magnificent trade-size volume. These three talented
authors bring stories that will give you thrills *and*
chills like never before!

Coming to your favorite retail outlet in August 2002.

HARLEQUIN®
Makes any time special ®

PHU